Yesterday I Cared

ASHLYN HARMON

I0693304

Dedication & Content Warnings

The universe gave Josie a best friend like Mia; but that wouldn't have been possible if it hadn't given Ashlyn a best friend like Claire first. Here's your book, bitch. I love you.

Dear Reader,

As an author, my goal is to provide readers with real and relatable characters. Stories they can see themselves in. Just like in real life, my characters don't live in a sunny, constantly perfect world.

This novel includes the following content that could potentially trigger some readers: drunk driving resulting in a fatal car accident (off page), chronic pain following an injury, discussions of mental health issues, verbally and emotionally abusive parents, minor fat-shaming, recreational alcohol consumption, sex between two consenting adults.

As always, please take care of yourself.

Love you all

Glossary

Here is a quick reference guide for all the swimming terminology used within this book.

- **Club swimming**: Club swimming differs from high school swim team mainly in their commitment level, competitive focus, and overall social environment. This is a year-round commitment that focuses more on competitive pursuit, offering more intense training and emphasis on individual performance as well as team performance. Club swimming typically comes with higher costs to athletes and parents.

- **Event**: A race of any given distance. (i.e. the 200-meter freestyle, the 200-meter individual medley, etc.)

- **Heat**: The preliminary sessions in the morning of a meet are composed of heats. When there are too many swimmers to compete in an event at the same time, it's broken into heats based on seed times posted by each swimmer.

- **Individual Medley (IM)**: All four strokes together in one race. Order is butterfly, backstroke, breaststroke, freestyle.

Equal distance must be swam in each stroke.

- **Long Course**: Refers to competitions held in a 50-meter pool, which is equivalent to an Olympic-size pool. These races are measured in meters. Long course seasons run from April to August.

- **Olympic-size Pool**: Also called a long course pool. It's 50 meters in length with a minimum depth of 6 ft 7 in, recommended to be 9 ft 10 in deep. Consists of ten lanes.

- **Olympic Trials**: A sanctioned long course meet held the year of the Olympic games to determine which swimmers will represent the USA on the team. A total of 52 athletes are named to the team, 26 men and 26 women.

- **Short Course**: Short course swimming utilizes a 25-meter or 25-yard pool. Short course season runs from September to March.

- **Underwaters**: Unequipped swimming beneath the surface of the water, typically seen after the swimmer leaves the blocks and after they push off the wall at turns.

- **Warm/cool down**: A recovery swim that's done after a race so the swimmer can rid their body of excess lactic acid that's generated during the race.

- **Warm-up**: A period of practice and chance for swimmers to loosen up prior to the start of a meet or their event.

Mia

"I think it's time you consider putting yourself back out there. Try finding someone you want to form a relationship with."

I stare at the woman across from me with a blank expression, waiting for her to crack and start laughing. Because I know she can't be serious right now. We had spent almost an hour talking about all the reasons I should avoid a relationship. Now she's telling me to get back on the horse. The very broken horse with a horrible sense of direction.

She holds my gaze, but I refuse to be the first one who breaks. We only have ten minutes left; I can sit here in awkward silence for that long. I don't need to use every moment offered to me in therapy. I don't need to dredge up a topic I don't want to talk about.

Nine minutes left.

Joy shifts in her seat, arching a brow at me. I'm not giving into whatever challenge she *thinks* we're having though.

Eight minutes.

Joy breaks with a sigh. "Mia, there is nothing wrong with being afraid to put yourself out there."

There's not really a good way to tell her how wrong she is without being rude. Being the center of attention has never been my problem, not in the way she seems to think. No, the issue isn't putting myself out there; it's what I'm supposed to do when it inevitably blows up in my face. Because it *will* blow up in my face and probably take a couple of other people down with me.

I have a knack for picking the absolute worst person to want to be with. They never want to stick around once life gets messy. Actually, scratch that. They get bored when my life gets too normal, and they want to help me blow it back up without caring about the wreckage they leave behind. I'm attracted to people who live for drama.

"You've been in Columbia for months; you've established yourself within your new community; you are surrounded by people who are in happy relationships," she continues. "You've said you want that for yourself one day."

"Of course I want it. Everyone wants it. That doesn't mean I'm going to get it, though." We still have six minutes left, and I know it's about to be the longest six minutes of my life. "As my therapist, aren't you the one who's supposed to remind me we don't always get what we want?"

"Of course we don't, but I can also promise you that you'll never get something if you don't go after it."

Therapy had been Josie's idea, reminding me of how much it had helped when I was younger. Plus, all my friends are regularly going, and I've seen firsthand how good it is to have a healthy outlet. They're basically peer pressuring me to better myself—it's kind of ridiculous.

"We've spent many sessions talking about your fear of being stuck in the same place while everyone around you moves on." Joy isn't ready to let this go, apparently. "This is a way to help you conquer that fear. By putting yourself out there, attempting to find a new relationship, you're pushing yourself forward. Sometimes we only need a push."

"I was thinking more along the lines of getting a goldfish." The unimpressed look she gives me only makes me groan. "Dating is exhausting. No one meets each other organically anymore. It's all through apps, and the apps are going to drive me nuts, Joy. Especially as a fat, queer person."

"But it's better than the alternative. Look, Mia, no one likes doing this because it opens us to the possibility of getting hurt. As humans, we do what we can to avoid feeling pain, but pain is a part of life. You shouldn't allow yourself to miss out on something wonderful because of fear."

I cross my arms over my chest as I allow my body to sink deeper into the couch. Why can't it swallow me whole? "You sound like my best friend."

Her eyes flicker with amusement. "Well, you already know I think Josie is a great friend. If you don't want to listen to me, maybe try listening to her."

I don't need my therapist to tell me how great Josie is; there's a reason we've been best friends for over a decade. My life would be in shambles without her, more than it already is. She's my person. No one sees me the way she does.

"Start slow," Joy advises. "Maybe try taking yourself on a date first or go on a double-date with Josie and Bryce so you have someone to lean on."

So I can have an audience for my failing love life and give the front-row seat to Bryce Clark? No way in hell.

The alarm on Joy's phone buzzes, signaling the end of our time. I shouldn't be surprised the longest ten minutes of my life come to an abrupt close right as I'm about to have some kind of lonely-single-woman breakthrough. At least this means I have two whole weeks to pack all these feelings back into their box.

I stand and gather my stuff. The end of a therapy session is always the most awkward for me, especially when there's nothing else to say. I know Joy will tell me we'll pick back up here next time, and I know I'll do everything I can between now and then to avoid that happening.

"We'll pick back up here next time." Called it. "I look forward to hearing your progress."

I freeze a couple of steps away from the door and turn to look at her with a frown. "Is this homework?"

I hate when she gives me homework. Last time she did, I had to call my mother.

Smiling slightly, she shakes her head. "Not officially. If you have an update in two weeks, great. If not, we'll continue to work through this together. See you next time, Mia."

With the final dismissal, I exit the room and head toward the front door, waving to the receptionist as I go. The entire session plays through my mind while I walk across the small parking lot to my car. Once I get there, I slide behind the wheel; the door rattling shut behind me. I stare straight ahead at nothing.

Dating terrifies me. Bianca was one of the few people I ever had a real relationship with, and I was naïve enough to think she could be the one. Until it ended and her mere presence was enough of a threat to my marketing career that I had to move to a different state. I learned two things in that relationship: don't date rich people who have everything handed to them, and don't date someone in the same field as you.

Thank god for Bryce Clark, Carter Abrams, and Adair Swimming. I now work for my best friend's boyfriend and our mutual friend, doing marketing for their swim club while also balancing some freelance clients. It's been great. I feel like I have control of my future again, and now my therapist wants me to go out and find love? Why the hell should I do that?

I need wine.

And thankfully, my best friend always has wine. I'm due over there for dinner in a couple of hours. She won't be upset if I head over early. Starting my car, I pull out of the parking lot, leaving everything that just happened behind me.

I don't need to date. I'm perfectly fine on my own.

When I get to Josie and Bryce's place, I exercise my "best friend with a key" rights and enter without even a knock. I can hear them talking quietly in the kitchen, so I call out to them as I close the door behind me and toe off my shoes. Josie's voice brightly calls back, summoning me toward the other room.

The second I enter the kitchen, I'm hit with the domesticity of it all. Bryce is at the stove, already working on something for the dinner our group of friends is set to have in a little over an hour, and Josie is sitting at the table with her laptop out in front of her, a notebook by her elbow. He's probably helping her work out a plot point for her next great romance novel.

Normally, this would make me hide a smile behind a gag, but it just makes the knife that was wedged into my heart during therapy twist painfully.

Josie grins at me. "Hey, how was your appointment?"

I make a beeline for the small wine fridge they have, offering a shrug as my only answer. I grab an open bottle and two glasses before turning back to my best friend.

"Sure, come on in and take our alcohol." Bryce's tone is teasing as he turns back to the stove and mutters, "Doesn't even say hello or offer me any."

Sliding into the chair next to Josie, I'm fighting back a grin for the first time since I left Joy's office. "Hello, Bryce! I'm pretty sure I bought this bottle and brought it over the last time Josie and I had a movie night with Kat."

Like the mature adult he is, Bryce sticks his tongue out at me. I instantly stick my tongue back out at him until Josie takes the bottle of wine from my hands.

"Calm down, children." She pops the cork and pours a small glass for each of us. I nudge my glass closer; she raises an eyebrow briefly before pouring more. "What happened at therapy that's making you want an extra-large glass of wine?"

I take a long sip, followed by a second, before I let out a groan. "She wants me to date."

Josie and Bryce exchange a look, having some kind of silent conversation the rest of the world will never be privy to. I don't know why it bugs me so much to see it right now, but there's an irritation crawling over my skin. Josie and I do the same thing all the time, but I don't love being on the outside of it this time.

"Just spit it out!"

Bryce's eyes go comically wide before he quickly focuses back on the stove. I should have known he wouldn't be the one to say anything, especially since he's still a little scared of me. A fact I will always take a little bit of pride in. Let it be a reminder of what happens when you screw over my best friend.

"It's nothing bad, but haven't I been saying that for weeks now?"

Heat creeps over my cheeks for some inexplicable reason, making it hard to make eye contact with her. Which is not something I'm used to doing. I've stared her in the eye and talked about everything from what to have for lunch to what toys are best to use, plus everything in between. We don't keep things from each other, we're open books. "I know, but it hits differently when a stranger says it."

"Can you really call your therapist a stranger?"

I shoot Bryce a glare over the top of my wineglass while I take another long drink.

"Shutting up now."

Even Josie sends a glare at her boyfriend before focusing back on me. "Bryce's point is that you and Joy have been working toward this the whole time you've been seeing her. Moving to Columbia was supposed to be a chance for you to start over, to move on from Bianca, and the reign of terror she left behind."

The most annoying thing about heartbreak is that the worst moment of a relationship never fully overshadows the good ones. I'm not grieving the relationship I lost; I'm grieving the one we could have had. If she'd respected my wishes or called me the fuck back, what could have happened? Would I even need to be here, hiding away from the life I escaped in Charlotte? Hindsight tells me it never would have lasted. I am used to working hard for the things I want in life, and she was far too used to her dad giving her everything she wanted, and more.

What I'll never understand is why she had to target me. Why did she have to attack me so personally that I had to leave a job I loved? What had I done to her except love her? And why was it not ever enough?

Josie takes my silence as her sign to continue, reaching out to squeeze my hand. "I'm worried you're holding yourself back. I'm not saying I want you to go out and jump on the first person who shows interest, but would it be so bad to go out and meet people who aren't us?"

A snarky comment sits on the tip of my tongue, ready to come tumbling out. The two of them have completely stayed in their own little bubble. I mean, they have Carter and Katrina, but that's Bryce's best friend and his girlfriend. They aren't building a community in the same way she wants me to.

Before I say anything, though, it hits me. They *have* their community. They brought it with them. I'm the only one on the outside—the one without a friend. Of course I have all of them separately, but they're in a world I can't access.

My stomach sinks as one of my worst fears unravels before me. I'm alone while they're surrounded by people in the same situation.

I suddenly find myself wanting to run far, far away from this place.

Josie's grip on my arm tightens, almost like she can hear the thoughts running through my head. Then again, with the way our friendship works, maybe she can. "Mia, I'm not sure that came out right. You know how much we all love you and want you around, but I don't want you to believe you can't have a life outside of us and Adair. I mean, Katrina has her clients, and I have my writing group. Bryce and Carter are far too codependent to ever stray far from one another."

I snort a small laugh out, knowing how true the statement is. I swear they follow each other around like lost puppies.

"Don't be jealous of the bromance, ladies." Bryce's grin is broad as he lowers the temperature on the stove before coming over to join us at the table.

As he steals his girlfriend's wineglass and takes a large drink, I allow myself to relax in this home. In the presence of the person who has always been there for me, and her boyfriend.

Josie rolls her eyes at him. "Please, Mia and I are so much better at friendship than you and Carter."

"That's only because you're slowly stealing him away from me," Bryce argues.

I grin at him over the rim of my wineglass. "And it's not our fault he has good taste." Bryce's eye roll makes me grin wider, but then he's leaning across the table with such a serious look on his face. I sink back in my chair. "Josie? What's your boyfriend about to do?"

Josie leans over, her voice nothing more than a whisper. "I think he's about to give you a motivational speech."

Stunned at this turn of events, I have no choice but to look back at Bryce and wait for whatever's about to come out of his mouth. Nothing on this Earth could prepare me to hear a motivational speech on my love life, or lack of it, from Bryce Clark. This is the man who spent *years* lying to himself, saying hooking up with my best friend was nothing more, but he also wasn't messing around with anyone else. Which is something that's only come to light recently, but still. What wisdom could he have to bestow on me?

"I know it's not my place to say anything, but I think you need to listen to Josie and Joy. I've always envied the easy confidence you seem to carry yourself with, but I also know what it's like to project that into the world. You do it to protect yourself, because you know opening up to someone means tearing that down a bit. I know it's terrifying, but trust me, it's worth it in the end."

Well, shit.

"You're in a new city that's full of people who could be the one, but they're not going to come to you," he continues. "You deserve to find someone who makes you happy. I never met Bianca, but I'm sure there was something there that had you falling, but it didn't work out. I'm not going to say it's for the best or there's a reason, but I am going to say you deserve to be treated better than that. I know you can find it."

I fight to keep my jaw from dropping open. Am I that transparent? And, more importantly, when did Bryce become so goddamn observant?

When I turn to look at Josie, she is beaming. "I told you there's a lot more to him than just a dumb swimmer!"

"You called me a dumb swimmer?" Hurt colors Bryce's tone, and he's pouting slightly when I look back at him. "I graduated with honors, thank you very much."

"I meant more in an emotionally stunted kind of way." I shrug. The hurt deepens. I quickly amend, "But that was back then—before you came back in Josie's life!"

He considers my words before sighing with a defeated nod. "That's fair, I guess. Therapy is a wonderful, wonderful thing."

"Except when it's pushing you to step out of your comfort zone," I grumble back.

His head tilts. "I disagree. I think it's exceptionally wonderful when it does that."

Ugh. I officially hate emotional growth when it's being showcased by Bryce. What kind of sick twist of fate is this? When did this man, who is two years younger than me, become the emotionally mature one? I just...

The ring of the doorbell cuts me off mid-thought.

"That'd be Carter and Kat," Josie reminds Bryce, who's already standing.

"Look at that, Mia, my best friend actually uses the doorbell." The door opens, and closes a second later, followed by Carter's voice calling out. I arch a brow, a smirk tugging at my lips while Bryce groans. "At least he rang it first before coming in."

"We're in the kitchen!" Josie calls, before looking at me, and lowering her voice. "We'll talk about this later?"

"Mm-hmm," is all I say before taking another large drink of my wine.

Carter and Kat walk into the room, already chatting a mile a minute. I allow myself to be pulled into hugs and small talk, relaxing as I let go of the therapy session more and more. Josie will want to bring it back up, but for now, I can pretend it didn't happen. I can be Mia and hang out with my friends, because there's no way a dinner with the most important people in my life can possibly throw me another curveball.

Tomorrow, I'll deal with the rest of my life. Tonight, I'll let it be.

Mia

Less than an hour later, the five of us are crowded around Josie and Bryce's dining room table, a whole spread of food laid out on the table in front of us. Wine has been poured, small talk is still happening all around me, but my focus is firmly planted on my best friend's boyfriend.

"Is there a reason you're staring at us all like you're about to recite some epic monologue?" The unimpressed look he gives me takes me right back to the conversation we had less than ninety minutes ago in his kitchen. "I'm really starting to hate this look on you, Clark."

Bryce glares at me from where he stands at the head of the table, waiting for the other four people in the group to take their seats. I simply grin back at him, taking a sip from my recently refilled wineglass as I hold his gaze.

"Maybe there is," he relents once everyone is seated. "Or maybe I have an announcement to make."

Involuntarily, my eyes dart to the left hand of my best friend. I relax when I realize it's bare. While I'm pretty confident Bryce will include me in the proposal process, or that I'd at least be one of the first to know, I'm not entirely sure what to expect from these two. They always have a way of surprising me.

"Well"—I motion around the table with my wineglass—"by all means, please proceed. Your captive audience is waiting."

Across the table, Josie gives me the exasperated eye roll I'm used to getting from her. Whatever happened earlier in their kitchen has left us and we're back to normal. Normal means I'm enjoying one of my favorite past times: irritating the hell out of her boyfriend. It's a special talent of mine, and one I take rather seriously. So seriously, in fact, that I put it on the résumé I gave Bryce and Carter as a formality when they hired me to do the marketing for their swim club, Adair Swimming. Carter had laughed so hard it took him nearly fifteen minutes to calm down, Bryce had glowered at me as he stuffed the résumé in a file folder with my name on it.

With the exclusion of Carter's girlfriend, Kat, I've known everyone at this table for over a decade. Though our lives weren't always so intertwined, I'd gotten to know how to push everyone's buttons, and there are certain people I've always enjoyed messing with more. That just so happened to always be Bryce.

Bryce clears his throat, which only makes me snicker. Josie lightly kicks me beneath the table.

"As you all know, Adair needs to hire another coach, so I can have time to focus on running the business," he begins. "Carter and I have been talking to several of our former teammates to make a decision. The contract has been signed, and our new coach starts in two weeks."

Excitement bubbles up in me at the prospect over them adding another elite swimmer to the coaching roster. We already have two Olympians; adding someone else of the same caliber will be an amazing marketing opportunity. It can also do wonders in helping us be taken seriously enough to host a professional meet. A club ran by a trifecta of Olympians and elite swimmers. Who wouldn't take an interest in that?

"Well, don't leave us in suspense." Josie laughs gleefully. My mind, however, is already running through a bunch of different ways to make the announcement. "Tell us who it is!"

First thing Monday morning, I'll get with Carter and Bryce to start strategizing—

"Ronan O'Brien."

My brain screeches to a halt as soon as the name registers. I blink up at Bryce. "I'm sorry, what?"

Everyone turns toward me, surprised by my reaction. A cold sweat settles on the back of my neck; the thumping of my heart against my chest is anything but pleasant. I've done everything I possibly can to not think about that man and now they're telling me we'll be working side by side? This is fucking fantastic.

"Why do you look so surprised?" Josie wears a frown. "I think Ronan will be a great addition."

Well, now I have to come up with an excuse, fast.

"I'm confused how this happened. I mean, why him? He's been out of the sport since 2017. I don't understand why you'd trust him with something like your business."

That's not entirely false, which I pat myself on the back for. To me, it's a gamble to trust someone as flaky as Ronan O'Brien with the well-being of their business. The same man who fell off the face of the Earth and only announced his retirement when allegations of him doping surfaced. He hasn't been seen or heard from since, that I'm aware of. Why would Bryce want a reputation like his associated with Adair?

"I don't know what you're talking about, Mia. He only took about two years off; he's been actively involved in the sport since early 2020." My brows arch at Carter's words. "Just because he hasn't been competing doesn't mean he hasn't been around."

Bryce quickly picks up where his best friend leaves off. "We've talked to a lot of people, Mia. Ronan was always our top pick. He's going to be an excellent addition to our team."

I still think they've lost their minds, but it's quickly becoming clear I won't be able to make them reconsider. According to Bryce, everything is in motion, and they have officially hired Ronan on. I'll have to find a way to ignore him, no matter how difficult that will be. I'll have to hope that Ronan does something to mess up this opportunity.

"This has been in the works for months before the decision was official. Bryce started talking to him at Trials and then more over the Olympics. He had a couple of things he needed to take care of, but he's signed on, and we're excited about where this can go," Carter explains.

Apparently, I'd been in the same room as Ronan O'Brien, multiple times, and had never even known.

My gaze drifts between Carter and Bryce, and I let out a small sigh. "Obviously, you don't have to convince me. It's your business and your decision."

Carter frowns. "But you're part of the team, Mia. We don't want you to be unhappy."

I wave him off. "Do not worry about me when making business decisions. I'm perfectly capable of going with the flow." I'm not capable of going with the flow, and everyone at this table knows that. Still, I'm grateful when they all choose to ignore it. "I'm worried this might not turn out the way you want it to. I only want you guys to be successful."

Bryce gives me what I'm sure he thinks is a comforting smile. "Trust us on this one, Mia. We know what we're doing."

With a smile, I nod, and raise my glass. "Congratulations, guys."

Everyone around the table cheers, but I can't help worrying about how horrible this is all going to go. The last thing I want is for Bryce and Carter to have to stand back and watch as the future of the club blows up in their faces. If there's one thing Ronan O'Brien is good at, it's ruining other people's plans.

The night at Bryce and Josie's might have ended up with me finding out I'd have to face the one man I swore I'd never think about again, but at least I didn't have to go back to the conversation about my lacking love life. And I'm in the business of loving small blessings right now.

The minute I left their house two nights ago, I forced myself back to never, *ever*, thinking about Ronan O'Brien again and I'd been quite successful until this moment.

"I don't know what you want me to say, Kat." I frown, stabbing away at something on my tablet. "If you're so curious about him, ask Carter."

I had arrived at her small office less than an hour ago, on time for our bi-weekly meeting on marketing for her design and renovation company, Effervescent Renovations. Watching Katrina walk away from the toxic company her stepfather ran and standing up for herself less than a year ago had been truly awe-inspiring. I still use it as a reminder to myself that it's okay to go after the things I want. While I know she doesn't necessarily see it, she does have it all—the doting boyfriend, the perfectly healthy relationship, and her dream job.

The last thing I expected, though, was for her to be the one to bring up my past. Especially because she's the only one who wasn't involved in that past. I know the other three well enough to know they suspect something happened. However, they are all, thankfully, too scared to push me into telling them. Either Kat hasn't learned that about me yet, or she's not scared of me.

"All Carter told me is that Ronan is a good guy and that they've discussed the concerns you've brought up." She says it casually as she flips through some tile samples. "Although he did tell me he thinks something happened between the two of you, but he's not sure what. That you and he used to be closer."

There's not a lie there. We had been closer once upon a time. Closer than anyone of our friends knew. I know Bryce doesn't know what happened because he would have told Josie by now. And Carter would have told Bryce. Overall, this group is really horrible at keeping secrets.

And then Ronan ruined it. Ruined it in a way that shouldn't have been surprising to me, but felt like a personal blow that I'll never recover from.

Instead of focusing on the part about him and me, I focus on the first part of her statement. "What do you mean, they talked about the concerns I brought up?" She shrugs. "And they still hired him?"

"I don't know what those concerns are, really," she admits. "All Carter told me was that anything you might be worried about has been handled. I feel a little like I'm in limbo here and wish someone would give me something to go off of."

I didn't want to spread rumors, especially because I'm still not sure they're true, but Kat has a point. Hiring Ronan could affect her life as well, and she has a right to know. "Back when Josie and I first started the blog, Ronan O'Brien was pretty famous in the swimming world. He was a hell of an athlete, charismatic, and pretty fucking gorgeous. He's the kind of guy who knows how pretty he is and isn't afraid to use it to get what he wants."

Understanding fell over her face. "The most dangerous kind of pretty."

"Exactly. He was a player and never really seemed to take anything too seriously. He had this air about him that said everything came easy and he didn't have to put in much work."

It's no secret that those are the kind of people I like least of all. That kind of behavior is one of the biggest reasons Bianca and I broke up. There was always something different about Ronan, though. Something I wanted to understand, because it felt like an act. He never let me get close enough to see the real him.

Her eyebrows crawled up her forehead. "And you were friends with him?"

"He was different with us." I'm not really sure how to explain what I mean to Katrina. "He never acted that way with us, or even around us. It was something we saw from the outside looking in."

Kat takes the seat across from me, tile samples forgotten as she gets more into the story.

"We all got along pretty well. He and I even spent some time hanging out alone after the 2016 Trials," I continue, forcing myself not to think back to those memories. They are more dangerous than anything else I'm about to tell her. "The following summer, though, something changed. I overheard Ronan say something to some younger swimmers, and it proved to me he's exactly the kind of person people always thought he was."

"Well, what did he say?"

A twisting feeling settles in my gut. I can still hear the way his deep, warm voice curved over each of the ugly words he said that day—the ones I wish would stop haunting me. "It's not important." I wave her off. "What is important is what happened next."

She sits completely enraptured as I finish off my tale—how that meet in 2017 was the last time we ever saw or spoke to Ronan. How less than a year later, he had refused to take a drug test, and all these doping scandals started surfacing, ruining the reputation he had left. He never denied them or fought against them; all he did was quietly announce his retirement on social media before they could formally pursue any allegations. The retirement post didn't make a single mention of the drama surrounding him.

By the time I finish, Katrina is staring at me with wide eyes. "Holy shit."

"Neither Josie nor I ever thought he was doping, not really," I say. "But when those rumors persist for years and there's no one around telling you the truth, it becomes kind of hard not to believe them, you know?"

"Do you really think Carter and Bryce would let him come out here if that were true, though?" That's the question I've been wrestling with since Bryce made the announcement, and the reality is, I don't know. "Or do you think maybe he's lying to them, and they don't know the truth?"

"Absolutely not." Ronan may be a lot of things, but a liar has never been one of them. "I think they know the truth of what happened, but don't feel like it's their story to tell. I guess I have to respect that."

"Then why are you so upset with him?"

I try not to let my frustration show. "Because, whatever happened, Josie and I deserved to know. We were all friends, and we deserved more than to have him fall off the face of the earth."

"But I thought the two of you weren't really talking at that point."

We weren't, but I still deserved to know. I would have listened if he reached out to me then. "That's true, but it's still something we should have known."

"That makes sense," she replies. "Can I ask you one more question? It's pretty personal."

Worry creeps up my spine, wondering how much more personal we can get. Still, I nod.

"Does Josie know you slept with him?"

"W...*What*?" How did she possibly guess that? It happened almost ten years ago; how could she possibly know that? "I...I don't have any idea what you're talking about."

"Don't act so surprised. I guessed about it last night, solely based on your reaction. Then this whole conversation kind of confirmed it for me." Even more panic claws its way up my throat. "Don't worry, though. I genuinely don't think Josie or the guys know."

"And they can't know, Kat." There is no denying the truth now. Instead, I need to focus on making sure my secret is kept a secret. "It was almost ten years ago. I never told them, and I know he didn't either. It was one of the biggest mistakes of my life."

Worry passes over her gaze. "Mia, what does that mean?"

"Nothing like that," I quickly assure her. "It was consensual, fully consensual. It wasn't something I expected to happen, but it led to me thinking he'd be different and all that got me was heartbreak."

I still dream about that night in Omaha—the way he walked me back to the hotel with an arm around my shoulder. How he kept pulling me in closer, the warmth of his breath against the top of my head. At nearly five-ten, I was used to being as tall as or taller than all my dates. The way he pressed a kiss to my head and how we agreed to watch a movie...something I never thought Ronan would be into.

It had been me that initiated everything that followed that night. Less than an hour into a movie I'd already seen, I'd gently taken the tablet from his hand and demanded to know why he wasn't trying to sleep with me. I wanted to know why he wasn't living up to the reputation I knew was true. His green eyes flashed with hurt before he admitted he thought I deserved better than him.

I'd swung a leg over his lap and was straddling him in seconds, wanting to know what his response was if I said all I wanted was him. The kiss he pulled me into still haunts me. No one has been able to kiss me like Ronan.

Katrina is staring at me expectantly, waiting to hear the rest of the story. "Look, I pushed him to give into his reputation because I wanted him. He wanted me, too, at least in that moment. Everything that came after, though, just proved to me I would never be good enough long-term."

"And that's why you don't want to see him? Because you don't want to relive that past?"

"I don't want to see him because Ronan O'Brien runs away. When things get hard, he bolts. The second something he doesn't like happens, he leaves. His way of handling things is not handling them. He might be a good person most of the time, Katrina, but reputations are created for a reason. Don't let him make you think otherwise."

I don't know if Katrina is willing to take my response at face value, but she nods and opens up a notebook, instantly bringing the conversation back to a safe area: work. Work, for us, means I don't have to think of Ronan or the way he humiliated me. Or the reality I've chosen to wear as a burden to protect the people around me. I saw the real him that day in Indianapolis, but it wasn't my place to share that with everyone else.

Ronan

As I lower myself into the only open kitchen chair, I groan in frustration. All the others are littered with random things that need to be put away, but I'll get to them, eventually. Right now, my focus shifts to making the pain in my leg subside; once I accomplish that, I can get back to unpacking my new place.

After living with this ache for over eight years, I should've known better than to overdo it. Every single time I move to a new place, this always happens. I somehow get in my head that I can accomplish anything and that chronic pain isn't something I have to worry about. Only to be proven wrong before the end of the day.

I should have grabbed an icepack from the freezer before I sat down, but it's too far away now. Instead, I gently massage the upper part of my calf, hoping some of the tension will melt away. I never would have guessed that, at thirty-four, parts of my body would already be betraying me. I've always taken care of myself, worked hard to stay in shape and eat healthy, but there are some things we can't control.

Like the consequences that come from a decision that wasn't your own.

My phone rings on the table by my elbow, Bryce Clark's name flashing across the screen. I grab it, fumbling for just a second before I accept the call. "Hey, man."

"Hey, how's it going?" Instead of a normal greeting, Bryce tends to get to the point. Which makes things easier if you're working for him. Which I am, or will be, in two weeks. "Are you sure you don't want some help getting moved in?"

I look around at the chaotic space and let out a small groan. More than anything, I want to be able to handle this on my own, but I know I can't. "Actually, I think I could use some help."

"That's great news," he happily replies, "because Carter and I are already here!"

Nothing about the statement surprises me, but I still laugh. Bryce has always been the kind of guy who anticipates what you need and gives it to you long before you ever ask. When it came to his own well-being and mental health, he was more resistant, but he'll never let a friend suffer in silence.

"And we brought pizza!" I let out another laugh at Carter's excited voice in the background.

"Just let yourselves in. It's unlocked," I tell them. "I just sat down and am not getting up for at least five minutes. I'm in the kitchen."

I toss my phone back onto the table once Bryce hangs up. A second later, I can hear them pushing their way into the house, declarations about how awesome the place is meeting my ears. I find myself looking around, trying to see it from their perspective. It's all sleek lines and modern edges that almost make it feel sterile. It was in my budget, though, and was the only house in the endless lineup of wealthy-bachelor-pad houses my realtor showed me that I actually kind of liked.

The house had potential, which is what drew me in. It's in a great neighborhood, had a huge yard, and was close enough to the pool to make commuting easy. If someone wanted to make it a home, it could easily be done with some remodeling, but that's not what I'm here to do. Settling down is so far outside my nature, I'm not sure I'll ever do it. I stay in a place long enough to accomplish what I needed to do, then I move on.

"This place is insane," Bryce compliments with a low whistle as soon as he steps into view. "Out of all the places you've lived, this might be my favorite."

"Yeah, it's pretty nice," I agree with a nod. "There's a huge backyard for Lezak to run around in."

"I bet he lost his shit when he saw it." I turn in time to see Bryce's gaze drift from where I'm working the sore muscle in my leg to my face, eyebrow raised. "You good, dude?"

I shrug, trying to hide any grimace of pain that might leak through. "Just overdid it a bit. It'll be fine in a minute."

Carter comes wandering in behind him, dropping the pizza boxes to the only free space on the table. "Then I suggest we eat first."

"You won't hear me argue."

Carter helps push some things off to the side, giving us more room. He doesn't even attempt to find plates, instead grabbing a stack of napkins off the counter. On his way to grab beers, the excited sound of a barking at the backdoor cuts through our small talk.

Bryce stops by the door, looking over at me with a raised brow.

I nod. "Just do *not* feed him any pizza."

"Why?" Carter asks with an amused grin. "'Cause that's your job?"

I roll my eyes, bending at the excited golden retriever puppy that comes barreling toward me. He's a mess of fur, aggressive tail wagging, and four limbs that still don't seem to work in any kind of synchronization. And he's the best thing to happen to me in literal years.

"I never saw you as a dog person, Ronan, but this dude is cute." Bryce sets an open beer in front of each of us. "Does Lezak know he has a dog named after him?"

My eyes roll. "I guarantee you I'm not the only person to have named a pet after him, but he did turn about seven different shades of red when I told him."

Both Carter and Bryce burst into laughter, probably picturing the exact reaction the older Olympian had when I told him. Jason Lezak, a freestyler like me, pulled off one of the greatest comebacks the sport has ever seen. He anchored the men's 4x100-meter freestyle at the 2008 Olympic Games in Beijing. He'd been a full-body length behind France at the start of his leg and didn't pull ahead until the final twenty-five meters. Team USA walked away with a gold medal and a new world record, and Lezak kind of went down in history.

"We told the girls about you joining the team yesterday." Bryce's swift change of subject nearly makes me choke on the bite of pizza I'd taken, but I can quickly wash it down with a swig of beer. "Mia seemed pretty upset about the news."

The name sends a cold shiver down my spine. Out of everyone I'd known back when I was professionally swimming, she was the one I didn't think I'd ever see again. At least, not in this capacity. Maybe in passing. Maybe at Bryce's wedding if he ever got his head out of his ass and told Josie Martin, her best friend, how he felt (thankfully, he did). Being in the same world, the same life, as her again, was a weird feeling. Mostly because I'm not sure what happened.

How did we go from an amazing night of sex, followed by a year of talking whenever we could, to her randomly deciding to hate me a year later?

It became obvious no one knew anything about what happened between us in Omaha. If she had told Josie, I'm sure Bryce or Carter would have heard. Following Olympic Trials, I spent the next few months constantly around the two men, and neither one of them said anything to me. No one in this group is necessarily great at minding their own business.

I know Bryce and Carter are going to be looking for answers, but those are answers I can't give. She stopped talking to me a couple of days into the National Championship meet in Indianapolis a year later, but those first few encounters had been completely normal and then a wall of ice went up. One I could never chisel my way through.

And no one seemed to know what happened.

"Are we surprised by that?" I ask Bryce, who shrugs. "I've told you this before, and nothing has changed since. I don't know what happened. She just got mad at me out of nowhere."

"Which would seem strange for most people, but somehow, with Mia, it makes sense." Both of us frown at Carter, who shrugs. "What? You know I love Mia, but if anyone is capable of hating someone and keeping those reasons completely to herself, it's Mia."

"Oh, she hates me now?" That's news to me. In the past, it's mostly been strong disdain and ignoring my existence. "Well, I guess that's good to know."

"'Hate' might be too strong of a word," Bryce counters.

"And I was thinking it's not strong enough." Bryce shoots Carter a glare. "Again, we all know Mia, and the capabilities that woman has. She scares me, guys."

Shaking his head, Bryce reaches for another piece of pizza. "Don't pretend like you and her aren't best friends."

"Exactly, I'm on her good side, which means I know what it means to be on her bad side. That's not something I'd really wish on anyone."

I know exactly what Carter means. There was a time when I was on her good side. Something I'm not sure Bryce has ever known. It's not that Mia is mean. It's more that she's a fierce force of nature and she's not to be messed with. She's fiercely protective of the people she loves, and fiercely protective of her own heart. Those who are lucky enough to be let in get to see a whole other side of her. She always reminded me of a sunflower in the way it turns toward light when it's ready to be nourished.

And when the light is on her, that woman shines brighter than anything I've ever seen.

"We wanted to give you a heads-up that things will probably be tense for a while," Bryce finishes.

"Whatever, dude." I'm attempting, and failing, to brush it off, but they don't need to know that. "I'm here to do a job—help you build up Adair Swim Club and establish a scholarship fund. That's what my focus is going to be on; I don't want to get caught up in whatever drama is left over from the past."

My plan for my time at Adair is to do what I've always done: accomplish the job I came here to do and move on. It's never good to get feelings messed up with that.

⋯⋯ + ∘ ✦ ⁺ ★ ⁺ ☾ ★ ✦ ∘ ⁺ ⋯⋯

On the Friday before I'm set to officially start as a coach at Adair Swim Club, Bryce and Carter decide to have me come in to meet the team of high school swimmers I'll be working with. Their primary focus is earning scholarships to four-year universities with the hope their swimming career can take them further. These athletes either come from area schools that don't have teams, or their swimming program isn't taken as seriously as other sports.

Bryce assures me their drive, determination, and heart is there. I'm looking for love of the sport, too, though. Whether any athlete wants to admit it or not, loving what you do is what gets you as far as you want to go.

I arrive at the club early Friday afternoon, wanting to take some time to get the lay of the land before meeting the kids that will be looking up to me.

As I approach the glass doors, I spot Josie standing at the front desk, chatting with someone. My steps slow as memories hit me. The last time I'd seen her, she'd barely been twenty-two. She'd still been shy and unsure around Bryce, trying to figure out her place in this world and in his heart. Now a confident woman stands in her place, looking at ease with who she is and where life has taken her.

She turns to greet me when I open the door, her eyes bright as her smile grows. "Ronan!"

A laugh escapes me as she tackles me in a hug of pure energy. Just the way she always was. "Hey, Josie."

She steps back to look up at me. "I can't believe you're here! When Bryce told me you'd accepted the job, I was surprised."

"Hopefully it was a good surprise?" The question comes out awkwardly. I stuff my hands in the pockets of my sweats. This is Mia's best friend—whatever resentment she harbors toward me could have been passed onto Josie.

"Only the best surprise!"

The tension in my shoulders relaxes. "Good. It's good to see you."

"You too. Now, Bryce and Mia are meeting about marketing for an upcoming meet or something—I don't know. I tried to keep his calendar straight for him since I'm, you know, the administrator. That lasted less than a month and resulted in him sleeping on the couch for two nights. So now he leaves me a sticky note with the day's plan on it."

"So, what you're secretly trying to tell me is that Bryce is still a huge control freak?"

Amusement glitters in her eyes, a sly smirk tugging up the corners of her lips. "I *knew* I was right to be excited about you joining the team!"

That obviously means there were people questioning it. Which I knew, because Bryce told me that Mia wasn't sure about what hiring me means. I want to ask Josie, find out what she thinks really happened to make me retire. Did Bryce tell her the truth? I wouldn't blame him if he did. I don't want to be the reason one of them is keeping something from the other.

"I'm guessing Bryce gave you a tour?" I nod in confirmation at Josie's question. "And I'm guessing it was all the important stuff you need to know in order to coach kids safely?"

My brow arches. "Seeing as that was what he hired me to do, yes. That's exactly what the tour was."

"Well, then, let me give you *another* tour. This time, it'll be more fun." Without asking, she links her arm through mine and starts leading me out to the outdoor pool. "We'll talk all about Bryce and Carter's visions and dreams, because you know those superstitious assholes won't tell anyone about them."

With a laugh, I allow her to lead me away.

Josie is still chatting my ear off as we head back to the lobby. All conversation about the facility is done, though, and she's moved on to sharing her wisdom about all the places they've visited since moving to Columbia. I've never even been to South Carolina, so most of this was new to me and I was taking her recommendations to heart. Sitting still or being alone all the time is not the best way for me to live my life.

When we round the corner and enter the main lobby again, it suddenly feels like the ground has opened up and I was free-falling.

Mia is standing at the desk, less than twenty feet from me, talking to another woman. I instantly suspect the other woman to be Carter's girlfriend, Katrina. With long blonde hair pulled into a messy bun, she is stunning, though not necessarily the type of person I'd expect Carter to be with. Based on what I've been told, I know they're happy together.

My entire focus, however, is on Mia Sheridan. She feels like a phantom that's been haunting me for years, yet now she's standing in front of me very much alive.

She's different from what I remember. Her long dark brown hair is loose around her shoulders. She's dressed casually, but professionally. Beneath the sleeves of her top, I can see several tattoos littered across her arms—not quite a sleeve, more like a random assortment of things she loves. All of them, I note, are black, and have either no other color or the bare minimum, which only makes them stick out more strikingly against her skin.

"Mia's gotten a couple dozen more tattoos since you've seen her last," Josie jokes. Her tone is low, probably to keep Mia from noticing us before I'm ready. "And please don't ask me how many she has; I lost track after twenty."

The surprised laugh bursts out of me before I can stop it. I don't know why that number is surprising, especially when I can see at least ten facing me. Unfortunately, the sound causes Mia and Katrina to both turn in surprise.

Time moves in slow motion as I clock every flicker of Mia's eyes. First, there's the faintest flash of happiness, but it's quickly masked behind a blank stare. Light green eyes track over my whole body, but not in the way that makes me feel weak in the knees. She's assessing me, looking for something. Too bad I don't know what that is.

When her eyes finally glance up at me, I offer the smallest smile and the world's most awkward wave. "Hey, Sheridan."

Her gaze snaps into a glare, her arms tightening around her bag. "O'Brien." She nods. "Nice of you to crawl out from beneath the rock you've been living under to join the land of the living."

My brows furrow, and I notice both Bryce and Carter behind the desk for the first time. Both look like they're holding their breaths. "I don't—"

"Don't." Her hand goes up, stopping me. "I don't have any interest in hearing your voice. We can be adults about this—you stay the hell away from me and I'll stay the hell away from you."

A stunned, awkward silence follows as Mia basically storms through the main entrance, never once looking back at us. I look around the room, but no one seems to know what to say. The air she left hanging in her place is tense with all the angry energy she put into it.

Almost eight years later, any questions I had remaining have evaporated: Whatever happened back in 2017 isn't something that's been healed with time. She's still pissed at me.

Bryce is the first one to break. "Honestly, that went better than I thought it would. What? Don't look at me like that, Ronan!"

I roll my eyes. "She hates me, Bryce."

When I look at Josie, she's looking anywhere but at me. Doubt settles in around me. Is this something we can work through?

"We'll deal with that later," Bryce decides. "Right now, you have a team to meet and practice to observe. Let's get set up."

With a sigh, I go to follow him but am stopped by Josie's hand squeezing my arm. "I'm happy you're here, Ronan."

I offer her a quick hug. I stop briefly to introduce myself to Katrina, who seems a little on edge around me, too. There's nothing rude about our interaction, but I'm not sure she's as happy to have me here as Josie. Before I have the chance to do anything to break the ice, Bryce is calling my name. I excuse myself and head out to the deck.

When I accepted the job, I told Bryce and Carter they'd have me for at least two years. Now, though, I'm wondering if I'll even make it two days.

Mia

I hate him. I hate his stupid, dark hair, and his grin. I hate the stubble he's let grow; it makes him look older and more mature. I hate the way he can still stand before me with all the confidence in the world and pretend he doesn't know how big of an asshole he is.

I've never hated someone more than I hate this man.

"You really rolled out the welcome mat back there."

I don't even startle at Josie's voice from behind me. It honestly took her longer than I thought it would to get back up to the offices and confront me about what happened. "He got what he deserved."

She moves further into the room, but I stay focused on the computer screen in front of me. "I'm not really in a position to judge that. You've never told me what happened between you."

"You don't need to know everything, Josie."

"I'd like to know when someone does something to hurt my best friend," she counters.

"And I'd like to keep things that could hurt my best friend away from her." Over the years, we've gotten good at this weird banter, where we actively avoid topics while still giving each other enough information in the hope the other will back off. "Just let me handle this."

"You haven't handled it, Mia."

They say the truth hurts, but it hurts more when it comes from your best friend.

I turn to look at her. She's sitting in her own desk chair, but she's watching me. "Josie, I need you to trust me on this one. I have handled it. This isn't something I can move on from and pretend everything is good. Whatever friendship Ronan and I had is gone, and it's not coming back. You know me. You know I wouldn't cut someone off like this unless it was absolutely necessary."

Her shoulders slump in defeat. "Yeah, you're right. I just...I always thought the two of you were into each other."

The laugh comes out sharply. "Trust me, nothing about me is something Ronan O'Brien wants unless it's just for sex."

"Do you really think he's still like that?"

I consider the question for a second. There had been a time in my life when I didn't think he was like that at all. That his whole reputation was nothing more than a mask for him to wear. Then his reputation—his truth—hit me in the face. "People can say they change—they can even show actions to support it, but who we are at our core is a lot harder to change."

Her frown deepens. "So that's a yes?"

"I don't know the man, Josie," I reply with a shrug. "I'm not sure I ever really did."

Sighing, she reaches for her mouse and wakes her computer up. I take that as a sign to turn back to my work. "I really wanted him to be different."

God, I thought to myself, *me too.*

Ronan O'Brien is *everywhere*.

I go to the gym to get in a quick workout before any of the swimmers get there, and he's already there. Lifting weights or doing yoga. Which is crazy because when the hell did Ronan start doing yoga? I remember him making *fun* of yoga, and insisting the intense stretching routine his coach had him doing wasn't that.

I leave the pool in the evening, and he's finishing up whatever he had going on for the day. There's no escaping him, especially now that he's settling into the seat across from me at my favorite local café.

I glare at him over the top of my laptop, but he shrugs. "There aren't any other seats. What do you expect me to do?"

I don't need to look around to know he's telling the truth; the café was already packed when I arrived, and it's gotten worse since students were released from classes. "Take it to go."

Those are the first words I've said to him in nearly a week. Every time we've bumped into one another, he's tried to start a conversation with me, but I haven't let him. I've walked away or ignored him. That's going to be harder to do now. Especially because he knows I won't back down. I'm not going to be the one to get up and leave. I was here first, and he's encroaching on my territory.

"Just say whatever you need to say to me, Ronan, and then you can leave."

His green eyes flick down to the drink by the edge of my laptop. "What the hell is that?"

"Frozen hot chocolate." Small talk I can do, if I have to.

His brow furrows. "I know you hate hot beverages, but doesn't that defeat the entire purpose of a hot chocolate?" He grins when he sees the surprise I know is written all over my face. "Yeah, Mia, I remember stuff like that about you. I did listen."

"But didn't stick around long enough for any real sort of connection."

His grin disappears, a blank look taking its place. "I think it's pretty clear you never told Josie about what happened that night in Omaha."

I *hate* him for bringing it up so casually. "What was there to tell?"

He doesn't back down. "The two of you tell each other everything. Why doesn't she know? Is it because you didn't want to steal her limelight? You know, two best friends are allowed to have their own separate hookups on the same night. One person doesn't get all the bragging rights."

No one gets under my skin as easily as he does. He knows all the buttons to push to irritate me. Once upon a time, it used to be funny and even a little cute. Now it felt patronizing. "What would I even tell her? That your reputation as a player and womanizer turned out to be true?"

Something flashes across his eyes, but I can't quite put my finger on it. "That's the fun thing about a reputation, I guess. It means you don't have to worry about disappointing people."

How many people has he said that to throughout the years? How many people were just another tally mark to him? And why is it so easy for him to brush people and their feelings aside?

"Do you remember the day we met? Back in Charlotte?"

A boyish grin tugs over his lips. The same one that caught my heart all those years ago, the one that led me to that hotel room with him, and the one that told me if I let go, this man would catch me. My heart would be safe with him. I was so naïve.

"Of course I do. As I recall, you brought a rather literal meaning to falling head over heels for me."

My eyes narrow. "Your bag tripped me."

"And I caught you," he brags. "What made you think about that day? I mean, besides the obvious fact that I'm sitting across from you."

"Sometimes I find myself thinking about what I would say to the younger version of myself if I were to go back in time."

His look is skeptical. "Okay, I'll bite. What would you tell her?"

"To run like hell from you." He blinks, utterly surprised. It's a personal victory of mine whenever I can make this man flustered. Whenever I can make his confidence slip. "I should have walked away and never looked back."

He blinks rapidly, my words soaking in. "Mia—"

"Please leave, Ronan. I have a deadline to meet for a client and I have nothing else to say to you."

He doesn't say anything else, just stands from his seat, and heads toward the exit. I take a deep, shaky breath before I slowly turn to watch him go. When I do, his head is already turned back toward me. He looks at me like he's staring at a stranger. I'm not a vindictive person by nature, but something about that felt right. I'd spent the last several years feeling like I was looking at someone I don't know. Now it's his turn.

When he catches me looking, he quickly turns, and leaves the café, the door swinging shut behind him. I don't know what this means or where this will lead us, but I'm pretty sure it's not going to help the work situation.

⋯⋯ + ∘ ✳ ★ ☾ ★ ✳ + ∘ + ⋯⋯

After a full week of Ronan being back in my life, I decide I need a distraction. I need to focus on something other than his stupidly handsome face that I want to punch.

The only thing I can think of is Joy's advice to get back out there. Maybe if I find someone else, I can stop thinking about the person I could have had something real with. If only he hadn't disappointed me the way everyone else does.

I download every single app I can find. Then immediately delete half of them.

I spend the night setting up my profiles, skimming through the options, deleting profiles, and repeating it all until I am left with only two apps and a handful of matches pouring in. Columbia is a huge college town, but there is still a surprising number of young professionals in the area, too. The more I flip through prospective match after prospective match, the more I begin to relax. I have options.

And none of these options are Ronan O'Brien.

There are few people who stand out more than others, which shouldn't be a surprise, but I'm almost alarmed at how easy it feels to fall back into dating like this. Which is probably because there aren't any stakes, not really. I match with someone, we either talk or don't. It starts to get tricky when an actual date is brought into the conversation. I'm not sure when I'll be ready for that part, though.

I don't do vulnerable well. Only the people closest to me get to see that side. Joy wanted progress, and I think downloading the app is more than enough progress. We can start there and see where the rest of the week takes us.

Ronan

"I don't know what I did, dude, but she really hates me."

Bryce is staring at me with wide eyes from the other side of the pool, both of us hanging on the lane lines in a way we'd yell at the kids for. Both of us are catching our breath, though it's coming a bit easier for Bryce than me. He's been determined to get me back in the pool, though, even for workouts.

"Yeah, I would say so," he agrees. "Mia can be scary and mean, but she's not hurtful. Those were shots aimed to kill. There's nothing you can tell me?" I hesitate for a second too long. "Ha! I knew it. Out with it."

"No way. I'm not telling you something she doesn't want known. Yes, there was an incident between us, but I really didn't think it'd result in this. In fact, it didn't. We were fine for that first day in Indianapolis and the whole year before that we were talking. Then, during the meet, everything just flipped on me."

"Yeah, I remember you guys were texting all during the Olympics. I'm not sure Josie knows that."

"Probably for the best, considering you didn't text her once," I counter.

He glares at me. "Hey, I fixed things with my half of *Adair Swimming Blog*. This is about helping you fix things with your half."

"I don't think there's anything to fix there, dude." I reach up, tugging on the edge of my cap. "Did they ask you to name the club after them?"

"Absolutely not. In fact, they both cried. Mia will deny it, but there were tears. Carter and I owe them a lot. You do, too. They were always rooting for us. The blog didn't work out for them, so what? It's still the reason we all met, and that's what we wanted to carry into the future. Now you're part of that."

Only for as long as they need me. Then I'll be moving on to whatever comes next. "Right, that's cool."

"You know you have a place here for as long as you want, right?" Bryce asks. "This isn't a timed commitment. You're not counting down to your last days."

Except I don't stay.

"Yeah, of course." My gaze drifts to the clock, desperate for a distraction. "Let's finish this workout before the kids get here."

I don't give Bryce the chance to respond before I duck below the water and push off the wall. There's a slight twinge in my leg, but I ignore it. Instead, I focus on a much slower freestyle than I'm used to and let the water calm my racing nerves.

⋯⋯ + ₒ ✦ᵗ ★ᵗ ☽ ★ ✦ ₒ ⁺ ⋯⋯

Lezak prances happily at my feet as I lead him into the main lobby of the pool. Bryce had initially been skeptical about what it'd mean to have a puppy around, but I'd managed to assure him it would be fine. Puppies, I've learned, help relax the swimmers (and the coaches). Lezak also takes to training easily, so I trust him to behave.

"Oh, screw you, Ronan O'Brien." I blink at Josie as she comes around the desk, probably to meet her new friend. "It's really not fair to us mortals, you know."

"No." I laugh. "I have no idea what you're talking about."

She motions to Lezak for permission to pet him, then she squats when I nod in approval. "It's really rude of you to be that pretty and have an adorable bundle of gold fluff as a pet."

Unable to hide my amusement at Josie's comments, I watch her sink the rest of the way to the floor. Within seconds, she has Lezak trying to catch her hand, giggling whenever he manages to change tactics and pounce on her.

"We're not getting a dog right now!" A new voice joins us, but I don't have to turn to know it's Bryce. Josie pouts up at him when he appears next to me. "Josie, no. We both have way too much going on right now."

Which doesn't make a lot of sense, if you ask me. They could bring a dog to work with them, just like I'm doing. It's not like Josie's on a massive book tour, yet, or like Bryce is still training. This could be a great time to get a dog. They could socialize him or her while Lezak and I are still here. Then they'd have a new Adair Swim Club mascot once I eventually move on.

"I hate you for bringing him here."

I gape at Bryce, shocked at his bluntness. "You were the one who told me to bring him here!"

"But I failed to think about how utterly enamored my girlfriend gets with any puppy she meets," he grumbles.

"Don't listen to him, Ronan!" Josie cuddles the dog closer, pressing kisses to his nose. "He's worried another man will take his place in my heart."

"She means the dog," Bryce declares before I can turn a teasing smirk his way. "Not you."

"It sounds more like you're trying to convince yourself, not me," I joke.

The door opens behind us, causing Lezak to perk up and swing his head toward the sound. There's a small gasp and then Lezak is off like a shot, bounding straight out of Josie's arms and toward whoever had just entered. I turn in time to see Mia Sheridan drop her bags and practically melt onto the floor to meet him.

For the blink of an eye, I see the woman who captured my attention all those years ago. Still a total badass who could take anything the world threw at her, but willing to let those hard edges soften for the right thing.

Everything about her shines brighter than before, though. Her laughs bounce off the surrounding walls before piercing me straight through my heart. A sharp reminder of how much I still miss what never was.

"Hi, baby," she coos at my dog, flopping his silky ears between her fingers. "And who is your human?" Her gaze lifts to her best friend. "I can't believe you let Bryce get you a puppy without me!"

"No!" Josie protests. "He still says I can't have one."

"Then who's..." She trails off when her eyes meet mine.

Shakily, I squat down, ignoring the slight twinge in my hip. I reach out to pet Lezak's head, and his tail thumps happily against her stomach. "This is Lezak. He's four months old."

I watch the brightness in her eyes dampen, a cloudiness settling in. In a move that's probably instinctive, she holds the puppy a little closer. "You named a dog after Jason Lezak?"

"When he gets the zoomies, you'll understand why." I'm trying to lighten the mood, but it doesn't seem to work. The iciness is settling around us once again, but god, do I miss the warmth. "Come on, Mia, you can't deny that you love it."

She turns her focus back to the dog. "Don't worry, Lezak. I won't hold your asshole human against you." My gaze snaps back up to Bryce, who's frowning down at us. "You can't help who adopted you and I'm sure he loves you."

"Of course I do," I snap. I may not be perfect at relationships, but I've always loved dogs and I'm a damn good dog dad. I refuse to let her think any differently. "Think what you want about me, Mia, but don't be that level of petty."

It's obvious I caught her off guard by calling her out. She loosens her hold on the puppy enough for him to wriggle from her grasp and immediately begin zooming between her and Josie.

Mia takes that moment to get back to her feet, but she doesn't say anything. Instead, she gathers her bags, gives my happy puppy another pet, and heads toward the office she shares with Josie.

Lezak sits at Josie's feet, looking between us, and the way his new friend just went, clearly conflicted on whether he should stay or go. The rest of us look at one another, the awkward tension in the air palpable. How lucky the little golden fluff is to not worry about petty things like someone not liking you when you're pretty sure they could end up meaning everything to you.

Josie breaks the silence first. "Okay, someone has got to tell me what happened."

I scowl at her. "If I knew, I would tell you. Or at least try to fix it myself."

She stands, dusting her leggings off. "Ronan, Mia only holds grudges like that when she's angry or been hurt. You have to know *something*."

"I haven't done a single thing that would warrant a grudge that has lasted almost eight years."

"That's exactly what someone would say if they messed up bad enough to warrant an eight-year grudge," Bryce protests.

Josie nods in agreement, eyes wide like her boyfriend made some profound point or solved a mystery. I kind of hate how in love the two of them are.

"That is the stupidest thing you've ever said to me, Clark," I snap. "And I knew you when you were a teenager."

And, god, did he say some stupid shit back then.

I bend down, quickly scooping Lezak into my arms before heading out to the pool, decidedly avoiding the office area. Mia Sheridan is the last person I want to be around right now. Besides, I have a dog who needs to get used to walking the pool deck with me if he's going to help motivate these kids.

Mia

"What happened between you and this guy?"

I've been in Joy's office for all of ten minutes and all I've done is complain about Ronan. I didn't delay the start of therapy by asking how she's been or if she and her wife are planning any fun vacations. No, instead I apparently decided to dive right into the actual session today. And, well, Joy seems to love it.

I sink back into the couch. "I don't want to talk about it."

Her brows arch. "Isn't the whole point of therapy to talk about the very things you don't want to talk about?"

"We can talk about anything else but that," I argue. "What about the dating apps? I downloaded those. Let's talk about them."

She crosses one leg over the other, hands folded neatly in her lap. "We can talk about whatever you want, Mia. This hour is yours. You're the one who immediately started talking about him. I'm worried that whatever happened between the two of you could be preventing you from moving on now."

"That makes no sense!" She's clearly forgetting the number my ex did on me that led me to this office in the first place. "If he was keeping me from moving on, Bianca would have never happened. Which, in hindsight, might not have been the worst thing."

"I didn't say he's always had that effect on you. I'm just saying he might be having it now," she counters. "Which would make sense, seeing as you're now in each other's lives again."

We're not just in each other's lives again, though. No matter how hard I try to avoid him, he's always there. And even though I've been nothing but an absolute jerk to him, he keeps up this polite, professional façade like nothing happened between us. And it infuriates me.

Maybe talking about it would help.

Joy seems to think so, too, based on the way she relaxes in her seat and reaches for her iced coffee. "Take me back to the moment everything changed between you two."

I groan, reaching up, and fiddle with the ends of my hair. I should have put it up before therapy; playing with my hair was a nervous habit of mine that I've never been able to break. "It was the last night of the Olympic Trials in 2016—we hooked up. It wasn't ever supposed to happen."

"Then why did it happen?"

"I don't know," I mumble. If I close my eyes, I can still see the two of us. We were so much younger, so unsure of what the world could bring us. I wonder if he was as blind to real heartbreak as I was back then. "He turned out to be different than I expected. It was the first time he and I had really hung out without everyone else around us and...I don't know. I guess he surprised me."

"In what ways?"

I twirl the strand of hair I'm playing with around my finger. "In every way. We only stayed out for two drinks and then we went back to his hotel to watch movies. He had been rooming with Bryce during the entire meet, but he'd gotten that room specifically to hookup on his last night. At least, that's what Bryce told Josie. But he never once came on to me, never pushed me for more, or even flirted with me."

"I thought it bothered you when he acted like the Olympic play-boy?"

Of course, Joy's going to ask the hard questions. Questions I don't know how to answer because the truth is, I did hate it. It drove me nuts and insulted my feminist heart, but more than that, something in me knew that it wasn't him. There was something about the entire reputation he carried with him that felt rather forced—or, at least, it did.

"It gave me a glimpse into the real him, and that made me put my guard down."

She nods, watching me closely. "Who made the first move?"

"I did." My hands drop to my lap and a new fidgeting starts; this time I'm picking at the chipped polish on my nails. "I don't even know what came over me, but I was the one who pushed it further. We were laughing about something and when our eyes met...it just, it felt like the moment was suspended in space. Does that make sense?"

"Like you were seeing everything you've ever wanted and if you took a breath, it'd all vanish around you."

I want to argue. God, do I want to argue. Ronan isn't everything I've always wanted, but in that moment, he was. I wasn't always fair to Josie when it came to her hooking up with Bryce, because I did the same thing. I saw the draw. I knew what it meant to see this gorgeous man—the exact kind of man we'd grown up hearing fat girls can't date. Yet I had this moment and I'd taken advantage of it. Worry crawls up my chest.

I bite my lip, looking at Joy. "Do you think I used Ronan to prove something to myself?"

"What would you need to prove to yourself?"

"That I was desirable...that I was sexy." Tears sting the corner of my eyes. "I don't want to be that kind of person, Joy."

"Do you think you are?" What kind of question is that? "Let me rephrase this. The Olympic swim team is full of attractive men and women, correct?" I nod slightly, wondering where she's going with this. "If you really wanted to prove to yourself that you could get someone attractive, would you have picked him?"

"Absolutely not. He's my friend. Or he was."

"Then I don't think you took advantage of him, Mia," she replies. "I think you're worried about that now because you still can't let yourself believe he wanted you back."

My stomach churns and twists. The walls feel like they're closing in on me, and everything starts to blur. The words hit me like a punch to the gut. Anxiety crawling up my arms; the need to hide away from my own insecurities too much to take right now. Before I can force myself to stand and flee, Joy's voice stops me.

"Mia." Her voice is steady and calm. Something I can focus on. "I need you to take a few deep breaths for me."

Together, Joy and I work to get the anxiety attack under control. By the time my breathing is back to normal, and a water bottle is pressed into my shaky hands, we've used about ten minutes of my session. Joy's warm smile and calm voice continue to center me.

As soon as I step into the building after therapy, Josie seems to know the session had been a long one. There must be something about the look on my face or something in my eyes because she glances up, offers me the smallest smile, and focuses back on the parent at the desk. I quietly move through the small crowd, heading up to our shared office with the hope no one else stops me.

Carter and Bryce are chatting outside the offices, in the small communal space we have there. Neither pay me any mind as I sneak into my office and close the door quietly behind me. Leaning back against it, I take a couple of deep, centering breaths. The smell of chlorine lingers in every part of this building and, while some people might find it annoying, it helps comfort me even more. It's something tangible I can hold on to and use as a centering tool; some of my fondest memories involve the smell of chlorine.

It's also involved in some of my least favorite memories, but I'm choosing not to focus on those.

It takes longer than I would like to admit for me to feel like the floor has settled beneath my feet, but once it does, it's time to focus my attention back on the mountain of work I need to do. I take my time, pulling everything I need from my bag and setting up my desk to be as productive as possible. I'm content to forget about pesky things like anxiety or feelings that get in my way. After all, I've always been pretty good at avoiding things I don't want to face.

I don't emerge from my office for a few hours. I allow myself to be fully emerged in the work I need to do and the way it can distract me from everything else. When I finally do come out, Ronan is standing at the coffeemaker. I curse under my breath and am just about to shut myself back into my office when he turns.

The frown on his features causes his eyebrows to furrow in a confused way that would look adorable on anyone else. But definitely not on him. "When did you get here?"

"Right after lunch," I reply, moving into the room. "Like I'm scheduled."

It's not that we have a schedule we need to keep track of. Neither Bryce nor Carter care when I come and go as long as I finish the things I need to. The days I have therapy, though, are marked that I'm unavailable until after lunch on the shared calendar, specifically to give me time to get my life sorted out. I wake up early, do some freelance work, go to therapy, and then come to work at Adair. Usually, I don't feel like I've been fileted open, but what can you do?

"I never saw you come in. I thought you were sick or something." His focus is fully on the coffee he's making; he doesn't even spare me a glance.

I shrug, walking over to the small fridge, reaching in to grab a Diet Coke. "I wasn't in the mood to talk. Next time, I'll be sure to announce my presence."

"That's not what I meant, and you know it. All I was saying is your presence is usually much more noticeable...wait, that didn't come out right either."

My eyes narrow at him while I reach for a small bag of chips to help me power through the rest of my day. "Do you want me to get you a shovel to help out with the hole you keep digging yourself?"

He finally looks at me. "You know, one of these days, we're actually going to have to talk about what happened, Mia." He sighs. "We won't be able to stay productive with snarky quips and a pool between us forever."

Fear rushes through me. There's no way he knows what I'm really mad about, right? If he knew the truth, he probably wouldn't even apologize. I wouldn't matter in the overall scheme of things, but he'd beg me not to tell Bryce, because we both know there's no way he'd be okay with someone, especially a friend, saying something like that.

"And what do you think we need to talk about?" I keep my voice even, hoping he can't pick up on the fear in it.

He glances around, like he's scared someone might overhear us. Then, in a low voice, he says the last thing I'm expecting. "What happened in Omaha."

I laugh, loudly. It comes so quickly, there's no way to get control of it before it's tumbling out. Ronan rears back like I'd just offended him. "You..." I take a deep breath, trying to calm myself down. "You think this is about sex?" Another laugh bubbles out as soon as I ask the question. "*Seriously?*"

"Of course," he snaps. I can see it, though, an emotion Ronan O'Brien doesn't wear all that often—he's uncomfortable. "What else could it be about, Mia? That's when everything changed."

But it's not.

I want to remind him of all the ways that night didn't change things, but allowed something new to happen. We spent the entire year between the summers of 2016 and 2017 talking. We'd text whenever we could, occasionally do video calls, and there were even a couple of times we met for dinner or coffee when we happened to be in the same city. We never tumbled back into bed together; we just enjoyed each other's company. I would never say this to my best friend, but in those twelve months, Ronan and I were closer to a real relationship than she and Bryce ever were when they hooked up.

And now I'm learning that a year that meant everything to me, meant nothing to him. Which only makes the anger burn hotter.

"This has nothing to do with Omaha. Nor does it have anything to do with the way you led me on for a whole year, Ronan," I snarl.

"Led you on?" If I didn't know the reputation he had—the way he played women—I would almost believe he looked confused. "What are you talking about, Mia?"

"Does it matter?" The last thing I really want to do is bring this all up. I'm in no place to have it out with Ronan, but I want to make something perfectly clear. "If you think this is about Omaha, then you need to do some self-examining. I should have known better than to let my guard fall around you. Everyone warned me."

He steps back, dark eyebrows furrowing further. "I don't think that's fair—"

"Isn't it?" I cut him off. "All the warning signs were there, and you ended up doing what I always knew you would."

"You were the one who straddled my lap. *You* initiated everything. I checked in constantly, making sure there was no regret. If you didn't want it, I would have stopped the second I knew. Hell, I stopped so many times to make sure you wanted it!"

That night comes back to me in flashes. Blunt nails trailing up my thighs, dark hair buried between my legs as stars lit up behind my eyes. The feel of him sinking into me. How it felt to be in this man's strong and comforting arms. How, for a blink, I believe I could have someone like him want me in return.

For twelve months after that night, I thought we were building something amazing. Something real. Laying the foundation for something that could last. Screw the reputation, screw the doubters—I knew Ronan O'Brien in a way no one else did and he was never going to hurt me.

What a fucking joke.

"You know what I want now? I want you to leave me alone, Ronan."

"Well, that's going to be hard when we work together."

"We work at the same swim club, but we don't actively work together. All my marketing goes through Bryce and Carter. You're a coach. You stay in your lane, and I'll stay in mine."

In the back of my head, I can hear Josie giggle. Of course, I would make a swimming pun to an Olympian in the middle of a heated argument. Ronan doesn't find it amusing, though.

"Do Bryce and Josie know about what happened?"

It's not a question, but a demand. He wants to know where he stands in the eyes of our friends. Which makes me think maybe he knows more than he's letting on. Neither one of them would care that we hooked up, especially because that same night was the start of their friends-with-benefits situation.

If he knows the truth, though, he'd be more concerned about who else might know.

"What was there to tell, Ronan?" Looking up at him, I know what I have to do. I need to get him to drop it. I need to give him a reason to stay away from me. "You were my biggest mistake, Ronan. I need you to know that."

The impact of my words is instantaneous. I can feel the way everything shifts, watch as Ronan seems to collapse in on himself. All the tension he was holding—all the bravado he seems to exude at all times—just vanishes. He blinks at me, stunned by my bluntness. And I feel a little sick.

I've never seen him look so small.

"I don't know what happened. I don't know what changed between us, but this..." He trails off in a low voice. "How long are you going to stay mad at the past, Mia?"

"I'm not mad at the past." The bag of chips crinkle beneath my grip. "I refuse to let it affect my future."

There's literally nothing else to say. I can hear footsteps coming up the stairs. It feels like the walls are closing in on me, the weight of our words pushing them closer and closer. I take a step back, ready to retreat back to my office. Ronan reaches for me, but his hand stops mid-air as he realizes what he's doing, then it drops.

And I know that whatever little shred of hope still hung between us is gone now. There's no coming back from the things I said. Just like there's no coming back from what he said. The past is going to define us; it's going to shape and influence everything that comes next. It will serve as a reminder that our words and actions have consequences, and we'll have to face those consequences one way or another. Even if it's eight years down the line.

The door to the stairwell swings open, pulling Ronan's gaze from me. In that brief moment of distraction, I do what every sensible woman would do in my position. I run.

I seek solace in my office; the door swinging closed behind me. I listen as Ronan chats with Bryce about some game that was on TV the night before, our friend clueless about what just happened. I used to want to hurt him the way he hurt me all those years ago, but seeing it unfold in real time made my stomach twist. Why did he have to make things happen this way?

We could have been happy. We had a chance to have everything, and he took it from us.

And I definitely never fought for it.

Ronan

Mia's words haunt me for days.

Every time I shut my eyes, memories flash through my mind. Good memories, great even. Only...now they're tainted with the truth I've learned. She regrets everything. She wishes it never happened. And I don't know what to do with that information.

Sure, she's not the first one to say those words to me. I've done a lot of things I'm not proud of, leaned a little too heavily into the playboy reputation swimming and media branded me with. I've had women scream at me in public, drinks thrown in my face, and unfortunately, even received a slap or two. They were all well-deserved reactions, but still.

None of those reactions mattered, though. They were reminders of what I was doing to myself, and of how I was filling my life with things I'd regret. Ultimately, they were fleeting moments in my life. Moments I wouldn't dwell on too long. I thought I would finally let go of them once the world seemed to understand I'd grown up. Except that never happened. I was never given the chance to be honest about who I am with anyone. Except Mia.

And that's why it hurt so badly. Because this one—this one matters.

For the first time in years, I had tried to build something with someone. I was dedicated to learning everything I possibly could about Mia Sheridan. To make her feel seen and heard. I wanted to get to know her on a level deeper than just the mutual attraction already there.

There has been something about her from the moment I caught her in my arms in Charlotte.

I slipped into the reputation I was known for with ease, but Mia never bought into it. No matter how flustered I made her—no matter how hard Josie was trying not to freak out—she just pulled herself together. She wasn't flustered for a minute; she went right to business and introduced them as the owners of *Adair Swimming*, the blog this club is named after. Even when I surprised her, she never broke her composure. It was one of the first things I learned to admire about Mia.

I was hesitant to push for anything more with Mia. I knew back then what I did to women, and I didn't want to put her through the same heartache. She deserved someone better—still does. When she pulled herself into my lap that night, every warning bell was blaring in my head, telling me to run before I fucked up one of the few good things in my life. But then I set my hands on her hips, and she was leaning in until our lips were barely touching. She brushed her long, silky dark hair to the side as she asked me to kiss her.

I was unable to resist.

I checked in so many times. She was the one who kept pulling me back in for more. More I was happy to give, but the fear was there. The very real possibility I would hurt this woman. We should have talked about it more that morning, but she was gone early. Woke me up long enough to let me walk her back to her room, hoping Josie wouldn't be too worried.

I kissed her goodbye at that door and held onto the fleeting feeling of *almost* for a whole year. A year I spent building something real. I thought we were doing it together, but I was very, very wrong.

When we met in Indianapolis the following summer, everything felt great. I had plans to see if she wanted to be something more, take it to an official level, and then it all came to a screeching halt. She went from being this bright light in my life to nothing but a cold shoulder. She wouldn't even look at me.

When I'd asked Josie if she knew what was going on, the way she joked about the reputation I had back then cut me deep. I'd put on a brave face, met her joke with one of my own, but I watched the way her smile faltered—she saw right through me. I spent weeks combing through messages, replaying every moment over, trying to figure out where I screwed it up; because it had to be something I did.

After a week's worth of text messages went unanswered, I finally took the hint and let her go.

Now she's throwing everything back in my face—proving my worst fear. Proving that it never meant anything to her.

When Bryce and Carter originally approached me about this position, I was hesitant because they mentioned Mia doing their media. It had nothing to do with me not wanting to see her. Over the last few years, whenever I let my mind wander, it always found her. Of course, I wanted to see her and what her life was like, but I respected her too much to force her to confront me and our past. It took a lot of convincing from the two Olympians and a quick glance at Mia in Paris for my resolve to crumble.

Whatever second chance I was hoping for clearly isn't on the table.

And that's fine, because we're two different people now. Who knows, we might not even be compatible anymore.

If I could only believe my own lie.

· · · · · + ₒ + ★ ★ ☽ ★ ★ + ₒ + · · · · ·

Mia lets out a small shriek of surprise when she rounds the corner to head outside. I somehow manage to stop the two of us from colliding and quickly drop my hands from her shoulders when she shoots me a glare. She mutters out her thanks before shoving past me.

"What the hell happened between you two now?" The whine in Bryce's voice has me turning toward him, eyebrow arched. "You were fine. Sure, you didn't get along, but I didn't have to worry about you becoming an HR nightmare!"

I cock my head. "Do we even have HR?"

He sets the stack of papers he was holding on the desk and leans against it. "Listen here, asshole. I am HR. I don't want to deal with a nightmare. Please don't make me."

The mental image of Bryce trying to recreate something that looks remotely like a human resources department is laughable to me. He's never been the type of person who will use buzz words or tiptoe around a problem in the guise of keeping things professional. He'd much rather tell it like it is. Which is one of the things I've always admired about him.

Especially when he used that specific talent to have my back and pushed me to keep fighting after the accident. But that's not something I should allow myself to dive into too much. Not when there are other things that need to be done.

"I promise you won't have to fire either one of us for unprofessional conduct." He doesn't look convinced. "Don't give me that look, man! I warned you this would happen."

He moves around the desk, wagging a finger at me. "No, you told me that the two of you wouldn't get along. Which is fine. We decided we could work around that. What you *failed* to mention was something could happen between you two that makes it worse. What happened?"

As if he's the only one who wants to know the answer to that question. "I don't know, man. We just talked."

His eyebrows shoot up his forehead. "You just *talked*? What the hell? Is that a euphemism for old people or something?"

I glower at him. "I'm only three years older than you, asshole. And it's not a euphemism for anything. We literally just talked."

"Then you need to not do that again," he decides with a nod. "Yeah, that's probably for the best."

I cross my arms over my chest. "And how is that going to work?"

"I don't know!" He throws his hands up. "Carter and I can be your carrier pigeons or some shit." He pokes me in the chest—actually pokes me. I fight to keep the laugh back when I see the seriousness in his gaze. "I have a delicate balance here, O'Brien, and I will not have the two of you messing it up! Got it?"

With one last poke to my chest, Bryce is turning to walk away from me, and I can't help but push his buttons a little more. "All right, we won't talk anymore. But are you going to give her the same lecture you gave me?"

He turns around. "No way in hell. She scares me."

I can no longer hold in the laugh, which only seems to irritate him more since he storms off with a scowl. From the very first moment he saw her, Bryce has always been a little afraid of Mia. And it's not him being dramatic. She's fiercely protective of her best friend, and Bryce was someone who didn't always treat Josie right. Of course, he was on her shit list.

But in the short few weeks I've been here, I've witnessed the shift in their dynamic. She knows Bryce loves Josie more than anything and will do whatever he can to keep her happy. She's stepped back a little, loosened the protective shield she's always had on the younger woman, and trusts Bryce to pick up the slack.

Hell, I'd even say a friendship between the two of them has been coming together.

He's lucky; he has Josie to help soften Mia's ire, whereas I am doomed to face it for the rest of our lives.

Over the next few days, I manage to listen to Bryce's demands. It helps that Mia seems to be going out of her way to avoid me whenever we have to be at work at the same time. Usually, she's shut in her and Josie's office or, when she needs marketing material, she'll turn around, and leave whenever she has the chance. Which is about to become harder, though, because Bryce has officially cleared me to take over the coaching of the high school team.

The team is made up of a number of kids from around the city who either don't have access to a swim team through their school, the team they're on isn't serious enough to help them with their goals, or their parents are determined to have their kid coached by an Olympian. Those kids are the ones I tend to check in on the most, not wanting to see their parents follow the same path mine did.

Overall, it's a solid team. Although they're young, I could already see several of them making time cuts for Olympic Trials in 2028, which is exactly what Bryce and Carter want to see for their small club. And now they're turning this team over to me while Carter focuses on some of the younger swimmers and Bryce takes a step back to focus on the business. I'm fulfilling everything I was brought here to do.

And it's no surprise I'm the one who breaks the silence between Mia and me.

I'm running the team through an efficiency workout—helping them nail the basics of knowing their stroke count and keeping it consistent—when Mia walks onto the deck. She hesitates when she sees me, before putting on a blank look of pure annoyance and walking down the deck to get better angles for photos.

My gaze drifts from swimmer to swimmer as I pace the length of the pool with them, trying to pick out the most consistent among them. As a group of them turn at the wall, heading back, while the rest of them are still making their way to the wall, I stop near Mia. She's determined to not pay me any attention, continuing to snap pictures. I break.

"You're going to have to get used to this," I tell her. "The team is all mine. Bryce's in his office and Carter is with the middle schoolers."

She's focused on scrolling through the pictures and, for a second, I don't think she'll respond to me. "I'm surprised they trust you to coach kids alone."

My gaze snaps toward her. "Excuse me?"

Surely Bryce and Carter told her what I do. Besides, there are so many steps involved in being cleared to coach, especially at a level where the kids would have to travel. Something I know she knows from her time doing media in the sport.

"We would hate for you to teach all those kids to be cocky, irresponsible assholes."

Is she really throwing that stupid reputation I had back in my face? The reputation she knows I hate and the one she and Josie worked hard to fight against? Was I always the picture-perfect athlete? No. Did I use my status as a world-class athlete to flirt? Sure. But I didn't have a string of girls waiting for me to give them a chance. I also hated the way swimming and sports media made me out to be this self-absorbed ass because of the way my parents paraded me around like a show pony.

She *knows* all that and now she's treating me like everyone else.

"You think you know me so well," I say lowly. "Don't you, Sheridan?"

I have never referred to her by her last name; she's always been Mia to me. And her name has always brought a smile to my face, until now.

Her eyes widen slightly, the brown line surrounding the greenish-blue looking impossibly dark, but her mask is quickly back up. She smiles smugly at me. "Yes, O'Brien, I do. Isn't that what I've been trying to tell you? You're not fooling anyone. You never have been."

My irritation grows. For the first time in my life, I want Mia to get as far away from me as possible. "Well, apparently, I fooled you once."

It's the wrong thing to say. I hate how her eyes shutter, how she seems to fold in on herself, and make herself smaller.

There's no emotion on her face when she looks back at me. She hops off the bleacher she was using for leverage, gripping her camera, and glaring at me. "And it'll never happen again."

My shoulders sag as I watch her walk back down the deck, probably ready to head up to her office. Hell, maybe she'll find Bryce and demand I be fired. This conversation would definitely fall under "HR nightmare," which he warned me against. Maybe he was right. I probably should have never opened my mouth.

I'm still cleaning up after my practice well into the start of free swim. One of the mothers had snagged my attention before I could stop it, asking about the schedule of meets and what the time standards would be. Although I calmly explained we were still finalizing the meet schedule, reminding her short course season doesn't start until September, she wanted something concrete. I mentioned a couple of the meets I knew we'd be looking at, which drew the attention of another parent who wanted to know why we weren't participating in long course season.

Which led to a whole other explanation of this team being new enough that swimmers are on different levels—levels we're still determining. Some of our athletes aren't familiar with long course, which requires a different approach to their races. Besides, since it's June, the long course season is well underway, and it could do more damage to the team to throw them into something they're unprepared for. There's a difference between the typical high school season and the club season, which we fall under, and keeping them in the club year-round will prohibit them from competing for their high school team.

Which then led me to learning all the reasons why swim parents know more than the coach. Something I'm not sure I'll ever get used to, but definitely know how to handle.

The point is, I'm already here later than I want to be, and I did not have enough caffeine to deal with this.

As I finish gathering the team's equipment, I think about the conversation I had with Mia. The way I'd pretty much burned every bridge that could have ever brought us together. Which is a shame because I'd really like to get her and Josie to put together a handout for parents to explain everything they need to know about club versus high school swimming. Maybe I could get Josie to bring it up; she doesn't hate me.

Or maybe she does. Mia's had a lot of time to tell her about what happened.

Something catches my attention out of the corner of my eye before I can finish cleaning up. Or, rather, someone. A swimmer has claimed one of our free swim lanes for herself and is gliding through the water in a gentle freestyle. She's better than any of the kids I currently have freestyling on the team.

I watch her swim a couple of laps, picking up pace occasionally before dropping back down. There are things that need improvement—her elbow position and turns are off, along with her breathing—but the basics are there. Not only are they there, but they're strong. She keeps her body in a great streamlined position—her head is low and in line with her body. Just looking at her, I feel like I'm looking at a younger Katie Ledecky or Simone Manuel. I want this girl on the team.

Forgetting my gear, I walk over to her lane, hoping to catch her when she stops for a break and a drink of water. Something else I've been able to easily pick up on is when someone is tiring themselves out. As predicted, she pulls to a stop at the wall as I'm approaching.

I approach carefully, fully aware of the fear that comes from a man approaching a young woman in public. I go in with the introduction. "Hey, my name is Ronan O'Brien. I'm one of the coaches here at Adair Swim Club. You're really talented, and I was wondering what team you swim for."

The young woman pulls her goggles off, resting them against her cap, and blinks up at me. Once, twice, three times. I don't know what to do.

"Holy shit," she breathes. Well, that wasn't what I was expecting. "I watched you at the Olympics. I mean...not in person because it was in Rio, and I was only five, but I remember watching you."

My face flushes. It's not often people recognize me anymore, even among young swimmers. My career ended in 2017 and most of the kids this girl's age were too young to remember, but she remembers me, and that will always be a weird feeling. "Uh, yeah, I retired in 2017."

She nods. "Yeah, I remember that. Holy shit, you were watching me swim and think I'm good? *Me*?"

"Yes," I exclaim, happy to pull the attention off me and back on her. "I was wondering what team you swim for? Is it a school team?"

If it's a school team, I have the chance to pull her away. If it's a club, it depends. Adair is the only one in the city who's registered with the US swimming governing body, which is a pull for a lot of people.

The young woman laughs in my face. "I don't swim for anyone! I'm not on a team. I just like swimming."

My scheming brain screeches to a halt. "What?" My astonishment is clear in my voice, and it's now my turn to blink at her. "But you're good enough to get a scholarship."

A scholarship. Go pro. Potentially go to the Olympics. Become one of the best female freestylers we've ever seen. But, you know, baby steps.

"I'm going to be a sophomore in high school, and I go to public school."

I bite back a smile. "Not high school, kid. College. I feel confident enough to say you could get a college scholarship if you took this seriously."

The wide-eyed wonderment is back, but it dims almost as quickly. "Swimming on a team is expensive. It's not something I can really afford."

Which tells me she's wanted this bad enough to look into it at some point.

Part of the reason Bryce and Carter brought me on is to build a scholarship. To give talented swimmers the chance to chase their dreams, even when their financial situation doesn't allow it. And she's right about swimming being expensive. It takes a toll on the swimmer's family.

And that's exactly why we want to push this scholarship. And I know who our first recipient should be.

"Would you want to swim on a team? More specifically here." She goes to argue, but I don't let her. "Let me talk to my boss, but there is a way we can get you on the team here—get you training and competing—without costing you a dollar."

There's something in her eyes that tells me she's been let down before. She doesn't want to hold on to too much hope around this. "I need to leave in fifteen minutes."

It's an opening; that's all I need. "That's all I need. What's your name?"

She's not convinced. "Emmie."

"Emmie," I repeat. "Great! Don't go anywhere, please!"

Ignoring the fundamental rule of no running on the deck, I take off toward the offices, determined to not be another person who lets this kid down.

Ronan

"Is everything okay?" Josie asks as I bypass the front desk, heading straight upstairs to the offices. "Ronan?"

I am fully aware I only have a short window of time to convince Bryce and Carter we need this girl on the team. If I can't offer her something in the next fifteen minutes—something that will convince her to stay—she'll go home and there's no guarantee I'll ever see her again. I'm not sure they'll be ready to commit to something like this so early on. Adair isn't even a year old, and I've only been here a month. We still have a lot we're trying to build and grow, but this girl could help us achieve every goal we've set for ourselves.

What we don't have with her, though, is time. I'm determined to give this kid a chance.

Bryce's office door is shut when I approach it, but I can see Carter through the window. Perfect.

I knock on the door once, not even waiting before I push it open. "Hey, can I talk to you guys?"

Mia is sitting in one of the chairs off to the side, mouth open like she was in the middle of saying something when I interrupted. I hadn't even seen her there, but her presence doesn't stop me from pushing further into the office. She's the one who said we needed to stay away from each other yet always seems to be around. She can get used to this.

"We're in a meeting right now." Exasperation drips from her tone while I shut the door behind me. "But sure, Ronan, come on in."

If this were her office, I might feel a bit guilty, but it's not. It's Bryce's and her opinion isn't my priority right now. "I'm sorry, but this is important."

"Yeah, of course." Bryce shuts his laptop, giving me his full attention. "Everything okay?"

To my left, Mia starts gathering her things. "I'll let you guys talk. We can finish our meeting later."

"Actually," I reply, "you should stay. This will probably end up involving you at some point, too."

The Mia I knew also loved cheering for the underdog. If I can get her on my side, at least in this one instance, she can help me get Bryce and Carter on board.

"Oh." She settles back into her seat.

Leaning back against the door, I cross my arms over my chest, and focus on the owners. "I want to talk about the scholarship program."

They exchange a quick look, but they all wait for me to continue.

"I found the kid who should get to the first one." Quick and straight to the point is the best way to get things to go my way. "She's downstairs right now."

For whatever reason, Mia is the first one to speak. "There is no way we can make something like that happen right now."

To my annoyance, Bryce nods. "That's still at least a year out, Ronan. We're doing great, but this is our first year and I can't be investing in a scholarship fund. Not right now."

An opportunity like this could open so many doors for this young woman. She could get into a good college, travel, and more. Plus, I can see it in her eyes—she loves being in the water, even if she's not doing it in a competitive way. The drive is there and a future full of whatever she wants is within reach. This is what I do. This is what I came to Adair to do.

I do feel a bit like a dick to just barge into Bryce's office and demand these two new business owners to take a chance on someone who could end up costing them a lot of money. There are ways to prevent that from happening, though. And the chance for this to go right far outweighs the likelihood it'll go wrong.

"You know how we feel about implementing a scholarship program, Ronan. We discussed it at length when we hired you." I focus on Carter, but don't miss the way Mia's jaw drops open a bit. Does she not know what they brought me on to do? "Give it another year and we can—"

"We don't have a year with this kid, guys!" I can picture the way my mother would purse her lips at my raised voice, but I press on. "She's a sophomore in high school and she's had no formal training. It is literally now or never."

Bryce looks at Carter, his frown deepening, and I know I said the wrong thing. I just made them even more concerned about what this could do—time and money could be wasted.

I have to fix it. "But she's good. She's *really* good. Her form is almost perfect. We all know what it means to see a kid who has that fire—something in them that tells you they're gonna be someone and do something incredible. She has that. All she needs is someone to give her a damn chance!"

Bryce lets out a sympathetic-sounding sigh, fingers roughly combing through dark blond curls. He's conflicted. The businessman in him is at odds with the swimmer who chased a dream. "Look, man, I get it, but the funds aren't there right now."

"And they won't be for years."

I turn to glare at Mia. "I thought you handled marketing, not money. Or coaching, for that matter."

She meets my glare with one of her own. "Well, you're not listening to the man in charge of the money. You know, your *boss*."

"She has a point," Carter cuts in. "Yes, we're starting to see a profit, but with four salaries, it's still tight. We don't have a lot of room to work with."

"Then stop paying me."

Mia chokes on air. A ragged cough overtakes her, and she reaches for her water. I clock her movements from the corner of my eyes, but my focus mostly stays on Bryce. I'm wearing him down.

He pinches the bridge of his nose. "We already told you we're not doing that, Ronan. We aren't hiring you, moving you across the country, and not paying you. Your salary is already way less than it should be."

It had taken months for the three of us to come to an agreement on that. I didn't need money. I managed and invested my earnings from my professional career well. That's what I live on, and I do so quite comfortably. There's not always a lot of money in swimming, but if you can get sponsorships and take on other side gigs like modeling, it adds up.

"And I told you I don't need it," I push back. "If my salary is the only thing preventing us from giving her a shot, then I don't want it."

Bryce glowers at me. "We're not doing it that way, Ronan. If you work for us, you get paid. That's how we're running this business. End of story."

I have never felt the urge to scream at the top of my lungs so strongly before.

"Bryce and Carter are running their business the way they want to," Mia says. I've also never felt this amount of frustration with her before—like she's purposefully getting in my way and making things difficult for me, no matter who else it could hurt. "It's ultimately their decision and you have to respect it."

"Fine." I cross my arms over my chest. "If that's how it's going to be, then I accept it."

Bryce raises a brow. "But?"

"I'll pay for her training."

With a groan, he drops his head in pure defeat. "Are you kidding me right now, man?"

"Seriously," Mia adds. "Is this really the time you want to throw your money around? We get it, Ronan, Mommy and Daddy are rich. Why do you always have to prove it to everyone around you?"

Her words sting, right down to my core. Nothing she's ever said to me has hurt this badly. I can see it written all over her face. She doesn't see me anymore. She sees the same person almost everyone else in the world does—the spoiled, rich kid party boy who has had everything handed to him.

I wish I knew what made her opinion of me shift like that. And more importantly, why does her believing this hurt me more than it ever has before?

I stare down at her, shoulders tense, and mouth pulled into a thin line. "I'm not trying to prove anything, Mia. I want to give her a shot. Isn't that what Adair Swim Club is supposed to be about?"

"No, you want the glory of paying for that kid's success," she seethes. "Let her finish the career you threw away."

Ouch.

"Now, wait a minute—"

I cut Bryce off before he can get into something I don't want to get into. "If that's really the way you see me, nothing I say will change that, but I always thought you were better than to stoop to shallow judgments. Turns out you're not the only one finding out people aren't who they seem."

Her cheeks flush, whether in embarrassment, or anger, I'm not sure. Still, fire flares in her eyes. "You think you're doing something noble here—"

"No. I'm supporting talent, Sheridan. Talent who might never get another chance without this. You can think whatever you want of me, but don't belittle this." I look back at Bryce and Carter. "Now, will one of you please come with me to see what I'm talking about?"

Bryce looks at Carter, who motions him to go ahead. "Your judgment is as good as mine. I'll wrap things up with Mia."

Bryce stands and heads toward the door. I take one last look at Mia, wondering if I'll ever have anything I want to say to her again, before I follow him.

We're halfway down the stairs when Bryce breaks the silence. "You're going to have to tell her, eventually."

I smirk to myself. "About what? My real job or the real reason I retired?"

He glares back, pulling open the door. "Both."

"Maybe." I shrug. "But not today."

······ + ₀ ✦ ✳ ✦ ☾ ✦ ✳ ✦ ₀ + ······

"Holy shit, dude."

Bryce's eyes are tracking every movement of the girl pulling herself through the water with practiced ease. He's stunned in the same way I was the first time I watched some of the biggest names in the sport swim in person for the first time. Forget about racing against someone that good—that kind of raw talent will always take your breath away. She could be the goldmine a small club like this needs.

"I really hate it when I have to say you were right." He rolls his eyes when he sees the smug smile on my face. "Don't get too cocky; she's not on the team yet. You said you talked to her?"

I nod. "Briefly, before I came into your office. She told me how old she was, and that she has no formal training, but has always loved swimming. Her technique is natural, Bryce. I asked if she'd be interested in swimming on a team, and she told me it's not something they could afford."

"Hence the scholarship program." His gaze has gone back to the young woman. "But she's interested?"

"She said it's always been a dream of hers. I'll work with her. Give her private lessons to help her get caught up with the rest of the team. This could work."

"Well, then, let's get her on the team."

Our time must be running out because Emmie has pulled herself from the water to wrap a towel around her shoulders, heading toward her stuff. Bryce and I follow.

"Emmie!" I call, hoping not to startle her. She looks up, eyes widening when we reach her. "This is one of the owners of Adair Swim Club, Bryce Clark."

"Nice to meet you, Emmie." Bryce holds out a hand. She stares up at him with a look I know well. It's the look that came whenever a young swimmer has met not one, but two Olympians in the span of twenty minutes. It's probably a good thing we didn't bring Carter with us.

She snaps out of it, shakily reaching forward to shake Bryce's hand. "Oh, my god, I'm sorry," she mutters, her gaze bouncing between the two of us. "I didn't think he was telling the truth. It's really nice to meet you, Mr. Clark."

He flinches in the same way every newly thirty-year-old basically gets told they're old by the younger generation, but he recovers quickly.

"Bryce." He smiles. "I'm surprised you didn't see all the headlines about two Olympians opening a club in Columbia. My marketing manager made sure to make a pretty big deal out of it."

She flushes. "Honestly, I didn't even know this place existed until my counselor told me you were letting high school students use the pool and gym for free."

Bryce glances at me quickly. "So, you don't have a pool or team at your high school?"

Her laugh is harsh and short. "No, not at all."

"How would you feel about swimming on a team?" Bryce presses, gently. Which is good, because Emmie is still looking at us like she's a deer caught in headlights. "Specifically, here, at Adair, on the team Ronan coaches."

"You seem to favor freestyle, and I have a lot of experience," I remind her. Bryce shoots me a *"Really, dude?"* look, but I don't care. I want this girl on my team. "And they agreed. You wouldn't pay for anything. We can handle talking to your parent or guardian, if you're worried about that."

She shakes her head, biting her lip. "No, I can talk to my mom. She won't mind, as long as she doesn't have to pay anything."

"It's a scholarship," I lie. "Tell her there's nothing that needs to come out of her own pocket."

She looks at me with vulnerable eyes. "And you really think I'm good enough to get a college scholarship?"

I hold her gaze, refusing to waver. "I do, but I don't want that to be the only reason you join this team. I want you to join it because you want to, because you love swimming, and want to see what you're capable of. The quickest way to burnout on something you love is to put a monetary value on it."

"He's right. You have to want to do this, Emmie," Bryce chimes in.

Her smile brightens. "It's all I've ever wanted, if I'm being honest."

Bryce takes that as her acceptance. "Great! We have some forms your parents will need to fill out. Ronan wants to do some private sessions with you before he pulls you into the team, since you've had no formal training. Is that alright with you?"

Emmie nods excitedly, her hands twisting the towel around. "Yes, absolutely!"

"And I have some stipulations," I tell her. She nods again. "School is your priority. You have to keep your grades up. I require all my swimmers to give me quarterly updates on their grades. If you slip below a C in any course, you're benched from meets until it goes up. You have to stay out of trouble; getting caught drinking underage or being apprehended will result in an immediate suspension. If you're on this team, you're committed. You show up on time for practices and meets, and you do your best. Swimming may feel like an individual sport, but your team is invaluable. And if you ever need something, you come to me, or any other adult working for Adair, okay?"

"We want our swimmers to know this is a safe space for them," Bryce adds. "If you're in trouble or need something, we're here to help."

"Exactly. Do you agree to these stipulations?"

"Absolutely. Thank you so much for this opportunity!" She reaches out to shake both of our hands.

"Welcome to Adair, Emmie." Bryce grins. "Let's get those forms and do a quick tour of the place."

"So, tell me more about him!"

Ronan, who was crossing the room to get a cup of coffee, stops dead in his tracks and turns to face Josie and me. "More about who?"

Ignoring his question, I look at my best friend. "There's nothing else I can say, Jos." I laugh. "You know how dating apps work; they don't give you a lot of room to get to know someone. That's what the dates are for."

From his spot in the other chair, Bryce scowls at the mere mention of his girlfriend ever being on a dating app, which makes me bite back a smile. Josie lasted all of one week on a dating app before swearing to never download one again; the lack of authenticity and taking the time to get to know someone was a huge turnoff for her. She wasn't in the market for a quick path, so she kept traveling the one she already was on, and it led her back to Bryce.

"But the two of you have been talking for *days*!" She drops her head back against the couch in annoyance, turning it to look at me. "Come on, there has to be something he's told you that's of note."

But he hasn't, not really. All of our conversations have been pretty shallow, not digging too deep into either of our personal lives. I know he works at the nearby university, but I don't know what he does there. I know he's a horrible texter and wouldn't know how to use a comma correctly if his life depended on it—which is something I won't be telling the writer sitting beside me.

"Oh!" Josie flinches at my outburst, but I don't care because I *do* have a fun fact about him. "He has a cat. It's named...Cat."

The fact sort of dies on my tongue as I remember just how lame it is.

Josie's anticipatory smile drops. "Oh...That's...not the most creative name I've ever heard, but it's hardly the cat's fault. I'm sure they're still adorable and it gets the point across."

Am I so pathetically alone that my best friend is trying to rationalize this lame tidbit of information I somehow managed to remember? The truth is that this guy is nothing special. He's a pretty basic, copy-paste white guy who doesn't seem to be interested in anything other than fishing—he even posed with a fish in his profile—and football. Our conversations are boring, and he barely asks about me, but it's what Joy would label as progress. My therapist has a point; I need to start moving on from the Bianca situation, and this is the first lame step.

"You're allergic to cats."

My gaze snaps up to Ronan, who is still frozen in place but also now frowning at me. I told him that in passing once, but he remembers it. Remembers it enough to bring it up in a moment like this. It shouldn't have an impact on me, not really, but I suddenly feel like some kind of way about it.

"I..." I trail off, not even knowing what I want to say.

"Oh, my god, you are!" Josie gasps, looking at me with wide eyes. "How is that going to work?"

I can't talk to Ronan—can't acknowledge that some of the information I shared with him is still there despite years of not speaking—but I can talk to Josie. More importantly, I can joke with Josie and make things seem better. Even if she doesn't fully believe me, Ronan will. He won't be able to see through the façade I put up. Or I hope not.

"We're not getting married," I joke. "I probably won't even end up at his house."

"But if he has a lot of cat hair on him—"

"Thank you for your concern, Ronan." I glare at him. "I know how to handle my own allergy. I'll be prepared."

He snorts, but finally finishes his path to the coffeepot to make himself a cup. "That's the start of a really healthy relationship, Mia. You have to medicate yourself just to be able to breathe around him? The Save the Dates practically write themselves."

"Don't all the romance novels talk about how romantic it is when someone takes your breath away?"

"Oh, please. There's a difference between that and a medical condition that prevents you from breathing."

"I'm touched by your concern, but it's none of your concern," I say to Ronan. "Dan and I are going out tonight, and we're going to have a wonderful time."

After grabbing his coffee, he collapses on the only free chair next to Bryce, raising his mug toward me in a salute. "I'll be sure to remind everyone those were your last words."

Bryce doesn't even try to hide his laughter, but does manage to catch the pair of goggles I throw at him. Which is honestly impressive for him.

I turn my focus back to Josie. "Why do we even have those up here?"

"Who knows." She shrugs. "Now, show me pictures again!"

Bryce groans as I grab my phone from where it's sitting on the couch to open up the app. I'm willing to take almost any distraction to keep Ronan from commenting on my love life.

The door swings open before I can even raise my arm to knock, revealing Bryce. "Hey, how was your date?"

Too exhausted to even utter a comeback, I raise my eyebrows, and give a little shrug. Thankfully, he takes my non-answer as an answer and steps aside to let me in.

Bryce and Josie's home envelopes me in its warm and cozy arms. I kick my shoes off to leave them with the rest crowded by the door, letting my purse fall with a gentle thud, and follow Bryce deeper into the house. In the living room, Carter and Ronan are watching a meet on low volume while Josie and Kat sit off to the side, talking about something. I can tell Josie's only somewhat paying attention, though, with the way her gaze keeps flickering over to the TV. The room smells like homemade brownies, which I know has to be Bryce's doing because I haven't brought anything over in weeks and baking is not Josie's strong suit.

When I spot the plate of said brownies on the table between Josie and Kat, I make a beeline toward it. I can feel the way each of my friends follows me with their eyes; concern seeped into their gazes. It's not often I allow myself to shut down like this in front of the group. This privilege is usually only reserved for Josie.

And my best friend is watching me with a steady gaze as I take a bite of brownie. I fight to let out a moan when the rich chocolate taste hits my tongue. I really wish I'd grabbed food before going on the date. "If you want to change, I laid some comfy clothes out on my bed for you."

The best thing about friends with similar body types to yours are moments like this. While Josie is a bit shorter than me and a tad smaller in certain areas, she loves her comfy clothes to be a size bigger for ultimate relaxation. And she knows me well enough to know if I made it over after the date, I wouldn't want to stay in the same outfit.

"Go change." She nods toward the stairs. "And then when you come back, you better tell me what happened tonight."

She left no room for any argument, so I shuffle upstairs and down the hall to the main bedroom. Just like with everything in the house, I instantly see my best friend's influence in the warm, cozy space. Despite living in South Carolina for over a year, she still hasn't been able to shake her Midwest roots. A thick, fuzzy blanket is draped across the edge of the bed and the bedside lamp is casting a warm glow.

I snag the sweatpants and T-shirt off the edge of the bed and duck into the bathroom to change. My smile only grows when I see makeup remover, a reusable cotton pad, hairbrush, and scrunchie on the counter. Bryce might be the love of her life, but she's my person just as much as I am hers.

About ten minutes later, I head back downstairs while pulling my hair up. In the living room, the boys are discussing the merits of some new training topic, with Ronan in the middle of a heated argument as to why it's a horrible idea. As I round the corner to head back to the girls, he trails off mid-sentence, his gaze clocking my every move.

It's been years since he's seen me this dressed down. The way his eyes rove over my body sends a little thrill up my spine. But I can't focus on that. Instead, I tell them, "It has inconsistent results, and a lot of swimmers have openly spoken out against it. I'm with Ronan on this one."

I don't miss the way surprise overtakes his features, but he quickly recovers with a triumphant smile. "Thank you, Mia!"

Josie appears out of nowhere, handing me a generous glass of wine. "Enough talk about work. I want to hear about what happened on Mia's date."

Groaning, I collapse into the only free chair, which gives me the perfect view to watch Ronan tense up. I'm suddenly aware that the two of us are the only single people in this room.

When he sees me looking at him, he clears his throat. "You really went on a date with someone who's pet could kill you?"

"Yes," I huff out. Did he think I made the whole thing up? No one could make up someone like Dan. "It's therapy mandated. She thinks I need to put myself out there more."

"Which is why you don't have to talk about it if you don't want to."

Who would have thought Bryce would be the one coming to my rescue? I don't mind talking about this one, though. It wasn't awful in the sense he's thinking, just an immature frat boy who missed the realization that it's time to be an adult.

"All he could talk about was his chicken."

All my friends blink at me in the same confused way I'd felt the first time Dan brought it up.

Carter's the first one to crack. "Like a pet chicken or...chicken, chicken?"

"Not a pet." I sigh. "Chicken he was cooking."

"I thought you went out to dinner?" Josie joined in, worry knitting her brows together. "I can't stop you from meeting these people at their houses, Mia, but I wish you'd tell one of us ahead of time if that's what's happening."

Josie and I share our locations with each other because, well, we're women in America who aren't stupid. Still, I know what she means about wanting a general idea of where I am. You can't really watch for anything strange if you don't think there's anything strange to watch out for.

I swallow a large drink of my wine. "We did go out. We went to that new bar downtown. It was really cool, good drinks. I didn't hang around long enough to try any of the food, but it all sounded good. We should all go one weekend."

"That sounds great, but let's get back to the chicken. Because I can't let that go."

"Ah, and that was Dan's main problem as well," I tell Ronan. "He had dinner cooking in a slow cooker back at home. He was concerned his chicken would either burn or he'd burn his whole house down. He called or texted his roommate fifteen times to check on said chicken."

The way Bryce's brows knit together, then his head tilts like he's trying to solve a hard puzzle, almost makes me laugh. "I have *so* many questions."

I wave my hand, signaling him to ask away.

"First, the whole point of a slow cooker recipe is that you can walk away from it while it cooks, and it'll be fine."

"Dan thinks that's a conspiracy theory."

The last of Bryce's resolve shatters, and a snort of laughter comes out. "*What?*"

I grin over the lip of my wineglass. "Next question."

"Fifteen text messages or phone calls in the, what, hour you were there?" Carter asks. "And you didn't even eat?"

"Forty minutes," I correct. "Dan was twenty minutes late because he was worried about his slow cooker. Then he took about twenty minutes telling me about his slow cooker. We'd just ordered when I fled."

"Is this real life?" Kat asks. "I feel like you're messing with us. Did he even want to go on this date?"

I nod. "He did. I asked him after the third phone call. He'd been looking forward to our date all week. He even asked me out again after I told him I couldn't do it."

"You said no, right?" I glare at Josie, who holds her hands up in surrender. "I'm just checking! We have got to find a better way to vet these people."

"Um, can I ask a question?"

I look toward Ronan, who I'd momentarily forgotten was here. "Sure, go for it."

"The guy was on a date with you, right?" I nod. "You were getting dinner together?" Another nod. "Why the hell was he cooking dinner in his slow cooker then? Was he meal-prepping for the week or for another date?"

"Very observant. You see, Dan wanted to get laid tonight. That was his ultimate goal. No shame in that. The slow cooker chicken was either for us after we hooked up or for his hookup buddy he had on standby if things with us didn't go his way."

Ronan's face screws up in pure disgust. "Please tell me he didn't tell you all that."

"He did. Proudly," I confirm. "He even asked me what position I prefer for my first time with a new partner."

Bryce chokes on the drink he'd just taken of his beer. Josie takes it from his hand while Carter claps him on the back. When he finally regains control, he looks at me with tears in his eyes. "What the *fuck*, Mia?"

"Dating apps are scary as hell, Bryce. Everyone seems normal until you get them out in the real world."

"Then I think you should stop. Therapy mandated or not," he argues.

I don't have to look at Josie to know she's nodding in agreement. I'm sure the two of them have their own plan for who I should end up with, especially since we've slowly started to talk again, but that's not happening. "Eh, I'll give it a few more shots. If nothing else, it's entertaining."

"That's not what this is supposed to be," Kat argues. "Don't you want to find someone you want to be with?"

"Well, it's definitely not going to be Dan," Ronan adds, saving me from answering a question I didn't want to get into tonight. "Let's leave him to his precious slow cooker and order some pizza so Mia doesn't starve."

Bryce is already pulling out his phone to order when I give Ronan a smile and mouthed, "*Thank you*." I get a nod and a small smile as he raises his beer bottle. "Okay, what does everyone want?"

Mia

Ronan's voice echoes off the mostly empty pool, yelling out some instruction to Emmie. The sound bounces off the walls, but there's no anger behind them. No harshness or sharp whistles that a lot of people attribute to coaches, especially ones who are trying to catch a kid up. It's solid instruction and gentle pushing.

Standing from the couch in the common area, I make my way over to the large windows overlooking the pool. Ronan is leaning against the starting block, stopwatch in hand, while Lezak is following Emmie down the length of the pool, offering supportive barks and yips whenever she turns her head toward him to breathe. It makes the corners of my lips tug up in a smile.

If someone had asked me all those years ago what I thought Ronan O'Brien would be doing after swimming, I would have never guessed this. I definitely wouldn't have pictured him advocating vehemently to get a young woman on a team at no cost to her, giving up his own time and money to help get her caught up with the rest of the team. The man who stormed into Bryce's office two weeks ago had taken me by such surprise, almost like he did when we were younger and his reputation was all anyone saw.

He was the classic rich boy who had things handed to him; that's the problem so many people had with him. But I never saw it that way. Sure, he comes from money, and his parents love to put the spotlight on their elite professional athlete son, but something always felt off about it. He never seemed to spend a lot of time with his family, choosing to train in California instead of staying close to them on the East Coast. Any interview that involved his parents never involved him, and the classic photos of parents congratulating their newly named Olympian child seemed forced.

I don't know where Ronan's money is coming from, and it's not any of my business, but I also can't help wondering if his relationship with his parents has been fixed enough to make Emmie's scholarship happen. There's not always a lot of money in swimming, but for someone like him, there was. He took on sponsors, did modeling on the side, and was a world-class swimmer with the medals, records, and titles to prove it. If he managed his money and paired it with his parents helping him out, I'm sure he'd be more than capable of handling Emmie and his lifestyle.

Hell, maybe his parents are covering Emmie's training. They seemed to have bankrolled most of his career, and I'm sure they'd love to have another shining athlete to attach their name to.

As soon as the thought crosses my mind, I shake it away. The O'Brien name is big in Massachusetts, his father taking on some multi-generational financial institution that makes the rich richer. Despite the tension between parents and son that was always obvious to me, the media never shied away from calling him out for being the spoiled rich kid.

A sharp whistle pulls me from my thoughts and sends my gaze back to the pool. Ronan is now squatting by its edge, demonstrating shoulder movement to Emmie, who is watching with rapt attention.

Even from here, I can see she's taking every piece of advice and feedback he gives her to heart.

A shoulder bumps against mine before the person settles beside me. I don't have to look to know it's my best friend. "I was too hard on him the other day, wasn't I?"

"You mean when you told him he shouldn't be allowed to coach children? Yeah, Mia, you were."

I turn to face my best friend, leaning against the window as I cross my arms. She stares back at me, not saying a single word. Instead, she's waiting for me to talk, wanting to see if I can offer up any kind of explanation for whatever's been going on between Ronan and me. But I can't. I don't want to talk. All I want to do is scream into the void. And while that might make me feel momentarily better, I doubt it'd do any good in the long run.

"Look, I don't know what happened between the two of you and I'm not going to ask, not again, but I do know what I see from the outside looking in." Josie points toward the window. "That man is confused as well. We all are. He can't fix what he doesn't know. I don't care about him, though, I care about you."

"Don't lie." I snort. "You care about everyone. Even when you shouldn't."

"Yeah, yeah." She waves me off. "I'm too nice for my own good. You're right, I do care about him because I don't want to see him hurt or anything. What I meant by that is I care about you more and in a different way. Whatever happened between you two happened almost a decade ago."

"Eight years!" I protest, not wanting to think how old I'm about to be and definitely not wanting to find a way to speed up time.

"Close enough." Josie laughs, which gets a smile out of me. "My point is, you have to be tired of holding the grudge, Mia. What if you never saw him again? Were you going to hold on to it forever? That would have been exhausting."

Taking a sudden interest in my nails, I shrug. "I don't know. I never thought that far."

"Let it go. For your sake. I'm not saying you need to forgive him or even start getting along with him, but this anger is not doing you any good."

Letting it go would mean letting my walls down again. And if I let my walls down around him again, aren't I just opening myself up to be hurt? Without the cover of the grudge, I'll become vulnerable. This man was able to get through my defenses once before. What would there be to stop him this time if I let it all go?

"I don't want to get hurt again," I admit to my best friend.

Reaching forward, she wraps me in a hug, and I sag against her. I should get her to hug me more often. The simple gesture has always been good for grounding me, reminding me that I'm not alone in this big, scary world.

"Pain is a part of life, Mia," she mutters, squeezing me tighter. "You know that as well as I do. I can't promise that you won't get hurt again, but I can promise you that you'll never have to go through pain alone." She pulls back to look me in the eye. "I'm always going to be here. That's our promise to each other, right?"

With a watery smile, I nod. "Right."

"Just promise me you'll think about it?" I hesitate for a moment before nodding. She grins at me. "Great, that's all I ask! Now, let's go."

I laugh at the sudden turn of events, Josie heads toward our office to gather her things. "Go? Go where?"

"Kat's place," she calls over her shoulder. "We're having a girl's night! Bryce and Carter are playing video games at my place. There'll be wine, snacks, and face masks."

"Well, if there's going to be face masks." I follow her into our office only to be hit in the face with a stuffed narwhal Bryce got her as a joke. Laughing, I toss it back to her. "Are you bringing your tarot cards or do we need to bring some of mine?"

Josie looks up from her bag with a sly grin. "Now you're talking."

When I come back from changing in the bathroom, Katrina's living room is in complete and utter chaos. There's a smorgasbord of food and drinks laid out on the tables and ottoman, an assortment of facemasks and other beauty treatments are laid out across the floor for perusal, *Practical Magic* is playing quietly on the TV, and I think I might be in my happy place. I'm wearing a pair of my comfiest pajamas—shorts and a T-shirt with a tarot card and rolling pin pattern Josie had made especially for me—and I can't wait for a nice, relaxing night with my girls.

Except Josie and Katrina are huddled over the masks while they talk quietly to one another. Pouring myself a glass of sangria, I assume they're discussing the masks until I hear Ronan's name. "Wait, what are you talking about?"

With a sheet mask in hand, Katrina moves onto one of the chairs while I take the couch. "Oh, just talking about how good Ronan is with Emmie. All the kids, actually. It's no wonder Operation Fly is such a success."

Tilting my head, I stare at her in confusion. "What do those two things have to do with each other?"

Josie tosses me a nourishing mask before taking the spot next to me, a bottle of nail polish in her hands. "You know Operation Fly? Ronan's organization."

The organization, I've heard of. It was just gaining traction when Josie and I stepped back from the sport. Operation Fly was a charitable organization specifically aimed at helping kids get access to the swim lessons and teams they wouldn't have otherwise. Whether through local clubs or schools, the organization offers clinics, and scholarships to get these young swimmers the chances they wouldn't otherwise have.

She just needs a chance. A chance we can give her.

Ronan's voice repeating those words are playing like a record in my mind. They sounded familiar when he'd stood in Bryce's office saying them, asking us to give Emmie a chance. I didn't connect the dots before. Out of every Olympian we knew, Ronan was the last one I'd expect to be behind something like this.

"Ronan swam freestyle." God, that was such a dumb thing to say because what he swam and what he, apparently, named his organization doesn't have to go hand-in-hand.

"Maybe he named it that on purpose," Josie says with a shrug, examining her nails before bringing out a file.

I can't help but frown as my eyes follow her. How long has she known and not told me?

And because she can read my mind, she frowns right back. "Did you not know?"

"No! What could possibly make you think I knew that?"

"I thought you knew! You were the one who was always doing research into stuff like this—deciding what organizations we wanted to support. You've donated to Operation Fly. I figured you knew and didn't want to talk about it."

"I did do research, but this never came up. There was nothing pointing this whole nationwide thing to him."

"You kind of have to go digging for it." Both Josie and I turn to Kat. I'd almost forgotten she was the one to bring this all up in the first place. "When Carter told me about it, I got curious. I think I was on their website, clicking around, for almost an hour before I even saw his name. Then it took even more digging to find out what his actual tie to the organization is."

Every single thing I was thinking back at the club an hour ago weighs heavily on my heart. Everything I said to him the day he saw Emmie feels like a punch to my gut. I'd been wrong. Not only had he gone on to do something amazing, but he also fought hard to keep the credit from coming back to him. I'd been accusing him of being someone so different when the truth was right in front of me all this time.

Josie nudges my leg with her foot when I've apparently been lost in thought for too long. "Did you really not know?"

Staring down at the mask that's still in my hand, I shake my head. "I had no idea."

Kat doesn't hesitate to introduce comfort. "I don't think he'll blame you for that, Mia. Especially because he's worked hard to keep his name off of it. He wants to do something good for the kids. During my deep dive, I also saw a lot of photos of him working directly with the kids. He's not just some president that funds the thing and runs; he puts the work in."

"Which is why Carter and Bryce fought so hard to get him here," Josie explains. "Ronan needed to make sure he could step away, which apparently, he can. He was able to leave the day-to-day running to his vice president, Mel."

I turn to look at Katrina with pleading eyes. "Please tell me you have ice cream."

Her eyes brighten as she jumps up, mask momentarily forgotten. "Oh, yeah, we got ice cream. I'll be right back."

"Hey," Josie murmurs when she's sure Kat is out of earshot. "I want to remind you that you knew Ronan. Once upon a time, we all knew him for who he is. Don't let whatever bullshit reputation he allowed to be put out there influence you away from that. I can promise you he's still the same guy he was back then, better even."

"But what happened?" I ask, frowning. "What made him disappear from the sport and decide not to tell anyone about this?"

Josie shifts in her seat, which tells me a serious conversation is about to happen. "We're best friends, and best friends tell each other the hard truth, right?" I hesitate before nodding. "Think about the last time you saw him, when everything changed, whether it was warranted, or not. Think about how you treated him. If you were him, would you want to reach out when you suddenly give up your whole world? Because that's what Bryce tells me it feels like, especially when it's not your choice."

"No," I whisper. "I wouldn't reach out to me if I were him, either."

"I'm not saying you need to forgive him, Mia. That's your business. But stop punishing yourself and him. If you can't forgive him, let the past go. It shouldn't matter anymore."

But it does matter! I want to scream. *It will always matter.* Because I'm pretty sure there will be some part of me that's always in love with him, but hating the person who broke your heart is always easier than facing the pain. Ronan was my first taste of someone wanting me exactly how I am, and he was also my first taste of being left for not being enough.

"I don't know if I can let it go, Jos," I admit. "I—I still don't want to tell you about it, but it was bad. It was the kind of hurt that you can't bounce back from. When he says he doesn't know what happened, he's not lying. Because...he doesn't know the truth. He doesn't know what I know."

She squeezes my hand, and the look she's giving me is so damn sad and soft. Like I'm a puppy in a shelter she's trying to convince Bryce to adopt to complete their small, child-free family. "Then don't let it go for him; let it go for yourself. Don't carry this anger anymore, bestie. It's not worth it. You deserve more."

"I've got ice cream!" Katrina dances into the room, showing off the various pints like the prize they are. Something tells me she had stood back long enough for Josie and me to wrap up our conversation. "Okay, Mia, what flavor do you want? I got you salty caramel and double cookie dough."

"Yes, please," I reply, reaching my hand out for both pints. Laughing, Katrina hands them over with a spoon before depositing the chocolate flavors to Josie and keeping the fruity ones for herself. She collapses back in her spot. "Okay, who wants to talk about how shitty men are?"

I pop the lid off the caramel ice cream. "Oh, please, you're both in amazingly healthy and loving relationships."

"Doesn't mean they don't piss us off," Kat replies. "Josie, you're up first. Spill."

She thinks for a second, eating a spoonful of ice cream before her eyes light up. "Oh, my god, Bryce started this new thing whenever he works out..."

And that's how I spend the rest of my night, hearing my very happy friends talk shit about their boyfriends. For the first time in a long time, I get to tell my own woes from the world of dating apps. It almost feels like we're back in high school or college with the whole world ahead of us. A movie about the power of sisterhood in whatever form it takes plays in the background, and I realize how lucky I am to have these ladies in my corner.

Ronan

Mia has been avoiding me more than usual. Which is saying something because her normal level of avoidance is pretending like I'm dead. But this is different, because when she's not avoiding me, I keep finding her watching me with an unreadable look on her face, like I'm a puzzle she's trying to solve. It's a look I've seen her make before, but to have it directed at me specifically is unnerving.

"Is everything okay with Mia?"

Carter looks up from his stopwatch to glance over at where she's pointedly not looking at me now and shrugs. "I think so. She's been normal with me."

"Well, that's not something I can measure up with, is it?" He frowns at me. "Come on, Carter, you know she hates me. Normal for you would be a miracle for me."

"All I know is that she and Josie crashed at our house the other night for a girl's night. She was fine in the morning—maybe a little quiet, but overall fine."

Frowning, I glance back at Mia, only to find her no longer there, and looked back to Carter. "All right, thanks, man."

He nods, already turning his focus back to the stopwatch and the kids in the water before I walk away. Emmie is supposed to be here in about half an hour for her next private lesson, and I have some prep to do, anyway.

When I enter the lobby, Josie smiles at me, and I know she's probably the only person with answers. "Hey, Josie." I lean against the counter, grinning down at her. "Is there anything going on with Mia I should know about?"

Her smile falters and I worry she's not going to tell me anything. Neither one of them is ever willing to betray the other, which is something I find admirable, but don't see how it could matter in this situation. It's not like she'd be betraying her trust too badly.

Still, I don't want to force her to tell me something she's not comfortable sharing. I stand straighter. "Never mind. It's not a big deal; I was worried."

"She didn't know you are the founder and president of Operation Fly." I lean back against the counter, frowning slightly. "Kat and I were talking about it the other night when we were hanging out. She overheard and asked about it. Honestly, I thought she knew the whole time and didn't want to talk about it because of whatever happened between you two."

There are a lot of things Mia doesn't know, but despite Bryce's comment when I first saw Emmie, I didn't think this was one of them. "She really didn't know?"

"I know, right?" Josie replies. "She was always the one doing research on things we should support, and she dug deep, making sure it was something we believed in. The only thing I can think of is that it was gaining traction as we were making our exit."

Or she somehow knew it was me behind it and chose not to support it. "Maybe."

Josie must sense my uncertainty because she's shaking her head. "She really didn't know, Ronan. Trust me, Mia can keep a lot of things concealed, but she cannot lie to me when I ask her something. She has a tell."

"A tell?" I don't want to use the information against Mia, but if I knew what her tell was, I could figure out if she's being truthful about Omaha not being the real issue. "What kind of tell?"

"Absolutely not." And just like that, Josie was back to being the defensive best friend. "I am not telling you that. She considers it a sign of weakness."

And the last thing Mia wants to do is let her guard down around me. "That's fair. Thanks for the information, Josie."

Her grin is back in place. "No problem."

Every time I talk to Josie, their friendship makes more and more sense to me. Mia's seen as the badass who's unafraid of anything, but there's a spark of that in Josie, too. The way she can bounce from a stone wall of protection to openly happy and warm can be startling. She might be underestimated, but she can easily hold her own.

As I'm heading up the stairs to my office, I pass Mia. She pointedly doesn't look at me, which isn't surprising. The part of me that's always tempted to push her buttons—see how long we can go before I push her too far—wants to make a comment, but I refrain.

She comes to a stop a couple of steps ahead of me, hazel eyes narrowing in such a glare that there's no green to be seen, only the thick dark ring surrounding it. "Let me guess, Josie told you?"

I slow to a stop, keeping a careful distance between us. "Told me what?"

"Don't play innocent, Ronan. You know what I'm talking about."

"I do, but I don't see why you're making a big deal out of it." Maybe if I go easy on her, it'll help ease the weird tension between us. "You didn't know I run a national charity, and now you do. It's not that big of a deal. I made sure to keep my name out of it as much as possible."

"But that's what I don't get," she snaps. "I know you, Ronan, you love the spotlight. Why wouldn't you want your name all over it?"

Something in me snaps—something that's been brewing from the moment I walked into this place. "You *do* know me, Mia! You're choosing to pretend you don't by parroting the bullshit the media spread about me. Every media outlet but you."

"Well, I've learned I'm blind to people sometimes." She crosses her arms over her chest and in the V-neck maroon T-shirt she's wearing, it's hard to ignore the way it accentuates her breasts. I fight to keep my gaze from drifting down, but I can't stop the quick peek, which makes a shriek leave Mia's mouth. "Are you shitting me right now, Ronan?"

"I'm sorry!" I say immediately, hands up in a defensive manner. It doesn't matter how attracted I still am to her, I shouldn't have objectified her like that. "I didn't mean to!"

"All you care about is the way a woman looks. And even then, it varies in the moment. What you wanted one day could be the next day's trash."

"What the fuck are you talking about?" I drop my hands, my anger rising. "You know that's not true!"

"No, I thought that wasn't true, but then the real you came out and I realized I was tricked."

"So this *is* about what happened in Omaha!"

She flinches away from me, and I really wish Josie had told me what her tell is because that right there tells me I'm right. "Stop bringing up Omaha! It has nothing to do with Omaha! I don't want to be around you anymore." She closes the distance between us, pushing me out of the way. "Why can't you get—"

What happens next happens so quickly it'll probably always be a blur in my mind. She hits the edge of the stair wrong and tumbles. I reach out to catch her before she goes down. Then, it's like we're in our early twenties again. Mia, in my arms, my gaze locked with the most beautiful hazel eyes I've ever seen, and everything shifts.

Those kids had no idea what was about to happen to them. They had no idea how many times their hearts would break and stubbornly come back together. They had no idea they would end up here, hating one another for something only one of them is aware of. Those kids—

The angle is awkward when Mia reaches around my neck and yanks me down into a heated kiss. I freeze for the briefest second, the reality of what's happening coming into focus.

But then I move my hands on the small of her back. I gently pull her up until we're both standing. I can feel her start to pull away, but I can't let that happen. I can't lose this moment. I pull her closer, taking control of the kiss. I feel her melt against me.

Maybe we stand there for seconds or years, but it's a connection I don't want to lose. Having her in my arms makes me feel like I'm standing in the eye of a hurricane as it all crashes around me. Everything outside of us is chaos, but we are beautifully still.

The moment Mia realizes what she's doing is evident. Every part of her tenses in my arms, and I immediately loosen my grip to make sure she knows she can pull away. She allows herself another second, and in that second, I feel nothing but hope.

That hope shatters when she pushes me back against the railing. Our lips separate and both of us breathe heavily.

Her glare is back. "We are never doing that again. Do you understand me?"

I hold my hands up in surrender. "You kissed me."

"*Never* again."

She jogs down the rest of the stairs, swinging the exit door open, and letting it slam shut. In the middle of an empty stairwell, I'm left in stunned silence. I press a finger against my lip, the ghost of her lips still pressed against mine.

I make the decision then and there to do whatever I can to fix this.

Because if I fix it, then there's a chance it'll happen again. And again. And again.

⋯⋯ + ₒ ✦ ✦ ★ ☾ ★ ✦ ✦ ₒ + ⋯⋯

"I'm coming!" I call out to whoever is on the other side of my door, knocking away. Lezak is happily trotting along at my heels. I pull the door open to see Bryce standing on the other end. My brow arches. "Hey, man, what are you doing here?"

Bryce holds up a six-pack of beer, looking like a sad puppy. "I'm officially pathetic, man. My girlfriend is hanging out with her best friend, and my best friend is hanging out with his girlfriend."

I step back, opening the door wider. "Wow, I'm not even the second choice."

Bryce steps into the house, handing me a beer out of the pack before heading straight for the couch. Lezak has found a new person to shadow. Neither one of us says anything, but I follow him, collapsing onto the couch beside him.

Twisting the cap off his bottle, he raises a brow at the one I set on the table. "Are we not drinking tonight?"

"You can go for it," I tell him, shifting the placement of my leg. "I took some painkillers earlier; my leg was acting up. I can drink on them, but it never ends well. I can drive you home if you need to drink more than one."

Bryce shrugs, taking a long pull from the bottle. If this was anyone else, the silence would make me uncomfortable, like something horrible had happened and he was waiting for the right moment to tell me. But this is Bryce, and the two of us grew a lot closer after I got hurt. We spent a lot of time in total silence; he was too stubborn to leave me alone, and I was too stubborn to let him in. I'm not sure what I would have done without him in those early months.

"You're doing great with Emmie, man," he finally says. "I haven't had a chance to tell you that, but I've noticed. The extra lessons are helping her catch up, but she's blended seamlessly into the team, too."

"Thanks." I nod. "She's a hell of an athlete. Just needed someone to recognize it. Plus, I'm always going to love having the opportunity to tell you I told you so."

He laughs, his gaze locked onto the bottle in his hand. "I'll gladly hear it as long as you stick around to say it."

The beer on the table in front of me was starting to look more appealing. "What do you mean by that?"

Sighing, he turns to face me. "Do you know why Carter and I asked you to come out here?"

"Because you needed another coach so you could handle the business."

"Yeah, but that's not the whole reason. We could have hired anyone, but we specifically sought you out, even though we knew we couldn't afford you."

This conversation is getting dangerously serious and I'm not about to cry over beers with a kid who has always been like a younger brother to me. "And you knew I'd show up for you guys."

"Of course, but showing up, and sticking around are two different things." Fuck, he's too perceptive for his own good. "I know you've only been out here for a couple of months, but I'm beginning to worry you don't see this position in your long-term plans."

Yup, definitely not going where I want it to go. I reach for the beer with a shrug. He's tracking my movements. "You know me, Clark. I never stay in one place for too long."

His frown deepens. "That's what I'm worried about, O'Brien. Don't you ever get tired of it? Not having a place to call your own?"

Someone once told me that you don't realize you're lonely until you learn you're alone. For better or worse, coming to Columbia proved that to be true. I'm suddenly on the outskirts of a group of people I'd once been a part of. We've all grown, we've all changed, but we're still the same in other ways. Except now I'm on the outside looking in. They found one another again without me because I was too busy running away.

And now I'm here, wanting to bring back what once was. I'm here forming a connection with a young athlete who I could see making it all the way to the Olympics, which is why I never let myself get close to any of the kids in Operation Fly. Yes, I trained them, but I wasn't their only coach. I was, once again, on the outside.

Bryce considers his words before saying, "I said something to you a long time ago, and it stuck with me. It's always been replaying in the back of my mind, and I want to say it to you again. I want you to hear me, really hear me, like you did before."

A long time ago...Shit, there were a lot of things he said to me back then that he could be bringing up now. And most of them are things I don't know if I'm in the mental position to hear again, even if I should. Maybe especially if I should.

I default to humor, like I always do.

"Quoting yourself and bragging about it? Damn, Clark, maybe you should have been the one with the asshole label." The look on his face says it all. I let out a sigh. "All right, lay it on me."

"Don't get so caught up in your own shit that you miss when life gives you another chance."

That was the one I didn't want to hear. Those words back then...they meant something different than they do now. They meant the difference between giving up on myself and pushing harder. They were said to me when he was one of the few people who were there for me, in the darkest moment of my life. When my parents didn't even have the decency to show up or check in on me. That sentence got me to where I am today.

And now he's giving it back to me again.

"It's not the same," I insist. Tears sting at the corners of my eyes against my will. I've cried in front of Bryce more times than I can ever count, but right now, it's the last thing I want to be doing. "Back then, it was different."

"Is it that different, though? Come on, Ronan, you're running from your fears, just like you were back then." I angrily wipe at the corner of my eye. "I'm not trying to make you upset, dude, but Carter and I wanted you here because we know what you can do. You were our team captain in 2016 and in other international meets. You have this magnetic personality that motivates people and makes them see what they're capable of. I don't understand why you don't see it for yourself."

It's frightening when someone sees everything you wish you could see in yourself. It's unnerving when they call it out and try to prove you deserve more, or at the very least, deserve to give yourself a break. That's something I've never been good at: giving myself a break. If I wasn't swimming perfectly, I was hard on myself. If I wasn't swimming perfectly, it meant I was a disappointment to my family. I didn't let myself get close or be real with anyone out of fear of ruining my career.

Until I met Josie and Mia and got closer to Bryce and Carter, that is. They were the first group of people who proved to me I can let people in without it being a distraction. Without it negatively impacting my career. I stopped caring about being the perfect athlete my parents wanted. I let myself love the sport again, only to have it taken from me.

"Have you..." Bryce clears his throat. "Have you told Mia anything?"

"She just found out about Operation Fly, man." The thought of telling her about this cloud lingering over my head—the seconds that changed everything—makes my palms sweat. The urge to run clouds my mind. "I don't want her to pity me."

"Mia Sheridan has never pitied someone a day in her life, not the way you're scared of. Just...consider it. Consider telling her. Consider sticking this out. Consider seeing what this chance holds." Bryce pauses before adding, "But if you do decide to take off, at least give me some warning, yeah?"

"Yeah, I will," I promise. It's the least I can do, especially when I'm not ready to face the other things. When I don't know if I can promise him I'll stick this out.

Silence settles once more. I stare down at the unopened beer in my hand, knowing I'll regret it if I drink it, and set it back down on the table. I reach for the remote instead. "There has to be some kind of sport on TV, man."

With a laugh, Bryce settles back in his seat. "When I left, a riveting game of shuffleboard was starting."

I snort and scroll through the channels in the hopes of finding something better. "They'll televise that, but not a non-Olympic swim meet. I see how it is."

"Stop fighting the media, Ronan."

"Never." I settle on a baseball game and silence falls again.

Mia

"Are you coming over for dinner tonight?" I glance up at Bryce and he lets out a long sigh. "We're having everyone over. Josie sent out a text."

A quick glance at my phone confirms I did get a group message. Kat had already confirmed for both of them, Bryce made a stupid joke about already living there. Besides myself, Ronan was the only one who hadn't answered. "Is Ronan going to be there?"

I know I'm not being fair to my friends by pushing them away in an effort to avoid Ronan, but what other choice do I have? The more we're around one another, the greater the chance of the past coming up. I've kept it all quiet for this long; I'm not slipping up now.

He frowns at me. "You know he will."

"Then you know I won't be."

"Are you going to make me tell your best friend, or can you be the one to disappoint her? Again."

"Okay, ouch." I frown. "But I'll tell her."

"This is getting old, Mia," Bryce complains. "You need to find a way to let go of whatever happened. Both of you. He's not going anywhere."

"You know, I miss when you were still scared of me."

"I'm still scared shitless of you." The admission makes me smile—at least I haven't completely lost my edge. "But I'm also your friend and I know something happened. We all know it. The two of you got along, until you didn't."

Dread pools in the pit of my stomach. He's calling out my lie, and he's probably able to pinpoint exactly when the shift happened. I need to get away from this conversation. Mature, observant Bryce, is too good at figuring things out.

"You need to stop listening to your girlfriend, Bryce." The words taste bitter on my tongue. "Nothing dramatic happened. Things change. People change."

But he's not about to let it go. "What changed? Did he say or do something? If this is going to be a real probl—"

"It's not a problem at all, Bryce. I'm capable of being professional around him."

He's not convinced. I can see it written all over his face. "I have no doubt about your professionalism, but I still think the two of you need to work this out. Whatever happened, communication is a two-way street."

I bite back a sarcastic reply about therapy really working for him, because it's a low blow. Sarcasm has always been my shield—a way to hide my real feelings from the rest of the world—but I don't need to project that onto Bryce. Especially when he's been working hard at things in his own life, and the life he shares with Josie. I refuse to poke fun at that to protect myself from my own insecurities.

I pull my bag onto my shoulder, facing my friend. "We'll figure it out. It just might take some time."

He nods. "Just...let me know if you need anything."

"Of course," I assure him. "The same goes for you, you know?"

I can see how uncomfortable the turn in the conversation has made him. A faint blush coats his cheeks and he's refusing to look at me. "Uh, yeah, sure. Thanks."

There's been something slightly off about him for a couple of weeks now. Nothing that makes me worried about him and Josie, but he's seemed lost in his own head. If there was something to worry about, Carter would know. And if Carter knew, I'd know. He has no problem calling Bryce out for being a dumbass.

So, for today, I continue to take pity on him. "I'm sure I'll see you sometime this weekend. Have a good night, Bryce."

"Yeah. You, too."

On my way out, I stop by my office to grab the rest of my stuff. In a true testament to our friendship, though, Josie and I have somehow managed to balance our different aesthetics and put together a cohesive space that works well for the small space. It makes me smile every time I step through the door, like it's real, tangible proof of our friendship.

It only takes me a couple of minutes to pack the rest of my stuff into my tote bag, but I quickly realize my water bottle is missing. The last place I'd had it was on the pool deck while I was taking some photos. Bryce had wanted to talk to me about marketing for an upcoming team fundraiser. Somehow, that conversation moved to his office and turned into a full-blown meeting. Apparently, I hadn't remembered to grab the bottle.

I glance at the window overlooking the main pool and can barely make out Ronan, pacing the length of the pool while Emmie does a freestyle lap. Crap.

I don't want to see Ronan right now. I've been doing my best to avoid him—especially since he got what he wanted and humbled me at the same time. I loathe his ability to do that.

For a moment, I consider leaving it there and getting it in the morning, but that would just make things worse. He knows it's mine, the cute stickers done in the colors of the pan flag that cover it is a dead giveaway. If I don't get it now, he'll give me shit about it tomorrow.

It'd be ridiculous to endure his taunting about how I hate him so much I can't get my water bottle. And, even worse, he'd be right.

With a groan, I gather the last of my things and trudge down the stairs. Ronan is sitting on the lowest bleacher now, elbows resting on his knees, stopwatch dangling from his neck, eyes trained on the water.

He barely glances away from his swimmer as he holds the water bottle out to me. I rapidly close the distance, taking it with a mumbled, "Thanks." My eyes drift over to the pool, watching Emmie cover a couple of meters.

A frown pulls at my lips. "Her elbow should be higher." The words come tumbling out of my mouth before I can stop them. Instantly, I want to take them back. I'm not her coach, and freestyle has never been my specialty.

"Thanks for the tip, but I think I know what I'm doing."

The apology dies on my lips. "Right, of course you do. The Olympian who ran away when he got caught doping, such a good role model for her."

His gaze snaps up to meet mine with narrowed eyes. "Is that really what you think happened?"

Of course I don't. I didn't believe it then, and I don't believe it now. When no one wants to tell you the truth, what other choice do you have?

I shrug. "It's what everyone was saying."

"Didn't think you listened to everyone."

The dismissiveness of his tone—the way he sounds utterly disappointed in me—hits me with a force so chill, I want to hide from it. I refuse to do that, though. "Well, what am I supposed to think when you fall off the face of the earth and rumors are all I have to go off of?"

He's as quick with his comeback. "You could have asked Bryce, or, you know, texted me? Remember, I wasn't the one who stopped talking first, Mia. You were mad at me long before this happened."

I groan, ready to stomp my foot like a child. "You know what, Ronan? Forget it. I'm not getting into this with you right now."

I'd only taken about four steps away when he spoke again. "I was in an accident."

I stop mid-step, frozen in time as the words sink in. *Accident.* Why hadn't Bryce or Carter told me?

Right, because I never gave them the chance.

I turn to face him. His gaze is still locked on Emmie, but he keeps talking. "I denied the drug test because I already knew I wasn't going to come back from this."

He stretches out his right leg, slowly. Little things I've noticed over the last couple of weeks start to add up in my mind. The evenings when his movements have been a little stiffer, or the times he'd need to sit for a bit, and the way I often caught him doing stretches in the middle of the day. Chronic pain from an injury he got from an accident.

How have I not noticed before now?

I bite back the sob that's caught in my throat, finding it hard to wrap my mind around how horrible I've been. "What happened?"

His shrug is casual, so flippant. "I was at a party, had too much to drink. I did the right thing and got an Uber. The guy who ran the red light going almost seventy in a thirty-five didn't make the right decision, though."

The slight sob escapes. Ronan doesn't pull his gaze from the pool. "Ronan—"

"The drunk driver walked away with only a broken arm and a concussion," he continues, a haunted shadow filling his features. "The driver of the car I was in died on impact. I was in pretty bad shape, too."

Visions of Ronan lying in a hospital bed, looking smaller than I've ever seen this man look, flashed through my mind. I hate them. I want to banish them all from my thoughts, but something tells me I'll never be able to. Not now; not after everything.

"I was still on pretty heavy pain medications when the drug test came up. I knew I wouldn't pass it. I also knew I'd never get back in the pool the same way, so I announced my retirement."

It doesn't make sense, though. Why he let all those rumors fly, why he let so many people think he was leaving behind the sport he loves because he was doping.

"Why didn't you tell me?" The question stumbles out of my mouth before I can stop it. "We defended you until your silence became too much."

He's quiet for a couple of seconds. I instantly hate the way that question sounded as it came out. When he finally looks at me, there's so much sadness in his eyes that my heart clenches yet again. "Why would I tell you, Mia? You'd already decided I wasn't worth your time. I never asked you to defend me—you could have gone with the story everyone else was using."

A frustrated sigh comes out. "Because, Ronan, you didn't deserve to go out like that!"

"Yet I deserved to be completely ignored and cast aside without an explanation." A harsh sting races down my spine; the words hitting me with a force I didn't know was possible. "I knew what I was doing, Mia."

Swallowing back my tears, I take a tentative step toward him. "Ronan, I'm—"

He holds up his hand. "There's nothing to apologize for, Mia. The past is the past. Neither of us can change them, but I want you to remember, you don't get to be the only victim here."

Ronan is dismissing me.

I want to fight back, argue that he somehow deliberately kept this information from me, but he's right. I was the one who forced him to keep stuff like this from me. I was the one who wouldn't answer his texts or social media messages. I was the one who, for the remainder of that trip to Indianapolis, would walk the other way whenever I saw him approaching.

If I had talked to him all those years ago, maybe things would be different between us now. Maybe I wouldn't be finding out about an accident that almost took his life years after the fact. Maybe I would have been there to support him throughout the recovery instead of seeing the effects that still linger.

And maybe...maybe the two of us would have been something more. Maybe we'd at least be friends. There are a whole bunch of maybes in there that I will never know the answer to and the only person to blame for that is myself.

"I need to focus on Emmie." Ronan's voice pulls me from my thoughts. When I look at him, he's still not looking at me. "We can talk about this some other time, if you want, but not today."

Another dismissal.

"Yeah, right, of course."

This time, I listen and turn to walk back down the length of the pool to head out. I peek back at him over my shoulder, but he's pointedly not looking at me each time. Clenched jaw, narrowed eyes, and stiff posture all focus in on the pool. Guilt rises from the pit of my stomach. I shouldn't have pushed him to share something he obviously wasn't ready to share.

This information doesn't magically fix what happened between us back in Indianapolis, but it does answer a lot of my questions. Questions I probably don't deserve to know the answer to after the way I've treated him.

Mostly, I'm angry at myself for letting one bad experience cloud my judgment to this extent. Just because I knew we'd never work out doesn't mean I should have immediately assumed he was cheating based solely on rumors and his silence. I have to do something to make things at least a little right between us.

······ + ₒ ✦ˑ ✦ˑ ☾ ✦ ˑ✦ ₒ + ······

I'm standing in front of Ronan's condo the next afternoon. It's exactly what I thought it'd look like; all natural colors and sleek, clean lines before I even step through the door. It screams rich bachelor pad. It's some place I would normally feel completely out of place in, but my own guilt, and kindness had won out. I need to make things right between us—at least in terms of his retirement and my feelings around that.

Yesterday I caught a glimpse of the Ronan I knew, and I want to acknowledge that man and all the things he's gone through. Part of me knows that, deep down, he's still the guy everyone warned me about, and that's the side I can stay mad at.

Because there's still this huge thing between us. Although we're ignoring it. Our relationship will never be the same—but the reaction to his sudden retirement is on me. I could have asked Bryce or Carter for further information. I never took the time to reach out to him, either, too worried the past would be brought up. I'm the reason I didn't know about the accident because he didn't owe me an explanation.

I let everyone else get inside my head. Let a reputation replace a part of him I knew in my heart—

The door swings open to reveal Ronan standing in the doorway, a wave of shock running straight down my spine. Suddenly, I'm back in Charlotte, North Carolina ten years ago and this man had caught me in his arms. He looks so much like the Ronan I knew back then—shirtless, Olympic rings tattoo visible on his forearm, sweats low on his hips, dark hair a damp mess, and green eyes that look straight into my soul.

"What are you doing here?"

It's not asked in a harsh or unwelcoming tone, which I deserve. Instead, it shows his surprise. While he's not mad to see me on his doorstep, he's hesitant about why I am.

My eyes flick from the tattoo that flexes as his grip on the door shifts and focus on those eyes. The eyes that make me feel like I'm floating in a calm pool every time I—*Focus, Mia*. "I made you bread."

His brow arches as I awkwardly hold the pan out to him. He presses his lips into a thin line, like he's fighting to keep in a laugh. My cheeks are aflame; he makes no move to take it. "Glad to see the baking stuck."

Yet again, Ronan is blowing my mind by remembering the smallest detail about me. Baking has always been an outlet, but I never had the chance to actually share that with him. We'd talked on the phone several times while I was baking and told him my favorite recipes, but this is different. And I think we both know it.

I grin smugly up at him. "And I've gotten better. Trust me, you don't want to turn this down."

"And you didn't poison it?"

Now it's my turn to laugh, which seems to help him relax slightly. "Do you think I'd tell you if I did?"

"Good point." He stares down at me, eyes narrowing like he's trying to figure me out. I wonder if he's trying to find the girl he knew, the one who hadn't been hardened with heartbreak and disappointment. Does he miss that girl? Sometimes I do. He opens the door wider. "Well, come in. Someone has to help me eat it and it can't be Lezak."

He doesn't wait for a response before turning and heading back into the condo, leaving the door open behind him. I only hesitate for a second before I follow him, shutting the door with a soft click, and toeing my sandals off right inside the entryway. Ronan's 6'6" height allows him to move much quicker than me. I manage to catch up quickly and step into a large, open concept kitchen.

My jaw drops open.

This kitchen is wasted on someone like Ronan, at least the version of him I knew. I would kill for a space like this, even if the overall slick, shiny bachelor style is not something I'm into. Still, it'd only take a couple of cosmetic upgrades to make this the kitchen of my dreams. Before I know it, I'm lost in the daydream of all the dishes I could create here—baking or cooking. I can envision the house parties I could host and the holidays a space like this would allow for. Except, this will never be my space and the man in the room with me will never be the one I share such memories with.

"What kind of bread is it?"

I startle at his voice, having momentarily forgotten he was there. I set the pan down on the spacious island. "Cinnamon swirl."

He sets two small plates on the counter before handing me a knife. "You should do the honor of cutting it. Can I get you something to drink? I can do iced coffee."

Iced coffee. He remembers my hatred for hot drinks and is willing to make me something specific. At least there's hope we can talk through this part. The rest of it, though, will take longer. I smile at him. "I'd appreciate that."

"Damn, is that a genuine Mia Sheridan smile I've been graced with?" He's teasing as he turns to a fancy coffee machine and starts pressing a bunch of buttons. "Please tell me that's not out of pity from what I told you yesterday because, if it is, I'm making you a hot coffee."

"No, it's nothing like that." I lean against the island to watch him work. "Just... the small things you remember kind of amaze me."

He gives me a skeptical look over his shoulder and shrugs. "I like knowing things about the people I care about."

"You don't care about me, Ronan," I challenge. "We haven't seen one another in years."

"Doesn't mean I ever stopped caring." He keeps his back to me when he says that, focusing on the task at hand, so I focus on the one I was given. A couple of minutes later, he sets two iced coffees on the counter and I hand him a plate. He takes one bite and lets out a loud, borderline sexual groan that has my eyes widening and cheeks flushing. "Holy shit, Mia. I knew you were good, but not this good."

Flushing even more, I duck my head and focus on nibbling on my own piece. He has a point, though. This is damn good if I do say so myself.

A few bites later, Ronan is reaching for his coffee when he speaks again. "All right, out with it. I know you're here because of what happened yesterday. Let's get it over with."

I set my fork down on the edge of my plate to take a sip of my own coffee. Now it was my turn to melt because this was the best iced coffee I've had in a while. The small smile Ronan tries to hide is enough to help me find my voice. "I'm not here because I feel sorry for you, Ronan. I'm here because I'm mad at myself."

He shifts from one foot to the other, looking at me out of the corner of his eye. "But why are you mad at yourself?"

"Because I let the stupid media get to me. I was so mad about everything else that had happened. I listened to the rumors when you didn't reach out to me."

"To be fair, I was a little busy," he replies. "I also didn't think you'd want to hear from me since every other message after Indianapolis went unanswered. You made it pretty damn hard for me to reach out."

"I know I did, and that's not something I can change, but I am sorry." I don't know what would have happened if I kept some kind of communication open between Ronan and I, but at least I would have known. "Did I miss something, though? Because no one knew what happened and I never remember seeing anything on the news about an Olympian being involved in a car accident."

Ronan picks at the bread on his plate. "My parents didn't want that kind of attention on me, especially since we didn't know what it meant for my career. They made the story go away."

That's not nearly as surprising as it probably should have been, but I still can't help but ask. "So they were supportive through the healing process? Your parents, I mean."

"God, no." The dry, choked laugh he let out breaks my heart. "I didn't expect them to be. They hired every nurse and physical therapist I needed, but they weren't there for me at all. I wasn't in a great place after the accident; there was a lot of survivor's guilt, and I was mad about losing swimming. Swimming was the last hope I had of ever having a normal relationship with my parents."

I could picture it, and I hated the mental image so much. Ronan doing the bare minimum to survive, ignoring advice and guidance from his doctors, drowning in the guilt of survival every second.

"What..." The question dies on my lips, not wanting to ask it. Not knowing how to ask it correctly.

"What got me back on track?" Of course, he knew what I was trying to get at. "You won't believe me if I said it."

I match the small grin he gives me with one of my own. "Try me."

He pauses for a moment, staring me down like he's trying to figure out what my reaction would be. "Did you know Bryce Clark is one stubborn asshole?"

My jaw drops open. "No way."

Ronan nods with a light laugh. "He flew out to California whenever he could—always made a point to be around when my physical therapist was there. When he found out there was no physical reason for me to not be walking on my own, he lost his shit, and gave me the tough love I needed. He reminded me that there was more to live for and refusing to do it was an insult to the person who didn't walk away from the crash."

Ronan clears his throat, combing his fingers through his dark hair. "The worst part is he was right then and is still right now. There are so many people out there who never get a second chance, not like this. Why would I waste it? And you know what? If there had never been a chance I would walk again—if I never got better in that way—my life wasn't over. And Bryce would have been there to remind me of that, too."

In the year after Ronan retired, there were meets Bryce didn't attend. Huge opportunities for the national team that he, and sometimes Carter, were absent from. When Josie or I asked about them, the team brushed us off, saying they had to take care of something personal. It was Ronan. Bryce stepped up to offer the support Ronan needed when his own family failed him.

"Does Josie know?"

Mouth full, Ronan shrugs. "I'm not sure what she knows. Between your reaction and the overall way she treats me, I don't think she knows. Which is something I need to talk to him about; I don't want any more secrets."

"The way she treats you? Are you referring to the way my empathetic best friend's eyes well up like a puppy whenever someone gets so much as a paper cut?"

He grins around his fork, nodding. "Yup. Imagine what she would do if she saw the scar on my hip and leg."

I laugh lightly, but my eyes dart to where I suspect the scar to be. If he notices the movement, he doesn't say anything. "But you're okay now, right?"

"Aside from chronic pain and a total shift in life, I'm good," he promises me. "Therapy has helped a lot. Both with dealing with my accident and everything else." I nod, chewing on my lip. That he notices. "Come on, Mia. You can't offend me. Ask me whatever you want to know."

That's a pretty dangerous request because I have a lot of questions, but I don't want to make him talk about this more than he should. "I'm assuming it was some kind of a crush injury in the leg?"

"Yeah, the car rolled a couple of times, and I was pinned beneath it when the fire department got there. They took me right into surgery to repair the leg, but they weren't sure they could save it. I don't remember the days after the surgery. I have the nerve damage mostly under control between therapy and occasional medications, but the pain flares up still. Thankfully, no complications came from the surgery or injury itself. I was in bad shape, though. Bryce told me he wouldn't have known it was me if he hadn't demanded answers from my parents when he couldn't get ahold of me."

"Okay, now that I can picture." I grin at him, taking another sip of coffee.

There's a small, fond smile on his face. It amazes me to see him look back on something traumatic in that light. To pull the positive memories from the negative ones. He could be angry, he could rage against the world and his parents, but instead he's chosen to move forward.

"And is this what made you start Operation Fly?" I ask, wanting to know everything. In a matter of hours, I went from not wanting to say a single word to him to needing to keep talking to him despite this cloud still looming over us.

"Kind of." He reaches for the bread pan and cuts us both another slice without even asking. Which is fine. I would have gone for my own once he was done. "The driver of the car I was in was a single dad; his kid went to his grandmother. I couldn't attend the funeral, but I made a sizable donation to the family to cover the costs and help get the kid settled into his new life more. I sent a card with my cell number and told them to let me know if they ever needed anything. About a year after the accident, I got a call from the grandmother. She wanted her grandson to learn how to swim, but couldn't afford the lessons. She knew who I was and asked if I knew of any community efforts to get him lessons for free."

"If you tell me you taught that little boy how to swim, I am going to cry." The tears are already stinging the corners of my eyes. His cheeks flushed pink. "Oh, my god, Ronan."

"He was a good kid," he explains, like this one little gesture didn't do something amazing for that kid. And lead to something bigger. "Plus, we all gotta start somewhere, right?"

"You're a good man, Ronan," I tell him, the truth slipping out before I can stop it. "I know I don't always act like I believe it, but it's true."

Ronan gives me a tighter smile. The reality that there's still something between us comes creeping back in. "I think I call this progress. What about you?"

"We'll go with progress because there's no way I'm leaving until we eat at least half of this."

I end up staying another hour, but the conversation never got as personal as it started. We talk about the club, Operation Fly, and Lezak, who, after waking up from a nap, decides I need to play with him. Which has the two of us running around Ronan's living room and earns me several laughs from Ronan. I don't pull out my phone until I'm walking back to my car, Ronan's door quietly closing behind me. New tears sting my eyes as I type a message.

> *Thank you for being the stubborn asshole you are.*

Bryce's reply is instant.

> **Bryce: He told you then?**

> *He did.*

> I'll fill Josie in tonight, then.

> How are you doing? I know it's a lot.

> *I don't know yet.*

Ronan

Josie is sitting at the picnic table outside the door when I arrive at Adair bright and early Monday morning. And I immediately have an answer to one of Mia's questions—Josie didn't know about the accident before, but she definitely knows now.

I stop at the bench she's sitting at with a raised eyebrow. "Did you lose your key or something?" Biting her lip, she shakes her head. "If there's a snake or something in there, Josie, you need to call Bryce because I don't fuck with snakes."

That at least earns me a small giggle, but then she's setting a cup of coffee on the table and a bag with something that smells delicious next to it. She pushes it toward me. I drop my bag on the ground and slowly lower myself onto the bench. "So he told you."

"I wish I would have known before," she admits while I unwrap my sandwich. "You don't have to worry. I'm not going to cry. I did that to Bryce over the weekend."

I pause before I take a bite of my sandwich. "Are you sure? You were looking pretty cow-eyed when I walked up."

She rolls her eyes, fiddling with a strand of her auburn hair. "I promise."

"You didn't have to do this, Josie. You don't owe me or anything like that," I tell her as I reach for my coffee.

Her smile is bright, nearly blinding. "I know, but I want to remind you that you don't have to do anything alone anymore. I'm sorry your parents suck. You and Kat could talk about crappy dads together. I'm sorry you felt like no one was there back then, but I want you to know we're here now. All of us."

Well, shit. I chew the bite of my sandwich, not trusting myself to say anything in response to that right away. "I'm assuming Bryce told you about his part in the whole thing."

"He did." She sighs. "But of course I think he downplayed it. He told me he did what he had to do, but I was talking to Mia about it, and we think he wasn't telling us the whole truth. There were a lot of unexplained absences in that timeframe."

"You talked to Mia about it?" I ask, surprised to have her telling me anything about herself.

Her gaze softens. "She feels guilty, Ronan. We both do. She's happy you finally told her, which led to me finding out, but there's still guilt there. We don't see you any differently or anything like that. We have to come to terms with someone we care about being in that much pain, even if it was years ago."

"Mia doesn't care about me, Josie. She's made that loud and clear. Baking me bread and spending time with my dog doesn't change that. Plus, I don't want pity."

"Oh, my god." She groans, kicking her head back. "You two are the most annoying idiots I've ever known. And I'm dating Bryce—that should tell you something."

"I don't know what you're talking about."

"I know you care for her," Josie insists, her tone completely changing. "At least as a friend, but I suspect as more than a friend. And I think it's always been that way with you."

"I never denied anything." I shrug. "The problem isn't me, though. It's Mia and her ability to hold a grudge. A grudge over something I'm clueless about. I want to fix it, but she's not exactly playing a fair game here."

"That's a sign she cares, Ronan. Look, you're not the only one who's had something traumatic happen in the years since you've seen one another. There's a reason she took a significant pay cut and step back in her career to be here. She's not going to let her guard down so easily again."

"Well, I don't think she's going to let me in."

"And I'm not telling you what happened to get her here, but it was bad." Josie looks over my shoulder, smile widening as she waves. I turn to see Mia walking toward us. Her steps falter slightly when she sees me sitting there. Josie's getting up when I face forward. "All I'll say is my boyfriend is a stubborn asshole for the people he loves. He doesn't like to see them hurting."

"Wait, what does—"

"Well," she declares loudly, "I need to get home and go full gremlin mode. I'll never publish a book if I don't write it!"

"Did you seriously come here at seven o'clock in the morning to bring me coffee?" I question. "You hate mornings."

"I sure do." She grins. "Just remember this moment if you ever question how much I love you, friend!"

Shaking my head, I finish off my sandwich while Josie and Mia talk briefly. The footsteps behind me grow louder before a shadow falls over the table. Mia is taking her best friend's spot. "How much do you want to bet she gets no writing done and is fast asleep within the hour?"

"Without a doubt," I agree.

Mia looks tired as she rests her chin in her palm, squinting at me. It's already starting to get hot out, and I wouldn't normally choose to sit in the sun to drink my coffee, but there's a peacefulness here I don't want to break.

"You told me something really shitty the other day," she says.

I ball up my trash and set it aside, focusing fully on her. "I did."

"I don't...This doesn't mean we're friends or everything is magically okay, Ronan." She frowns. "I'm still mad about the past. I believe you when you say you don't know what I'm talking about, but I do, and I'm not ready to talk to you about it."

I press my lips into a thin line, trying to keep my frustrations at bay. She's talking to me, at least that's something. "I can't fix it if I don't know what it is."

"I know." She nods. "I just...I won't hold that against you, okay?"

Resigned, I nod slowly. "What does this have to do with the shitty thing I told you the other day?"

"I want to share a shitty thing that happened to me."

"This isn't a competition, Mia. We don't need to compare trauma."

She looks startled at the idea. "That's not what I want to do at all!"

Exhaustion is seeping into my bones. I'm tired of this back and forth with Mia that seems to never get us anywhere. "Then why tell me?"

"I can't talk to you about what happened between us right now—"

"I know." I groan, dropping my head into my hands. "I get it, Mia!"

"*But*," she stresses, "that doesn't mean I won't ever want to talk about it. If I tell you my shitty thing, I'm hoping it'll be proof to you that I'm working on being ready because there are only three people who know the whole story besides me, and that's Josie, Bryce, and my therapist."

Hope and despair are weird feelings to have fighting against each other in the pit of my stomach. On one hand, Mia just told me I could still get forgiveness and the chance to fix things, but she wants to share something that changed her forever. And if there's one thing I'm not sure I'd ever be able to handle, it's seeing Mia's heartbreak. I know from experience that every time you tell a story like this, that's exactly what happens.

She takes my silence as a prompt to continue. "Has Bryce ever told you about my ex? Her name is Bianca."

"You know Bryce would never tell me about an ex unless it involved your safety," I remind her.

"True." She sighs. "All right, Bianca and I were together for a couple of years. I thought we were going to end up married. She came from money, her parents coddled her, and wanted to give her everything she wanted. You know that's not my style, but she tried to change that."

The story unfolds from there, how Bianca wanted to open a marketing firm with Mia but have her parents give them money to cover all the upfront costs and how offended she was when Mia didn't want to take such a generous gift. While Mia loves being able to help small business owners see their dreams come true, Bianca only wanted to make money for being on social media all the time—even I know that's not all there is to marketing.

Mia had thought they'd figured it out and everything would be fine, until she came home one day to find all of Bianca's stuff gone. A few moments later, she'd received a text message that declared their relationship done and a waste of time.

"Shit, Mia." I frown, reaching out to squeeze her arm. She lets me, wiping angrily at the corners of her eyes. "That's horrible. No one deserves to be walked out on like that."

"That's not even the worst part." She laughs bitterly. "The worst part is that she decided ruining my trust wasn't good enough; she wanted to ruin my career, too. She moved forward with opening the firm, then proceeded to steal my clients from underneath me. She ran my name through the mud. My reputation in Charlotte plummeted and the firm I worked for was ready to fire me rather than protect me. Which further broke my heart because that action went against everything I thought they stood for."

The pieces of this puzzle, the explanation for what Mia's doing here, slowly comes together. "And that's why you're here?"

She wipes her eyes again, nodding. "Bryce offered me a job. It was the chance to get away from it all, to start over surrounded by people I could trust. He pretends what he did wasn't a big deal, but we all know it was."

"He does have that tendency," I reply thoughtfully.

She agrees before taking a deep breath. "So there's my story and part of the reason why my already shaky trust issues have completely taken over. It's part of the reason I'm not ready to face the past, Ronan."

Shaking my head, I offer her a smile. "You don't need to explain it to me, Mia. Take as long as you need. Maybe we can be friends, at least?"

She considers the words for a second, biting her lip. "See, *friend* is making warning bells go off in my head."

Because she doesn't trust me anymore. Whatever I did—whatever happened—added to her shaky foundation, and Bianca sent everything tumbling down. Where I had a chance before her ex, I now have to fight for my life because someone didn't realize the good thing they had and destroyed it instead.

But I won't pressure her. I won't force her to make decisions she's not ready to make. Not now; not ever. "All right, not friends. What would you call us?"

"What about frenemies?"

I snort at the word I haven't heard since high school but can't fight my smile when she holds her hand out to me. I shake it. I could still have some fun with this. "Fine, we'll be frenemies. I think I'll like this."

Her brow arches. "Yeah?"

"Oh, yeah. I can still tease the hell out of you, but still know you like me just a little bit."

She rolls her eyes, then squints up at me when I stand. "And why would you want to do that?"

I lean down until our noses are practically brushing. She takes in a sharp breath and her eyes flutter closed, which makes me smirk. "Because, Mia, you're still hot as hell when you're mad."

Her hazel eyes snap open and lower into a glare as I pull back, laughing. "Grow up!"

"Oh, trust me." I smirk at her, allowing my eyes to track down the amazing view I have before me. "I'm plenty grown up and you already know that."

"Oh, my god." She groans, exasperated. "You're seriously annoy-ing."

"Sure," I call over to her as I make my way to the door to unlock it. I hear her get up to follow me. "Pretend all you want, Mia, but I happen to know something important about how this situation will end."

She stops a couple of feet from where I'm holding the door open for her, putting her hands on her hips. "Yeah, and what's that?"

"The enemies—or frenemies—always become lovers in the end."

Her eyebrows shoot up her forehead, eyes going wide, and a faint blush coats her cheeks as she stomps inside. "I should have never come here this morning; I should go back to yesterday."

"What was so great about yesterday?" I flip the lobby light on, turning to lock the door behind us since we're not open yet.

"Well, yesterday I liked you. Yesterday I cared about you."

The declaration has me spinning to look at her, a thick lump forming in my throat. "Oh, yeah?" She lets out an affirmative "mm-hmm." "Well, what about today?"

"Today I'm back to finding you annoying as hell!"

My smile grows with each annoyed thump her feet make on the stairs as she heads to her office. Seconds later, I hear the door close. Shaking my head, I head up the same stairs to get up to the gym for my workout. When I reach the top, I have to cross through the common area to get to the gym, and she is peeking up at me out of the fringe that's fallen in her face. Her cheeks turn bright red when I give her a wink.

Yeah, frenemies can be fun.

Mia

I laugh loudly when Katrina turns to glare at Carter. "What are you going to do?"

"I don't know!" He scrambles to look at the cards laid out on the table, actively looking for some kind of clue into his own potential future actions before giving me a panicked look. "Mia, why would you tell her that?"

Laughing, I gather the cards, the offending Five of Wands the last to be picked up. "Do you think I have any say in what cards are going to show up? Besides, it doesn't mean something *will* happen, just suggests there could be disagreement or tension in this situation."

"Besides, even if it does come true, it doesn't mean you're the one who will mess up, dude," Bryce comforts. "It could just as easily be Katrina."

Kat crosses her arms over her chest with a scowl. "What makes you think it'll be me?"

Bryce holds his hands up in defense. "See, this is why group tarot readings are dangerous. It's bad enough when Josie does her own and ends up scowling at me but never tells me why."

"I can't believe any of you are taking this seriously."

We all turn to face Ronan, who has been silently watching the whole exchange from the corner of the kitchen. It hadn't been lost on me the way he kept his distance, with a look of uncertainty directed at the cards, like the deck could curse him from afar or something.

"What? You don't believe in having your future read?"

"No, Katrina, I don't." He pushes off the counter, but then his steps falter when I start shuffling the cards. I bite back a smile. "It's not realistic to think a deck of cards can give you any insight into what's coming next."

Bryce is shaking his head before Ronan even finishes his sentence. "Hey, man, I don't know if I believe in it all, but I know Josie's been doing this since before we got back together. And I spent enough time at her apartment back in Omaha to know that between the tarot cards and the friendly ghost who lived there, to learn there are definitely things out of our depth of understanding."

"We don't know if I had a friendly ghost for sure," Josie protests.

Bryce gives her an unimpressed look. "My shoes moved overnight, babe. As I recall, we were too busy with other activities to do it ourselves. You tell me how they ended up neatly lined up by the door."

"Your apartment was definitely haunted," I tell Josie before turning to Ronan. "And you are being extremely closed minded."

He gives a casual shrug, then sits at the barstool Kat just freed up across from me, eyes tracking my every movement while I shuffle the deck. "I think we're in charge of our own destiny, and using something like tarot cards helps us make excuses for our own shortcomings."

"Oh, shit," Bryce mutters under his breath. "They were starting to get along."

I tilt my head as I look at Ronan, saying, "That's pessimistic. The cards aren't meant to be excuses; they're meant to help amplify the voice within that you should already be listening to."

"What kind of voice is that?" He smirks, tone teasing. "My heart?"

"Ew, no." I make a face. "Your intuition. Most of the questions asked in tarot readings are things you already know the answer to. The cards help you trust your gut."

"Yet it told Kat she'd have a small spat with her boyfriend in the future. How do the cards know what to say about my future?"

"She asked for a past, present, future spread based on her love life. The goal in this kind of spread is to help sort out your priorities. It doesn't mean they'll fight five minutes or years from now, but it is a reminder to not let something simmer under the surface," I explain. "The longer you let agitation simmer, the more likely it is to blow up in your face and be worse. Maybe one of them has picked up a new habit that the other finds annoying, but if they don't talk about it soon, it could blow up."

"Oh, my god." Kat gasps, spinning to face Carter. "She's right, you *have* picked up a new habit. You haven't been closing the drawer on the dresser all the way. Dust is getting on the clothes; I keep tripping over it and getting things snagged. It's been really annoying."

He blinks, a small frown on his face. "I didn't even notice I've been doing that. I'll try to be better about it."

Leaning back in my seat, I motion to our friends like they just proved my point. Mainly because they had.

Ronan, however, is not convinced. "You could have planned that or, at the very least, you put the idea in her head, and she went searching for something."

"Okay, now I'm getting offended," I reply, setting the cards down. "How could I have planned to pull that exact card? How could I even know something petty like that could be bothering Kat?"

"*Hey!*"

I flash her an apologetic smile but keep my focus on Ronan. "Do you want to know what I think is going on here? I think you're intimidated."

He snorts. "By what? You or a deck of cards?"

"Both. But definitely the cards. You're pretending not to be curious because you're scared of what they'll say about you."

"I'm not scared of anything," he replies coolly. "Especially witchy fortune cookies."

I keep a cool, even expression, reaching for the deck again. "Then prove it. Let me do a reading for you."

I can instantly tell how much he hates the idea, but I know him well enough to know he hates being challenged even more. "I think I'm good."

"I repeat, you're scared of the cards."

"Seriously, dude, just let her do the reading," Carter comments, arms slung around Katrina.

"Yeah." Bryce smirks. "Letting her give you a reading will prove you're not scared of them."

For a brief moment, I think we have him cornered bad enough that he's going to give in, admit he's unsure of my hobby, and what it might make him examine. Then he gets the same cocky, confident smirk I'm used to seeing on him, and sits up straighter. "Let's do this."

"Seriously?" I cough to cover up the light squeak my voice gave.

He leans closer to me. "Seriously, let's see what you've got, Sheridan."

"All right." I reach up with trembling hands to push my hair back out of my face. "It's best if you get comfortable. Try to relax."

Ronan makes a show of getting more comfortable in the seat across from me while I try to calm my rapidly beating heart. I've always found reading tarot for someone else to be a little intimate, which is why I only do it for the people I truly know and love. Whenever I do this, I'm asking them to take a deep look at their own lives, seeing if anything I'm getting from a line of cards resonates with them. Because of this, I can't promise it'll be something they want to hear.

"The first thing I always do is remind people I'm not a professional," I begin, which only makes his brow arch more. "Yes, I've been doing this for years, and I taught Josie, but I primarily only do it for myself, not other people. Hopefully, something will resonate with you, but I can't make promises. That would be true even if I was a professional."

"Do people really get paid to do this?"

I ignore his dig, focusing on his green eyes even though they make my heart beat even faster. "Now, what do you want to know? No yes or no questions; the cards don't work that way."

"I want the same kind of reading you did for Kat, for scientific purposes." Of course, he's taking this to such a level, trying to determine how much he believes in it. But it feels a little like he's determining how much he believes in me. "But I want to know about my life. My past, my present, and where I'm going with my future."

My eyes widen. "You don't want to zero in on anything specific? Maybe your career or your love life?"

"Nope," he declares, eyes alight with amusement. "I want to see what you come up with for my entire life."

"I should have known you'd make this as difficult as possible," I mutter under my breath. I raise it to say, "Such a broad topic may mean the cards don't feel as relevant as they could. Are you okay with that?"

"I think I'll be the one who judges that, right?" God, why is he being so cocky? And why is it making my heart beat a little erratically and my stomach twist in an annoying way? "So, what's going to happen here?"

"I'm going to shuffle the cards, focusing in on your question, and the pattern of the spread." Instinctively, I start a casual shuffle, the cards moving easily through my hands. "I feel I give the best readings if I'm in control of the cards the entire time. I want to avoid breaking the intention behind the reason. Does that work for you?"

Ronan nods, but the wary look is back in his eye as he watches the cards move. "And how do you know which ones to pull?"

"I use the fall technique," I tell him. "Which basically means I keep shuffling until three cards fall out. Now, as for turning over the cards, I'll give you a choice. I can either turn them as they fall or turn them after all are pulled. I turn them; I don't flip them."

"There's a difference?"

"Cards have different meanings if they're reversed," Josie explains from my left. "If she flips them instead of turning them, the meaning of the reading could change."

Ronan glances my way, and I nod in confirmation. "All right. Turn them as they fall. I like watching the story play out in real time."

Shifting in my seat, I zero in on Ronan's question. The room goes almost eerily silent as I start shuffling with more intention, building the connection with the cards, and letting my intention flow through me. The first card falls within seconds of starting.

In the past position, I turn over the Four of Cups reversed. I take notice, immediately finding it interesting. No one says a word as I start shuffling again. The Seven of Wands falls up to take the present position. My breath catches in my throat when I turn over the final card, The Lovers.

"Oh!" Ronan howls with laughter. "Would you look at that? The Lovers are in my future. I think I can interpret that one all on my own, don't you agree?"

Playing it cool, I straighten the cards, and use the time to gather my thoughts. I don't want him to know the last card caught me off guard, too. I'm not sure I like any possible meaning that card could have in this situation. "Maybe you should let me tell you what all this means, especially since the cards aren't always as they appear."

He motions to the spread on the table. "By all means, tell me my future, Miss Sheridan."

With a roll of my eyes, I take a look to find the connecting pieces. Once I describe what each card means, I'll pull it together and relate it back to his question. I think this is going to be much more relevant than he anticipated.

"We'll start with the meaning of each card." I point to the one in the past position. "This is the Four of Cups, but in reverse. This suggests that you took on a new outlook on life. You stopped dwelling on where you were and decided to take steps toward your future—the future you wanted."

Ronan sits up a little straighter, his green eyes glancing over at Bryce. I want to see his reaction, but I'm too focused on watching the doubter before me.

I move to the second card. "The Seven of Wands is telling you to take a stand. I can't tell you what this is in regard to, only you can do that. It's a message on how it's time to fight for yourself and that future you decided to chase. Push back, don't worry about the odds being against you. This is your moment."

Another glance toward Bryce and Carter has me wondering what they know about Ronan that I don't.

"That might make a bit of sense," he murmurs, but then the small smirk is back. "How about we talk about the last card?"

"The Lovers..." I trail off, trying to find the best way to describe this card. "In this instance, it could mean finding love, but it doesn't necessarily mean you've already found it."

"Well, that's good," Bryce murmurs, "because everyone who's an option is literally taken."

I bite back a grin at the idea of him not seeing me as an option for Ronan. At least he still thinks I hate him. Because I do.

I absolutely do.

"So, what does it mean, exactly?" Ronan asks, ignoring his friend.

"In this instance, I would say it's reminding you to follow your heart, but be careful to make sure you're looking at what the best option is. It can be a warning to not give your heart away too easily."

The smirk slowly slides off his face. "Oh."

"Yeah, so to sum it all up..." I take a glance back at the cards. "I would say you made the right decision by focusing in on a new outlook and taking a chance. In the present, you need to prepare to stand up for the things you believe in and defend them when necessary, or you run the risk of losing them and yourself. That needs to be your priority right now. In the future, you can start looking for romance based on good communication, but be careful not to mistake lust for love. Do you have any questions?"

He looks at the cards, like there might be some secret within them that we've both missed. The crease in his forehead deepens with his frown, green eyes jumping between them all. I'd give anything to be able to read his mind right now—figure out if he's panicking over how relevant this reading seems. I feel like I know nothing about his life at this point. I'm still trying to get used to this new version of him I'm being exposed to, but even I can connect the dots.

"What else can you tell me about The Lovers card?"

Bryce groans at the question. "I'm officially bored with this. We're supposed to be having a game night, and this doesn't count."

Ronan waves him, and everyone else, off, but stays exactly where he is, waiting.

"What do you want to know?" The rest of our group filters out, heading toward the living room to set up the game night.

"Everything."

"I mean, there are a lot of ways to interpret it, and it usually depends on the question being asked," I tell him. "Typically speaking, it signifies a perfect union, but we need to know what that union is. It could mean learning to love and accept yourself. It could mean romantically, or even, in some cases, deep friendships. If you're focusing on your own health, it could be a reminder that your support system is here and never goes away. It can also be related to heart health."

"Oh, so now they can tell me if I'm going to have a heart attack?"

"Seriously?" I grab the box with more force than I mean to. "You're the one who's asking follow-up questions. You don't get to be a judgmental ass."

"You're right, I'm sorry. Please continue."

I narrow my eyes, trying to show him my dislike for this whole conversation. "If it's in a reading focusing on your career, it could signify that you're entering a partnership that's going to be great and successful. In relationship readings, it signifies a strong bond. It can also signify sparks starting to fly within your love life. It doesn't mean the person you're thinking about is the one."

"And who do you think is on my mind?"

"That's it." I snatch up the cards that I'd laid out and add them to the deck to put them away. "I'm done doing this with you."

"Oh, come on, Mia," he pleads. I get up, gathering the dishes still sitting on the island from dinner. "I'm messing with you! I just find it hard to believe you take this seriously!"

After depositing my dishes into the sink, I start washing my hands to have something to do. "As I said earlier, tarot cards are rooted in intuition, Ronan. Part of the point is to help you learn to trust your own instincts and that's something I need to do."

"That's not an answer, though, is it?"

Letting an eye roll loose, I turn to face him. "The world isn't that black and white. They help me see and find clarity with what has happened and what's currently happening in my life."

His brow arches up. "And what's going to happen in the future?"

"Why does it matter to you?" My arms cross over my chest. "Weren't you always the one talking about not shutting down what other people are into? Especially when it comes to their belief system?"

He's clearly startled by my question and seems a little chastised. Which I take as a win in the conversation.

"Besides," I continue, "can you honestly tell me nothing I said in that reading resonated with you?"

"I never said it didn't!" Defensiveness is back in his tone. "But I also never thought you'd be into something like this and find merit in it. You always like to see things the way they are."

He wasn't getting it, and I don't feel the need to keep repeating myself. I don't owe him any more of an explanation. I don't need to tell him how I got into reading tarot when I was forced to make decisions about where my future was going to take me. I don't need to tell him how reading those cards helped me cope with things that happened in the past, things that involved him. I don't need to keep telling him that these cards help me find comfort in the things I already know. That they feel like they're backing me up.

Especially when he used to tell me how staring at a black line for hours upon hours was his form of therapy.

"Well, I'm not sure you know me well enough to make that call. And sometimes people find answers in unique places. Just because what I do doesn't make sense to you, doesn't mean it's wrong."

"That's not what I'm trying to say, Mia!"

"You know, maybe that's your problem. You say a lot of shit, Ronan, but does anyone even know what you mean? Do we know if there's any truth to what you say at all?"

Ronan's pale cheeks flush a shade of red I've never seen before. "What the fuck is that supposed to mean? I have *never* lied to you, Mia."

"Forget it." I wave him off. I don't want to do this anymore. I don't want to have this conversation. I've avoided it for eight years. Why not make it a lifetime?

As I turn to leave, he reaches out, and gently grabs my arm, keeping me in place. My gaze snaps down to where his fingers are holding me, not wanting to think about the last time we were in a position like this. And I refuse to pay attention to the way my heart is thudding against my chest.

"You are not doing that, Mia," he seethes, stepping closer. Somehow, I know Ronan wouldn't hold me here if I asked him to let me go. He wouldn't hesitate to release me, but my morbid sense of curiosity keeps me rooted in place. "You've done nothing but treat me like shit since I got here. Longer, actually. Every time I feel like we take a step forward, you go five back. You refuse to tell me what I did, and now you're calling me a liar? Fuck that."

My gaze locks with his. "It's not my job to tell you when you make a mistake, Ronan. You're a big boy."

"But I don't know what mistake I made," he says through gritted teeth. "I can't fix whatever this is if I don't know what happened. Please, tell me what happened. I'm tired of this shit."

"I don't want an apology, Ronan." I fight to keep my voice from raising, the last thing we need is for everyone to come in here and witness this stupid argument.

"Then what do you want from me, Mia?"

I glare up at him. "To leave me the hell alone."

"And if I don't want to?"

The question catches me off guard. I shrink back. "W—what?"

It's the first time either one of us has said anything like that out loud, despite our actions obviously proving the question right. There's still something between us. Sure, it might be sparking with relentless rage, but it's there. And eventually, it'll pull us together until we explode.

He takes a deep breath, and then a step closer to me. I don't back up. I can feel his chest rise and fall. His green eyes search my face before they settle on my lips. "What if I don't want to leave you alone?"

The question is asked in barely a whisper. His warm breath fanning against my face with each word. It sends a shiver down my spine, and I should walk away. I should step back, put as much distance between us as possible, and keep it that way. The last thing I need to do is prove he still has some kind of hold on me. That's what I should do.

Instead, I surge forward, and he meets me in the middle, our lips crashing together in a kiss that is both passionate and uncertain.

I don't go back to that day in the stairwell because this kiss feels different. This kiss is us, through and through. Suddenly, I'm in my early twenties, chasing a dream with my best friend. I'm in Charlotte, North Carolina again, staring up at swimming's golden boy after he caught me in his arms. Things look brighter. I've never known the kind of heartbreak I know now. Everything's possible. Nothing is without reach, including this man.

But that's not reality.

As soon as his lips move to deepen the kiss. I pull back with a gasp. Ronan's staring down at me, jaw slack, breathing a little heavier. Somewhere in the kiss, his grip on my arm had dropped. I take a step back. "That cannot happen again."

Ronan follows me. "Right, I agree."

"Ronan!" I take another step back, and he follows. "I'm serious."

"So am I." I'm pressed between a kitchen island and solid muscle. Except I don't want to escape. "Completely serious."

Everything is different about the next kiss. Ronan's hand is cupping the back of my neck, tilting my head toward him to angle it just right. There's no hesitation, as a quick swipe against my bottom lip and the small gasp I release is all he needs before sliding his tongue inside and taking control of the kiss.

Oh, my god. My fingers reach up until they're combing the dark hair at the nape of his neck. *This man is always going to ruin me.*

With his other hand, he grips me tighter around the hip and takes another step closer. There's not a single part of our body that isn't touching, and I feel my resolve melting away. I don't want to be mad at this man. I don't want to be hurt over the things of the past. I want to know this version of him. I want to see how he's grown and changed. I want to know how much of the guy I knew is still inside him and whether our lives can be entwined the same way they once were.

I want more, I finally admit to myself.

We break apart at the sound of a loud thump and laughter from the living room. Both of us are turned toward the doorway, frozen like we're about to be walked in on, breathing hard.

Reality starts to come back into focus. We're in Josie and Bryce's kitchen and we just had a fight. An angry kiss between enemies might be hot in a romance novel, but in real life, it'll complicate things. And I can't allow for things to be more complicated.

I gently push Ronan back. He stumbles away from me, swallowing thickly, and bringing a hand up to fix his hair.

"That will never happen again."

"What?"

I glare at him, taking a second to pull myself together. If I go out there right now, my best friend will know what happened with a single look. "Both kisses were mistakes. I'll never let it happen again."

Ronan opens his mouth to say something, green eyes going a little wide, but he never gets the chance. Carter enters the kitchen. He stops as soon as he enters the room, frowning at both of us.

"Are you guys good?" Carter focuses his attention fully on me. He might not know what happened between Ronan and me, but he's more than aware of what his guy friends are capable of. And he's not afraid to call them out. "Josie sent me in here to make sure you hadn't killed each other yet."

"If I have to be alone with him for a second longer, I might kill him." I push past Ronan, purposefully heading toward the living room. "What was that thump?"

Carter follows behind me. "Bryce fell off the arm of the couch."

I laugh, but it sounds a little strained. "Of course he did."

"Mia." Carter's voice is lowered. "Are you good?"

"Fucking peachy, Carter." The sarcasm is evident, and I know he'll want to follow-up about it, but I don't know what else to say to him. He doesn't deserve my lies.

He hums in understanding, murmuring, "We'll talk about this later," as we enter the living room.

Mia

Carter and Josie corner me at work on Monday morning.

I don't know why I'm surprised, but the way they storm in and shut the door of our office and snap the lock behind them makes it feel like an ambush. Then Josie pulls the blinds, and I absolutely feel like I'm being held hostage.

"What's going on?" I ask, warily looking between the two of them. "Should I be worried?"

"Carter told me what he saw, and I think we need to talk." Josie plops down in her chair, staring at me expectantly. Carter sits in the cramped chair in the corner. I almost laugh at the way he has to fold his long limbs to sit properly. "Start talking."

I turn to Carter. "What exactly did you see?"

His cheeks turn bright red, his eyes widening slightly. "Um...well, I..."

"Yes?"

He clears his throat. "I saw you and Ronan. The other night at Bryce and Josie's? After you did the tarot reading."

Well, so much for trying to play it cool. We're getting right to the point. "We were talking in the kitchen."

"That's not what it looked like to Carter," Josie replies. "To Carter, it looked like the two of you were fighting and, more specifically, it looked like you were fighting against him."

I suck in a breath, realizing what it actually looked like to him. Coming in from another room with me trying to push past Ronan, anger and embarrassment burning my cheeks. I swallow thickly. "Uh, does Bryce know?"

"If Bryce knew what he saw, do you think Ronan would still be employed?" Josie questions. "I know my boyfriend's protective streak; he takes action first and asks questions later. I wanted to hear the whole story from you before we told Bryce. You know, to decide whether it's something he needs to know."

"Right," I breathe out. "Getting answers is probably a good first step."

Even if I've never done that a day in my life. My god, I have too much in common with Bryce and it's starting to freak me out a bit.

"So, as your best friend, I'm going to ask this once and only once. What happened?"

The locked door, pulled blinds, and presence of our favorite cinnamon roll suddenly makes sense. "We kissed." They both look at each other with blank stares I can't read, and I hate it. "Actually, *I* kissed him...again."

Josie jumps up from her seat in a move so fluid it startles me. "What do you mean again? When did you kiss him the first time?"

"I'd actually be interested in knowing the answer to that, too." Carter frowns. "Last I knew, you hated one another, and that tidbit of information dates back eight years."

Oh, you poor, sweet, oblivious boy. You couldn't be further from the truth.

Do I lie? Do I say the kiss in the stairwell was the first and only? Do I lightly allude to something happening in Omaha? What lines am I willing to cross here?

"We kissed right after I found out about Operation Fly." Is it really a lie? It was the first time we'd kissed since everything happened in Omaha. As far as they both know, that was the first time we'd kissed. They don't need the details of whatever happened years ago. That won't do them any good.

"But what does that mean for right now?" Carter asks. "Are the two of you into each other? Are you going to try dating? Do you even like one another?"

The last question is the most complicated one. The more time I spend around him, the more I realize whatever crush I had on him never fully went away. I'm not going to be the same naïve girl I was then, though. I wasn't going to fall the first time he sends a wink my way, nor am I going to let my guard down. Two kisses shared mostly in anger doesn't change what happened before.

I shrug. "He's an attractive man. No one in this room can deny that and—I don't know, it just happened. Maybe it's because I've been going on these dates, but nothing happens with any of them. Maybe I'm a little lonely, but the reality is, nothing more is going to happen between Ronan and me. Two kisses don't mean we're ready to fall into bed or walk down the aisle."

Something about the way Josie is looking at me has me shifting in my seat. She knows there's more to the way I look at Ronan. I've never been able to deny when I was into someone. No matter how much I argued against it, she's always known.

"Just...be careful. I don't want to see you get hurt again. Especially not this close to moving on from Bianca. Yes, I want to see you get out there and find someone else, but not at the expense of your heart breaking again."

"Aren't you the queen of second chances?" I ask, wanting that probing look to be directed anywhere but at me. "You and Bryce had this whole thing you came back from. I thought you'd be happy to see Ronan and I making any sort of progress."

Why do I do this? Why do I turn the attention off me by directing a spotlight on something that makes someone else uncomfortable? I know I do it, Josie knows I do it, and even though she's never been hurt by it, my deflection makes her relive things. Yet to avoid my own pain, I take her back to a time when the man who loves her more than anything on this Earth broke her heart. Back to a time when she felt humiliated and ostracized from a sport she loved, all because he was too young and too scared to face the truth.

It took them a long time to get where they are, but I'm certain from the moment they met, there hasn't been a day when Josie Martin wasn't Bryce Clark's everything.

She doesn't take the bait, though. Rather than shrink in on herself or try to change the subject, stubbornness rolls off her in waves. A burst of pride shoots through me. "Don't use me to get us off your back, Mia. I know what you're doing."

The fight drains out of me. "You know I don't mean to do that, right? It's something—"

"You're working on it, I know. I don't take offense. I know you too well and I know what you're doing. You don't mean to hurt people, but you feel the need to protect yourself."

"Doesn't make it right," I mutter.

"No, but forgiveness is easily given in these moments," Carter adds. "Because we know the real you, and we know what you hide behind when you don't want to share that with the world."

Josie nods in agreement. "And I might be the queen of second chances, but you know how hard I worked to get here. You know how hard he worked and how hard we work together still. I don't know what happened between you and Ronan—whatever you're hurt by—but I'm going to share some important advice I once got. You're allowed to be mad at the people who hurt you. You're allowed to decide who gets to be part of your life moving forward."

The words ring in my ears with a familiarity I can't seem to put my finger on. My mouth drops open a bit, hoping the words will find me. That they'd come tumbling out, but nothing does.

"You said it to me once, when Bryce came back into my life," Josie reminds me.

The realization dawns on me; it was right after he brought her coffee, and she wasn't sure where she wanted him to be in her life.

She goes on to say, "I had to decide whether the person who hurt me got to be part of my life going forward. Despite everything, I've never regretted the decision I made, not really. Now it's your turn to decide that for yourself."

"But what if I get hurt?"

It takes me a second to realize the sad, scared whispered question came from me, but once I do, the weight of it settles around me. Because that's the real question, the one I've been avoiding this entire time. If I give him a chance—if I tell him the truth—I'm opening myself up for heartbreak. And that's always scary.

"Then we'll be here to help you put yourself back together," Carter replies. When I turn to look at him, he's leaning forward with his arms resting against his knees, brown hair a tousled mess. "You know you can't avoid pain, but not everyone is going to leave you, Mia. You won't know who's going to stay until you give them a chance."

The two people in this room with me will never leave. They're going to be the ones who stay. Ronan could run. He could run far away from me and never look back, but he'd still be there. Just out of reach in my heart and mind, and I'd be forced to live with it for the rest of my life.

"It's your choice, Mia. It's always been your choice," Josie mutters.

I know that. I just don't know how to make it.

⸳⸳⸳⸳⸳ ✦ ✦ ★ ✶ ☾ ✶ ★ ✦ ✦ ⸳⸳⸳⸳⸳

"What are you doing here?"

Carter is walking toward me, hands stuffed in the pocket of his hoodie. Further behind him, Ronan trails in with Lezak prancing at his feet. My heart thumps against my chest—clearly more excited to see the puppy than the man holding the leash.

I don't get a chance to answer Carter because the second Ronan unhooks the leash, the small bundle of golden fluff charges straight at me. Laughing, I reach down to scoop him into my arms, happily accepting all the kisses he eagerly gives. "Hi, puppy!"

"Should I be offended that he zoomed right past me to get to her?" Carter's sad tone barely pushes into my puppy-induced haze of happiness. "I think he hates me."

When I look at the two men, I find Ronan wearing a fond smile, fully focused on me and his dog. Unable to be on the receiving end of a grin like that for too long, I look away. "Don't take it personally, Carter. I think he'd pick Mia over me, too."

I hide my own grin in the fuzzy fur of the golden retriever's head. "What can I say? Dogs love me."

"They're not the only ones," Carter mutters under his breath, then groans when Ronan elbows him in the side.

I set Lezak back on the deck, looking between the two of them with a frown. "What was all of that about?"

"Ignore him," Ronan insists. I don't miss the glare he sends Carter. "I'm guessing we all got the same cryptic text message?"

"You mean the one from Bryce that told me to meet him here at eight o'clock at night and to make sure Josie doesn't know?" Carter squats to give the puppy a belly rub, but his eyes stay locked on us. "Do either of you know what this is about?"

Ronan takes a seat next to me, sighing as he stretches his bad leg out in front of him. "No idea."

I resist the urge to check him over for any obvious sign of something being wrong. He's had a long couple of days, which I know get to him. "He better get here soon, though, because mysterious Bryce freaks me out."

Ronan laughs, reaching down to scratch Lezak between the ears now that the puppy has made his way back over to his human. "It's because he's bad at it." Lezak playfully nips on his fingers. My heart swoops at the soft smile he gives his dog. "He either acts way too dramatic or not dramatic enough."

Carter stands once he's sure he's lost the attention of the dog. He chews at his bottom lip. "You don't think they're breaking up again, do you?"

"Absolutely not." There's not a lot in my life I'm certain of, but this is one of them. "They're too disgustingly in love to ever break up...again."

Ronan nods in agreement. "They've gone through too much shit to let anything get between them now."

Carter doesn't look as certain.

Footsteps echo and all of us turn in time to see Bryce emerge from the side door. Predictably, Lezak barks and takes off toward him. Bryce cheerfully greets us, stopping long enough to scoop the dog into his arms, and closes the distance between us.

"What's going on, dude?" The nerves are evident in Carter's voice. "If you're breaking her heart again, I'm on her side this time."

Bryce squints at his best friend, mouth set in a firm line. "What the hell are you talking about?"

"Abrams is worried he's about to be the child of divorce," Ronan explains. "Do you blame him, though? That text message was cryptic."

Bryce frowns at Carter. "You would really take her side?"

Honestly, he doesn't sound at all surprised, which is probably good.

I reach for Lezak, who Bryce hands over immediately. The puppy cuddles against me, worn out from all the activity. "We would all take her side, Bryce."

"Even Lezak." Ronan reaches over to pet his dog. "Now, what are we doing here?"

Bryce's gaze lands on me, his bottom lip disappearing between his teeth. "Please don't be mad at me. I was going to involve you in the whole process, but then I saw it, and I knew. It's perfect."

"What are you..." My question trails off as realization clicks into place. My jaw drops open. If I didn't have a cuddly puppy in my lap, I'd probably spring up to attack him in a hug. "Oh, my god! Let me see it!"

"Let you see what?" It's Ronan who voices the question, but one fleeting glance at Carter tells me he's just as confused.

"Ugh, men." I roll my eyes, making grabby hands toward Bryce, who laughs.

He drops a deep blue velvet box in my hand and my breath catches in my throat. The weight of it makes this all the more real. Tears are already stinging the corners of my eyes when I look up at Bryce. He's watching me cautiously. My best friend is about to get engaged!

The appearance of the box must make something click in the guys' heads because they both lean closer to get a peek. I shy away from them. They can wait their turn. I've waited years to have this moment.

I'm not mad Bryce didn't include me in the purchasing process, but I will be the first of our friends to see it.

I lift the lid, half expecting to see something big, something flashy. Instead, my breath is literally taken from me. Nestled in the velvet cushion is the perfect ring for Josie. An oval cut blue-green sapphire set in a yellow-gold band, small diamonds accenting the gem on either side.

I look back up at Bryce. "It's not a diamond."

He shakes his head, shifting his weight from one foot to the other, a sure sign of his uncertainty. "I...uh, I had a list. Of all the big stores you're supposed to go to when you look for a ring, but I got bored one night and started looking online. I found this one and I...I just knew. It's her."

I hand the ring over to Ronan so he and Carter can take a look, but I don't look away from Bryce. "Josie would hate a flashy diamond."

Biting back a smile, he laughs. "She would, but she'd pretend to love it because it came from me. I didn't want that, though. I want her to actually love it. Screw what society thinks."

"You know it's not about the ring, right? She just wants you."

His gaze drifts to the ring. "She deserves this." His tone is so firm, leaving no room for doubt. He wants forever with her. "She deserves the whole world."

I set Lezak on the bench beside me before I tackle Bryce in a hug. I laugh at the surprised sound he makes. He freezes for the briefest second before hugging me back.

My eyes are even mistier when we separate, but I still manage to pull off a serious look. "You better treat her well, Bryce Clark. She's my person as much as she is yours."

His grin is soft. "Always."

"Dude." Carter claps his best friend on his back. "This is huge! Just don't mess it up this time."

Bryce allows Carter to pull him into a hug with a groan. "Oh, my god, it was one time. Can we let it go?"

"Technically, it was three times, right?" Ronan looks to me for confirmation. I nod. "Fourth time's the charm then, right?"

Scowling, Bryce accepts a congratulatory hug from Ronan as well.

If someone had told me we'd be here one day eight years ago, I would have laughed in their face. I never thought we'd make it. Not like this. Not as a group of friends running a business together, and definitely not with Josie and Bryce heading down the aisle. It was too good to be true back then. Sometimes, I worry it still is.

An elbow nudges my arm. Ronan is standing far too close now, concern in his eyes. "You got quiet."

"Just thinking." He nudges me again, urging me to say more. "I'm happy for them. They're good for each other. Always have been, don't you think?"

He hums in agreement. "But you thought you'd be first?"

"Not at all." I laugh softly. "I was actually thinking more about how everyone around me seems to be moving on while I feel stuck. A common topic in therapy as well."

"What are you talking about? You're not stuck. You're doing a lot with your life, Mia."

"Sure." I snort. "Says the Olympian turned philanthropist."

"No. Says the man who had the only thing that made him anything taken from him and had to figure out how to be a contributing member of society."

Swimming isn't the only thing that made him someone. I've always seen him for who he is, and that is someone who deeply cares about helping those he can. Someone who is determined to break away from his family's hold and create a life he can be proud of. Someone who is as gorgeous on the inside as he is on the outside. Even when I was mad at him, I never only saw the heartless, playboy reputation he projected out to the world. I'd always been able to see Ronan.

I don't get the chance to say any of that to him.

He steps up to Bryce again. "I'm happy for you, dude. She's going to love it." Bryce grins at him. Pure happiness radiates off him, and he hasn't even asked her yet. "If there's nothing else, though, I'm going to head home. I had a long day and need to feed Lezak."

Bryce's gaze moves from Ronan to me, observing the moment. "Yeah, of course." He nods. "Thanks for coming."

With another quick hug, Ronan is scooping the sleepy puppy from the bench to head for the door. No one says a word until he's fully left the building. The pool is eerily quiet, and I need it to stop.

"Mia—"

"It's fine, Bryce." My eyes plead with him to drop it. I'm not even sure what I'd say. What even happened? "Show me the ring again."

He hesitates and is about to check in on me before thinking better of it.

"When are you going to do it?" I ask once I have my breath back from looking at it again.

That's how I spend the next forty-five minutes, sitting on the uncomfortable bleachers, throwing out random ideas for Carter and Bryce to either shoot down or turn into a theatrical production. I may not have helped pick the ring, but Bryce will definitely need my input on the proposal because Josie would hate a sky writer.

And it gives me something to focus on other than Ronan.

Ronan

With my arms firmly crossed over my chest, I watch the mayhem of teenagers performing drills in the pool. My gaze flicks from swimmer to swimmer, taking quick mental notes about what needs to be adjusted and worked on. When I glance at the clock on the wall, I notice Bryce walking toward me. I try not to let myself tense.

Where the hell is she?

"Looking good," he comments when he reaches me. He stands beside me in a position that mirrors my own, watching silently for a minute or so. "Aren't you missing someone, though?"

"Yup," I mutter through gritted teeth.

From the beginning, I've made it clear to Emmie that if she wants to do this, she needs to commit. She'd promised she would and has been following through on that promise, until recently. In the last ten days, she's been late to over half the practices with little to no explanation. Whenever I try to ask her about it, she gets out of the water or runs off to the locker room to change and go home.

"How many times has she been late?"

"Enough," I bite out. "The last two weeks have been the worst. I'm going to talk to her."

"The season is coming up, dude. You don't want a swimmer who doesn't show up for her team. I thought she wanted to swim relays?"

I'd already put several swimmers through mock relay races, trying to figure out our strengths and what areas we need to strengthen. What athletes swim it well together, and which ones don't. Swimming may seem like an individual sport, but it's not. And when you commit to a team, you're expected to show up when you're supposed to.

I turn to Bryce. "She's usually about ten to fifteen minutes late. If she comes in, tell her not to change but to come talk to me. Get Carter to bring me the kickboards his group used, and she'll clean them."

A slow smile spreads across his face. "Are we about to see hard-ass Coach O'Brien?"

Rolling my eyes, I bite back a smile. "Don't pretend like the hard-ass coaches weren't the ones who made all the difference."

"Hell yeah they did." He raises a fist, and I bump mine against it. "I'll keep an eye out."

As requested, Carter brings out a couple of large bags full of the used kickboards with the disinfectant she'll need to use. He doesn't say anything, but he knows exactly why I'd ask for something like this.

Less than fifteen minutes later, Emmie is heading down the length of the pool, still dressed, a bashful smile in place.

The rest of the team is taking a water break. I turn my focus to them and blow my whistle. Their gazes snapped toward me, listening as I give them a set I know will keep them occupied while I talk to Emmie. Once they are all back to what they were doing, I turn to Emmie.

"Coach Bryce told me not to change?" She gnaws on her lip in uncertainty. "I'm sorry I was late—"

"Again," I add. "You were late again. I told you there would be consequences if you weren't taking this seriously."

Panic washes over her. "Are you kicking me off the team?"

"No." I frown, a little surprised that's the conclusion she jumped to. "But you will not be participating in tonight's practice. Instead, you'll sit on the bleachers and clean the kickboards Coach Abrams used. They're used for the ten and under team, and then during open swim. They need to be disinfected thoroughly."

"But, Coach—"

I cut her protests off with a raised hand. "You will also pay attention to your teammates while they're practicing. Since we're still working on your form and technique, I want you to spot a minimum of ten things that need to be improved."

As I hand her a spare sheet of paper and pen from my clipboard, she opens her mouth to protest again, but shuts it when my brow arches. "Yes, Coach."

Throughout the rest of practice, I look over to check in on Emmie. I don't like punishing swimmers, but I know the value of committed teammates and how those teammates who aren't can drag a team down. Every single kid on this team has their own goals, whether to continue in this sport professionally or to use it as an avenue to other paths, and it would make me a bad coach if I prioritized one swimmer over the rest. Especially when that swimmer isn't showing up.

To my relief, every time I look at her, she's doing what I asked. She diligently cleans the kickboards, making sure to go over them at least twice before placing them in the clean bin. Her attention is still completely on her teammates, though, eyes tracking their movements the same way mine do. When she finishes the kickboards, she moves off the bleacher and comes to sit at the edge of the pool. She stays there until I blow the whistle, dismiss practice, and all her teammates head toward the locker room. She only offers small waves as they pass her.

"We need to talk, Emmie," I tell her once the rest of the kids are out of earshot. I move to sit on the bleacher she'd vacated, and she turns to face me. If my leg wasn't killing me, I'd consider getting down to her level, but the likelihood of me getting up is too slim. "And I need real answers this time."

"I don't mean to be late, Coach," she begins, without any prompting. "Things have been a little...hectic at home."

I notice her hesitation. "Hectic how?"

"I'm a little overwhelmed." She frowns, taking a moment to think through what she's going to say. "My mom has been working crazy hours, and I'm trying to keep things organized at home, but things are slipping through."

"If you're too overwhelmed, you can take a step—"

"No!" She looks at me with wide, pleading eyes. "Swimming is the best thing I have going right now. It's *my* only thing. Everything else is for my family, and I don't mind that, but I can't lose the one thing I love."

I see a lot of my younger self in her. I clung to swimming for a long time. It was the only lifeline I had to a life that was mine and not the life my parents wanted me to have. It wasn't until they started noticing just how good I was at the sport that things started to shift. Slowly, it changed from the thing I loved more than anything to the thing that let me feel like myself while not being mine. I got lost in the expectations of my parents within the sport.

Emmie's family isn't using her talent for their own gain, but they are keeping her from her passions by having her pick up their slack. It's not the first time I've seen this, and it's not the first time I've worked around it. I'm happy to do it again, but I need to know she still wants it.

"I understand where you're coming from, but you also have to consider your team and the promises you made them," I remind her. I won't hold the scholarship over her head, never wanting to be that coach who puts a monetary value on a kid's place on their team. I've met too many of those, too. "Clearly, if you want to continue on this team, we need to figure out how to help you balance your responsibilities. Tell me what I can do."

There's a flash of *something* in her eyes, but it's gone before I can even begin to decipher it. "There's nothing to do," she tells me. "My mother's schedule is going to go back to normal by next practice; I'll be able to get to practice on time like I've been doing. I promise, this won't happen again."

"That's not a promise a fifteen-year-old can make, Emmie." Real life will always come before swimming, no matter how much the kids might wish it otherwise. "Being late to practice every once in a while is going to happen, Emmie. I need you to communicate with me—call the front desk, send me an email, text me. Just let me know you'll be late, and we can work around it. If I wanted to do relay drills with you tonight, I could restructure the order of practice, but I can't do that if I don't know you'll be late."

She nods with a chastised look. "I didn't mean to let you or the team down, Coach."

"It's okay." The last thing I want is for her to beat herself up over this. "Commitment can look different from what you initially expect. Learning to adjust when things don't go according to plan is part of what I'm hoping to teach you guys."

"You can plan and practice all you want," she parrots, making me smile, "but you never know how a race will go until you swim it."

I grin back at her. "Glad to know someone is paying attention." She laughs. "Get out of here. I don't want to keep you too late."

She's still laughing as she stands, but then it fades, and she smiles shyly. "Thanks, Coach."

My brow arches. "For?"

"Believing in me?" she replies with a shy shrug. "Not giving up on me? Maybe both? I don't know. I'm not used to either one."

"First of all, you're worth believing in and I don't give up on anyone. You're here because you're talented, and there are a lot of people backing you up."

Cheeks flushed, she nods, and ducks her head, heading toward the locker room. I can't ignore the gnawing feeling in my gut that something else is going on, that there's *something* she's not sharing.

"Emmie!" She turns to face me. "If you ever need help, no matter what it is, we're all here for you. Do you understand?"

Her mouth opens slowly, but then promptly snaps shut. She nods quickly before turning back to hustle to the locker room. I realize in that moment, the look I couldn't read was fear. Which confirms there's something more going on, but I can't burst in and demand answers. I have no proof, nothing to base those concerns on. There's no physical evidence, and she's never asked for help, but I'll make sure every adult in this building knows to keep an eye out for her.

I've done this enough times to know when a kid needs help.

"Oh, my god, Lezak! Get back here!"

Looking up from the clipboard in my hand, I see my dog sprinting toward me with something in his mouth. Not even a second later, Mia appears in the doorway, dark hair flying, and a frantic look on her face as she chases after him. My curiosity is instantly piqued.

"Lezak, stop!" The dog keeps running. "Lezak, heel!"

"We haven't learned that one yet," I call. Which only earns me a groan from her.

I squat down to meet the puppy at the same time Carter blows his whistle and yells, "Walk!"

Mia flips him off over her shoulder and speeds up. Thankfully, there are no kids here because we'd never get them to walk on the deck again. "Ronan, do not touch that!"

"Hey, boy," I greet the pleased puppy once he reaches me. I pet him between his ears with one hand while I take what I now realize is a bra from his mouth. It's deep purple and lacey. Well, shit. "Are you taking things that aren't yours again?"

Mia slows to a stop right by us. "I'll take that back."

When I look up, she's flushed, and holding her hand out. I'm not sure if it's embarrassment or the jog that's painted her cheeks. I stand, but keep the bra out of her reach.

"Ronan, come on!" She still has her hand out, toes tapping against the deck, but the red I can see on her ears confirms she's embarrassed. "Give me the bra back. Your dog stole it!"

"'Stole' seems like a harsh word, don't you think? He's a retriever, he retrieves." Being the glutton for punishment I am, I unfold the bra, and take a look at it, letting out a low whistle. "Damn."

With a gasp, Mia lunges for it, but I move quicker. "Ronan, what the hell?"

I'm teasing her, making her squirm for fun. I'm definitely not picturing this against her pale skin or wondering why she has it at work but isn't wearing it. That would be a bad idea.

"You've shown no proof of ownership. I've heard bras are expensive. How do I know—"

Smirking, she crosses her arms over her chest. "I'm at least a cup size bigger than both Kat and Josie, who are the only other women here. Does that suffice?"

Although the statement has some interesting information in it, I don't want to think about the bras my friends' girlfriends wear. I hand it over to her. "How did he even get it?"

Huffing, she awkwardly holds it in her hand, not having anywhere to put it. "The strap on my bag broke. Your dog decided it was a prized possession and took off with it before I could pick everything up."

"Maybe he just has good taste." Giddy flutters whirl in my stomach when I see the flush come up her cheeks again. "Correct me if I'm wrong, but don't you usually wear bras? Not bring them with you to work?"

A small smirk tugs at the corners of her lips, and I'm suddenly less sure about my teasing. "Because I have a date tonight and I need to leave right from work to get there."

My breath catches in my throat, forcing me to make an embarrassing sound I refuse to put a name on. Her smirk grows, and I clear my throat. "And you need this bra over the others you own?"

"Well, sure." She shrugs. "It's pretty, right? And a girl should always wear a pretty bra on a date—whether it'll end in hooking up or not."

Instinctively, I take a step closer, my senses being assaulted by the faintest fragrance of her perfume—something fresh and airy that blends with the chlorine. "And are you planning on the night ending with a hookup?"

Mia gnaws at the corner of her lip, looking a little less sure of herself. "Who knows? I haven't met this person yet. I don't know if I'll connect with them."

A quick glance around the deck tells me we're the only ones here. No one is watching us. I reach out, pulling her closer. She allows me. "Well, just remember, there is someone you have a connection with."

Her eyes flutter closed, and I fully expect her to close the distance between us, give into the growing tension. At the last second, she steps back, leaving me stunned. "What?"

"Let's give this person a chance, Ronan," she teases with a flirty smile. "Maybe I'll find a connection with them. If not, I know where to find you."

With a wink, she turns to head back toward the lobby, leaving me a stunned, sputtering mess. I've always been the one to flirt. Mia tends to go where I lead her, but this will-she-won't-she thing is new. And I think I like it.

I look down at Lezak, who's staring up at me with his tongue hanging out. "Next time you steal her bra, I better get a kiss out of it."

He barks in response before sprinting after her.

Later that night, I'm standing outside a trendy restaurant dressed in a button-down and dress pants. Waiting for a blind date to arrive is not how I wanted to spend my evening, but here I am. Kat's been bugging me about meeting one of her clients, believing we'd hit it off, and I'd been avoiding the topic. But after holding Mia's lacy bra in my hand, something shifted in me. Especially knowing she was planning to wear it for someone else.

If Mia is being serious about finding someone special, someone who isn't me, then I need to let go of whatever pipe dream I have surrounding her. And the only way to do that is to start getting out there myself.

Jasmine had jumped at the opportunity to go out tonight. She'd replied to Katrina's message within mere minutes, and suddenly I had a date and a new contact in my phone.

I spent any free time I had during the day texting her, trying to get to know her even a little before sitting across the table from one another. She didn't budge, too interested in finding out where we were going and what she should wear.

I hate dates like this, where they require too much effort. I'd much rather go out to a casual place, dressed in an outfit that doesn't require the world's most uncomfortable shoes and have a great time then feel like I'm putting on a performance.

A woman in a well-fitted gray dress that would look more at home in a courtroom than on a date approaches me. Which made sense, considering all Kat told me was that she's a lawyer and might be coming straight from work.

Katrina hadn't been lying about how beautiful Jasmine was. But she's a beautiful woman in a conventional way; the kind of beautiful a lot of people attribute to athletes. Her beauty pales into comparison to the one person I'm trying to forget.

I give her a warm, charming smile as she approaches. "You must be Jasmine."

Her smile is tight, but polite. "Are you Roman?"

My hand falters mid-shake as the name registers, but I quickly recover. "It's Ronan, actually."

She tilts her head in confusion. "What is?"

"My name." I frown. "My name is Ronan, not Roman."

"Oh, I'm sorry." She laughs, flicking her long caramel hair over her shoulder. "I'm horrible with names."

A trait that makes me question her ability as a lawyer, but whatever. "Should we get our table?"

She nods and then waits with an arched eyebrow until I move to pull the door open for her and lead her up to the hostess stand. "Hi, I have a reservation under O'Brien."

The hostess glances over the list before offering me a bright smile. "Right this way, Mr. O'Brien."

Neither Jasmine nor I say anything on our way to the table, which is on the large patio off the back of the restaurant. It's a warm, but beautiful night. Small fire pits are scattered throughout the patio for cooler nights, but string lights with Edison bulbs create a warm atmosphere, especially when paired with the small lanterns adorning each table.

It's simple, but welcoming, and creates the perfect atmosphere for a first date. As soon as Jasmine is situated across from me, though, I conclude she doesn't agree.

"Is this all right with you?"

Startled, she looks up, and gives me another tight smile. "Fine."

"I don't mean to push, but I'm not sure I believe you?"

She shakes her head. "It's fine, I promise. I just don't like eating outside that much because outside has bugs."

"Oh, I should have asked. I love eating outside." Her grimace tells me this bit of information isn't something she wants to hear. "I can see if they're able to move us inside?"

"I said it's fine, Roman," she bites out and picks up her menu.

Sighing to myself, I ignore the name, and do the same.

Silence settles around us while we both look over the menu. So much silence that we're both ready to order when our server approaches. She orders the salmon and an expensive glass of wine, while I order a steak and a local beer.

"I have to say, you're not what I expected when Katrina told me you're an Olympian."

Huh. I haven't heard that one before, and I'm not sure what it's supposed to mean.

"Well, I am," I reply. "I went in 2012 and 2016. I swam professionally from the time I graduated from college until I retired at the beginning of 2018."

She picks up her wineglass as soon as it hits the table, taking a long sip while studying me. "And what sport did you do?"

"Swimming." I smile and thank the server for my beer. "It's been part of my life for as long as I can remember, basically."

She hums under her breath. "Well, like I said, not what I was expecting."

I want to ask more questions, push the issue, and figure out what she means, but someone at a nearby table catches my attention. Apparently, I wasn't the only person who thought this was a great place for a first date, because Mia's here with hers. The one the bra was for. My brain short circuits.

She looks beautiful, with her hair styled in dark waves and make-up fairly neutral except for the deep red lipstick. The loose-fitting cropped tee she's wearing showcases her tattoos, but the grimace at whatever her date is saying is the thing I notice most.

"You know, I looked you up."

My attention snaps back to Jasmine, a frown forming on my lips. "I'm sorry, what?"

She rolls her eyes, leaning back against her seat. "I said I looked you up online, but you can't be surprised by that, right? Katrina told me your name, and it's a pretty common thing for women to do these days. Plus, you're a professional athlete—"

"Was," I correct, but she doesn't seem to care. It makes sense I have to correct her, she looked me up and still can't get my name right.

"So I knew it'd be easy to get some information on you. Which is part of the reason I'm shocked we're here for our date. Everything I saw tells me you're a party boy who only wants to have a good time. Definitely not the 'sit in a cozy restaurant and talk about our days' kind of guy."

"And I'm guessing that's a problem for you?" I hear the irritation in my voice, but I can't help it. "You knew where we were going. Why did you say yes?"

Jasmine shrugs, running a long red nail around the rim of her wineglass. "I was bored and have never dated an Olympian. I thought it could be fun."

I know what those words mean. I've been the one to say them more times than I care to admit, in some variation. I wanted to hang out, to get drunk, maybe hookup, but at the end of the day, this isn't going anywhere. Jasmine isn't looking for a serious relationship; I'm not sure she's even looking for a real date.

Still, Kat set this up, and I owe it to her to see if I can salvage it.

"Well, that's not who I am anymore." I want to set those expectations right away. "I've grown up a lot over the last few years. Hopefully, this night isn't a big disappointment to you."

She gives me a flirty smile over her wineglass. "Well, that depends on where we end it."

I bite back the grimace at the forward comment as she sips her wine. I didn't come here with any intention to hookup, but it's clear she did. And while I am not opposed to hookups on the first date, I've done it more than enough times, I can't shake the feeling she came to this conclusion based on articles she read about a man who hasn't existed in a long time.

"Look, I would prefer we lay this all out on the table before we waste our time. I am not sleeping with you tonight."

Her brow climbs up her forehead in surprise. "And you know that after only fifteen minutes?"

"I knew it before I even met you. It's not personal—you are a very beautiful woman, but I am looking for something real. Something more serious and I don't do hookups anymore."

Her eyes flit across my face like she's looking for some kind of tell—a sign that what I said isn't true. Maybe she thinks I'm pulling some kind of test on her, but it doesn't matter. I'm not wavering on this. I don't want to hookup with anyone.

"Are you using me as a rebound?"

Her question catches me off guard, but I'm quickly distracted by the sound of someone coughing loudly across the patio. My gaze snaps to Mia in time to see her take a gulp from her water, cheeks flushed. Jasmine must notice when my attention is lost because she follows my eyes over her own shoulder.

"Is that your ex?" Her gaze lingers on Mia for a minute. "Her tattoos are cool as hell."

I don't know, but the compliment makes a smile tug across my lips. I don't know why, but Jasmine didn't strike me as the type to be jealous of someone else's tattoos, especially when it comes to as many as Mia. Though, personally, I can't agree with her more.

"Not my ex. Just a friend I've known for a while," I tell her.

Jasmine turns back to me with a shrug. "If you say so, but I still think you're looking at this like a rebound."

I have no interest in pouring my heart out to this woman I barely know, and don't particularly like. Especially about a woman I barely had before I fucked it up and spent years in a miscommunication-based hell just to get a sliver of her back in my life. And now I'm too terrified to even let myself consider something happening between the two of us.

"I have no intention of treating you like a rebound," I assure her, my gaze flicking back over to Mia, who is looking increasingly uncomfortable, before focusing back on my date. "I'm sorry if I gave you that impression."

"It wouldn't be the first time things ended that way." A flirty smirk crosses her features. "We could still have fun."

Dear god, how many times am I going to have to tell this woman I'm not sleeping with her?

Out of the corner of my eye, I see Mia starting to look around for something or someone. I manage to ignore Jasmine long enough for my gaze to lock with the person I'd rather be with.

Surprise flashes across Mia's features before it settles into something calmer. Her attention turns back to her date when they start speaking again. When our eyes meet again, she gives me a look of pure panic.

The look in her eyes screaming one thing. *Help me.*

I don't know what's going on, but my instincts are kicked into overdrive. I fish my wallet out of my pocket, pulling out all the cash I have in there. It's more than enough to cover dinner for both of us, but I feel bad for what I'm about to do.

"I'm sorry," I tell Jasmine. "I swear I never bail on dates, but I need to go."

"What?" She gasps, face turning red. "What do you mean, you're leaving?"

"This was never going to work, Jasmine." I set the money on the table. "This will cover both meals—feel free to get some dessert or something."

"Are you telling me to keep the change? What the fuck is wrong with you?"

"I'm sorry," I say once more before I'm up.

I have no plan, no strategy for what to do or say. I don't even know what's going on. I feel the need to get Mia out of here. As I make my way across the patio, I can still feel Jasmine's gaze on me. I silently send up a prayer to anything that's listening that she won't make a scene.

But she'd be totally in the right to do so if she wanted.

When Mia realizes I'm coming to her aid, a smile tugs across her lips, and she feigns surprise. "Oh, hi Ronan!"

"Hey, Mia," I greet, coming to a stop at her table. She stands to briefly hug me, and it takes everything in me to not pull her closer.

"Ronan, this is my date, Georgie." I smile at them, bidding them a small hello. "Ronan and I work together at the swim club I was telling you about. He's one of the coaches."

"Oh, right," Georgie replies, focusing on me. "She tells me you have an outdoor pool. You must struggle with keeping backswimmers and other insects out of the water. You wouldn't want the kids getting bit."

Huh, that's an interesting way to greet someone.

"We do a lot of maintenance to keep any bugs to a minimum," I quickly say, praying no one can overhear this. Bryce will kill me if I somehow make people think we have a bug infestation. "I guess I never knew what those were called."

Lies. If you ever spent any time around water, especially lakes and streams, you've dealt with those assholes.

Georgie shrugs. "Well, I'm an entomologist; it's kind of my job to know about bugs."

The quiet groan Mia makes before downing the rest of her wine tells me everything I need to know.

"That's cool." I turn to her. "Mia, I hate to bug you, but we have an emergency at work and are needed back at the club."

"We are?" she asks, eyebrows furrowed. I silently plead for her to go with it.

"Yes," I stress. "Bryce has been texting us, but you must have your phone on silent. I saw you sitting here and decided to come grab you."

"What kind of emergency can you have at a closed swimming pool at eight o'clock at night?"

Well, gee, Georgie, I think, *give me a second to come up with one.*

"It's the lane lines." The words come stumbling out, so I guess that's what I'm going with. "Carter was bringing them in and got tangled in them again. Apparently, it's pretty bad this time."

"Oh." Her eyes go comically wide. "Not again."

She immediately starts gathering her things to stand. "Carter is a disaster. I don't know why Bryce keeps letting him do this. I'm so sorry, Georgie, but I should go."

"It's fine," they reply, standing to bid Mia goodbye. "Emergencies happen."

"It was great meeting you, Georgie. I hate that it had to be in these circumstances," I say.

"Come on, Ronan, we need to go," Mia urges, tugging my arm. "I had a lovely time, Georgie."

Mia is already dragging me through the restaurant before I can even wrap my mind around what we just did. When we finally get out, she turns to me with a relieved look.

"I don't think I've ever been so happy to see someone in my life," she breathes out. "All we talked about was bugs."

I grin at the full-body shiver that goes through her at the mere mention. "Well, they are an entomologist. I'm sure there are a lot of facts to share, considering there are thousands of species out in the world."

She glares up at me. "But they should have more than one subject to talk about on a date, Ronan. Besides, you didn't necessarily look like you'd found the one with your date."

"Kat set us up," I admit. "I guess she doesn't know me all that well yet. Jasmine came to the date because she'd looked me up and felt confident we'd end up in bed."

I see the rage flare up in Mia's eyes, but she quickly morphs it into a comforting smile. "That's a shitty way to approach a date. I'm sorry, Ronan."

With a small shrug, I squint against the setting sun. "Both our dates are over now, which means our night is over. Unless you'd like to grab some dessert?"

She hesitates for a second, and I fully expect her to decline. I'll take her home, make sure she gets in all right, and then go find some food for myself. But if there's even the slightest chance she might want to spend time with me, I'm going to take it.

"We had only gotten to the appetizers, and I couldn't even stomach those because of the conversation."

"You mean creepy, crawly bugs." I watch her tense up. "Most of whom have more than a normal amount of legs."

"Stop that!" She swats me across the chest but smiles when I laugh. "There will be no more talk of bugs tonight. I want food, real food. And then we should definitely get dessert."

"Are you sure we don't need to go save Carter from evil lane lines?" I joke, following as she leads me down the street. I have no idea where she's taking me, but to be honest, I don't care. I think I'd follow Mia Sheridan almost anywhere.

Mia turns to give me a smirk, continuing to walk backward. "It's almost nine o'clock on a Saturday night and he's in love with his girlfriend. I think our pal is tangled up in some*one* else tonight."

I groan, pinching the bridge of my nose. "Why did you have to go there?"

Laughing, she turns back around, her skirt flowing in the soft summer breeze. "Come on, O'Brien, there's usually a food truck around the corner and you have not *lived* until you've had their burritos."

"We're having a nice night. I'm almost scared to ruin it."

I turn to look up at him in surprise. "Okay, well, now you have to tell me whatever you were about to say. I don't care if you ruin it."

He hesitates for a moment, and I wonder if he realizes he even said that out loud. "This kind of feels like how things felt before, you know?"

The word "before" hits me hard, all the different ways he means it is evident. Before we slept together and changed everything. Before we spent every spare moment of a year talking, talking more than our friends, who are in a committed relationship. Before I treated him normally one day in Indianapolis, only to hate him with everything in me the next day. Before, before, before. I miss the before.

"Yeah, it does" I admit.

"You have to throw me a bone here, Mia," he pleads. "I can't fix things between us if I don't know what I did, and I promise you I don't know what I did."

I swallow, and try to find the words, but they simply won't come. Which is ridiculous because I can vividly picture the day everything changed. The day I heard those awful things he said and knew I'd never be more than a hookup to him. If he wasn't willing to defend my best friend, there's no way in hell he'd defend me.

"All I know is that we were fine that first day in Indianapolis," he recalls. My heart drops to the pit of my stomach. "I was signing autographs with Bryce, who was having a small fight with Josie. We were fine. Then, after they worked everything out, you and I suddenly weren't fine."

God, he knows. He knows exactly when everything happened. Remembers it eight years later.

"I heard you."

His head tilts. And despite those words sliding out of my mouth without my permission, the look is pretty freaking adorable. "What?"

Well, I guess there's no turning back now.

I inhale a long breath. "I had gotten up to stretch my legs. I was walking around, and I saw you watching the meet with a couple of college kids I didn't recognize." His eyes are wide. He *knows*. "I was going to come down and sit with you, but stopped when I heard what you said."

A panicked look crosses his features. "What did you hear, though?"

"They were talking shit about Josie, Ronan. Somehow, they'd figured out that she and Bryce were sleeping together and were being horrible to her."

"I didn't say anything bad about Josie!" he defends, holding his hands up in mock surrender. "I would *never* say anything bad about Josie."

Frustration bubbles inside me, almost to the boiling point. "That asshole called my best friend desperate and said no one in their right mind would want her. You didn't correct him! You said, and I quote, 'people are entitled to fuck who they want.' I left when he said he'd never sleep with a whale."

"And if you would have stuck around for even thirty seconds longer, you would have heard me tell him to shut the fuck up!" Ronan's voice has risen with mine, emotions running high between the both of us. "Do you really think I wouldn't jump to her defense, Mia? Are you kidding me?"

"You didn't initially!" I challenge.

"Yeah, because it was their secret!" he spits back. "They wanted to keep it quiet. I was in a pretty hard position there; I couldn't let them know they were right. And it wasn't even for Bryce, he could handle it. I didn't want idiots like that ruining things for *you*."

"What are you talking about?" I cross my arms across my chest, trying to stabilize myself as yet another thing I thought I had figured out was suddenly on shaky ground. "We didn't need your protection."

"Oh, believe me, I know that. The blog was starting to pick up traction. You were doing well; I didn't want some asshole kid ruining that for you by starting rumors. Josie didn't deserve to have her name dragged through mud, and I didn't want them to spread something about how you're nothing more than groupies looking for sex."

It all crashes around me, this illusion I had of Ronan for the last few years. Everything I thought had been wrong. It'd been a lie. He wasn't the villain of the story. And he only came across that way because I decided to cast him in that role.

"I was protecting my friends." He's taking deep breaths, in through his nose and out through his mouth. "All of them. I never agreed with Bryce wanting to keep things quiet. I told him he'd risk losing everything, but I respected his wishes. Carter and I were put in a weird place because people asked us all the time. Fans, the media, other swimmers, and even random strangers wanted to know if Bryce and Josie were together. So yeah, sometimes I had to laugh at some cruel jokes, but I never let it get personal."

That... That's something I never thought about. We all give Bryce and Josie so much shit for keeping things quiet and refusing to acknowledge what was between them for so long, but I never stopped to think about how their decision affected us. Me, Carter, and Ronan were pulled into something we weren't part of. I only had to worry about Josie, who didn't have the focus of as many people as Bryce did. With the eyes of so many people on them, those two went to bat for not only Bryce, but Josie, too.

No one on the outside would look at Josie, or myself, and think *that girl is hooking up with a swimmer*. Because it didn't fit whatever bullshit narrative society painted. When people talk about the girlfriend of a professional athlete, they have an extremely specific picture in their head. I've always known that, and I'd wanted to protect Josie from it.

"I was up in the stands to watch a few races," he continues, pulling me from my thoughts. "When they saw me there, they came over, and started talking, like we were bros, or something. I mostly ignored what they were saying, but eventually, I had to say something. They were being obnoxious. The comment you heard was meant to shut them up, but it egged them on. When their comments started to get more personal and pointed, I got pissed."

It's so ridiculous—the need I suddenly feel to defend Josie. This all happened almost eight years ago, but was the manifestation of all my worst fears. The rage is still there, even though I know she doesn't need me to protect her. In those rare moments when she isn't capable of handling herself, she has Bryce.

"I don't think they expected me to start yelling at them about the importance of respecting people and not making comments about someone else's love life or their personal appearance." Ronan's voice pulls me back from the edge as I'm about to tumble into a spiral, questioning whether, or not I'm still needed. "They definitely didn't expect me to tell their coach."

I gape up at him. "You didn't."

God, the look of pure pride he has shouldn't be as sexy as it is. "She was pretty mad, which wasn't all that surprising. She benched them for at least three meets."

A laugh sputters out of me, and he grins, an amused glint in his eyes. He watches as I finally fall apart. There are tears stinging the corners of my eyes from laughing so hard before he finally joins in. Somewhere along the way, tears start streaming down my face.

I can't believe I stayed so mad over something I hadn't fully witnessed. I disregarded the person I knew and started to believe the rumors because, when I heard those words leave his mouth, I let myself think the worst. I let myself believe that if he could say something cruel like that about Josie, there was no way he didn't regret what had happened between us.

I let myself believe rumors and facades over what I knew in my own heart and soul to be true. And I have a lot to make up for.

Strong arms pull me against a solid chest. It's a strange sensation to be hugged while you're simultaneously laughing and crying. I don't push him away.

"Does this mean you don't hate me anymore?" Another laugh escapes him as he steps back, hands resting on my shoulders. "Because I missed being your friend."

"No, I don't hate you." I wipe the corners of my eyes. "And I'm sorry, Ronan. For letting your reputation cloud my own judgment, I knew you better than that. I should have come and talked to you."

"Why didn't you? You have to know I'd never lie to you."

"I...I think I was scared," I admit. "Even though everything was fine between us, I never let myself believe we'd be okay after what happened in Omaha and, I guess, hearing you say that solidified it for me."

"Mia." I turn away at the broken sound of his voice, but a gentle hand grips my arm and turns me back to face him. "Is that why you said that night was the biggest mistake you've ever made?"

God, I *did* say that. There are so many things I wish I'd never said and never done now that I know the whole truth. Or, at least, what I think is all the truth. "I was hurt, Ronan. It's not an excuse, but it's my truth."

"I know, and we can go back and forth apologizing for what we each should have done or said, but it's pointless. We're not there anymore; we're not those people. All I'm asking is for the truth now."

The way his piercing green eyes stare at me sends a shiver up my spine; it was a gaze similar to the one I got when I straddled his lap all those years ago. "Yeah, I guess it was."

His bottom lip disappears between his teeth, and I want to free it, to get him to say whatever he was trying so hard not to say right now. "Whatever you may have thought, I want you to know that I don't regret that night. I never wanted to pressure you into anything, but I wanted you then. That night was pretty great, if you ask me."

A faint blush coats my cheeks. "It was, wasn't it?"

The cheeky grin that is known for getting women into trouble with him appears, and all the tension between us disappears. This is the man I missed, the one who was my friend and who could always make me laugh. "I've never gotten any complaints, you know."

I laugh, shoving him lightly. His laugh floats through the air as I link my arm through his so we can keep walking. "I'm glad we're friends again, Ronan."

His hands slide into his pockets, keeping step with me. "Me too."

"Joy is going to be so proud of me." My comment earns me a snort of laughter. "What? She is! I've officially been on five dates, and I fixed a longtime feud with someone."

"Does this one count? Because I definitely saved you from this one."

My eyes widen as I look up at him. "Because the only thing they could talk about were bugs, Ronan."

"That's because they're an entomologist, Mia."

"Yes, in food production and disease prevention." I shiver. "I'm going to have nightmares about bugs crawling on my food and giving me diseases."

"I think it's safe to say you and the entomologist don't have a future together."

"Stop making fun of me," I whine. "This also means I'll have to tell Bryce and Josie the real reason I've been a jerk to you."

"Bryce knows. I mean, about what happened in Indianapolis. I told him when it happened, because I wanted him to know. He doesn't know that's why you've been so mean."

For the second time tonight, my jaw drops open. "He *what*?"

"Yeah." Ronan grins. "And I think that he told Josie."

"So, this whole time I've been keeping this from them to protect her and they've known?" He nods and I groan. "God, I'm never going to hear the end of this."

⁕

A couple of days later, the six of us are at Bryce and Josie's, ready for another game night. Honestly, I don't know why we keep doing this to ourselves. The night always ends with one of the guy's pouting and us girls moving out to the patio with glasses of wine while they argue about the real winner. I guess that's what happens when you try to do anything competitive with a bunch of Olympians. They always like to win.

The first thing everyone notices is that Ronan and I drove together. He offered to pick me up since he passes my apartment on the way from his condo. Carter is getting out of his own car with Kat when we pull in, his eyes widening when he spots me in the passenger seat.

He's storming into the house ahead of us, calling for Bryce.

"What?" Bryce questions, coming out of the kitchen with a towel in his hands. "Why are you screaming at me, dude?"

"Am I dead? Because I think I'm in some alternate universe."

"What?" I want to roll my eyes at how overly dramatic Carter is being. Bryce is just more confused. "What are you talking about?"

"Your boyfriend is the most dramatic person I have ever met," I tell Kat, who's standing next to me in the entranceway.

Josie comes jogging down the stairs, brows furrowed. "What the hell is going on?"

"That's what I'm trying to figure out," Bryce says. "Carter came running in here and asked if he's dead."

Josie's brow furrows. "What? Why would he be dead?"

"Carter is freaking out because I drove Mia here and he happened to arrive at basically the same time."

At Ronan's explanation, it goes deadly silent. Carter and Kat seem to wait with bated breath for the other two's reactions. Josie and Bryce, however, are doing that annoying silent communication thing she and I perfected years ago.

"Stop that." I snap my fingers in front of Bryce's face. "It's only cute when Josie and I do it. Just say whatever you want to say."

"Did you kidnap her?" Bryce asks hesitantly.

Josie jogs down the rest of the stairs, coming to a stop in front of me and grabbing my face in both hands. "Did you hit your head? Do you have amnesia?"

"I will count to two and you better—"

Her hands drop immediately. "Nope, definitely still our normal Mia." She turns a glare to Ronan. "What happened?"

I kick off my sandals by the door. "And here I thought you'd all be happy we made up."

As I walk into the living room to get comfortable, four voices are fighting to be heard over one another. I can barely make out Ronan's amused laugh. When I collapse on the couch, he takes a seat next to me. Everyone else gathers around like I'm about to tell them a ghost story or something.

"We need to know what happened!" Josie demands, but she's looking a little too pleased for my liking.

I look at Ronan, only for him to shrug.

"Remember the dates we both had the other day?" I ask. "Well, they suck."

Katrina looked at Ronan with a gasp. "Jasmine sucks?"

He grimaces, clearly embarrassed about having to talk badly about one of her clients, but he seems to recover rather quickly. "Kind of the worst, actually. She was mad that I didn't live up to the reputation she'd found online."

"No." Kat groans, leaning against Carter. He pats her shoulder comfortingly. "She always seemed to be so put together, I thought she was looking for someone more serious."

He frowns. "I think the only way she's settling down is by renovating her house." A moment passes before he adds, "But mine wasn't nearly as bad as Mia's!"

"Don't listen to Ronan!" I protest. "Georgie wasn't that bad, they just...could only talk about their work."

Josie's brow furrows. "But isn't Georgie an entomologist?"

"Mm-hmm. We only talked about bugs for the forty-five minutes we were together. Which, did you know cockroaches can live almost seven days without their head? I didn't, but now I do."

"Oh, ew." Bryce grimaces. "At least the conversation shifted when you were eating?"

"Oh, no." I shake my head. "No, the facts just shifted to bugs in food. Which is a thing, even if you can't see them."

I swear Bryce turns a little green.

"I finally intervened the third time I saw Mia gagging while trying to eat flatbread," Ronan jumps in. "Jasmine didn't seem too sad to see me go."

"But how does any of this get us here?"

"After Ronan saved me, we talked. A lot," I explain, looking over at him. "To be honest, I was getting tired of holding it in. I opened up to him about why I was mad, got some answers, and found out that I didn't need to hide it from you, because everyone knew. Except Kat."

Confused, Bryce looks at Ronan, who immediately answers. "Summer Nationals in 2017, asshole college kids."

His confusion deepens for a whole second before realization dawns on him. "Oh! Those assholes. Wait, you were mad at him for that? He told me about it immediately. Carter, too. I told Josie that night."

I can feel how red my cheeks are. "Well, I know that now! I had no way of knowing that then and Josie had already been pissed off at you once that trip."

Josie's looking at me in amusement. "Well, I guess I was wrong."

"What do you mean?"

"She thought it had to do with you guys hooking up in Omaha," Bryce responds.

"*What?*"

The exclamation comes from three people: me, Ronan, and, surprisingly, Carter.

"Oh, come on. You were not as sneaky as you thought you were. I ran into Ronan in the hallway going back to his room."

"And you were wearing the same clothes with your makeup from the previous night smeared." Josie points at me. "You never sleep in the shirt you wore all day, and you *always* take your makeup off."

Well, fuck. Apparently, there never were any secrets between us. They all knew what I was so upset about and the secret we thought we managed to keep was clocked by everyone but Carter.

Ronan clears his throat. "Well, this has been an enlightening evening so far. Are there any other questions before we stop talking about the past?"

In that moment, I want to hug him. I'm not ready to face every aspect of the past. The last few days have been more than enough for me. It feels almost like my entire viewpoint is shifting, and I don't know what to do.

"Are you two together now?" The question comes from the only person in our little group who hasn't talked much, Katrina.

"No," Ronan and I reply in unison, the unsaid *but* lingering in the silence that follows.

"Okay, then," Bryce replies. "What do we want to play first?"

I'm in the kitchen for another drink when Carter comes in. I nod to the bottle of wine I'm opening, and he comes over to me with a nod.

"I'm a little embarrassed to admit I'm apparently the only one who was clueless about you guys hooking up."

I hand him the full glass, leaning against the counter. It's been a while since I've had a good chat with him and now seems as good as time as any. "Honestly, that makes me feel a little relieved. Maybe we weren't so obvious." I take a sip of my wine before remembering my conversation with Kat months ago. "But I do need to tell you that your girlfriend clocked it immediately."

He groans into his wineglass. "Why would you tell me that? Now I feel really dumb."

"You had a lot going on back then," I argue, smiling at him. "You'd just made your first Olympic team, and I didn't see you much after that night. Not until the next summer when everything went to hell."

"I was so confused in Indianapolis. First, Josie was pissed at Bryce, then you were pissed at Ronan—I was getting whiplash. Not that both instances weren't justified. I get it. I don't blame you for being angry with him."

"Really?" The surprise is clear in my voice. "You don't?"

"Not at all." He sets his glass down on the counter before leaning against it. "When he told us what happened, my initial reaction was anger, too. Anger at him for even putting himself in that situation and anger toward the assholes who said it. It took me a while to realize he was in a different position than I would ever be and that his reaction would be different.

"I mean, yeah, people knew Bryce and Ronan got along, but they never guessed how close they were. When it came to me, Bryce and I were always lumped together. Which makes sense with us being best friends forever and me transferring to his team. Still, it meant no one would attempt to talk about Bryce in front of me. Not the way they would with Ronan."

"And his reputation probably didn't stop them from thinking they could," I point out.

"Exactly," Carter agrees. "It took me a while to realize he was defending them in the only way he knew how."

"I can't believe I never considered it. I was so worried Josie would end up heartbroken that I took everything at face value and went with it. I was so angry for so long and he couldn't even tell me the truth because I never let him know where the anger came from."

"He understands," he assures me. "Ronan...He dealt with the consequences that came from his reputation more than he alluded to. People never took him seriously and people tended to make a spectacle of him instead of being honest. I actually think the way you handled it might have been a relief to him, because you continued to prove you were different."

But I haven't been doing that over the last several months. Instead, I've been treating him horribly, letting him think that I truly believed the rumors and the stereotypes. I used his reputation to hide my own hurt, to pretend like this man couldn't touch me when, in reality, he was always one of the few who cut through my own bullshit.

"Forget everything that's happened since you started at Adair," Carter says. "I know what you're thinking, Mia. That was a defense mechanism, and he knows that."

My gaze drifts toward the living room, where I could hear Ronan's laugh before settling back on Carter. "But how does he know that?"

"When he retired and everyone was accusing him of doping, you stood by him. You didn't listen to any of those rumors and never once let your anger cloud your judgment. When every other media outlet turned their back on him, you refused."

Flushing, I look down at the wineglass in my hand. "That was a joint statement from both Josie and me."

"You wrote it, though."

He laughs when I look up at him with wide-eyed surprise. "How do you know that?"

"Come on, Mia, you and Josie have distinct voices. Even back then. Bryce and I knew it came from you, and Ronan did, too."

A thick lump is forming in my throat, but I swallow against it. I'm determined not to cry in this kitchen because Ronan and Josie will see it the second I join the rest of the group. "I knew he didn't cheat."

Carter nods, reaching for his wine, and pushing off the counter. "Like I said, the two of you have always seen each other for who you are. That's why you're here. Don't doubt that."

He gives my arm a gentle squeeze before he heads to the living room. I take a few deep, steadying breaths, pulling myself together before I go out to face everyone again. Everything shifted between us tonight and I don't know where it's going to go, but I hope we get the chance we should have taken all those years ago. This can be our fresh beginning.

Ronan is laughing at something Josie had said when I enter the room, but his eyes brighten, and his grin grows when he sees me. Contentment settles in the pit of my stomach as I settle beside him on the couch. "What were you laughing at?"

"Did you know Bryce and Carter have matching tattoos?"

I turn my head to gape at him. "*No!*"

Bryce groans, but Carter lets out an indigent, "What the fuck, man?"

My gaze snaps back to Josie and her wide grin.

"Don't look at me." Bryce points a finger at Carter. "You told your girlfriend, so I had to tell my girlfriend."

"But we didn't have to tell the whole group!"

Josie hides behind her glass of wine. "Oops. Must have had a little too much wine."

"Oh, please." Bryce rolls his eyes. "You knew exactly what you were doing."

"They're waves," Ronan murmurs to me.

"*Oh, my god,*" I breathe, shifting to look at my best friend. "You have to tell me everything!"

Ronan

"Hey, Kat!" I jog across the parking lot to catch her before she reaches her car. She turns at the sound of her name and waits for me to catch up. "Hey, do you have a minute?"

She arches a brow. "Sure, but something about the look in your eye is making me a little unsure if that's the right answer."

"I need to ask you a favor. I want to ask Mia out on a date."

In the two weeks since we talked everything out, I've seen a shift in the two of us. The way we still gravitate toward one another, find each other across a room. We've worked at getting that foundation back underneath us. I'm not going to waste it this time. They always say you have to ask for the things you want, and I am more than ready to ask.

"Okay, but that's usually a one-person job." She leans against her car, crossing her arms over her chest. "What could you possibly need me for?"

"I want to surprise her. I'm not sure she'll say yes if I ask. Things are better, but they're not perfect and I'm not sure she's ready to fully look past everything that happened."

"So you want to trick her? That doesn't seem like it's going to go any better."

Well, when she says it like that, it makes me feel like a dick.

"Be honest with me, Kat. Do you think Mia and I could be good together?" I ask.

She sighs out in defeat. "Yes, I think you guys could be great together, actually. Mia deserves to be happy, and you already follow her around like a lovesick puppy. I mean, seriously, you're worse than your dog."

"Don't I deserve to be happy, too?"

"Like I said, Mia deserves to be happy. Tell me the plan and then I'll decide if I want to help you."

Well, I guess I better really sell it, then. "Okay, so..."

⋯⋯ + ₒ ＊ ★ ＊ ☾ ★ ＊ ＊ ₒ + ⋯⋯

Even as I walk up to Mia's door, I can't believe Katrina actually agreed to help me and managed to pull it off. I made her promise not to tell *anyone* about tonight, in case it blows up in my face. The plan is simple: Kat was supposed to offer to set Mia up on a date, a show of support in her mission to get back out there. I then told her, in detail, every plan I have for the date and asked her to pass it on to Mia.

Apparently, she'd been intrigued by everything going through Kat instead of being forced to share awkward text messages with someone she didn't know. Kat also made sure to point out that Mia had no qualms about getting set up by her, despite my situation with Jasmine.

I let Kat have the win.

I reach Mia's door and inhale a deep breath before reaching up and knocking. I hear movement on the other side before the door opens to reveal Mia. Confusion instantly overcomes her features.

My breath is taken in that instant. She looks stunning; comfortable, like I requested, but stunning enough to stand out in any crowd. Her wide-leg pants flow and the old school band tee knotted at her waist highlights two things I love about her: her tattoos and her waist.

"Ronan?" She leans against the open door with a frown. My focus is pulled to the muted rose color on her lips. "What are you doing here? I can't talk long. I have a date."

Despite knowing a date is coming, she isn't kicking me out. She is focusing on the friend who's at her door instead of worrying about someone who's coming, like I had known she would.

"What time is your date supposed to be here?"

She glances down at the dainty gold watch on her wrist, a frown forming. "Right now."

I frown back. "Oh, he's late."

She peeks her head out to look down the hall before ducking back in with a shrug. "Life happens; people are late sometimes."

"Don't even try to pull that with me, Mia." I grin. "I know tardiness is one of your least favorite things, so it's a good thing your date is standing right here."

Her arms cross over her chest. "What are you talking about, Ronan? Kat set me up—"

"With a new client who is looking to update his bachelor pad," I recite. "He's new to the city and wants a fun evening out with no commitment required."

"How do you possibly know all that?" she demands, hands on her hips now. "Did you set Kat up to this?"

"His name is Ryan, right?" I ask with a smirk.

"Oh, my god, you asshole!" She's laughing as she shoves me lightly, so I don't take the insult to heart. "Come in while I finish grabbing my things."

I step inside the apartment, shutting the door behind me and watch as Mia walks over to the couch. Her place is exactly how I pictured it. A workstation is set up at the window in the living room, overlooking whatever view she has. The couch has blankets folded across the back, pillows on either end to create a cozy atmosphere. There are pictures hanging on the walls, showcasing her eclectic taste, and somehow pulling it all together to make it unquestionably Mia.

"Why didn't you ask me out like a normal person?" She's sitting on the arm of the couch, slipping on a pair of flats. "You tricked Katrina into asking me for you."

I stuff my hands in the pockets of my jeans, suddenly unsure if I want to own up to this—own up to the truth that I wasn't sure it'd work in my favor if I asked her myself. I hadn't been brave enough to face what felt like the very real possibility that Mia would reject me.

"I wasn't sure you'd say yes," I admit quietly. She looks up from her shoes to stare at me with wide eyes. I shrug. "Having Katrina tell you she wanted to set you up seemed like a safer option."

"After the success rate she has with you, I'm surprised you took the chance." She stands, grabbing her bag. "All right, what are we doing tonight?"

She's not turning me down, not kicking me out. Instead, she's standing before me, looking like a realization of every dream I never let myself dream, ready to go out with me.

"Well, that's for me to know and you to find out." I grin. "Are you ready to go?"

We fall into easy small talk as she leads me out, locking her apartment behind us. She tells me about some of the marketing clients she has right now, and I fill her in on how I'm concerned Emmie might not be taking this as serious as I'd hoped. We keep talking about whatever comes to mind as I navigate toward downtown.

I manage to find a parking spot fairly close and lead her to the small cafe the date will be taking place at. For this first date, we're doing something completely out of my comfort zone. It'll hopefully give me the chance to show Mia I'm the man she always believed me to be by showing that I listen to her interests and take her desires into account.

But if I accidentally burn anything, I hope she takes some pity on me.

"So we're doing dinner?" she speculates. She linked our arms together the second I came around my SUV to join her on the sidewalk and hasn't let go since. "Is that the plan?"

"We are technically doing dinner," I reply, reaching for the door to the cafe. "But it might not happen in the way you're expecting."

Eyeing me curiously, she steps through the door and stops at the hostess stand. I give the hostess my name and she marks us off before leading us up a winding staircase in the back. Mia gasps when we reach the top, but says nothing else as we're led to our stations.

The hostess takes our drink order before disappearing back downstairs.

The second we're alone, Mia turns to me. "Are you serious, Ronan? A cooking class?"

Her hazel eyes are practically gleaming with excitement, and I don't care how many things I burn if it means I get to see this. Grinning down at her, I nod. "Yeah, are you surprised?"

"Um, yes, absolutely! I never would have guessed you'd pick something like this. I know why you're always eating at Bryce and Josie's."

"When you have the same delivery person five days in a row, it gets a little pathetic," I reply, my cheeks flush. "I can't promise I'm going to be good at this."

She bumps her shoulder into mine. "Well, it's a good thing you have someone who's excellent at this on your team."

"And I'm the one with the ego?"

Over the next three hours, I have one of the best nights of my life. The menu is so far over the limited skill set I have. Mia, on the other hand, looked in her element, only brightening even more when we got to the dessert portion. I already knew this is where she excels the most, but doing it with her was something else entirely. With an ease only someone like Mia could possess, she guided me when I became lost, but didn't make me feel awkward about it.

The couple across from us, however, was a totally different story. In between our own cooking, Mia and I spent time listening in on the fight they were having; it was fueled by competitive natures at war with one another, each unable to give up control. We weren't the only ones paying attention to them, either.

At the end of the night, Mia links our arms together again, allowing me to lead her back to the car. Only then do we actually bring up the couple.

"I have never heard such petty arguments before," she comments. "And if you want this night to keep being as magical as possible, you will say nothing about the last couple of months."

"I was going to say years," I tease. "But, yeah, months work, too."

"What did I just say?"

We come to a stop at my car, and I set the leftovers on the hood right before she wraps her arms around my neck, pulling my focus down to her. My hands land on her hips.

"Do you think they're going to breakup or make up?"

"To be honest? I don't care." I lean in until my forehead is resting against hers. I squeeze her hips lightly. "I'm more interested in our fate. You said tonight has been magical?"

She bites at the corner of her lip, trying to hide her growing smirk. I want to pull it free, relish in the feeling of it moving against mine.

So that's what I do.

Her gasp of surprise is quickly swallowed, and I can feel the way she melts against me. All the tension she seems to carry at all times eases in my arms. That is more than enough for me.

Mia closes the rest of the distance between us. Taking any excuse to deepen the kiss. I grasp her chin in one hand, tilting her head until the angle is just right.

For better or worse, I've kissed a lot of women in my life; I've experienced kisses so bad they made me want to flee the country, and I've experienced kisses so good they made my toes curl. But this...this is better than anything I have ever and will ever experience in my life. It's better than the angry kisses we'd exchanged. Better than the kisses we shared in Omaha.

Because with each glide of our lips, this starts to feel more real. There's hope in this kiss—hope that reminds me we can still have everything we wanted, even though we left it broken at one time. Hope that I have someone in my life who wants to hold on to me. Someone who will prove to me it's worth it to stay.

She pulls away with a deep breath, heavy-lidded hazel eyes looking up at me through dark lashes. We're both trying to catch our breath, chests heaving against one another. There's only one thing on my mind, but I can't utter the words out loud. I can't ask that of her.

"Ronan," she breathes, brushing her fingers through the hair at the back of my head.

"Hmm?" I hum, leaning down to steal one more quick kiss.

"I think I'd like to go home now."

Fuck. The moment crashes around me the way I should have anticipated it doing. Still, there's nothing worse than watching things you long for be snatched away before your very eyes.

Dropping my hands to my side, I try to put as much space between us as I can with me pressed against the hood of my car. She doesn't give me any room to move. "Right." I clear my throat. "I'll take you home."

"Ronan." She grabs my wrist, forcing me to a stop before I can squirm away from her. I meet her gaze, waiting for the rejection I'm sure to get. "Would you like to stay the night?"

Double fuck.

With one small question, every hope I'd been holding onto comes flooding back. I don't know why it takes my breath away, but I'm shocked by the forwardness of it all. She was the one who crawled into my lap all those years ago; she was the one who made me lose my mind with a few small movements and words. Now here she is doing it again.

I clear my throat once, then twice more, not trusting myself to say anything coherent right now. This is Mia, for crying out loud. I've wanted this for longer than I care to admit.

She flashes a flirtatious smile, and I can't help but wonder how her goddamn lipstick is still perfect when we've spent the evening eating and drinking.

I can think of a few ways to mess it up, though.

"Are you going to answer me or just stand there, looking at me like you're ready to do this here and now?"

"Can we pick up my dog?" Why the fuck is that the first thing I say?

Her amusement just grows, hazel eyes twinkling with it. "Yes, we can break the rules of my lease and sneak the puppy in."

I surge forward, pulling her into a kiss that's also different from all the rest of them. This one is deep, passionate. It has intent from the second our lips connect.

She groans into me, her body practically going boneless. I scoop an arm around her, keeping her upright.

When I pull away this time, a dazed look has replaced the flirty smile. It brings a smirk to my own lips. I give her one last peck on the cheek, removing my arm from her waist. "Get in the truck, Sheridan."

······ + ₀ ✶ ✦ ☾ ✦ ✶ ₊ ₀ + ······

This time is nothing like last time.

There's no TV playing in the background, no blinding lights surrounding us, no adrenaline from making an Olympic team, nor the impending fear that someone will end up walking in on us.

This time, it's just Mia and me. And a confused golden retriever on a leash. By the time we reach her apartment, heavy rain pours down around us, making the streetlights look hazy as they glimmer off every raindrop on Mia's face.

She's holding my hand, and I can't help but stop and pull her closer. She holds my gaze with an intense look. I want her more than I've ever wanted anyone. I want to feel her underneath me as I press her into the mattress. I want to know if her light scent tastes as good as it smells. I want to relive every moment from that night so long ago, but make it better. Because this means something different now.

We're not kids figuring our lives out anymore; we're confident adults, looking for someone to build a life with.

"Mia," I murmur right before I capture her top lip between mine. With a shiver, she curls closer to me. I move to deepen the kiss.

We stand in the rain, lost in each other, until her hands reach up to run along my jaw. That's when I feel the tremble in them and remember we should get inside.

Once I pull away, I press a lingering kiss to the top of her forehead, breathing in the scent of her shampoo.

"We should go inside," she breathes out before I get the chance.

Reluctantly, I pull away from her enough to allow her to lead me into her building. I have every intention of dragging her closer and resuming the moment the elevator doors slide closed, but at the last minute, an older woman calls out for us to hold the door.

And she lives two floors above Mia.

So instead of pressing her against the wall and making her melt, I keep my hands to myself and try to be on my best behavior, while Mia makes small talk with her neighbor. Eventually, the doors slide open on Mia's floor, and we depart with a wave before rushing down the hall.

I try to wait patiently behind her as she unlocks the door, but the anticipation is too much. I slide an arm around her waist and pull at her shirt until it's untucked, fingers sneaking underneath to touch bare skin. Mia gasps, the door finally open.

I'm done behaving.

As soon as we step into her entryway, I let the dog off his leash, barely paying attention to where he darts off to, I spin her around until I can kiss her. I hear her bag and keys clatter to the floor but am too distracted to care. Instead, I bend slightly, my arms winding around her thighs before I lift her into my arms, the action immediately breaking our kiss.

"Ronan!" Her hands scramble to grip my shoulders, her legs tightening around my waist.

My attention, however, is drawn to her neck. I kick the door shut behind me. With a groan, she cranes her neck back to give me more access. When I take a step toward the hall, her legs tighten around me in a quick warning.

Breathing hard, I pull myself away from her neck and look at her with a frown. Has she changed her mind?

"The door," she breathes out, fingers tangling in my arms.

I stare at her for less than a second before the meaning of her words catches up with me. I step closer to the door, reaching behind me for the lock as I dive back into her neck. She giggles before squirming in my arms until she can reach the lock.

I rest my forehead against her shoulder, catching my breath until I hear the click of the lock. "Now can I take you to bed?"

Mia's smiling when she leans down to connect our lips again, both her hands cradling my jaw. This kiss is softer than the others, but I don't care, because with this kiss, I get to remember what it feels like to have her smile pressed against mine.

I groan when she pulls away again, but she just presses a kiss to the corner of my mouth and squirms until I put her down. "Let me get Lezak some water and make sure he's comfortable."

Her simply caring about my dog shouldn't be the turn on that it is, but I stand there dumbfounded as she grabs her bag and keys, stashing them on a table he can't reach, fills a bowl of water, and makes him a warm spot on the floor with blankets. In less than a couple minutes, she's coming back to where I still stand and my body moves on instinct, lifting her into my arms again.

Once we make it to the bedroom, I relax, and let Mia take control for a bit. Just as I suspected, she's immediately into it. Her fingers move under the hem of my shirt, swiftly pulling it up, and over my head. Both of us smiling as we separate for that brief moment.

In that space, I take a second to look at her. Her makeup slightly smudged from the rain and the kissing, her hair in disarray. I reach behind her, removing the clip holding the strands in place, watching as it tumbles around her shoulders. With a gentle touch, I cradle her chin, watching as her hazel eyes darken ever so slightly.

She'd left a lamp on in her bedroom, which now casts a warm glow over the room that gives her an almost ethereal look.

I press our lips together once more, groaning as a hand traces over me before she reaches for my belt. In a blur of heated kisses and roaming hands, we get ourselves stripped down to our underwear. I groan when I trace along Mia's left breast, feeling the lace beneath my fingertips. I pull back long enough to look at the bra, seeing the familiar purple lace.

"You wore it for someone else, again?" I frown, tracing the intricate floral pattern, feeling Mia shiver in my arms. "Purple is my favorite color."

"I know." She sighs. "It was a deciding factor."

My gaze snaps to her eyes, my frown deepening. "Mia, if you tell me you knew I was going to show up at your door—"

"You're going to what?" She's got an intimidating, and sexy, as hell teasing smirk on her face as she shoves me toward what I hope is the bed. In all honesty, I've been too distracted to pay attention to the room's layout. "Isn't this ending exactly how you wanted it to?"

Does it make me an asshole to say yes?

The back of my legs hit the edge of the bed, and I sit. Her hands go to my shoulders, gripping tightly. "I asked Kat—"

"Kat didn't tell me anything. I saw the two of you talking in the parking lot and then she called me. I was kind of hoping it'd be you."

"Glad I didn't disappoint," I whisper, running my hands along her bare sides, feeling the soft, smooth skin beneath my fingers.

She squeezes my shoulders, and I pull her closer until she climbs onto my lap. Her thighs rest on either side of my hips as she settles against me in a way that has both of us hissing in pleasure.

She sighs, slowly moving her hips in a circular motion that has me instantly harder, the movement offering just enough friction through the thin layers of fabric separating us. "I never thought this would happen again."

Her admission sends another wave of want through me. My hands grip her hips, leading her in the slow movements. I want to clear all barriers between us, feel her sink down on my dick, and watch the blush spread up her whole body as she rides me.

I place lingering, open-mouthed kisses along the edge of her bra, reaching behind her to take it off, and instantly replace the fabric with my mouth.

"Ugh." She groans, hips moving a little more frantically as I move to give the other the same attention. "I need you."

I lean up until I can press our foreheads together, stealing a lingering kiss. "I need you," I admit, "and I've spent the last nine years hoping this would happen again."

She pulls me into another kiss and guides me down against the bed until she can lean over me, our bare chests coming together. She trails kisses down my chest, her hand reaching below the waistband of my briefs, wrapping around me.

I can't help but grind into her warm hand as she strokes me, clearly enjoying teasing me. She presses kisses along the band of my boxer briefs. Heat flares in my chest as I realize what she's offering.

"No." I groan, tangling my fingers in her hair. She looks up at me, startled. I lead her back up my body and roll us so I'm hovering over her one more time. "I need you, Mia," I whisper against her cheek.

"Condoms are in the nightstand." She turns her head to pull me into another kiss, her leg wrapping around my hips in an attempt to pull me closer while I fumble for a condom.

"Fuck." I grunt when I realize the box is still sealed. I can feel her gaze as I move to tear into it, grinning triumphantly when I have one.

She's looking at me in amusement. "Has it been just you and your hand for a while, babe?"

"I haven't slept with anyone in eight months." I move back over her, finding the spot on her neck I know makes her squirm. Her instant reaction makes me smile. "I'm clean, but we should do this safe, right? What about you?"

She nods. "Not since Bianca, but at least I have toys."

The mental images popping up in my head are magnificent, but definitely not better than having her beneath me. "Fuck, baby," I push down the lace underwear, which matches the bra. "We'll revisit that another night."

"Promise?" She bats her eyelashes at me, her foot attempting to push my briefs down. I finish the job for her and instantly start kissing my way down her chest and stomach, stopping randomly to suck bruises into the pale skin.

"Ronan." She gasps when I make it between her legs. "Not now," she pleads. "I want you."

Well, I'm definitely not one to disappoint a woman.

The moan we both let out as I push in takes me back to the first time, and I hope I can feel it again and again. I still for a second, letting us both get used to the feeling.

But her legs wrap around me, pushing at me, her head laid back against a pillow. "Ronan," she whines, pulling me in again. "Move."

Ronan

Nothing pulls you out of a dead sleep as effectively as a phone call in the middle of the night.

The shrill ringing breaks through the still silence of Mia's bedroom, jerking me from a blissful dream featuring the woman beside me. A second before reality catches up with me, I stare up at the ceiling. Then I reach for the phone, fumbling to answer it, barely glancing at the screen.

Mia's bedside clock glares 1:42 a.m. back at me in a harsh blue light. "'ello?"

"Coach Ronan?" Emmie's voice sounds like she's a hundred miles away instead of speaking directly into the receiver. "I...I need help."

Twenty minutes later, Mia and I are pulling to a stop at the address Emmie texted. The red and blue lights bouncing off the houses blur my vision as we make our way toward the house. I'm looking everywhere; my gaze barely lands on one person before blinking to the next, trying to find Emmie.

Finally, I see her.

She's dressed in pajama pants with an Adair hoodie on. Her hair is a mess, arms wrapped around herself for either protection or to keep out the chill. She's talking to a female officer who has a stoic look on her face. Just off to the side, there's a woman around my age dressed in a pantsuit, talking on the phone, but she's keeping a close eye on Emmie. And I know, instantly, that this woman is a social worker.

Mia must see her at the same time as I do, because we both start heading toward her. Until a hand on my chest stops me dead in my tracks.

I blink at the officer, who came out of nowhere. "Sir, you need to stay back."

"I..." The words die on my tongue as I look toward Emmie. How had I missed so many signs? "She..."

Emmie's gaze jumps toward us then, her eyes widening before she crumbles. She says something to the officer she's talking to, motioning toward us. Mia and I are being waved forward.

Mia's there first, pulling the teen into a one-armed hug, asking her if she's all right. I let my girl—I let Mia fret over her, but I squeeze her shoulder before facing the officer and social worker.

"Ronan O'Brien," I introduce myself, shaking hands with both women. "I'm Emmie's coach at Adair Swim Club. This is Mia Sheridan, who also works there."

"Mr. O'Brien, my name is Penny Smith. I'm the social worker who's been assigned to this case."

I let my eyes scan over Emmie, who has no obvious injuries, before I focus back on Penny. "What happened?"

Penny and the officer exchange a glance before looking at Emmie. The officer is able to convince the young girl to go get checked over by the paramedics. She glances back at us, eyes wide with fear, exhaustion, and unshed tears. I give her my best reassuring smile, even though adrenaline is still pumping through my own veins. She turns to face the paramedic who met them.

My focus is pulled back to Penny, who starts filling us in on what's been going on for years before having escalated in the last few months. In the year they've been here, the authorities have been called almost a dozen times by concerned neighbors and at least one teacher. Each time, Emmie's mother has managed to skate by when CPS would follow-up on calls. She'd charm them with a wonderful personality, discussions of going back to school, and Emmie would stand by her mother. A well-practiced routine that managed to fool everyone. Until tonight.

Tonight, it was Emmie herself who called. She'd told the dispatcher that there was no food in the house, no electricity, or running water. Her mother had only been awake a handful of hours over the last few days, and she was worried about her. She'd shared how she'd been forced to lie in the past, not able to let the police know what her life is like, or that her mother is an addict incapable of taking care of anyone.

I feel bile rise in my throat. Mia's grip around my bicep tightens with every word, and I try to remember what it'd been like when I was in her shoes. The first time I was confronted with a story like this. Over the years, it hasn't gotten any easier to hear. I'm not sure it ever will. Which is probably for the best.

"So, what happens now?" Mia asks, looking between the social worker and officer.

"Emmie informed me that she has a half brother who is twenty-seven," Penny explains, glancing down at her phone. "We're still trying to get a good number for him."

"Does he know anything about what Emmie has gone through?"

"According to Emmie, he tried getting her out the last time she saw him. Their mother was clean for a few years there and refused to relinquish her rights. Records indicate he tried to pursue it legally, but it didn't go anywhere. The mother's response to his attempt was to cut all contact between the sibling. Emmie doesn't even know if he's still in the state."

I'll never understand what people in positions of authority are thinking when children are involved in cases like this. The ultimate desire should be to keep them with their parents, but when a pattern is present, and a sibling is trying to protect another by getting them out of the situation they've already been in, they should be listened to. How much grief would it have saved Emmie if someone had listened to her brother?

Penny clears a message away from her phone. "The number Emmie was able to find is no longer in service. We're hoping to get in contact with him tonight, though."

Mia's grip on my arm tightens even more. "What happens in the meantime?"

I already know the answer to her question.

Twenty minutes later, I've been cleared to take Emmie back to my place for the night. Penny assures me she'll keep trying to get information on the brother and call me as soon as she gets in contact with him. We can only hope that he's as receptive to getting her out of a horrible situation now as he was back then. Either way, I don't think any of us are going to get much sleep tonight.

Before we leave, I go into the house with Emmie to grab a bag, and my heart breaks even more. Though it's clear there's not much money, the house is clean and well organized. I know it's all Emmie's doing. Emmie's attempt at giving herself a normal, more stable life. I wonder if that's what her brother had done for her before he got out.

On the way home, I pull into the first open drive-thru I see, getting us all at least something to eat.

"Are they calling my brother?" Emmie's voice is quiet, subdued in a way I've never heard before.

I miss the sassy, defiant kid I'd come to know.

"They're trying to." I look in the rearview mirror, hoping to catch a glimpse of her eyes, but hers are locked on the world passing us by. "Are you okay with that?"

She nods. "I miss him. I hope he remembers me."

Fucking hell. I hate her mother.

"He does, Emmie," Mia pipes up, turning in her seat to face her best she can. Her smile is gentle and comforting. "Trust me, no one could forget you."

"Mom did." She shrugs. "All the time."

"Your mom needs a lot of help, Emmie." My grip tightens on the steering wheel. "None of that is your fault."

"What if he makes me move back to Charleston?" I hate that I don't have those answers for her. Her brother could do that, or he could decide he doesn't want anything to do with his sibling anymore. I doubt it, but it's a possibility. "I don't want to leave Columbia."

"Don't worry about that," I insist. "We'll get answers soon enough, and we'll help you however we can."

Silence falls over the car. I glance at Mia out of the corner of my eye. There are tears running down her cheeks. I don't want to say anything, especially when I'm pushing back my own, so I reach out to squeeze her knee. She gives me a watery smile, then tangles our hands together.

The last twelve hours have officially changed everything. I'm not sure if it's for better or worse.

My phone rings almost as soon as I collapse onto the couch. It's an unknown number, so I quickly answer. "This is Ronan."

"Hello, Mr. O'Brien." Penny's voice rings in my ear. "I was able to get in contact with Emmie's brother, Liam. As next of kin, he's been granted full guardianship, effective immediately. I will work on expediting the paperwork to grant him full custody over the child."

Despite the fact she can't see me, I find myself nodding along. I've heard variations of this exact speech so many times, I could probably give it myself.

"I have him on the other line so we can coordinate a pickup. Do you have any questions for me before I connect the calls?"

"No, ma'am."

There's a slight fumbling on her end before a click sounds in my ear. "Mr. Campbell, I have Emmie's swim coach, Ronan O'Brien, on the line with us."

"How's Emmie?" This instant question eases my anxiety slightly. I wish every guardian I've been on the phone with prioritized the child the way he is. "No one will tell me anything other than the fact she's safe."

"She *is* safe," I stress. "She's finally asleep and seems to be handling this all okay, given the circumstances. She was pretty quiet, but I know it took a lot for her to be the one to ask for help."

He lets out a tired, defeated sigh. "I didn't even know they were in South Carolina. Last I knew, they were headed to Georgia. They've been this close; I could have done something."

"You're doing something now." I'm not sure if the words are a comfort to him or not, but they're what I'd want to hear if our roles were reversed. "Are you in Columbia?"

"Charleston. I can be there in less than three hours."

"I understand your urgency to get to her and see she's okay for yourself, but she's asleep. It's almost five o'clock in the morning; she needs rest. Get some of your own and get here later this afternoon."

"I agree with Mr. O'Brien," Penny adds. I'd almost forgotten she was even on the line. "She's in capable hands. He's done this before."

"You have?"

"Yes." More times than I care to count. The kids we work with sometimes have shitty home lives. I step in until other, more stable, arrangements can be made. More often than not, those arrangements meant the child either moved or had to give up swimming, which was always harder to swallow. Hopefully, it doesn't come to that with Emmie. "It's summer, so the only priority she has right now is swimming. As far as I'm concerned, she's not expected at regular practice until she's ready. That gives you some time. My advice to you is to take the morning and come up with a plan, because she'll have questions."

"Showing her you have some sort of plan will give her back some of the stability she's lost," Penny agrees. Clearly, it's not her first time doing this either. "Given the fact you haven't seen one another since she was nine, we should also plan to meet somewhere she's comfortable."

"Let's go to the club," I offer. "She's comfortable there and there are distractions she can use while we talk. She can swim or workout. No one else will be there until the evening except for us and her other coaches."

"Right," Liam replies. "Yeah, that's probably a good idea."

"Let's plan to meet at Adair Swim Club tomorrow afternoon at two."

"That works for me," I agree.

"I'll be there."

We take the time to coordinate the rest of the logistics and answer some basic questions Liam has; like whether or not she has stuff with her or if they have the chance to go back and get more. Then we're hanging up. But, almost immediately, my phone rings again.

This time, I recognize the number. "Hey, beautiful."

"I should have known Ronan O'Brien would still be charming even when he's dead on his feet."

"You know it." I might be smiling, but she's not wrong. I feel the exhaustion deep within me, but it's paired with a rage that comes whenever I have to deal with shitty parents. They come in every shape and size. Every kid who has them can tell you the effect they have on you will last a lifetime, constantly altering your view of yourself, other people, and life in general.

"Did Penny get ahold of the brother?"

"Yeah." I drop my head back against the couch, finally allowing myself to relax. "He's meeting us at the club in the afternoon. He wanted to drive out right now, but we both advised everyone gets some rest."

"That's a good idea, and I'll be there tomorrow." I didn't have to ask, she anticipated not only my needs, but Emmie's, too. The more people she sees in her corner, the more supported she'll feel. "You should get some sleep, Ronan. You've had a long night, too."

I'm about to argue, but I can feel my body relaxing more. When I don't say anything, she launches into some ridiculous story about Bryce and Carter, trying to build her entertainment center when she first moved to Columbia. It's ridiculous, in the most comforting way.

"Next time, I'll build it," I promise.

"Absolutely," she agrees. "Now where was I?"

Somewhere around the moment they start throwing things at each other, I succumb to sleep.

Ronan

I don't pull myself out of bed until around eleven. I clung to sleep as long as possible, but my need to check on Emmie won out. When I peek my head through the cracked door to her room, she's still fast asleep, with Lezak curled up beside her. He barely lifts his head to glare at me before settling back down. His message is clear: don't wake her up.

He probably needs to go out soon, but I trust the puppy to let me know when it's necessary. Leaving the door propped open, I head down the hall toward the living room, yawning as I go. I'm in desperate need of coffee.

Just as I pass the front door, a quick knock sounds. The sound is so quiet I'm not sure I would have heard it in any other room. I look out the window to see Mia standing on my porch, reusable grocery bags in both her hands.

I quietly open the door and motion her in.

Neither of us say anything as I shut the door and take some bags from her. She follows me into the kitchen, settling her bags on the island beside the ones I carried. Too curious for my own good, I look inside, and see everything you could ever want for a delicious breakfast.

"What's all this?" I keep my voice low, hoping not to wake Emmie up.

I take a second to look at Mia. With her dark hair thrown in a messy bun, no makeup on her face, and dressed in leggings, and a sports bra with a jacket thrown over it, she looks like she just rolled out of bed herself. I pull her into my arms.

She leans into my chest, wrapping her arms around me, keeping us as close as possible. I take a second to bury my face in her hair. Well, as much as I can with the bun on the top of her head.

For the first time since I got the phone call, I allow myself to relax, melting into her arms. We stay like that for a couple of minutes before she takes a step back, heading right for the bags.

"You both need to eat," she explains, pulling things out. "I wasn't sure what she would be in the mood for, so I got a little bit of everything."

"You know I have stuff here, right?" I tease, kissing her temple before helping her start to unload. "You didn't have to buy all this."

"Your protein shakes and power meals aren't going to be enough to sustain a teenage girl after the night she had. She's going to want comfort food."

"Okay then." I grin, looking over the array of food. "Tell me what to do."

She points to one of the bags we haven't touched yet. "There's fruit in there. Think you can throw together a fruit salad?"

With a roll of my eyes, I reach for the bag. "I can't mess things up with that, can I?"

"There are strawberries, and the melons need to be cut smaller." She motions toward where she knows I keep my knives. Which would have been a pretty scary thought a month ago. "Do you think you can handle that without hurting yourself?"

I make a face at her and grab the strawberries to rinse them off in the sink. The two of us work in silent tandem for a while; Mia taking on the more detailed responsibilities while I'm left to put out the fruit, get the drinks, and set the table. She wouldn't even let me make a waffle, but that's honestly probably for the better.

Just as nearly everything is set on the table and Mia has finished cooking, I hear shuffling from upstairs. We barely exchange a glance before Lezak comes bounding into the room, tail wagging as he slides toward Mia. Since she's still in the middle of cooking, she laughs, and uses her foot to give him some gentle pets. I call him over and open the backdoor so he can do his business and get some of his morning zoomies out while we eat.

Despite the teenager sleeping in my guest bedroom, I can't help but note how domestic all this feels. Which is a thought I shouldn't have because we're not even technically together—we went on one date and then all hell broke loose. I don't even know what we are.

Emmie comes shuffling in, looking exhausted, but I can tell she got some sleep.

"Good morning!"

Mia's chipper greeting is the right level of enthusiasm. She's not trying to make it sound like everything was normal and this is the start of a brand-new day; she didn't talk to her like a scared animal; and she didn't overly do it in a way that makes you feel like you need to tiptoe around everyone, pretending like you didn't have what will probably be one of the worst nights of your life.

Emmie shyly waves at Mia before taking the seat I pulled out for her at the table. She brings her knees up to chest and takes us in. "Thank you, Coach," she mumbles. "I don't remember if I said that last night."

I take the seat opposite of her. "There's nothing to thank me for, Emmie. I've always told you guys that you can call me in an emergency, especially if it's about your safety. You did exactly what you were supposed to."

Mia brings over a plate of waffles before sitting beside me. "Ronan's right. You were in a situation you couldn't fix on your own, and you called someone you trusted to help."

Emmie's gnawing on her bottom lip again, eyes darting around the food laid out. She's probably starving.

"Why don't we eat breakfast before we go to the club to meet up with your brother?"

Her eyes bug out of her head. "Wait, Liam's coming here? They got a hold of him?"

"You haven't told her?" Mia swats my shoulder. "Ronan!"

I hold my hands up in defense, suddenly feeling like I'm caught in a precarious situation. "She was asleep when Penny called! I wasn't going to wake you up, Emmie. We were all exhausted. If he talked to you, I think he would have made the drive here in the middle of the night, and that's not what any of us needed last night. He's meeting us at the club with Penny in a couple of hours."

"But...he's actually coming?" she asks. "Does it sound like he wants to help me? Take me in or whatever?"

My heart clenches for this child, because she is still just a child—a child who's been carrying a level of responsibility that shouldn't have been hers for far too long. Now she's probably questioning her place in the lives of those she loves, maybe even within her own life.

"I refuse to make any promises." I learned early on that hearing about a sibling or family member in need pulls a reaction out of people, a reaction they sometimes can't follow through on when faced with the reality. "But it did sound promising. He's anxious to see you, to make sure you're okay, and then we'll go from there."

She's back to picking at her nail polish and avoiding eye contact. "I don't want to leave Columbia or Adair. And I don't want to go into foster care or group homes."

Mia and I exchange grim looks, neither one of us knowing what to say. The future is uncertain right now; how do you comfort a child when that's true?

"Let's not get ahead of ourselves," Mia advises. "Let's eat as much food as we want for breakfast and then see what the day brings us. Regardless of what happens, Emmie, you have a lot of people on your side. Try not to worry too much."

I don't know if it's Mia's words or her overall comforting presence, but Emmie finally starts to relax. When she looks back at the food this time, her eyes light up, and her stomach lets out a loud growl that has us all laughing. Mia starts handing dishes around the table, asking Emmie about school and swim team.

Emmie lights up as she talks about her favorite classes, teachers, and the friends she's made through both school and swimming.

I'm suddenly privy to way more information than I care to know about my team, including who's fighting, who's crushing on who, and what drama they all have at their respective schools. It's information overload, and Mia listens with rapt attention, asking follow-up questions, and coaxing Emmie out of her shell.

By the time we make it to Adair, they've moved onto discussing the latest fan theories on Taylor Swift's next album, and I'm kind of grateful I'm an only child.

Bryce and Carter are waiting in the lobby when we arrive, awkwardly hovering. I'm sure they wished this wasn't something they'd have to deal with, but unfortunately, dealing with kids means you're forced to see an uglier side sometimes.

"You told them?" Emmie groans, hiding her face.

"Yeah, I did," I admit, not wanting to lie to her. "I had no choice. They own the club, and therefore, need to be informed when things like this happen."

Surprisingly, Bryce is the first one to speak up. "When we first met, I made it pretty clear that the entirety of Adair Swim Club should feel like a family; that means when someone is down, we're all there to help."

Carter nods in agreement. "We're here to answer any questions your brother or social worker might have about your scholarship or the club in general. This matter will stay private, though. If anyone else finds out, it'll be because you've decided you're comfortable enough to tell them."

She glances around at the adults nodding in confirmation before relaxing and mumbling out her gratitude.

We don't have to wait long before two people approach the building. One of them is Penny, looking as professional and put together as she did at almost three o'clock this morning. The other is a man who's probably in his late twenties, with cropped brown hair, and dressed like he rolled out of bed to get here as quickly as possible. It must be Liam.

Bryce lets them in, briefly introducing himself, but the man's eyes keep darting all over the place. When they finally land on Emmie, who just came back from getting a phone charger we have upstairs, the tension in his shoulders eases, a look of relief washing over him.

"Liam!" Emmie drops the charging cord and beelines for her big brother.

"Hey, Em," I hear him say back after pulling her into a tight hug.

All the adults take a step back, trying to give the siblings a moment, especially when Emmie's shoulders start shaking and Liam's follow soon after. Bryce and Carter make a small huddle with Penny, quietly answering her questions. I avert my eyes, but before I do, I can't help the swell of hope in my chest.

Maybe this one will work out.

Once Emmie and Liam head out to spend the day with Penny to determine what'll happen next and what the best course of action for her is, I head upstairs to the office. Bryce and Carter are sequestered in theirs, both of them offering to take over my practices for the day, but Mia is lounging on the couch in the common area.

When she sees me walk through the door, she closes her laptop, and sets it on the table. I collapse on the other end of the couch, casually pulling her legs into my lap and running my fingers along her calf.

"How did it go?"

When I turn toward her, she has her elbow on the back of the couch, watching me closely. "Pretty good, actually. Liam seems like a good guy. He also seems committed to keeping Emmie here despite what it'll mean for him."

"So you think this is going to work out?"

"I can't say for sure, but I do think he's the best thing for her right now. He clearly cares about her and has tried to fight for her before. I'm not worried he won't show up for her, but there are circumstances outside of our control. Even his control. I like to think I know the kids I coach, but I've seen kids who come from similar situations react in ways I never could have anticipated."

"Well, I know I don't have experience with this, but I think you made the right calls and did everything you could," she says. "And I think Emmie is grateful for you showing up. I think all these kids are pretty damn lucky to have you as their coach, Ronan. At least they know someone's looking out for them."

Despite everything I've spent the last few years doing, I've never had someone tell me I'm doing the right thing. Or even that what I did was good. Tears sting the corners of my eyes a little bit, causing me to look straight ahead, and will them away.

It's not that I'm scared to cry in front of Mia—it's quite the opposite actually. I'm scared that once I start, I won't be able to stop. Between the exhaustion and being with someone I trust whole-heartedly, a few tears might lead to a full breakdown. I am too tired to deal with that today.

Mia's foot nudges against my stomach, pulling my attention back to her. She's looking at me with a goofy grin, which must mean I missed something.

"I'm sorry, I zoned out there for a second," I admit, resuming the gentle movement of my fingers against her bare leg.

"Yeah, you did." I must hit a ticklish spot because the way she squirms brings a smile to my face. "I was trying to ask you a question. A very serious question."

Brows furrowed, I sit up a little straighter, my hand stilling on her leg. "Sure, what's up?"

"I was thinking about last night..."

My brain short circuits for a second, trying to come up with what she could possibly be talking about. Last night? When I had to take one of my swimmers out of a neglectful home? Weren't we already talking—*Oh.*

"You mean our date?" Despite my exhaustion and evident brain fog—because how the hell was that only last night?—a smile manages to tug at the corner of my lips. "Please, tell me more."

A faint blush coats her cheeks, so I give her calf a squeeze, hoping I help ease her embarrassment. "I know I told you this already, but I had a lot of fun and it was great to spend so much time together."

"I had fun, too. It felt like old times, didn't it?"

"No." She laughs. "You would have never taken a cooking class with me back then, no matter how much you liked me and liked spending time with me."

"It is not my fault I didn't learn to use a stove properly until I was thirty," I argue. "Blame my parents. I would have started a fire back then."

Her laugh seems to dance around the room, her eyes bright with a joy I want to bask in forever. God, do I want to keep being the person who makes her smile like that.

But right now, I'm anxious to see where this conversation is going. "Don't get distracted, Sheridan. You were thinking about last night and how much fun we had...what comes next?"

She pushes back strands of hair that have fallen out of her ponytail, giving me a shy look. "Despite your inability to use a stove all those years ago, I always thought we were building something. A real foundation after that night in Omaha, you know?"

I nod along. "Yeah, I agree. I think we both recognized we couldn't commit to anything in the moment, with our lives taking us all over the place, but I thought we were doing the same. And we were doing it with the intention of being ready when we got the chance."

She frowns. "And then I went and blew it all up."

I reach out and take her hand in mine, our fingers tangling together. "Hey, no. Don't think like that. I'm not mad at you for what happened. You were protecting yourself and Josie—there's no shame in that."

"I was protecting us from someone who would never hurt us. I was too insecure to believe that."

"I forgave you, Mia. Even when you were still mad at me, I knew whatever happened, I'd already forgiven you. I've missed having you in my life and I'm not about to chance that now."

"What if I ask you to?"

"What are you talking about?"

She fiddles with the hem of her shirt, but keeps her gaze locked on me. "What if I told you I wanted to take a chance, together? On the two of us?"

"For real?" I ask, dumbfounded. I can't seem to find any better words in the moment. "You mean as a real, serious couple?"

"Yeah." She drops the hem of her shirt and shifts on the couch until she's facing me, her legs tucked underneath her. I turn to give her my full attention.

"I know you probably don't want to have this conversation at work—"

"I don't care where we have it. I'm still having a hard time believing we're having it. Mia, are you sure?"

"I'm tired of wasting time, Ronan," she admits. "I'm tired of denying myself the person I want because I'm scared of getting hurt again. I think we owe it to ourselves to see where this could take us."

The people we were before—the ones fumbling around in that hotel bed in Omaha—never could have fathomed what we'd go through. They were on top of the world, and reality had no way of touching them. The two people sitting here now have had nothing but reality thrown at them. A car accident, a shitty ex who destroyed a career, and a chance we never thought we'd have again.

I'm taking that chance. I've been wanting to take that chance from the moment my eyes landed on her again and I can't believe how lucky I am for her to want to take such a chance with me.

"I wish you would say something," she anxiously replies.

Oh, shit, right. That part. That's how conversations work.

From that moment on, it's like I couldn't even contain my grin if I wanted to. Leaning closer, I pull her into a soft, sweet kiss. Something chaste and mild; something that definitely won't make Bryce feel like he has to start a real HR department.

She's a bit breathless when we pull away, and I try not to feel smug about being able to do that during a romantic moment happening in a not-so-romantic setting. "I'll take that as a yes?"

"I was planning on asking you the same thing in a couple of days," I finally say. "I wanted everything to die down a bit. I didn't want you to think I got caught up in the moment or something like that. I'm happy you were the one who brought it up."

In fact, it might mean even more to me that she was the one to ask. I always pride myself on being the kind of guy who lets his girlfriend take the lead when she wants or needs to, but there's never been an instance where I haven't been the one to initiate this kind of conversation. Not that there are a lot of them to make it count, but still.

She's beaming. The smile lighting up every aspect of her face, like the sun is shining down directly on her. "You realize this means we'll have to tell our friends, right?"

"You get to tell Bryce," I rush to say. "He already threatened me about creating a workplace nightmare—called himself HR and everything."

She snorts out a laugh. "Bryce would be horrible at HR."

"Right?" I exclaim.

"Do you even have any experience with a real HR department?"

"Um, yeah," I scoff, but she doesn't look convinced. "Operation Fly has one, but I've never dealt with them hands-on because I'm the founder and president who mostly stays out of that side of the organization."

"So that's a no, then," she teases.

"Not everyone's professional path looks the same, Mia."

One of the office doors open. "Hey!"

"Hey, man." I wave awkwardly.

"No kissing at work," Bryce warns. "Don't make me write you up."

"Do we even have a process for that?"

"I can make one," he cautions. "And, Mia, you're supposed to call Josie and tell her what she hopes is good news and that you're not going off the deep end."

"Bryce!" she screeches. "You told my best friend before I could?"

"I was on the phone with her and the two of you were about to have sex, what was I supposed to do?"

"We were *not* about to have sex; we had one sweet kiss." Mia groans, hiding her embarrassed expression behind her hands.

"When you're on the clock, any amount of kissing will be viewed ten times worse."

"Technically, we never clock into this jo—"

"O'Brien, I will kick your ass." Bryce doesn't give me any chance to reply before he steps back into his office, closing the door tightly behind him.

"We really are going to cause a workplace incident." I turn to her with a grin, but snort out a laugh instead. "Carter just gave me a thumbs up through his window."

"Well, at least someone approves." She laughs.

"Nah, Bryce approves. He's just being an ass."

As if to prove my point, I lean forward to kiss her again. Bryce yelling our names through his barely open door is the only thing that makes us spring apart, but then we're laughing.

"Ronan, stop!"

A deep chuckle sounds in my ear, sending shivers down my spine before he nuzzles against my neck, placing soft, closed mouth kisses along the sensitive skin. He pulls me tighter against him when I squirm. "And if I don't?"

The grip I have on the spatula tightens, but my head tilts, giving him as much access to my neck as possible. "I promised Carter I'd get him these cupcakes for the ten and under group. Do not make me disappoint a bunch of children."

"You've been working on them forever," he whines. "Why does Carter get your attention? He can make cupcakes himself."

"Yeah, from a box!" I argue, completely scandalized by the idea. "Those kids deserve something better for their celebration."

"They're children, babe," he deadpans. "If it has sugar, chocolate, and sprinkles, they're going to be happy."

Gasping, I spin in his arms to glare at him. "You did not just say that!"

With a laugh, he holds his hands up in surrender and takes a small step away from me. "I'm sorry, babe, but someone has to tell you the truth. Those will be devoured in seconds. They won't care how good they tast—"

My mouth drops open as the batter splatters across Ronan's face. I flicked the spatula at him without even realizing I was doing it, and now he's blinking at me while I fight to hold in the laugh.

"Seriously, Mia?" He groans, but I can see the small smile threatening to come out. "We're being that petty right now?"

The batter drips down his nose and I can't hold in the laughter anymore. "Oh—oh, my god. I am so sorr—"

I shriek as batter splatters across my own face. Holding a whisk in his hand, Ronan looks at me with a proud grin. "There. Now we're even."

I move on instinct, grabbing the pastry bag of frosting and aiming it at him. He opens his mouth to protest, but promptly closes it as the frosting smears across his chin and cheek.

Then it's on. In a matter of minutes, Ronan's kitchen is destroyed. Batter decorates every single thing I had out for cupcakes, and neither one of us care.

It came to an end when I slipped on some batter and almost went down. In a move so reminiscent of the first time we met, Ronan caught me in his arms. This time, though, it wasn't quick enough, and we both tumbled to the floor. Now we're laying on our backs on his kitchen floor, side by side, shoulders brushing, and we can't stop laughing.

I can't remember the last time I laughed like this with someone. I know I've never been in a relationship that feels as easy as this. But things with Ronan and me have always been easy. He's one of the few people I've let my guard down around, allowed myself to be vulnerable; and it means more than he'll ever know that he does the same around me.

I meet his bright green eyes, and they still manage to take my breath away. He turns his head to look at me and sprinkles fall out of his hair, which sends me into another round of giggles.

He shifts until he's leaning over me, strong arms on either side of my head, keeping me upright. He leans down until he can kiss a smear of frosting off my cheek, and my breath catches again.

I can feel the smirk against my skin when he feels the change in my breath. Smug asshole. He moves to the other cheek and repeats the motion.

"We need to clean the kitchen," I tell him. "Almost all of this could kill Lezak."

"Good thing I don't pick him up from doggy day care for another four hours," Ronan murmurs against my skin, moving his kisses down my neck. I can't help but tilt my head back, granting him more access. "We've got plenty of time."

With a groan, I wind my arms around his shoulders, pulling him closer as he gently nips and sucks at the skin of my neck. He settles fully against me, content to stay right where we are, not move a single inch.

"Ro—" I gasp when he licks at more frosting that's settled around my collarbone. "*Ronan.*"

"What, gorgeous?"

Oh, my god. The gravelly tone of that question has instant heat pooling in my stomach. I can't believe this is happening, again. For the third time.

He moves back up my neck until he can capture my lips in a searing kiss.

"We...we *can't.*" The last word is said in a whine when he reaches down to squeeze my breast. "Fuck."

With a smile, he places a few quick kisses against my lips, his hand sliding down until it can sneak beneath my shirt. "What excuse do you have for me now?"

Every possible excuse I could ever come up with practically flies out of my head. My fingers tangle in his hair while his fingers skim up and down my ribcage.

Everything is different with Ronan. There's no moment of hesitation when his hands first glide over a layer of fat. There's no admiring me when I'm spread out on my back, looking thin. There's awe and reverence with every gaze, every touch, and every kiss. I feel cherished by him in a way I never have before.

He chuckles against my neck before pushing the fabric of my shirt up, revealing my stomach. I let out a tiny moan as he starts kissing down my neck toward my collarbone again.

"Did I make you speechless, baby?"

When I look down at him, he's resting his chin against my chest, smirking up at me. His eyes are hazy, pupils so dilated I can barely make out the bright green iris. It's physical proof that I'm as capable of wrecking him as he is of wrecking me.

"We should move," I decide, finally remembering what I had started to say moments ago. I nod when he looks at me, confused. "We're on the floor, Ronan. We're both in our thirties."

"Trying to tell me I'm only good for the missionary position or something?" As though he wants to prove a point, he grinds down against me. "I'm not that old, and neither are you."

I bite back a smile, but the laugh still comes bubbling out. What is with this man and his ability to make me laugh during sex? It's still new to me.

"That's not what I was talking about," I tell him, his hand skimming down to trace the waistband of my leggings. Goose bumps prickle my skin. "Your leg—"

"My leg is fine," he assures me. "I'd tell you if it wasn't."

"But, Ronan—" I cut myself off with another gasp as warm fingers slide beneath the waistband of my leggings. "Oh, god."

He's still watching me, eyes dark and heady as my head lolls back, all thoughts of his leg forgotten.

As his finger finds my clit, starting with slow circles, he buries his face against my neck, offering soft kisses to the skin.

This man is going to ruin me. There are small whimpers coming from somewhere, but it isn't until he pulls back with a deep kiss to my lips that I realize it was me.

"Babe." I gasp against his lips. "Please."

"I'm not fingering you without lube, baby. We have a couple of options here, though. We can go upstairs and finish what we started, or I can take you against the counter."

Despite the heat shooting through me, melting me into a puddle right on Ronan's kitchen floor, I can't help but laugh. "You don't have lube down here, but you have supplies to do that."

Dark eyes take me in and sinful lips smirk down at me. "Come on, baby, you and I both know I can get you ready to take me with just a condom."

He doesn't give me a chance to answer before he's pulling back, the sudden removal of his body heat enough to make shivers run through me. Next thing I know, I'm being pulled to my feet and back onto the counter with his lips connected to mine.

There's still batter in places where there shouldn't be, still plenty of small messes for us to clean up later, but once he has me worked up enough that I'm a quivering mess, I don't care. And when he turns me around, my back pressing against his chest, and he's sinking into me at the most delicious angle, I care even less.

······ + ∘ ✦ ✶ ★ ☾ ★ ✶ ✦ ∘ + ······

One of my favorite things about living so close to my friends is the weekly get-togethers. If we go to Josie and Bryce's, it's usually a game night with a side of whatever Bryce feels like cooking that night. When it's my turn, Bryce is usually trying to keep Josie away from lighting my apartment on fire while we bake whatever recipe I found that week. And when it's Carter and Kat's turn, we know we're getting takeout and crappy movies we spend the night talking over. We haven't figured out what Ronan's week is, but not using that kitchen is a damn shame.

No matter where we go, though, I live for these nights.

This week it's Carter and Kat's turn to host and their townhouse is a flurry of activity when we get there. The delivery driver pulls up as we walk up to the door. Carter barely moves out of our way enough to let Lezak dart inside, let alone the two of us.

"No, it's fine," he calls when we walk past him. "I don't need help carrying things. Just go, keep walking."

With a dramatic sigh, Ronan presses a kiss to the top of my head and turns to help our friend. The closer I get to the kitchen, where we usually gather, and pile our plates high with food, I can hear laughter, but the combination of so many voices makes it hard to decipher who's actually talking.

"Mia!" As soon as I round the corner, I'm attacked by my best friend in a hug. She's practically vibrating with energy. When we separate, I take a quick glance down at her left hand to see—nothing.

I shoot a glare at Bryce, who seems to slink behind Katrina.

"Did someone give her an extra shot of espresso?" I question the room. Kat's beaming, shaking her head. "Why's she so hyper?"

"I feel like I haven't seen you in *weeks*," Josie replies, linking her arm through mine. "So tell me, what's been happening? How's the new relationship going?"

Groaning, I turn my head to yell over my shoulder. "Babe, Josie's interrogating me. Get in here, please!"

"Aw, that is so cute!" Josie gushes. "She's asking him to come defend her. Bryce, why aren't we this cute anymore?"

Ronan comes in carrying bags of what smells like pasta, and my mouth waters at the sight of that gorgeous man holding carbs.

"Please," he says, setting the bag on the counter. "I literally watched him pout because you left a room without telling him you love him. You guys are disgustingly adorable."

"Exactly!" I agree, helping him unload the bag onto the counter. "Leave me and Ronan alone. All you need to know is things are going good."

"Well, I would hope things are good," Carter adds, trailing behind Ronan with more food. "You promised me homemade cupcakes and those kids got cupcakes from a box. Which means someone or something—maybe both—distracted you and then you couldn't follow through on your promise."

Ronan and I exchange looks of pure shock. "How do you possibly know that?"

He raises a brow. "Come on, Mia, I may be shit in the kitchen, but I can tell the difference between cupcakes that are homemade and from a box. They were dry as hell and tasted like fake chocolate."

"My apologies," Ronan says. "I didn't realize you've developed such a refined palate. Next time I decide to seduce my girlfriend in my kitchen, I'll make sure you're not who she's cooking for."

As my cheeks turn fire engine red, Bryce lets out a loud groan. "Please don't say 'seduced' in my presence."

"Did the kids have a problem with them?"

"No, Ronan." Carter frowns. "I barely managed to grab one for myself before the kids tore them apart."

"Then does it really matter how the cupcakes were made?" Katrina turns to her boyfriend with a frown. "Why did they need to be homemade?"

"That's what I said!" Ronan grins.

Carter is pouting though and looking at his girlfriend like she committed the ultimate betrayal. "Et tu Brute?"

Kat simply rolls her eyes, pats his cheek, and goes about grabbing everything we need. Josie jumps into help, but Carter refuses to let the topic go.

"It's not always about the kids, you know. I worked hard this summer. I deserve a reward, too. But then Ronan had to go and defile cupcakes."

The wink my boyfriend sends me makes another blush coat my cheeks. This time, both Bryce and Carter groan, but the girls look at me with wide eyes.

"This isn't my house, so I can't ban sex talk," Bryce says. "But for the love of God, can we keep it PG?"

"We haven't even said anything!" Ronan protests. "If your mind is going somewhere dirty, that's on you and not us. Get your minds out of the gutters."

"Are you saying we're making too much out of this? That we're actually taking it somewhere dirty?"

Ronan grins at Carter. "Well, no, we never said that."

"Jesus Christ," Bryce mutters.

"If you act like this when Liam gets here, I'm going to kick all of your asses." Kat points at each of us individually. "Not only is he my new employee, but he's the guardian of one of the kids you coach. I know you guys—I know how welcoming you can be—so don't screw this up. He's feeling very much like a fish out of water and needs friends his own age he can talk to."

"He's twenty-seven," I point out. "That's practically a toddler to Ronan."

"Oh, fuck you." He laughs, leaning over to press a kiss to my head. I grin up at him.

After that, everything kind of goes to chaos. Liam arrives and Kat is making sure he knows everyone, which of course, he does. Apparently, when they both worked under her stepfather, she hadn't been shy about telling him, or their friend Nadine, all about us. Including how annoying she initially found Bryce to be, which is probably my favorite part.

Liam blends into the group, not afraid to jump in on the teasing, and is a naturally relaxed person. We learn that he went to school in Virginia, mostly on scholarships, and working his ass off to get where he is now. If there's one thing this group appreciates, it's working hard to get the things you want. He tells us about how Emmie is settling in, that he feels like he's not quite reaching her. We give him as much advice as a group of thirty-year-olds who are only children and all childless can give, but he's grateful, nonetheless. He gives us all the drama about Dalton Enterprises and what happened after Katrina made her dramatic exit.

Overall, it's a good night with the opportunity to meet someone new and see if they're someone who will get folded into our tiny, tight-knit family. More than likely, the answer is yes, because it's who we are. All of us are so far from our families, either physically or emotionally, but we recognize the need for that connection and believe in families that are found through life. Almost more than the ones we're born into.

Ronan

"I haven't had this much sex since I was in my twenties."

Mia laughs, rolling over to snuggle against my side. "I find that hard to believe. You're mister reformed playboy Olympian."

I graze my fingers down her bare back, tracing the tattoo of a crystal I'd already memorized. A citrine tower, she'd told me when I first asked about it, because it enhances mental clarity for manifesting dreams and goals.

"You know that's a lie. I got caught having fun a couple of times in my early twenties, and it became my whole identity." Her kiss to my pec tells me she knows this to be true and a reminder that she sees the real me. "Besides, having to learn how to walk again put a bit of a damper on my love life. Did you know Bryce is the worst wingman to ever exist in history?"

"Considering all the help he needed from literally everyone else, I'm not at all surprised."

We lie there in silence for a few more minutes, enjoying one another's company. Before too long, though, the stiffness that's been building in my leg for the last several days becomes unbearable. Groaning, I gently push her back so I can sit up and stretch out my leg. Her eyes are locked on my back.

"Do you need me to get you anything?"

I shake my head, slowly standing. I turn to face her and nod toward my bathroom. Which I think might be the one place in the house she hasn't seen yet. "Come on, let's take a bath."

She balks at the suggestion. "You're joking, right? You must be joking."

"Why would I be joking? My leg is stiff as hell, and I want to soak in the tub with my gorgeous girlfriend, who I had another round of mind-blowing sex with."

"Your leg hurts because you keep insisting on having mind-blowing sex with your girlfriend on hard surfaces or insist on carrying her."

"I'm willing to deal with the consequences to my actions," I reply, holding out my hand. "Now come on, let's take a bath."

"It's not going to work, Ronan. You're a giant and I'm a size twenty or twenty-two. There is no way in hell the two of us are going to fit in a standard sized bathtub."

I bend forward to grab her wrist and tug her toward me. I may not be a professional athlete anymore, but I haven't let up on my strength training. "Good thing it's not a standard bathtub then. Come on, baby."

Reluctantly, she gets out of bed and follows me to the bathroom. As soon as I flick on the light, she lets out a surprised gasp, just as I expected she would. The bathtub was one of the selling points for this place, because I definitely cannot soak in a standard one. This one, however, is extra wide and long, practically the size of a small hot tub, with depth that allows a good soak. The two of us will be rather comfortable in there.

I lead her over to sit on the edge while I start the water, making it as warm as possible without burning on skin so we can stay in longer. Another selling point was the brand-new water heater. She watches me with amusement as I get the Epsom salts from the shelf and add them to the water.

Before long, the two of us are sinking into the warmth of the bath with relieved sighs. She rests between my legs, leaning most of her weight against my chest.

Despite how intimate we've been the last four or so weeks, this takes it to a whole other level, and it might be one of my favorite moments. Silence fills the room, neither one of us feeling the need to break it. Mia's fingers mess with my hand, where it rests on her stomach, turning it over to trace her nails along the lines of my palms. Both of us are as content as could be.

"Don't tell me you know palmistry, too?" I keep my tone low and quiet, not willing to be the one who breaks the silence.

She lets out a breathy laugh, shaking her head. "No, but it's kind of fascinating, isn't it? The way these lines can tell a story—how they reflect your life?"

I press a kiss against her temple, breathing in the scent of her shampoo. "Is there anything witchy or witchy adjacent you don't find fascinating?"

"Curses," she answers immediately. "I may be the mean friend, but I'm not mean enough to curse anyone."

"I don't think you're mean," I murmur. "You're protective of yourself and the people you love. There's a difference."

"Then why is Bryce scared of me?"

I tangle our fingers together. "Because he hurt someone you are protective of, and he knows it. He's probably going to spend the rest of his life trying to prove to you how sorry he is and that he'll never do it again."

"He can make it up to me by proposing to her already," she grumbles. "I hate keeping secrets from Josie, but that ring needs to be on her finger. He keeps texting me ideas and I keep shooting them down. Josie won't want it to be public or overly extravagant."

There are days there where I forget our friend's impending engagement. The moment Bryce told us felt odd to me. I'm only a little older than him, but for a good chunk of those years, it felt like a bigger gap. He was still in his early twenties, barely an adult, when I had my accident and the way he stepped up as a friend, as someone who looked up to me, made me realize how fleeting moments are for each of us.

It happens slowly and then all at once. One day, you still feel like a kid who's fighting to be seen for who they really are, but also not quite ready to handle serious things, and the next, you're staring adulthood straight in the face and wondering where your youth went.

"I can't believe they're going to get married."

"They're not getting married because he's too much of a chicken shit to propose to her. I swear, if he doesn't do it soon, I will."

I can almost picture it. Mia, too frustrated waiting, finding the ring, and dragging Bryce along with her until they find Josie. There would be no ceremony, no pomp or circumstance, she'd plop down on one knee and do it for him. But I can't let her do that; they deserve their moment. "Give him time. He wants it as perfect as you do."

With a long, drawn-out sigh, she tilts her head back to look at me. Unable to resist, I lean down to kiss her. I don't know if she was planning to say anything else, or plead her case, but the kiss seems to relax her. When we separate, she settles further against me, her eyes drifting closed as I hold her tighter, relaxing into the silence.

"You all did a great job tonight!" I tell the team, who are all beaming up at me. "Our first meet is the second week of September, so just over a month away. And we're hosting it here."

The entire team cheers, getting pumped up for the first meet as a team. Most of them are coming off high school teams, deciding to go the club route all year. Since we're registered with the National Swimming Federation, we must adhere to their rules, which means we can race against high schools, but our swimmers cannot be on both teams. For a lot of them, this will be their first time facing their high school friends as rivals, and I'm anxious to see how it goes.

"Go home and get some rest. Tomorrow you have a weight training session," I remind them. "I'll see you all at six tomorrow morning."

I bite back a grin as I'm met with nothing but groans from annoyed teenagers. As a new club and a new team, I tried to keep early morning practices to a minimum, preferring evening or daytime practices during the summer. The closer we've gotten to competition season, I've started moving the practices to better reflect what the schedule will look like during the school year. Which typically means practices every morning, and an occasional practice or workout after school. A couple of the kids stop to ask me questions, or talk about their practices, so it's surprising to me when I turn and find Emmie patiently sitting on the bench.

"Hey, you okay?"

When she looks up at me, there's something in her eyes that I can't quite read, but I don't think I like it. Immediately, a hundred thoughts run through my head. Has something happened with Liam? Has he decided he can't take being a caregiver? I know he got a new job, but what if it's not what he wants, and he's decided to move back to Charleston with Emmie?

"I need to talk to you," she admits.

"Sure." I smile, taking a seat on the bleachers. "What's going on? Getting nervous about the meet?"

While this may be the first meet some of these kids experience swimming for a club, it'll be her first meet ever. I don't remember my first meet ever; I was too young to retain the memory. I do, however, remember what it felt like the first time I stepped up to a block and realized I loved racing and I loved swimming. It's still in the list of my most life-changing moments. Emmie will get both experiences rolled into one.

"No." She grins, relaxing in a way that screams confident swimmer. A second later, though, her shoulders hunch back up. "Because I won't be swimming in the meet."

My brain comes to a screeching halt. I knew this was a possibility, especially given everything she has going on, but I never let myself fully consider it happening. That she could still walk away from this sport despite all the time we put into improving her swimming, despite how much she loves it, and despite her natural talent.

"May I ask why?" I question. "And why now?"

She shrugs, not meeting my gaze anymore. "I just...everything has changed in my life and this isn't what I want anymore."

Bullshit. I know it's bullshit, but I won't call her out on it. Just like I don't want any kid to feel like they have to swim for their parents' approval, I don't want any kid to feel like they're forced to see it through to avoid disappointing me.

"I will not ask you to stay, if this is truly the decision you want to make." I'm trying to keep my voice steady when every fiber of my being wants to demand real answers.

"It is." She won't look me in the eye, but I'm feeling pretty hopeless about getting a real answer out of her.

Swallowing hard, I have no choice but to let her go. "All right then. If you change your mind, I don't know if you'll be able to come back. We haven't discussed what it would mean if a scholarship swimmer walked away from the team."

When I look back at her, I can see she's trying to school her look of pure panic into one of indifference. She nods and mumbles, "I understand."

I want her to talk to me, to tell me where this is coming from. I want to see if I can offer her some kind of help, but her walls are tall this time, and I'm not going to be the one knocking them down.

"I need to get home." She hops up from the bleacher, heading toward the locker room before stopping to turn back. "Thank you, Coach. For taking a chance on me."

Now take a chance on yourself, I silently plead. Out loud, though, I reply, "I stand by what I said the day we met. I think you're worth taking the chance on."

Ducking her head, she turns away to continue down the deck. She passes Mia on the way, who smiles at her, and slows to a stop to chat. Emmie says something to her before scurrying away. Mia frowns before looking down the deck toward me. I stand to greet her as she picks up her pace.

"What is that all about?" Her eyes are searching my face the second she reaches me, probably able to see the disappointment clearly written out. "Ronan?"

I shrug, stuffing my hands in the pockets of my sweats. "I don't know. She wouldn't talk to me. Just told me she couldn't do it anymore and quit."

Mia's eyes widen, her jaw dropping open on a gasp. "*What*? No way. That can't be what she wants!"

"I don't think it is, but I'm not going to push her, Mia." I don't know if she gets the underlying message, that I don't want to do to another kid what my parents did to me, but I need her to believe me. "She wouldn't talk to me."

She glances over her shoulder to watch Emmie disappear into the locker rooms, then looks back up at me. "Do you think she'll talk to me? She loves swimming, Ronan. You were there when she lit up at your kitchen table. There's something else going on. There has to be."

She's right. The way Emmie looks whenever she's in the water or talking about swimming is pure passion. It's the same look I saw light up the eyes of my friends and competitors long after my parents dimmed it in my own. If there's even a slight chance that Mia could get her to open up, and I'm thinking there's a pretty good one, then we might be able to forget about this.

"Maybe," I tell her. "I do think it'd be good for you to try."

She doesn't waste a second, leaning to press a kiss to my cheek, and give my arm a squeeze before she's jogging down the deck toward the locker room.

A harsh whistle blows from somewhere behind me, followed by Carter yelling, "Walk!"

But Mia doesn't listen. She also doesn't flip him off this time, so it might be progress all around.

"Rude of her to not listen to me."

"*Fuck,*" I exclaim, practically jumping out of my skin. Carter is standing next to me, looking a little smug. "Where the hell did you come from?"

He grins. "I wasn't quiet, man. Where is she going in such a hurry?"

"She's trying to talk Emmie out of quitting."

"Oh, shit," Carter breathes.

"Yeah." I turn to look at him. "I'm hoping she can change that, though."

Mia

"Ronan told me you quit."

Emmie's eyes narrow into a glare, but she doesn't pay attention to me. Instead, she focuses intently on stuffing her towel in her bag.

I move to sit on the bench across from the lockers, careful to give her enough room. "Don't get me wrong, if you don't want to do this anymore, you shouldn't have to. It just seems like it's coming out of nowhere."

She hesitates for the briefest second before she returns to packing her bag. My eyes track her movements, trying to catch a glimpse of her face. She refuses to look at me, though. "I don't think this is what you want. I think you want to do this, want to see where this could take you. You're a talented swimmer, Emmie. If you weren't, your coach wouldn't have fought so hard for you to be here."

With a huff, she turns to face me with her hands on her hips—pure defiance. "What do you want me to say, Miss Sheridan?"

I ignore the formality, knowing she'll never be anything but polite and respectful, especially at the club. "I want you to be honest. If not with your coaches or me, then at least with yourself. If you're scared, that's a valid feeling, and we can work on it, together."

I hum under my breath, picking at a stray thread on my jeans. "Maybe you're right. Did you know I had my first public anxiety attack when I was seventeen? It was over a bad grade on a test. I'd studied so hard—worked my ass off in that class—and still came up short."

She glares at me in pure teenage rage. "This is nothing like a bad grade on a test."

"Humor me for five minutes, please?" I motion to the bench across from me and wait for her to take a seat, huffing while crossing her arms over her chest. "Now, where was I? Oh, right. The test. It was the most important test of the semester, and I knew I needed a good grade in the class to get into all my top colleges. While I was a swimmer in high school, I wasn't good enough to depend on a scholarship.

"So, I studied hard, dedicated myself to school and swimming, hoping for the best. The problem was, those two things became my entire identity. And my best was never good enough. When one slipped, the other wasn't there to catch me, and it terrified me. I put so much pressure on myself to not disappoint anyone—my parents, my teachers, my coaches. I didn't care if I disappointed myself as long as everyone else was happy."

She gnaws at her bottom lip, eyes suddenly glistening with the tears. From how she's fighting to hold them back, I know I've hit a nerve. "It sounds like you put a lot of pressure on yourself."

I nod. "And I'm starting to think you know something about that?"

With a groan, she drops her head into her hands, eyes shutting on the way. My heart aches for her, for all she's been through. I see a lot of myself in this young woman and want to help her in a way no one helped me. She deserves to be in control of her life, chasing after what she wants instead of giving it up to be who someone else needs her to be.

All the work I put into my schooling was never enough for anyone. Never enough for my parents, who wanted nothing short of perfection. Never enough for my teachers or coaches, who wanted my time and attention focused on different things. But Emmie still has a chance. She's surrounded by people who want her to find balance, to learn how to prioritize her own happiness.

I nudge her with the toe of my boot. "You know, your brother is pretty badass."

She looks at me, a few tears making their way down her cheeks. "Is he? Because he gave up everything to move here and take care of me."

"He didn't give up anything, Emmie." I frown. "He made this decision because he wants to do what's best for you. He didn't want to make you give up swimming, school, your friends, your life, move somewhere new."

"He shouldn't have had to make that decision! I should have been able to handle it!" Her head drops back into her hands, but this time, her shoulders start shaking with sobs. "I shouldn't need his help."

I drop to the floor before her, ready to offer whatever comfort I can. The water on the damp concrete instantly soaks through my jeans, sending a shiver down my spine. "Hey, no, Emmie. Look at me, sweetheart." Teary eyes barely meet my own gaze. "You are fifteen years old—you shouldn't have to raise yourself and parent your own mother. That was her job, and she failed you both. If Liam had it his way, you would have never been stuck there for as long as you were. You know that. Why do you think he'd feel any differently now?"

A shaky hand comes up to aggressively wipe at her eyes. "I wanted to prove to him I could do it the way he did. It was his turn to make it out and have a life for himself, which he had. I was supposed to take care of everything. I didn't want to be the reason he got pulled back in. He gave up his life for me!"

"No." I shake my head, squeezing her knee. "He wanted to get you out. He wanted to give you the life you deserved, but she wouldn't let him. She kept you apart for her own selfish reasons."

"And then I went and messed it all up," she cries. "He's going to hate me, Mia."

I push the hair out of her face as gently as I can, the locks already tangling from the chlorinated air. "*No*. You didn't do anything wrong. You're a child. You're supposed to be building your life."

"And I took his away from him!"

"Emmie, listen to me. Your brother is never going to hate you or resent the fact that you brought him here. Do you really think Ronan would let you be with someone like that? He'd tell Penny in an instant and fight like hell to get you somewhere else. Liam is so proud of how strong you are, but he doesn't want you to feel like you have to be strong forever. He wants you to enjoy the rest of your childhood and to make a new life together.

"I want you to talk to your brother about this, because you shouldn't be putting this much pressure on yourself. You don't have to prove something to him or prove you're worthy of his love. Do you understand me?"

She nods, hiccupping slightly. "What if I can't get a scholarship?"

Dear god, this girl is bound and determined to break my heart. "Is that why you want to quit? Because you're scared it's not going to pay off in a monetary way?"

She hesitates before crumbling. "I want to go to college, Mia. I want to be better than my mom."

"And you're going to do that, Emmie. No one here doubts that, but you cannot put this much pressure on yourself. Do you think

Liam isn't worried about what happens in three years? Of course he is. Everyone here is invested in your future; we're invested in the future of every kid that walks through that door, but swimming isn't the only thing that matters."

"It could open so many doors for me, though." She frowns, sounding exactly like Ronan.

"But it won't do that if you hate it," I counter. She deflates a little, almost like I voiced something she was already thinking. "You're a great student, Emmie. You're wickedly smart, and swimming will add to that. There is more than one path to your future. Let me ask you a question, if there were no swimming scholarships in the world but the sport required the same level of commitment, would you want to quit?"

She's shaking her head before I even finish asking the question. "No, I love it."

"Then don't run away from it because you're scared." I squeeze her knee again. "Take the day off, go home, and talk to your brother about all this. Then, we'll see you tomorrow. I'll tell Ronan you changed your mind."

She groans. "He's going to be so mad at me."

"Not a chance," I say, standing. "He's going to get it, Emmie, because he knows what it's like to be in your shoes."

The only difference is that Emmie is fighting for a future; Ronan fought for the love and acceptance of his family. I'll never say that to her, though. That's his secret to share.

"I'll see you tomorrow," I promise her, with a smile.

Nodding, she goes back to packing her bag. I'm on my way back out onto the pool deck when she calls my name. When I turn back, she's shyly smiling. "Thanks for talking to me."

"Anytime, kiddo."

Emmie and I talk for a few more minutes before I make my way back out to the deck, all the guys are standing nearby, anxiously waiting for news. Between the anxiety rolling off them both and their pacing, they could easily be cast in any medical show as a family waiting for news.

"She's alive," I joke.

Ronan stops dead in his tracks, staring at me with wide eyes. "Was there ever a question about that?"

I shake my head. The joke went right over his tall head. "She's not quitting; she's going to be here tomorrow and will want to work extra hard to prove her dedication to you." Ronan immediately starts arguing, so I hold a hand up. "That's between the two of you. I told her she doesn't have to do it, and that you wouldn't like it."

"Did she say why she even thought about quitting?"

I bite my lip, wondering how much I want to tell them. Of course, they need to know some of it in case it comes up again, but she confided a lot in me, and I don't want to disrespect that bond. "She's falling into old habits. I don't think she knows what stability looks like and keeps waiting for her homelife to blow up in her face."

"But things are good, right?" Bryce asks. "I thought Liam got a job working for Kat. They worked together at Dalton Enterprises, right?"

Carter nods. "She's been wanting to expand her business, but needed an architect for it. His timing was kind of perfect. It doesn't match what he made at Dalton Enterprises, but it's more than enough."

"Things at home are fine," I assure them. "She just doesn't trust when things are going well, and I don't blame her. She's worried Liam will end up resenting her for making him give up his life. She was thinking about getting a job to help with the bills or help around the apartment by spending less time at the pool. Basically, she wants to prove to him that she's capable of taking care of herself and he can go on living his life."

"That's not why he came down here, though," Ronan says. "Liam wants her to be a kid; he doesn't want her doing what she had to do when it was only her and her mom."

"I'm sure that's been communicated to her, but she's not getting it yet."

Ronan fishes his phone out of his pocket and starts scrolling through his contacts. "I'm going to give him a heads-up before she gets home."

"Good idea." I watch him walk away, then turn to the other two. "She's in a position none of us have ever been in and she's going to respond to things the way she thinks is best. It's our job, and Liam's, to show her supportive environments."

Bryce and Carter both agree, and we hang back until Ronan is done with his phone call, and heads back over to us.

"Well?" I ask.

"Liam thanked me for the heads-up. He'd been worried something like this might happen. Apparently, she was acting distant. He assured me that their financial situation is fine—there's no need for her to get a job or give up swimming, especially with the scholarship. He's going to talk to her again, find out what he needs to do to make her understand her only job is being a fifteen-year-old."

I nod, relieved to know Liam is falling back into the role of big brother so easily. That was my piece of advice to him that night at Kat and Carter's, to trust his instincts and not be afraid to reach out to us. While none of us know anything about raising a child, we all know what it was like to be a teenager. We can help him figure out the best moves. Plus, if asked, I don't think Emmie has any problem telling people what she needs.

"Will you tell me what you said to her?"

Ronan and I are walking across the parking lot, his arm draped over my shoulder, and the summer night air is practically suffocating with its humidity. "I told her about how I put too much pressure on myself to grow up when I was her age—how it led to panic attacks and, eventually, me not wanting to swim competitively anymore."

He turns to face me when he reaches his car and leans against the SUV. "You never told me that."

I shrug, reaching for his hand. "It's not something I like talking about. I wasn't good enough to get a scholarship, or a full ride, so I ran myself ragged in high school. When it came time to make the decision about swimming in college, I decided not to. I was worried it would happen again and, as much as I loved the sport, I didn't love it the way you or Emmie do. I didn't need to be in the water to be part of it."

"Which is what led to you and Josie starting Adair."

"Which led me to meeting some pretty amazing people." I grin at him. "That blog changed my life in ways I'm still figuring out. Most importantly, it brought me Josie. She's always going to be my person, even when I find my one. But it also gave me an incredible family, even if we had to do some falling apart before coming back together."

"Watching you and Josie together is something I don't have words for—your friendship is literally like fireworks. You could take over the world and I think the world would let you."

I bite my lip to keep my wide grin from bursting any bigger. "Those sound like pretty good words to me."

He laughs, raising our joint hands to kiss my knuckles. "And this finding your one? Is that something you're actively looking for?"

"Maybe." I shrug shyly. "I don't know if it's on my radar right now."

"Is it because you're tired of looking, or could it be because you found something?"

"I'm pan, Ronan. The entire world is my oyster when it comes to potential love interests," I tease. "Besides, I'm still in the middle of my story. You never know who gets the happy ending."

"What if the story never ends?"

The picture paints itself so vividly in my mind. What it would look like for us to spend whatever forever looks like for us side by side. I can see lazy mornings spent in bed or wandering around local festivals; I can see us celebrating holidays with our friends, taking Lezak on long walks. The kisses, the hugs, and the never questioning our place in each other's lives. It's a beautiful picture, and I want so badly to see it come true. But I can't jinx it. I refuse to.

I stand on my tippy-toes until I can brush our noses together and whisper, "Even better."

Ronan drops one of my hands to wrap it around my waist, pulling me in for a deep kiss.

I'm not ready to say the words yet, not by a long shot, but the idea of him and I having a story that never ends sounds pretty damn good to me.

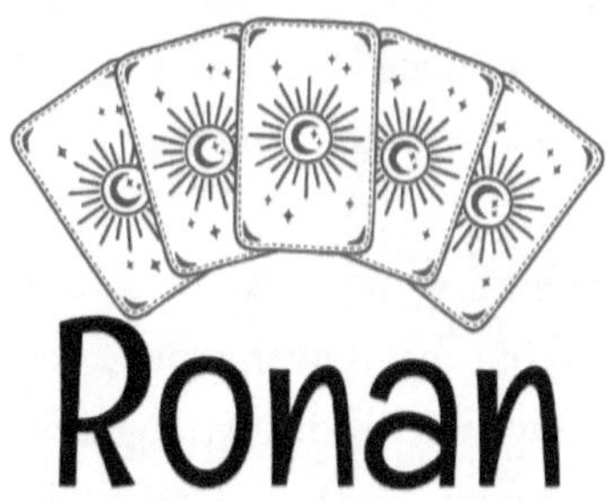

Ronan

It's shocking how quickly everything you work so hard for can collapse around you. Love, a career, a relationship—all of it can crumble. Nothing is permanent, so it shouldn't be treated like it is.

That's the way I've lived most of my life, especially the last eight years. The day I woke up in the hospital bed, with no one but a kind nurse holding my hand while the doctor slowly dismantled my life, haunts me. From that point on, everything fell apart. I lost what felt like everything, including the final proof that I never had my parents' love. I only had their attention, and even that was fleeting.

Instead of focusing on the people who did show up and convinced me to fight for what I still had, I focused on all the things I'd lost. Since starting Operation Fly, I'd pick new clubs and swimming programs to oversee whenever I felt the need to run. To get away before I'm standing in the rubble of my life once more.

The last week or so, I've started feeling that itch again. The restlessness, the need to run. This time, it pisses me off. What do I possibly have to run away from? Everything I could have ever wanted is here; why can't I stick around to see it through for once?

When the itch started, I made an appointment with my therapist. I'm still getting to know him; I'm still determining whether he's who

I'd like to see going forward, should I stay. I also haven't been as good about going as I usually am, which makes the process harder.

The appointment was two hours ago. I'd walked into that office so sure I was about to hear the same thing I'd heard countless times. My previous therapist told me I had a restless soul, which isn't a bad thing, but I needed to wait for the thing that felt real. I'd been happy to let her believe that.

This guy, though, he saw right fucking through me. In less than an hour, he'd figured out that it wasn't me searching for something real; it was me running away from anything that felt too good, too tangible. He was the first person to call it what I've always known it to be: fear.

By the end of the session, I felt ripped open and raw in the way only therapy could make you feel. Worse, I know he's right, and now that a stranger has spoken the words out loud, there is no denying it. I don't want to run away anymore, though.

And I'm fighting against every instinct I have to stay, but my behavior is defaulting to patterns. Which my therapist, who I now have regularly scheduled appointments with, thinks is a defense mechanism. That I'm allowing myself to fall into those old habits, despite my brain saying otherwise, out of fear that things won't work out.

My phone lights up on the table, an incoming call from Mel, reminding me of the other obligations I have. Watching Lezak dart around my backyard, I press the phone against my ear. "Hey."

"Wow, you sound like an absolute delight this afternoon," she greets sarcastically. "Is it a bad time?"

I pinch the bridge of my nose, hoping to keep the headache I can feel coming on at bay. "Nah, it's fine; just came from an appointment. What's going on?"

"The start date for the new build in Santa Fe is closing in on us, Ronan," she reminds me. "You told me you wanted to take it. I need an answer, soon."

When Bryce and Carter asked me to come out to Adair, the Santa Fe project was already in the works. It was going to be a large undertaking—building a new facility at a high school in an underprivileged area and bringing kids from surrounding high schools to swim for the same team, while also providing water safety classes free to the community.

It was supposed to be my way out of Adair. It'd give me six months to make sure my friends were good, and then I could leave. Onto the next thing.

"Send Jon," I say, surprising even myself. "And have him take Morgan with him. She needs the experience." Mel stays silent on the other end for a little too long. "Mel?"

"I'm sorry. Is this some kind of a joke?"

"Not a joke." I lean back in the chair, squinting against the sun. "Jon is a strong coach who's great with people at all levels and Morgan is excellent at water safety. She just needs more coaching experience. Jon will be good with that. Did you have someone else in mind?"

"Yeah, you," she deadpans. "Since when do you turn down a project in a city you've never been to?"

"I can't leave Adair yet. Bryce and Carter still need some help."

It's a bald-face lie. Both, or either, of them could run this place completely on their own. Sure, I made a commitment to my team, but there's no reason for me to stay. Even Bryce had a feeling I wouldn't stick around months ago.

"Okay, if you're sure." I can hear the uncertainty in her voice. "What about future projects? Are there any you want me to put you on?"

"Not yet. I don't know how long I'm going to be out here."

Why can't I just say I'm planning to stay? That she's more than capable of taking over the day-to-day operations of Operation Fly? Why can't I tell her I've found everything I've been looking for my entire adult life and don't want to leave it behind? Why can't I be honest with her?

"All right, I'll keep you updated," Mel relents.

"I actually need to come out to California soon. We need to have a meeting with the board to talk about some things regarding the future and it's best if we do it in person. I'll try to get out there in the next two or three weeks. Does that work for you?"

"That should be fine. Ronan, can I ask you a serious question?"

"Yeah, of course."

"Are you staying in Columbia?"

Dropping my head into my free hand, I let out a breath. "I'd like to see what we can do about making that happen, yeah. What are your thoughts?"

"That maybe there is a God after all."

Hearing my very atheist VP say that makes me snort out a laugh. "Yeah, maybe."

"We'll talk more about it when you get out here. Just let me know when you have your travel plans."

"Will do," I promise her before hanging up.

I watch my dog roll around in the grass, clearly enjoying himself. Just letting Mel in on my thought process makes me feel lighter, like I can have everything I want. I'm not ready to tell the others yet, in case something happens, but I'm moving forward, and trying to create a future I can truly be proud of.

Bryce glides into the wall before turning to relax against it. He's barely breathing hard despite doing more laps than me, and at a pace that's much quicker than mine. Part of me hates him for it, and I think I always will. Not in the real way, but in the way you hold a grudge against the people who can still do the things you can't.

A living, breathing reminder of what I lost that night.

"Is the leg bothering you?" He rips his cap and goggles off, tossing them to the deck before reaching for his water bottle.

I wince at the movement. "Your hairline is going to start receding from the way you rip that cap off your head."

He rolls his eyes mid-drink before setting the bottle back down on the edge. "Stop being so dramatic."

I shrug, draping my arms over the lane line to support myself. "Don't come crying to me when Josie starts freaking out because you're balding before forty. The leg is fine, just a little stiff. Swimming helps."

He nods. "How are things going with Mia?"

I could almost get whiplash with how quickly he changes subjects. It's not something we ever really talk about, not the way I know he and Carter do. She is the last thing I expected him to bring up this morning. Sure, Mia's his girlfriend's best friend, but he's never jumped into any of my relationships like this before. Then again, none of them were nearly as serious as this, and I bet he probably knows that.

"Fine," I reply slowly, reaching for my own water.

"Just fine?"

"What are we doing here, man?" I question with a sigh. "Are you really about to give me the shovel talk?"

He shrugs. "Someone has to do it, don't they?"

I frown at him. "Yeah, I guess, but I was expecting it to come from Josie, not you. You were my friend first, you know."

"Yeah, I was, but she needs people looking out for her more than you, sometimes. I know she told you about it, but you weren't here for the Bianca aftermath. She was a mess, and I want to make sure she's good. I'm sure you'll get a similar talk from Josie, too."

"Let's add Carter and Kat to the list, too."

"I wouldn't be surprised," he admits. "Again, you weren't here when she first moved here. We can support both of you and still be happy to kick your ass if you hurt her."

"I think Mia is more than capable of kicking my ass," I reply. "And if she doesn't, Josie will. Hell, they'd probably take turns."

"Great," Bryce replies in a much more serious tone than I'm used to him using. "Consider me third in line."

I almost tell him the truth—that if I'm stupid enough to screw this up, I'll let them all take turns. "I have no intention of screwing this up, Bryce. Not again. I'm acknowledging this second chance."

He nods, reaching for his cap and goggles again. "Good. Just make sure you don't fuck things up this time, Ronan. I know you're serious about her, but I need you to also recognize that she doesn't give third chances."

Before I can say anything else, he pushes off the wall into an easy breaststroke. Every word he said to me runs through my mind, but before long, I find my focus shifting to him. He's picked up speed, cutting through the water effortlessly and with nearly perfect form. Breaststroke might not be my area of expertise, but I've been around the sport of swimming long enough to realize he's counting his strokes. Maintaining consistency in a way that could monitor progress isn't something I've seen him do in a long time.

It's something we're all used to, but once we lose the pressure of competition, it's not something we need to do. For a lot of swimmers I know, it's the first thing they get rid of. From the other side of the pool, I watch him turn at the wall before gliding underwater.

He comes up before the fifteen-meter mark, transitioning into a freestyle, and that's where I can immediately tell he needs some work.

"Is he swimming the back half of an IM?"

I didn't hear Carter approach, but he's standing on the deck, dressed in a black brief with a cap and goggles in his hand. His entire focus, though, is on Bryce.

"It looks like it, doesn't it?"

I'm curious to see if he's wondering the same thing I am. Whenever he and I would swim, he tended to stick to either breaststroke or backstroke, two of his strongest areas. I'm pretty sure the last time I saw him do any sort of IM swim was when he was still competing.

"Yeah," Carter admits, pulling his cap over his head. "What do you think that's about?"

It's definitely not for me to say, because I'm not Bryce. I don't know what his physical fitness goals are or what he hopes to achieve from a workout. I do, however, think how he's switching up his swims and has started to pay more attention to the details is interesting. Why he's doing this, though, isn't my business.

"I don't know, man," I reply. "Maybe he felt like switching up his workout?"

Carter shrugs. "Makes sense."

Without another word, he dives into the pool, picking up a well-paced freestyle. I continued to watch Bryce, though. Even after I pull myself out of the pool, I watch him. There has been something different about him recently, and I can't put my finger on it.

Ronan

When Josie called and told me I had someone at the front desk wanting to see me, a million different people ran through my mind. Each more unlikely than the last. Because the truth is, the longer I'm in Columbia, the tighter-knit my circle becomes. Which isn't necessarily a bad thing because I've never felt more supported or as much a part of a family as I do here.

In this job, being surrounded by these people every day makes it harder to keep up fake friendships and appearances. The only person outside of our group that I talk to consistently is Mel Segal, and that's only because she's second-in-command at Operation Fly. Honestly, I don't mind that my circle is dwindling to the people who really matter.

The one person I should have expected to see, however, is the one waiting at the desk when I get down to my office.

"Liam," I greet warmly, shaking the younger man's hand when I reach him. "How's it going?"

"About as well as it could be," he replies with a sheepish shrug.

"Yeah, I can imagine." It's true, though. As much as Emmie's life was thrown upside down, so was his.

"Do you have a second to talk?"

Confused and a bit curious, I lead him up to my office, where he takes the seat across from my desk. "What can I do for you?"

"I think we should talk about Emmie almost quitting?"

"I agree," I say with a slow nod. "She and Mia talked in the locker room after she made the declaration, and she ended up changing her mind. Did she ever talk to you about it?"

"Not ahead of time," he confirms my unasked question. "I had no idea that was even a thought running through her head. I'm glad Mia was able to talk her out of it, though, and I wanted to stop by to personally thank you for it. And thank you for the call."

When Emmie had talked to me about quitting, I was worried she might have had something to really be concerned about. That maybe Liam was guilting her into taking on more responsibility because of everything he had given up. The more I thought about it, though, the less likely it seemed. Liam hadn't even questioned any of the decisions he was forced to make. He had listened to what we thought were the best options for his sister and went above and beyond with it all.

While it isn't totally out of the realm of possibility, I doubt Liam will be one to go back on his word like that.

"I want to make sure we're on the same page. As two people who care about her success, you don't want her to quit the team?"

"Not at all," he assures me. "From the first day we were reunited, all she could talk about was the team and how much she loved swimming. It made me so happy to see she found an outlet, to find something she loves, and is passionate about. It's something I could never do for myself until I left home."

"Emmie mentioned that you tried to come get her when she was younger?" It's not a question I should necessarily be asking, but the more I know about the situation, the more I can help Emmie in the future as well.

He nods. "Straight out of college, I graduated and drove to their house. I thought my mother would be thrilled to not have to worry about a child that she never wanted to take care of in the first place. But then she heard I graduated with an architectural degree and decided it meant I had instantaneous money. Like you graduate and they hand you a check with your diploma or something."

"That would be nice," I joke.

"Yeah." He chuckles. "But needless to say, I had nothing. I wanted to save my little sister from dealing with the same shitty life I had. I had a place to live, a job that kept me stable through college, but I knew I'd never get a judge to sign off on it."

"Which is why you attempted to get your mother to see reason. It makes sense. I would have done the same thing in your shoes. Especially if you could get her to sign her rights away and put you as Emmie's sole caregiver."

"I had all the paperwork, man." He groans. "I had a lawyer friend draw it up, all it needed was her signature, but I failed Emmie."

"No, your mother's selfishness failed Emmie. You can't blame yourself for that," I remind him. "Did Emmie tell you anything about what her and Mia talked about?"

"Yeah, she did. Which was a hard conversation to have, because it was literally history repeating itself. She was doing the same thing for our mom that I did for years. She saw me getting out of there as an accomplishment."

"And it was." He doesn't look convinced. "Liam, if you hadn't gotten out of there, you might not be in a position to take care of her now. No one knows what would have happened if you had stayed. You can't change the past, so show up for the future."

"You're right. I know you're right. I just...I don't know how to do that. I don't know how to make her understand that I want her to be a kid. I don't want her to worry about paying bills or making sure I have the freedom to do whatever she thinks I need to do."

"I've owned Operation Fly since 2019, and I've worked with a lot of kids in very similar situations. All they want is someone to say those exact words to them. To say, 'hey, I've got this, don't worry.'"

"And you really think that'll get through to her?"

"Maybe, but I also know she's been doing this for a long time. The words are a great place to start, but follow it up with actions. And try to show up for her."

"Oh, I'm planning to," Liam promises. "I already gave Katrina the meet schedule and the school schedule, so she knows when I won't be available. Though in hindsight, she probably doesn't need the meet schedule because she could ask you for it."

With a laugh, I nod. "Yeah, she helped write the schedule."

"Can I ask you something as someone who knows Emmie better than I do at this point?"

I know it's going to be something that seeks validation, because as unstable as Emmie's life is, Liam's is as well. He needs to know he made the right choices, that he's doing everything he can to help Emmie. He's including her in big moments like finding an apartment that caters to both their needs, helps her both feel in control, and capable of letting it all go.

"If you're about to ask me if you made the right decisions, I say yes," I tell him. "This can be a second chance for both of you, if you let it. Plus, I have some bad news for you."

"What?" The panic on his face makes me grin.

"You're Emmie's guardian, which ties you to Adair; and you're Katrina's friend and new employee," I say. "These people adopt people. You're not getting away from this group."

He looks a little uncertain as he lets out a nervous laugh. "It sounds like you're saying it from experience. Should I run?"

Through the window of my office, I see Bryce and Carter arguing about something and then Mia hits them both with a folder, flashes me a grin, and heads into her office. I look back at Liam with my own grin. "Nah, I wouldn't run."

From the moment Emmie walked back through the doors of Adair Swim Club after quitting, she's been on fire. Putting in extra work, pushing herself harder, and doing whatever she can to prove to me she's taking this seriously. Knowing that so many people—both here and at home—want to see her achieve whatever dreams she has seems to have ignited more sparks in her. She's not ignoring instruction or allowing her teammates to distract her. She's shown up early to practice with races queued up on her phone, some of them mine or Carter's, asking why certain technique decisions were made or what could have been changed to achieve a better outcome.

Hell, she even showed a brief interest in the IMs. Bryce ran her through a quick training session, assessing her skills in the other strokes, and then had her race Carter. They were both dead on their feet by the end of it, and Emmie loudly declared she was never doing it again and asked Bryce why he had a death wish. A question I still ask most IMers.

At least I know she's interested in other strokes, though. As long as I don't put them together in one race.

She's proven to me how stability at home can impact kids. It's given her the freedom to start finding herself and to chase her dreams. It's a constant reminder to all of us about why we do what we do.

Although, she's not happy when I announce I need to head to California for a couple of days. Neither is the rest of the team.

Because they're kids and I'm about to upset their routine. They don't understand why the trip has to interfere with their practices. Or maybe they don't associate the state of California with having real business hours. Either way, they aren't happy.

Mia agrees with them, if her distant behavior is anything to go off of. The way the light faded from her eyes when I told her about the trip was almost enough for me to break and tell her all about my plans. About how I can't promise it would work out the way we want, but this is what I want. I held myself back, though, determined not to disappoint her if this doesn't go the way I want it to. It would hurt more than holding in the truth for a few days.

I know what they're all worried about, and yeah, I should tell them; but there's still the smallest chance the board gives me a reason not to step down as president, or Mel decides she's not ready for the step up. Both of them seem highly unlikely to me, but I'd rather not get anyone's hopes up.

My plan is to get to San Francisco, get through the meetings, and not let anything else hold me up. If all goes according to plan, I'll be back in Columbia before anyone can miss me. This time, for good.

Mia

Normally, I love the stillness of Ronan's place. Especially when I'm snuggled into his insanely comfortable bed with a wall of muscle against my back and a tiny, but rapidly growing, fluff ball at my side. But this morning, I hate it.

I can usually sleep through his alarms, but this morning, it has my eyes blearily blinking open at 4:15 a.m. I keep still while he slides out of bed after brushing a quick kiss to the top of my head. He scoops Lezak up before quietly padding out of the room. I feel the loss of heat from both of them. I know he's making the dog, who's also used to waking up early, go to the bathroom so he can let me sleep a little longer, but it makes me feel more alone in the massive bed.

He leaves for California today.

He plans to be in San Fracisco for three days, and though he booked his return flight and everything, something about it doesn't feel right. His vagueness about what he's doing out there isn't sitting well with me. I know he has a business in need of his attention, but telling me he's got meetings about the future of it and the places it'll go, has fear settling heavy in the pit of my stomach.

He never realizes I'm awake, and I'm okay with it. I don't feel like talking. I don't feel like trying to figure out if his vagueness is to keep me from getting my hopes up or if it's because he already knows he might end up breaking my heart. He's always been restless. He has always loved traveling for meets or modeling gigs; I've always known that. This time, though, I let myself believe he'd found something to make him want to stay.

And now I'm facing the consequences. The second he walks out the door, I feel like it's the beginning of goodbye.

My back is still to the door when I hear him come back into the room. A second later, I feel Lezak curl into the bend of my legs. It pulls a small smile from me, the way he doesn't care about personal space like his owner.

I lie completely still, listening as he finishes moving around the room to gather the rest of his things. Hearing the sound of his bag zipping is like nails on a chalkboard. I squeeze my eyes shut when I feel him kneel on the bed, leaning toward me.

A warm hand gently squeezes my arm. "Baby," he whispers, squeezing again. "Wake up, gorgeous."

"Hmm?" I roll over, disturbing the puppy in the process, but I try my best to act like I'd just woken up. I blink up at him sleepily. "What's going on?"

His smile is soft, adoring even. He pushes a strand of hair from my face. My eyes flutter closed as his skin brushes my temple. "Hi, baby. You can go back to sleep, but I wanted to tell you goodbye and that I'll miss you."

My eyes drift closed again when he presses a kiss to my lips. I want to reach out, pull him back into bed, and refuse to let him go. Once I have him back in my arms, I'll beg him not to go.

Instead of doing that, I kiss him once more and ask him to keep me updated. "I love you" is on the tip of my tongue, but I swallow it down. He gives me one more kiss and another pet to Lezak before he's leaving.

I listen as he moves through the house. I don't hear the front door open or close, which makes me hold my breath. Maybe he changed his mind. Maybe he isn't actually leaving, and he'll be back in my arms any second.

But then I hear the garage door open and the sound of his SUV starting.

The tears are falling before I even know they've welled up. It's so stupid to be crying over this. I don't even know what's going to happen. It's not like he stood in front of me and declared he was moving back to California. It's not like he told me he was choosing a different state over me.

But I do know history repeats itself and my history shows that people never stick around forever. And history also tells me Ronan O'Brien doesn't stick around in one place for too long, regardless of who he leaves behind.

And this time, it looks like I'm the one he's leaving.

⁕ ⁕ ⁕

"Shit," I curse under my breath.

Lezak lifts his head, watching me frantically pick up piles of notebooks and other things thrown over Ronan's counter in search of my phone. The ringing stops but picks back up seconds later. Which tells me it's Ronan, and he's trying to tell me to take a break. Which, when I glance at the time on my laptop, I realize I haven't done for a couple of hours.

"Aha!" I declare, showing the dog my phone. He looks unimpressed, dropping his head back to his paws. I answer the phone. "Your dog has a problem with judging people."

Ronan's deep laugh echoes in my ear. I'd give anything to be in his arms right now, feeling the way that laugh rumbles through his chest. His arms would hold me tighter. It's fine, though. I need to wait a few more hours. A few more hours and he'll be back home.

"Is he actually judging you or are you doing something ridiculous in front of him, only to be disappointed in his lack of validation?"

I sputter at the joke that hits too close to home, and he laughs again. "Therapy isn't until Monday, Ronan," I grumble. "You're lucky I'm letting you get away with a joke like that."

"I know. I thought only Josie would be able to."

"And you were willing to risk it?"

"Eh," he says, probably with a shrug of his shoulders. "What's that saying about no guts, no glory? Besides, your reaction helped me prove a point to myself."

"Oh, yeah?" I lean back in my chair. "And what point would that be?"

"That you like me," he says smugly.

Well, two can play that game. "Gee, what gave it away? The fact I'm on the phone with you or the fact I moved into your stupidly big condo for the week you've been in California?"

"About California…"

Everything shifts. He goes from lighthearted to unnervingly quiet. Warning lights are flashing in my mind, telling me to brace for the impact I've been ignoring but subconsciously waiting for. Ronan is the type of person who belongs in California, after all.

"I need to extend my trip." The statement feels like a stab through my heart. I didn't brace hard enough. "Only for two days. Can you watch Lezak for a couple more days?"

The life I allowed myself to dream of is starting to crumble around me. And the only person I have to blame for it is myself. I can't believe I let myself do this again, let myself actually believe that a woman like me could get someone like Ronan to stick around.

He must take my silence as a no. "It's okay if you're busy, babe. I can see if Bryce or Carter can take him—"

"No, it's fine. I can watch him." I might as well get all the puppy time I can. "Sorry, I was thinking over my schedule. Besides, they would be the worst dog sitters."

"What makes you think that?" His tone is adoring, and I really wish he'd stop talking to me like that. Especially if he's going to end up breaking my heart.

"Bryce would never agree to watch him because Josie would be able to talk him into getting a dog. And Carter would have Lezak so spoiled so quickly." I shake my head even though he can't see me. "I'm not convinced you'd ever get him back."

Ronan lets out another one of those laughs, but this time it feels bittersweet, and I want to run away from it. "Did you just accuse our friend of dognapping?"

"I accused him of having the potential to be a dognapper," I correct. "Tell me I'm wrong."

"I can't," he admits, which makes me feel a little smug.

Silence settles between us again, which means the one question that's on the tip of my tongue comes bubbling out. "So, only two days and then you'll be back?"

The way he sighs into the phone doesn't help my mounting anxiety. "Yeah, that's the plan. We'll see what the next few days bring after this meeting."

"What's the meeting about?" I'm not even sure it's really my place to ask a question like this, but I can't help wondering.

"Just something to do with finances. I'll tell you more about it later. When I get back, though, we should go to dinner. There are some things we need to talk about."

What kind of things? Things like, "They need me back here, so I have to move back to California"? Things like, "There are projects all over the nation that absolutely need Ronan O'Brien and his restless heart can't turn them down"? I don't want to force him to choose between me and Operation Fly. I wish I could know if there was a reason the choice needed to be made.

"Yeah, I think we do," I agree quietly.

"Don't worry about it, baby. I'll be home before you know it."

I wonder if the promise feels as hollow to him as it does to me.

"I'll see you in a couple of days," I assure him. "I gotta go."

Hanging up the phone, I look down at Lezak, who's staring up at me with wide-eyed love. I don't want to lose this. I don't want to lose him—Ronan or the dog—but I feel like I'm sitting on a ticking time bomb and everything's about to go up in pieces. Including my heart.

I look up at the knock on my office door to find Bryce standing there, phone in hand and a grim look on his face. "I heard from Ronan. Do you want to talk about it?"

My brow arches. "Do you want to talk about why you still haven't proposed to Josie?"

He takes a tentative step into the room. "I'll talk if you talk."

Normally, Bryce wouldn't be the first person I'd go to with a feeling like this, but we're on equal footing now. He knows sides of Ronan—pieces of Ronan's life—that I can only hope to. I'm still learning how things shifted for him following the accident. Still learning how to exist in the same place as him, instead of seeing him a couple of times a year. It took me a long time to realize that sometimes it's much easier to have a relationship over the phone than in person.

And I know Josie better than anyone. Maybe aside from the man standing in my office. In that instance, it's not that he knows her better; he knows her differently. I've been there from the beginning of them. I know how anxious he is to get this right; I need to make him understand that there's no such thing as perfect. It has to be right.

"Sit down." I wave him in. He quickly moves into the office, the door swinging shut behind him. If Josie, or anyone else, were to come up here now, they'd assume we're having a marketing meeting and wouldn't disturb us. "Who goes first?"

"You," he spits out before I can say the opposite. I glower at him, but he just smiles. "Mainly because I'm not sure I trust you to hold up your end of the deal. You're not exactly known for opening up, Mia, especially to me."

"So you're holding the information I want to know hostage?"

"Yeah." He chuckles, nodding. "Pretty much."

Bryce Clark is a lot smarter than I give him credit for. "Fair enough. Did Ronan tell you anything about these meetings? He told me they're regarding the future of Operation Fly, but that's it."

Bryce's look is sympathetic, which almost hurts as much as the vagueness of Ronan's explanation. "You're worried it may mean he's not sticking around."

"Obviously," I reply flatly. "I know both you and Carter have talked to him about this. He doesn't stay in one place. He runs."

"He won't run from you, Mia. I can promise you that."

"Do you think he's staying?"

"I think..." He trails off and I want to scream. "I don't think any of us know what Ronan's next move is. Just because I know he won't run from you doesn't mean I necessarily believe he's here to stay."

"If he leaves now, he will break my heart. I don't think I can do that again."

"Mia, you are one of the strongest people I know. If he breaks your heart, we'll break him, and then you'll figure it out. You didn't let Bianca's heartbreak define you and you sure as hell won't let Ronan's, if it even comes to that."

"Didn't I let Bianca's heartache define me? I moved down here, I took the job my best friend's boyfriend offered me—"

"Oh, come on, Mia. We've known each other for over a decade; can't we at least acknowledge we're friends now?" he says.

In the heart of a serious conversation, a laugh bursts from me, which leads to him laughing just as hard. It takes us a minute to settle down, but the moment is still nice. I don't think I've ever had a conversation like this with Bryce; usually we talk about work or I'm threatening him not to break Josie's heart. The truth is, we became friends a long time ago. The first time I saw the way my best friend looked at him, I knew this man was going to break her heart, but I also hoped he'd be the one to put it back together.

"Okay friend, I need your advice then." I wipe the corner of my eye as my laugh dies down. "What do you think I should do about all of this?"

He collects himself. "Ronan and I have a lot in common. We both screwed up things in the past. We're living, breathing proof that people grow up and change for the better. But we're also not perfect. We make mistakes and we run away from our fears sometimes."

"Which brings us to the ring that you've had in your possession for almost *two months*, Bryce."

Bryce holds up a hand, stopping me before I can go any further. "We're still talking about you, Mia." I let out a grumble under my breath. "What do you want to say to Ronan?"

"We are not role playing a conversation with my boyfriend, Bryce. Those conversations are for us to have."

"Maybe, but maybe not. If you tell me everything you want to tell him, you can pick through it and figure out the real message. Push past your own insecurities, push past the pain that still lingers from before, because believe me, I know there's still pain from before, and focus on the now. Top three things you want to say to him, go."

I hate that his logic makes sense. I hate that Bryce is suddenly being more mature than me, especially since he's in a whole different place in his life. One I never thought he'd reach before me. There are things I want to say to Ronan—things that aren't going to be helpful, things that will hurt because of my own fears, and things I want to scream at him for the past.

"I'm waiting," Bryce says.

"Give me a second—damn." Taking a deep breath, I look at Bryce and begin, "Number one, I'm not someone he can come back to when it's convenient for him. Number two, I'm worried there will be a day when I'm not enough for him. Number three, every chance I get, I'll pick him."

Bryce leans back in his chair, looking a little smug. "I asked you to pick the three things you want to say to Ronan but don't feel like you can, and you tell me the three things I think you need to say to him the most."

This whole conversation is becoming frustrating as fuck. When did this asshole get so wise? When did he get so goddamn observant? And how the hell can he pull me out of my shell better than a therapist I've been seeing for months can?

"And if I never get the chance?"

"Then that's on him; not on you," he replies. "I think you need to find a way to say them, for both of you. As your friend, I want you to realize it's okay to be real with people who care about you.

You can tell them when you're hurting or scared. Me, Carter, Kat, and obviously Josie—we're all here for you, no matter what. Ronan is, too. On the off chance you find that he's not, then let him go."

I blink several times to keep the tears at bay. A few break through. "Fuck, Bryce." I wipe at the tears. "You need to warn a girl if you're going to make her cry."

"So, I should preface my proposal by telling Josie she might cry?"

It's an opening. He's said everything he needs to say and is giving me the chance to move on. I appreciate the gesture because I'm not sure I can even fathom words about myself right now. Let alone the precarious place my relationship is teetering in.

"No." I shake my head, grabbing a tissue to dab my eyes. "Do not ruin it. Just tell me why it hasn't happened yet."

He shrugs, picking at a thread on the arm of the chair. "I guess I've been putting a lot of pressure on it—wanting it to be perfect."

"Then hear me when I say nothing public and nothing over the top," I press, repeating myself for what feels like the hundredth time. "Josie will say yes, because it's you, but she won't like it."

"Yeah, I know, I know. I unsubscribed from the extreme proposals newsletter I was getting."

"That exists?" I ask, eyes wide. "Who on Earth would subscribe to—I mean, it makes total sense for someone who has photographers following them around everywhere."

"Thank you," he replies. "I don't want to feel like it'll need a do-over. I want to be absolutely sure she'll love it. She's given me more second chances than I deserve."

"If someone's important enough, I'm not sure we ever run out of second chances," I tell him. "Stop worrying about perfection and start paying attention to timing. The right moment is going to hit you like jamming your finger in a lane line." I grin as he hisses in pain at the metaphor. "Exactly like that. You might have already lost some of those moments by trying to make it bigger and better. Your instincts are good, especially when it comes to Josie."

He looks down, thinking my words over. "Yeah, you're right." He sighs after a few moments. "I need to relax a bit."

"Exactly, but when the time comes, do not tell her you have a surprise for her. Mainly because it's weird; mostly because she will think you got her a puppy and I am not dealing with puppy-less Josie. That might be the only time she says no."

"The no would be a reaction to it not being a puppy, though," he argues, "not the proposal."

"Whatever helps you sleep at night, bud."

He groans, standing from his chair. "Promise me you're not doing anything to encourage her. We cannot get a dog right now."

"I'm doing nothing to encourage her," I swear, holding out my fist. "Thanks for the talk, Bryce."

He raises an eyebrow, but bumps his fist against mine. "Anytime, Mia. And remember—"

"No dog!" I call as he leaves my office.

They're going to have a dog by Halloween, I just know it.

Ronan

"I can't believe you're really doing this." Mel is staring down the paperwork I laid in front of her with wide-eyed bemusement. "Operation Fly is your baby."

I shrug, completely content with my decision, but understanding why she might have some doubts. "I'm still the chairman of the board. I'm just not the president anymore. You are."

"I haven't signed the paperwork yet, Ronan."

I place a pen on top of the stack. "No, but you will. And I know that because you love this place as much as I do. Besides, I've seen all the work you've put into the mission of Operation Fly and in diversifying the sport as a whole. There was never any question about who I wanted to take my place."

Even while she was competing, she made a point of challenging the racial disparities that continue to exist within the sport. Often pointing out that she was only one of four Black people to ever receive a full ride swimming scholarship from her college, and the only woman. Whenever she was in a new city, she would try to do a clinic specifically targeted for Black children who didn't have access to proper swimming lessons, stressing the importance of water safety and the economic challenges that kept these fundamental skills out of reach from marginalized communities.

Although she was a couple years older than me, I'd followed her career closely. The economic divide was evident from the day I started swimming, and the racial divide only became more obvious the longer I was active. Mel is part of the reason I decided to start Operation Fy, her determination to not just talk about change, but make it happen, inspired the hell out of me. I had money from my grandparents that I had done nothing to earn, and I wanted to be part of the change. I just knew I couldn't do it alone.

"And you knew I'd say yes?"

I shrug. "I hoped you would, but that's why I didn't tell anyone back home what the meetings were about; just in case you wanted me to stay on for a little longer while you got used to the position."

Mel is grinning, fiddling with the pen. "You called Columbia home. I don't think I've ever heard you say that word."

I hadn't meant to use it, either. It still scares the shit out of me. "Shut up," I grumble, "and sign the damn papers, Mel."

Still smiling, she pulls the stack closer and uncaps the pen. I watch as she flips through the papers, signing where she needs to. In a few quick flicks of the pen, it's done. I'm no longer doing the day-to-day running of Operation Fly. The business I built from the ground up, the thing that had a real role in bringing me back to life. It doesn't hurt nearly as much as I expected it to. Whether it's because I'm handing it over to someone I trust completely, or because I have a future I want to see through, I don't know.

"Congratulations," I offer, shaking her hand. "You're officially the boss."

"Of everyone else," she corrects, handing over my copy for safe-keeping and tucking her own into her backpack. "Technically, you're the president of the board, so you're still my boss."

"Funny how that works, right?" I grin cheekily at her. "I'll still be hovering, making sure you don't get into trouble."

"What kind of trouble could I possibly get into?"

"I don't want to find out. Please don't make me find out."

With a laugh, she pulls her bag onto her shoulder and follows me out of the conference room. Both of us greet several people as we walk back to my office. Mel's office is right next to it. This office is bigger than the one at Adair, but there's a sterility to it that I'll never have there. Still, there are some things I want to pick up to take back with me. We enter the mostly glass room, Mel immediately collapsing on the comfortable chair I have in the corner.

"Thanks for agreeing not to give me your office." She kicks her feet up onto the small table. I roll my eyes and ignore her. "I did not want to move all my shit."

"Your office is literally next door; it wouldn't have been that hard. But no problem. I'll still need it when I come back to visit anyway."

"Are you selling your condo here?"

"I talked to my realtor yesterday, but nothing is concrete about it," I say, picking up a framed picture of the whole crew from after I made my final Olympics, and Bryce and Carter made their first in 2016. Mia and I were practically on top of each other, Bryce and Josie trying to avoid looking at each other, and Carter was all by himself. Poor guy. The fact that this was the photo I chose to put on my desk should have clued me in faster. "I want to talk to Mia about it."

"Right, Mia!" Mel said her name in a sing-songy way that had me groaning. "Are you blushing, O'Brien?"

"So what if I am?" I teased back, not even trying to deny it. "It's called a love life, Segal. You should try getting one."

Her face scrunched up in defense. "Ew, no thank you. Speaking of your love life, though, are you heading back to her tomorrow?"

The question takes me back to my call with Mia yesterday. While I had reassured her again that I'd be coming home, I had also dropped the bomb that I'd be there two days later. She'd sounded so disappointed and a little lost in her own thoughts. The call started with her normally bubbly self, but by the end of it, I felt like more than one country was between us.

"I had to extend my trip by two days," I tell her, continuing to pack. "I got the summoning call from Declan O'Brien. Text messages, emails, even the receptionist here got them for me."

"Well, there's a name I haven't heard in a while. What does he want?"

"Probably the usual, to scare me into being a good, spoiled rich kid."

"Ugh." She groans. "The travesty. How did he even know you were here? Why is he even here?"

I shrug, turning to lean against my desk. "I don't know. Somehow, he's keeping tabs on me. He either had business here already or he made sure he had a reason to be in the California office. Either way, it's going to suck."

"Better you than me."

⋯⋯ + ₒ ✦ ˙ ✦ ☽ ✦ ˙ ✦ ₒ + ⋯⋯

"I didn't expect to see you."

"Really?" I lean against the back of the chair, ignoring his motion for me to take a seat. I know better than to get too comfortable around Declan O'Brien. "You sent me numerous calendar invites and text messages demanding my presence. I didn't think I had much of a choice. Believe me, I'd rather be almost anywhere else."

"Don't be petulant, son," my father replies. "I called you here to have an adult conversation about what you're doing with your life. Do you think you're capable of that?"

"You want to talk about the life you've purposely ensured you have no part of, unless I'm standing on a podium with a medal around my neck?"

My father sighs, steepling his fingers together and looking at me evenly. "There you go again, making something out of nothing. Why can't you understand that being an O'Brien comes with certain responsibilities that involve making sacrifices?"

My grip on the back of the chair tightens. "I've always been well aware of those responsibilities. When you pushed me until I ended up hating the sport I love, I was aware. When more people fawned over you for it, I was aware. When you only spoke to me when I had a big win or impressive race, I was aware. But how about when I got in an accident that almost cost me my life and neither of you ever came to see me? Or when Bryce Clark had to demand information from you because you didn't even know what hospital I was in? Pretty sure it was him and Carter Abrams who pushed me to learn how to walk again. Are those the sacrifices you made?"

He waves me off. "Your mother and I had meetings. Besides, we'd already taught you to walk once, son. Did you really need us to do it again?"

It's his idea of a joke and he actually thinks he's funny. That accident changed the way I look at a lot of things, including my parents. If this was ten years ago, I would have internally screamed at him to pay a goddamn ounce of attention to me, only to fold, and give in to whatever he wants. Not this time, though.

"Don't kid yourself. You didn't even do it the first time. Sacrifices have to be made, right?" My heart is pounding against my chest, but this is it. This is my moment to tell him everything I've always wanted to and I'm not holding back. "Which nanny was it again, Declan?" Eyes that match mine flash with anger at the use of his first name. "Or did you even keep her around long enough to learn her name?"

He points a bony finger at the chair I'm leaning against. "Sit down, Ronan, and speak to me like an adult."

I stand straight. The only sign of any tension in my body are the fists I keep clenched at my sides. "I'm fine standing. Just say what you need to say so I can go home."

Home. The word bounces around in my head. I can't remember the last time I called some place home and actually meant it. But that's what Columbia is to me now. More importantly, the people who are there make it home.

Mia Sheridan captured my heart the day I caught her in my arms, the Charlotte sun beating down on us. Although we haven't always been in each other's lives, she's never strayed too far from my mind. She was always there, reminding me what it means to lose something good. I'm not going to make that mistake again because, when I think about home, she's who comes to mind.

"It's time we talk about where your future is going," my father says. "You're in your mid-thirties, Ronan. It's time you grew up."

"Pretty sure I've already done that," I say. "I own a nonprofit that has national recognition, I own a condo, survived a life-altering injury, and have several Olympic medals. Maybe your continued absence from my life has caused you to miss some of those milestones."

He doesn't say anything initially, opening a file on his desk and taking the time to scan it instead. "You're throwing away the trust fund your grandparents left you for this silly little project of yours. I will not sit back and watch you throw away their hard work."

"That fund was left for me to do with what I pleased. Besides the age restriction, there were no stipulations placed on it. How do you even know any of this? You haven't had access to my finances in years."

He laughs mirthlessly. "Don't look so surprised, son. You may have taken me off your accounts, but there are still ways around it. I'm one of the richest men in the country and you're my son. Money is power, my boy, you know that."

I hate that he's right. Time and time again, I've witnessed what money can do in the hands of someone who only loves power. It hurts, it ruins, and it destroys. Long ago, I vowed to never be like the man in front of me.

I keep my tone even. "What I do with my money is not your concern. I will be taking extra precautions going forward to ensure you're denied access to that information. I'm well aware of the power money gives you, Declan, but it doesn't give you power over me. Not anymore."

His whole body seems to freeze with a tension I've never seen before, and it's exhilarating. All the things my therapist has said to me over the years about deserving to be free of the power he has over me is making sense. This feeling is intoxicating.

"You don't know what you're saying. Don't be ridiculous." There's a quiver to his voice, the restrained anger threatening to burst through.

I step around the chair to take a seat, a move that makes his eye twitch. Leaning forward with my elbows resting against my arms. "I know exactly what I'm saying. The only reason you called me here is because I'm not following whatever precious plan you had for me, where you could use me to help make you richer."

The corners of his mouth pinch the same way they always did before he started screaming at me; but I'm not a kid anymore, so he can't banish me to my bedroom. "You are wasting your money. You don't take a paycheck from this place. If you put your face on the company more—"

"Nonprofit," I correct. Nonprofit and charity were the equivalent of swear words in my house. My father could never fathom why someone would care about something that didn't immediately benefit him. "I don't need to take a paycheck; I'm doing just fine. I invested the money I made swimming correctly, so that's more than enough to live off. I would rather pay my employees fairly for the amazing work they do, then make myself richer at their expense."

The anger was manifesting itself in the splotchy redness creeping across his cheeks and up his bald head. "You're a disappointment to this family, Ronan."

I lean back in my chair with a casual shrug. "That's not the first time you've said that to me, but here's something I've never said to you: I'm embarrassed to be part of this family, so your disappointment can't hurt me anymore."

"You ungrateful little—"

"On that note"—I stand, ready to be done with this conversation—"there's nothing else for me here. Thanks for the chat—hope it cleared some things up."

I take a step toward the door. I hear things on my father's desk jostle, then a hand is squeezing my arm so hard, I can almost feel a bruise forming. I look down at the hand, then up at my father, who is staring me down. Up this close, I can see the signs of his aging—the wrinkles around his eyes and jaw, the slight sagging of his skin, but I also realize I'm not looking him in the eye anymore. The man who always towered over me and made me feel small even when our heights were matched was now an inch—maybe even two—shorter than me.

"You will regret this. You won't get a damn penny from me!"

I wrench my arm from his grip, watching as it causes him to stumble slightly. "I don't want anything from you. Either of you."

I'm at the door when he speaks again, voice shaking. "You're no longer part of this family, Ronan. Do you hear me?"

The last shred of hope I've spent my whole life hanging onto snaps. "I can't lose what I was never part of, right? You made that decision a long time ago, Declan. I hope life treats you better than you treat it."

The door shakes when I slam it shut behind me. I can hear him screaming my name, followed by a loud crash. His secretary, a woman I've known most of my life because she's never stood up to him, is staring at me with wide, stunned eyes. I stop at her desk, giving her a tight smile. "You might want to add me to the list of banned visitors, Gina."

Her face relaxes, offering me a small smile. "Heading home, dear?"

I smile down at her in return. "I am. Have a good day."

Mia

"Excuse me, Miss Sheridan?"

I spin around to face the woman who'd spoken my name in a polite but firm tone. I'm surprised to be staring at someone who looks like the poster child for swim moms everywhere with a tone that deserves to be commanding boardrooms. Her smile is warm, but professional.

"That's me." I smile, tucking a strand of hair behind my ear. "What can I help you with?"

"It's nice to meet you! My name is Rachel Smith. My daughter Daisy swims on Coach Ronan's team." The girl in question instantly pops into my mind. She and Emmie have gotten close, clicking almost immediately. I've heard Ronan and Bryce, reminding them to focus on practice.

"Right." I shake her hand. "It's nice to meet you, too. Daisy is a great kid and a wonderful swimmer."

Rachel flushes in the way all doting parents do when someone compliments their kid. It's the same prideful look Ronan gets when Lezak learns a new trick. "Thank you. I was wondering if I could speak with you about a job offer?"

Well, that's certainly not what I was expecting to hear right as practice is about to start. I was about to retreat to the gym for a quick workout. "Oh, that's very nice, but I'm in the process of building—"

"Your own freelance marketing business, I know. Bryce told me when I asked who does the marketing for Adair. I'm looking to hire an independent marketing professional for the business I run with my wife. Is there somewhere quiet we can talk?"

I blink, but recover my surprise quickly. "Sure. We can go up to my office or go outside?"

Rachel agrees to stepping outside, since it's not too hot. Before long, the two of us are sitting across from one another at a picnic table. Rachel slides a dark green folder across the table to me.

"My wife and I own a number of restaurants and bars in both Columbia and Charleston," she begins. "Bryce told me you like to work with people who have causes. I'd like to chat about some of the things we believe in. First, we locally source as much product from South Carolina farmers as possible, but all our products are organic and ethically sourced, regardless. Secondly, and most importantly, my wife was formerly a social worker and has seen firsthand the difficulty children face when they age out of a system that doesn't always work in their favor. Over seventy-five percent of our workforce is made up of kids who are about to age out or have aged out but don't know where to go."

I feel an itch under my skin, a dozen or more ideas already bubbling up in my head. "And you would want me to handle the marketing for the restaurants?"

She smiles. "Exactly. Our last marketing person didn't seem to care about the vision we had or the difference we were making in these kids' lives. We provide a sense of normalcy, teach them a positive work ethic, and help them learn what to expect from the outside world. I think you'd be perfect to take this over."

"I would love the opportunity to present my portfolio and a list of references—"

"Mia, I've looked through your portfolio, read the testimonials, and even looked at the work you did under your former employer in Charlotte. As far as we're concerned, this is a done deal if you agree. The contract, description of work, and everything else can be found in this folder. Take your time, look it all over—even have a lawyer look it over if you'd like. I'm willing to wait for you. The only way we're pursuing any other options is if you turn us down."

From the window overlooking the deck, I can see Ronan and Bryce talking. It doesn't take me long to realize they're talking about me. Between Ronan's look of frustrated confusion and the way Bryce keeps motioning toward the window, despite neither one of them knowing I'm in the building tells me enough. I don't know what they're saying, but part of me wants to go down there and handle it myself instead of making Bryce do it. The other half of me is tired of being the only one who fights for me. So, I let it go this time.

I still haven't decided what to do about the Ronan situation. He hasn't given me any sort of honest explanation about what kept him in California and whether or not it'll take him away again. But I also haven't given him the chance to explain. He got in late last night after I told him I couldn't pick him up at the airport due to a freelance client, but then I was already in bed when he got home. He'd called my name in the dark, but I'd pretended to be asleep, my heart twinging when he pressed a kiss to my shoulder. After not getting much sleep, and his exhaustion from a cross-country trip, I was able to sneak out before he woke up.

I've been avoiding him since.

I'm surrounded by Olympic gold medalists, but if there was a chance to win one in avoiding conflict, I'd be the most decorated Olympian of all time—not Michael Phelps.

Ronan glances up toward the window, eyes lighting up when he sees me. He gives me a wink that has me frozen on the spot before excusing himself and heading down the deck. I watch Bryce sigh before looking up toward the window, shaking his head when he sees me.

I think we might be getting written up by HR.

I grab my drink and settle onto the couch with my laptop and the folder Rachel gave me. I'm not in the mood to have some long, drawn-out reunion with Ronan, but it'd probably be in our best interest if I didn't completely ignore him.

"Hey, gorgeous," he greets when he enters the room.

I look up at him and fight the swooping feeling of my heart. He looks good. Well-rested and refreshed in a way I've always associated with California. And that's just another pierce to my heart. Because why would he want to stay here when California treats him like that?

"When did you get here?" I don't get up, keeping my tone casual as I flip open the folder, looking through the paperwork but not really taking in any of it.

He hesitates by the chair. "About an hour ago. What are you up to?"

"Hmm?" I feign being interested in what's in front of me, looking up at him with a smile. "Oh. I'm looking over some information a potential client gave me. Figuring out if it's something I want to move forward with."

It is. I know it is. I read the package front to back a couple times and showed it to both Bryce, who sang Rachel's praises the way he apparently sang mine, and Josie. Both of them are in agreement that this is an opportunity I should take.

I'm not sure I'm ready to share this news with Ronan, though. What difference does it make if he knows the truth when he's probably not going to stick around long enough to see it come true?

"Yeah?" he asks. "Are you thinking about taking it?"

"I am. It's a long-term contract. I'll have a better idea of my monthly income with it." The vagueness of my answer puts a bitter taste in my mouth. Hadn't we just spent glorious weeks tearing those walls down brick by brick? And now I'm building them back up.

I'm tired of destroying, only to rebuild.

"That sounds like a great opportunity. I'm happy for you."

He's happy for me, but not happy enough with me to stay, to see where this thing could really take us and find out if it'd be as magical as I always wondered.

"Mia." His tone is gentler now, quieter. "I think there's been a misunderstanding about what's going on here."

I fake a look of pure innocence when I tilt my head. "I have no idea what you mean, Ronan."

"Can you come over tonight?"

That's the last thing I want to do. Why would I give him the opportunity to break up with me in person?

But there's still a small part of me that's holding onto the hope that I'm wrong. Maybe he doesn't want to break up with me. Maybe he doesn't want to tell me he's moving back to California.

It's stupid to hold any hope around this, but I can't help it. I want to believe he's not capable of abandoning people the way he was before.

"Mia, please. I have news I want to share with you, and there are some things we need to clear up."

"Fine," I relent. "Do you have practice tonight?"

"Uh, no. Bryce wasn't sure when I'd get back, so he was already planning to lead it. He wants us to figure things out first."

Because Ronan is moving away and Bryce would be the one to take over, having the most experience as a freestyler.

"I'll be there at six." I stand from the couch. "Now, if you'll excuse me, I need to call the owner of this company and tell her I accept her offer."

"I can't wait to hear about it!" Ronan calls happily, but I close my office door behind me.

Ronan

Dressed in jeans and a burnt orange top, Mia is standing on my porch. She has been standing on my porch for a few minutes now, actually. Except she's not knocking on the door, she's not ringing the doorbell, and she's not using the copy of the key I know she still has. I look down at Lezak, who's sitting patiently by my side. He looks back up at me, tail swishing across the floor.

Neither of us have an answer to her behavior.

Eventually, I swing the door open and stare down at her with a frown. "How long have you been out here and why do you hate knocking so much?"

Normally, that would make her smile, but this time, her face remains stoic. Something in my gut twists. Is this not about to be the kind of conversation I thought we were having?

As much as I don't want to admit it, there's only one way to find out.

"Come in, baby." I feel her relax slightly as I take her hand in mine, leading her inside. "I hope you haven't eaten yet."

She's chewing at her bottom lip. "I haven't, but—"

"Great." I don't want to hear an excuse as to why she can't stay. I have things to say; she has things to say. "I ordered takeout."

She grabs my wrist, pulling me to a stop before I can lead her to the kitchen. I look down at her. "Ronan, we need to talk."

"Yeah. I thought we could do it while we eat?"

She's shaking her head, tears clouding her eyes. "I can't eat. I need answers."

"Baby," I mutter, reaching out to stop a tear before it can fall. "Why are you crying?"

"Bryce and I talked after you extended your trip—two friends sitting down and talking." That's a confusing way for her to start a story. "I wanted to know why he wasn't proposing to Josie, and he wanted to know how I was feeling about you leaving."

"What?" I frown. "Why would that be any of his business? He knew I was coming back. You both did."

A wounded look on her face takes my breath away. "We weren't sure we believed it," she whispers, and my heart drops to my stomach. "And I'm not sure I believe your presence here now isn't the beginning of goodbye. I just...he made me realize there are some things I need to say to you—a lot of things actually—but there are three things I have to tell you."

"Okay." I'm frowning down at her, and Lezak is weaving around between us, like he can sense the tension, too. Of course he can; he just doesn't understand. Which makes two of us. "What is it?"

"I want a partner, Ronan," she whispers. "I can't be someone you pick when it's convenient for you."

I take a step closer, reaching up to cup her cheek. The way she leans into it lights a spark of hope. "Baby, I want that, too."

Her eyes flutter open. "The second thing. If this is going to work out, you need to know there's a part of me that's scared I won't be enough for you one day."

One sentence. That's all it took for my heart to break. Not for me, but for someone else. For someone who brings so much joy, happiness, and light to this world but can't see it in herself. For the woman before me who loves so deeply, scientists will spend forever trying to figure out the depth she holds. I'm going to bask in it for as long as she lets me.

"I can be a lot for people," she rattles on. "I try not to be, but something always slips up. And I know there are things I should fix—"

"Hey, hey," I soothe, pushing her hair back. "Mia Sheridan, you are enough for me. You're too good for me in a lot of ways. As for this idea of fixing things, there's not a single thing I see that needs fixing."

Her lip wobbles again, but she sucks in a deep breath. "Bianca—"

"Fuck Bianca. She's the one who wasn't enough; she's the one who wanted to make you into what she wanted. Mia, I'm telling you, right here, where I stand, you are whole and beautiful. You are more than I could ever dream of having and if you choose me for the rest of your life, or the rest of the week, I know how lucky I am to have you."

A beautiful, blinding smile breaks across her features, so blinding I can't bring myself to look at it. I lean down, brushing the softest of kisses against her lips, but pull back as she tries to chase me for more. My lips move to both of her cheeks, kissing away tears and the tracks they left.

Her hand tightens on my wrist. "Wait, Ronan, I still have another thing."

Right, a third thing. I pull back, giving her my full attention. "Okay, what is it?"

"That every chance I get, I'll pick you."

I stare at her, dumbfounded. Did those words really come out of her mouth? Did she almost take my thunder away from me? Not that I care. I'm not one of those guys who has to say the four-letter word first, but I had a whole damn date night—The date night!

With a grin, I tangle our fingers together and tug her toward the kitchen. Lezak trots ahead of us.

I'd missed hearing her laugh bouncing off the walls of my house when I was in California. Hearing it now reminds me that this is home. She is home. The people in our lives are home. "Ronan, aren't you going...Oh, my god."

She skids to a stop in the doorway of the kitchen, taking in the sight before her. The table is set with dark purple napkins and ombre purple glasses, lit with dark candles. Our dinner is in the oven, waiting to be served. There is a huge bouquet sitting in the middle of the table, three cards worked into the display.

"Kat helped with the setting," I murmur. "The flowers are for you."

"Ronan, what..." I cut her off with a nudge toward the flowers. She closes the distance, letting out a wet laugh when she sees the tarot cards nestled into the bouquet. She turns to me. "I thought you didn't believe in tarot?"

I wind my arms around her, pressing her back against my chest and resting my chin on her shoulder. Her hands come up to rub my forearms, one finger dipping down to trace the outline of my Olympic rings tattoo. I turn it until she has full access. "It's kind of hard not to believe when the person who read the cards got everything right."

She tilts her head to look at me, smirking. "I did, did I?"

"Mm-hmm. I could have taken whatever my father offered me. I could have lived a life without responsibilities, but that's not what I wanted. It wouldn't be a life and I'd always be under his thumb. So, I took a chance to focus on a new outlook. As for standing up for what I believe in, that's what I was doing in California."

She turns in my arms; her surprised eyes searching mine. Her hands are resting on my chest now, mine having dropped to her waist. "What do you mean?"

"I'm no longer president of Operation Fly," I admit. "I resigned and promoted my VP, Mel Segal."

She gasps. "Ronan, why would you do that?"

"Because that position would eventually take me away from my home, sometimes for months at a time, and I didn't want that. I'm still the chairman of the board and I'll still need to be in San Francisco occasionally, but this gives me more flexibility to be here." I rub gentle circles against her side. "It gives me the flexibility to work with my team, support my friends, and continue to fall in love."

"Love?" she whispers.

I press my grin against hers. "I'm still on the Seven of Wands, baby. My priority is living my life and finding a home for myself. When my father called, I knew I needed to deal with it. I called to ask you to watch Lezak a little longer so I could do that. We fought. The kind of fight you can't come back from, but in the end, he's happy because he gets to keep his money and wash his hands of his washed-up son."

I can see the way she wants to protest. She wants to try to figure out ways to fix it, so I kiss her again before she can. This one a little longer, a little deeper, but still a kiss for the sake of a kiss.

When we part, I tell her, "Don't try to fix it, gorgeous. I made my choice a long time ago. I feel free in a way I didn't before, but I hope you weren't banking your happy ending on another trust fund coming my way because that thing has been dissolved."

"Another?" She arches her brow. "And you lost it? Well, that might change everything."

I pull her closer when she tries to pull away, both of us laughing. This time, when we try to come back together, it's a disaster, our smiles getting in the way.

"And The Lovers card?"

"That one's easy," I tell her, winding my arms around her to pull her close again. "You see, there's this woman I know who will pick me every time, but that's not really necessary. Recently, I realized something important—something I'd been blissfully blind to before."

"Yeah? What's that?"

I press my forehead against hers. "You. It's always been you, Mia. When I think of home, I think of the people we surround ourselves with. I think of us turning this place into something warm and cozy, having Lezak with me at the pool, but at the center of it all is *you*. Because you are my home and I'm sorry I spent so long away."

"Ronan," she breathes. "I love you, Ronan."

She still beat me to those three words, but at least I got to say everything I needed to. At least I got the chance to say what has been weighing me down for so long.

As she collapses against me, both of us allowing ourselves to be lost in a kiss, I'm happier than I've ever been. I've spent my whole life looking for somewhere I belong, but it turns out that it's not a place. It's someone. It's many people. It's a small family I've spent years building, constructing it out of the people I can't be without.

"I love you, too," I murmur.

Mia shifts in my arms, turning her face to press against my side. Her warm breath ghosts against my skin. The house is still and quiet in the early morning. Not even Lezak is up yet, but I can't bring myself to go back to sleep. An anxious buzz has taken over me, but it's not in a bad way this time.

Mia and I talked a lot over dinner last night. I explained why I kept things from her and expressed my fears behind them, elaborated on how ruin follows me wherever I go. She shared her own fears of being left and how my lack of communication ignited those fears. We worked through those remaining issues, apologizing when those needed to be said. We made commitments to one another and the relationship we were hoping to build. We talked for hours, with Lezak asleep at my feet and the dishes left forgotten, when we finally made our way to bed.

We had tumbled into the covers, clothes lazily coming off one another. There was no frenzy, no biting passion. We took our time with one another, got to know each other's bodies as fully as possible. She found a spot on the inside of my upper thigh that I didn't know could bring the sounds out of me that it did. Then again, maybe it's Mia. I finally got to see what it looked like when she came apart on my tongue and fingers. Each second that passed between us was charged with something different from burning passion. It was contentment.

And as I pulled her into my arms, watching her fight sleep after the magical night we had, I knew this was where I wanted to be. I wanted to be here yesterday, today, tomorrow, and forever if she'll have me.

I will be the luckiest man alive if this gets to be my forever. If there's any higher being out there listening to me, I beg and plead that I don't do anything stupid to mess this up again.

With my free hand, I reach out to grab my phone from the nightstand. I scan the notifications to see if I missed any important messages. Part of me contemplates sending Bryce and Carter a text to tell them I'm staying, but it doesn't feel right. Text messages, avoiding confrontation, and taking the easy way out are how I handled things before. If I'm serious about this being a fresh start, I should probably work on changing that approach.

"You better not text them."

I look down, expecting to be met with eyes that make my heart soar, but Mia's eyes are still closed. And her face is still pressed against me.

"How did you possibly know what I was thinking?"

One hazel eye pops open and I can see half her smile. "Because I know you, Ronan. You may not be running away, but you hate confrontation and that's not going to vanish. But you owe them more than that."

I set the phone down on the bed with a groan. "Guys text each other their big news; we don't make some big declaration."

"Bryce and Carter do."

"Yeah, but Bryce and Carter also have matching tattoos." It's a joke, but I know what she means by it. "Unfortunately, there are still a lot of men out there who do the bro thing instead of being real with their friends."

"And is that the type of man you want to be? Especially to two guys who stepped up for you in your darkest moment?" Her questions are quiet. I wonder if she's scared to ask them, despite already knowing the answer.

The truth is, I don't know how to have the kind of friendship Bryce and Carter have. Besides them, I've never had real friends. People have always wanted something from me. While she's working on believing me when I tell her I'm staying, I'm working on opening up to people and trusting them to accept me as I am. And whether she realizes it extends to friendship or not, these are the traits that made her think I wasn't coming back.

"Put yourself in their shoes. If either one of them worked for you and thought about quitting—"

"I haven't thought about quitting in over a month," I argue. "I had to sort some stuff out before I told anyone I was staying."

"And decided not to let any of us in on your thought process," she replies with a poke to my chest.

I can tell by her teasing tone that she's not mad at me about what happened, not anymore. But she isn't going to let this go until I figure out a better way to tell our friends the truth. For that, I think I'll need her help.

"What do you think I should do?"

She shrugs. "How about you look them in the eye and tell them the truth?"

I know it's that simple, but I've never allowed myself to believe it. I've never allowed myself to trust that I can be transparent with someone and they'll accept what I tell them. I know my job isn't in jeopardy, and I know the two of them would never kick me out or be mad at me for wanting to stay. They've repeatedly told me they want me to stay. Being this vulnerable with them, though, is something I haven't done since we were all in a hospital room and rehabilitation center.

Mia and I barely make it to the club in time for my practice. I had every intention of arriving early and having plenty of time to talk to them, but when a beautiful woman pulls you on top of her with a wicked smile, you lose sense of time. Or, rather, you forget to set an alarm to wake you up from the nap that's sure to follow.

When we walk into the lobby, Bryce and Carter are going over the workout plan I had given them. Loud teenager chatter echoes from the locker room. It feels good to walk through the doors of Adair, knowing I have no plans of ever walking out of them indefinitely. It is yet another space where I feel comfortable and confident in my own skin—a space I can keep coming back to.

"That took me months to come up with—don't fuck it up!"

Their heads snap toward me, confusion creasing their brows as I stand before them with a smile.

Bryce is the first to crack. "You're back. And you're here."

I hold in my groan. "I was never not coming back! Jesus."

"Well, Mia can be pretty convincing when she's sure of something. So, when are you leaving?"

The question stings. I can't pretend it doesn't. Despite him pointing the blame toward Mia, it's clear he was expecting me to come in here and announce that I think they have a handle on things and wish them luck with it before I head out to the next great adventure. Except this is the greatest adventure I've ever had, and I want to stick around to see it through.

Mia nudges me in the side. I guess now is as good a time as any.

"About that...I'm not."

Bryce and Carter exchange a look that's full of silent communication. It's the same look Mia and Josie give one another. Then they look back at me with small frowns. They really do spend too much time together.

"Not what?" Carter finally asks.

"Not leaving," I reply with a bright smile. "That trip to California was never meant to be a precursor of me leaving. It was me tying up some loose ends with who I'm handing the reins to at Operation Fly."

Bryce balks. "Wait, what? You're giving up your organization to come out here and work for us? That's not what we wanted you to do, Ronan."

"Operation Fly is in good hands. I have enough coaches and other team members for it to run without me. I'm still on the board, so there will obviously be times I need to be there for something, but the day-to-day is not my responsibility anymore. It hasn't been for a long time; I just made it official. And then I came home."

Bryce looks to Mia. I don't know what he sees in her features. I keep my gaze locked on him. Whatever he sees, though, must calm him since he turns back to me and holds out the clipboard and stopwatch. "You got a bunch of teenagers to coach. That's what I hired you for."

I reach out and grab everything. I turn to give Mia a quick kiss before I head out onto the deck, needing to make sure everything is in order for today's practice. Just as I'm about to walk out of the lobby, I hear Mia murmur a "Shut up, Clark" and my grin grows.

"What do you want to talk about today?"

Over the last several months, Joy and I have started a lot of sessions this way. Mostly during our sessions when I felt like being stubbornly quiet despite the thoughts and emotions whirling around in my head. She'd ask the question, a gentle prod to get me to open up, but I rarely ever did. Today, though, is going to be different.

"Ronan is staying."

I'm smiling so big my cheeks hurt. I see the briefest flash of surprise on Joy's face before she's smiling with me. She's not radiating the same elated happiness I am—not that I expect her to, but I can tell she's happy with the news. Happy about what it means for me going forward. Which is good, because I'm happy, too.

"That's wonderful news, Mia." She sets her pen down on her notebook. "I know you've had concerns about his ability to settle down and stay in one place. How are you feeling about this announcement?"

"Like I can finally let the past go and focus on my future," I admit, which earns me a brighter smile. "The whole time he was in California, I was terrified that was it. Something would happen and he'd decide to stay, even though he kept telling me he was coming back."

Joy picks her pen up, scratching a quick note across the page. "That makes sense, though. Humans base their fears off experiences. You have had a history of people choosing themselves over you, despite how hard you try and of no fault of your own. Have you talked about these fears with Ronan?"

"We talked about it a lot over the last couple of days," I tell her. "He promised to be better at giving me the details I need to be assured I'm not getting left, and I promised to work on fearing he won't come home every time he leaves."

"Do you know what that sounds like to me, Mia?"

"Healthy communication within a relationship?" This is something Joy and I discussed a lot in the aftermath of Bianca—all the ways she refused to give me that basic necessity of a relationship.

"Yes! Now, talk to me about what this is bringing up for you in regards to your past relationships."

"Ronan is helping me realize where things fell through with Bianca, like lack of communication," I explain, picking my words carefully. "I know I wasn't perfect in my last relationship, and that she probably views me as the villain in her story, but it's okay to be both the villain and the victim in a relationship. As long as you're willing to admit that, while you were hurt almost irreparably, you also weren't perfect."

"That's a wise observation." Joy nods, jotting something down. "I like how you recognize that you can be the bad guy in her variation and still be the victim in yours. You don't know what she says about your relationship, and there's no reason for you to know or care if she's taking any responsibility. The important thing is you're recognizing the parts that hurt you and the parts you might have slipped up."

"And I don't want to make those same mistakes again. I know our lives will not always be perfect. This isn't some fairy tale or movie—it's life and we both have baggage. But we want to get better at communication. We've already started discussing couples therapy to help us with that. I want to stop thinking everyone is going to leave."

"I think therapy is a wonderful idea, Mia," Joy nods encouragingly. "I want to focus on that last bit, though. People leaving. Remind me again who's left."

My skin prickles at the shift in topic. "My parents, Bianca, and…"

I can't think of anyone else, but I know that when she first asked me that question there were four people total, and now, I can only think of three.

She's smiling knowingly at me. "The first time I asked you that question, you listed some guy you used to know. The absence of that person tells me it was Ronan."

She's right, I realize. I used to include Ronan in that last, but I never gave her details or shared how much it hurt. But I guess it doesn't hurt anymore.

"And you know what that tells me? That even though people sometimes leave, they can come back. Just like Ronan did."

"I don't know where I'd be if he didn't," I admit.

"You would have been fine, Mia. The dependence of happiness does not rest on him alone. He's part of your happiness, yes. The same way every other person is and, guess what, those people have left and might come back. Just like Ronan."

"Josie has never left," I point out.

"Yes, because Josie is your person. You know I've always liked Josie and I'm sure she wouldn't go even if she was dragged away."

"No, I know she's not going anywhere." It's a relief to know she's always going to be by my side and have my back. Just like I have hers.

"Do you want those other people to come back?" Joy questions. "Would they enrich your life if they came back?"

My parents are living their lives, the lives they always dreamed about having once I graduated. It might have hurt like hell to have them leave, but their happiness matters as much as mine. I don't even have a bad relationship with them, and I know how content they are. I wouldn't want to take that from them. And Bianca is a simple answer. Had there been a time I wanted her to come back? Maybe, but it's long gone.

"No," I admit. "Definitely not Bianca. My parents coming back would enrich my life, but at the cost of their own happiness, and I won't do that to them."

Joy nods, resting her hands on her notepad with a smile. "You've found your people, Mia. You don't need to cling to them; they're not going anywhere."

Did I just win therapy?

"Now, we're out of time for today, but I'll see you back here in two weeks."

Nope, I guess not.

······ + ₒ ✦ ✫ ☽ ✫ ✦ ₒ + ······

A couple of nights later, Ronan and I are surprised to see Emmie sitting at the picnic table when we leave Adair. Practice ended almost half an hour ago, but there she was, reading a book.

"Hey, kiddo," I greet, moving away from my boyfriend. She turns to smile up at me, nodding when I motion to the bench across from her. "What are you doing here? Where's Liam?"

She bites back a grin. "He was on a job site with Katrina. Apparently, there was an accident. He's fine!" She adds the last part when

Ronan, who had taken the seat beside me, and I exchange worried looks. "Something about paint exploding all over him. He got stuck there longer, texted to tell me what happened, but I told him to stop by the apartment to change and shower. I know Coach Bryce is here for at least another hour, usually, so I told Liam he approved it."

I suck my bottom lip in to keep from laughing; Ronan is fighting his own amusement.

"Next time, come tell one of us, okay?" he says. "I know you can navigate this whole city on your own, but we have a responsibility and want to know if you're staying on property late."

"Ronan's right," I add with a nod. "Did you want us to give you a ride home?"

"No, it's okay. He should be here in like ten minutes. Can I ask you something, Coach?"

"Of course," he replies immediately.

"I saw some articles about what you were like when you were younger."

A hot flush works its way up my boyfriend's cheeks, and I reach out to grab his hand. He clears his throat. "What about them?"

"Were you really that big of a jerk?"

"He was never a jerk," I cut in before he has the chance to say anything. Emmie's eyes drift to me, clearly confused. "Josie and I met these guys for the first time in 2015, so I'm a trustworthy source. He was young, popular, and talented, and he fell into some partying. The newspapers got a hold of it thanks to his popularity and blew it out of proportion."

"I'm not going to pretend like I don't have a past, Emmie," Ronan jumps in. "Sticking to this sport for the fame and attention and sticking to it for love and passion have two different outcomes. I'm proof of that. There are things I did in my early twenties that I regret, but I can't change them. That's why I always want to make sure you guys are doing this because you want to. Along the way in my career, it became a job I dreaded going to, and I didn't have the opportunity to regain my love for it until I couldn't compete."

"The accident," she murmurs.

He must have told his team about the accident. Since his parents erased every trace of their golden boy's fall, there's no way any of us would know he was involved without being told. He did everything right, and a drunk driver took his career from him, and the life of his Uber driver.

He sighs. "Yes. A couple of stupid actions turned into who I was in the eye of the swimming world. There were times I leaned into it—because having a reputation means you're less likely to disappoint people—but it's not who I was. Just like with any sport, especially at a level you're aspiring to be at, it can have its downfalls and its dangerous areas. You'll be faced with choices, and I can't make them for you. I can only remind you, and every one of your teammates, that your past follows you. You can't run from it because it will outrun you. So, try to make choices you can always be proud of. It won't be perfect, but owning your decisions makes them yours."

"And if you ever need someone to talk to, your brother is there for you," I add, reaching out to squeeze her arm. "Ronan, Carter, and Bryce have all faced the choices you'll have to face, so use them as the resources they are. They're going to do their best to guide you, but they can't help you with what they don't know about."

"And you?" she asks, surprising me. "Can I come to you for advice? I know it may be weird, but I'm a girl surrounded by a ton of testosterone. I need girl power."

"Absolutely. But you want to know a secret?" She perks up and nods. "These guys aren't fazed by anything, and they may surprise you. They're hardcore feminists, all three of them."

Her eyes go comically wide as she turns to Ronan. My boyfriend nods. "Screw the patriarchy."

She beams at me. "That's really cool."

I wonder what it must feel like to be her age and know there are men out there who are as pissed off as we are. That are willing to stand up and help us fight until our voices are heard. Women and young girls are ignored every single day, especially in their sports and in their jobs; and every single day, Emmie gets to come to a club that will fight for her right to be there, to be seen, to be heard, and to be taken seriously. At Adair, her role in her sport is as important as any of her male identifying teammates. It warms my heart to know I get to be part of it.

"But I'm still not asking Coach Ronan if he has a tampon."

Ronan's face turns bright red at the out-of-nowhere statement, but clears his throat. "They're always in my bag."

"Really?" Even that surprises me. I was about to tell her where she could find them in our office.

"Yeah, of course," he replies. "Being a coach means showing up for my entire team, no matter what."

A car horn blares as it pulls into the parking lot. Emmie barely glances at it before standing and darting toward it. She waves over her shoulder with a shout that she will see us tomorrow.

I lean into Ronan's side. "You're pretty incredible, you know that?"

He kisses the top of my head. "It's nice to be reminded. I looked at what you brought over when you stayed; my bathroom is stocked, by the way. Pain relief supplies, too."

I squint up at him. "Are you sure you don't have a little sister hiding somewhere?"

"My parents hated me. Why would they have another?"

It's so easy for him to make light of the situation, and I have to respect that, but with each self-deprecating joke, I need to remind him of how loved he is. I kiss his shoulder, looking up at him through my lashes. "If anyone ever calls you a jerk again, they'll have me to answer to."

"Oh, thank god. I was getting so tired of defending myself. I've been waiting for a badass woman to come into my life to do it for me."

"You joke, but I know there's a part of you that feels that way."

He kisses me, laughing against my lips. "We're the kind of couple that fights for each other."

Yes, we are. Him and me against the world. Plus, a family that we sort of adopted tagging along. Still, us against the world.

Ronan

Adair Swim Club has never been this packed, and it sends a thrill through me. The meet is nothing major, but it's the first in the season. And, more importantly, for some of my swimmers, it's the first time they'll get on a block. It could go about a hundred different ways because a swimmer never knows how a race is going to turn out until they get in the water and swim it.

I pull my gaze from the warm-up pool to scan the crowd for familiar faces. Both Carter and Bryce are helping me out by keeping the kids organized and motivated, making sure they get to their lane on time. It's a single day meet, and I can already see some of them starting to drag.

The rest of the Adair Swim support is out in full swing, and almost everyone is wearing the shirts Mia designed. My eyes land on the section with my girlfriend in it and immediately find her. She's grinning brightly, talking to Josie about something, and her dark hair is flowing with every movement of her head. Kat is next to them, with Liam at her side, who looks like he might throw up. I bite back a grin. If Emmie goes as far as I think she can go, Liam has a lot more nauseating moments ahead of him. He should pace himself.

Emmie's final is up next, she has the top time going into the final. I remember when I raced at her age, desperate to pull out a fast time to impress my parents. Emmie, though, is relaxed as she shakes her muscles out. A cool confidence about her that comes from trusting in herself, in her training, and in knowing she won't lose love if she doesn't win.

It's her first final she's ever swam. The hundred-yard freestyle.

I might be feeling as sick to my stomach as Liam is. I don't have favorite swimmers, but there are definitely ones closer to my heart.

"You ready?" I ask her. She's fixing the braid her hair is in before she puts on her cap. She nods. "This is your first final ever, Emmie. No one is expecting fireworks, but if you trust yourself and everything we've been working on—"

"I could have fireworks?" She grins cheekily.

"Let's start with sparklers and work up to fireworks," I offer with a laugh.

The swimmers are called for the race. Emmie flashes me one last grin and I move to stand next to Bryce, crossing my arms over my chest and training my eyes on the blocks. I don't know why I have this nervous energy in me, why I feel the need to jump up and down to try and work it out. I feel like we're on the edge of something, but I don't know if it's good or bad. Maybe I should have had Mia do a tarot reading for the outcome of this meet.

No, that would be a bad idea.

"Dude, you need to chill," Bryce mutters, the coach of the high school standing on his other side. "She's going to do fine."

"I know," I reply. But do I know? "This is her first final, and she's been working so hard. Plus, her reaction time isn't exactly where we want to see it and—"

"And all that can be fixed in practice later. Let's focus on the now."

Take your marks.

My gaze jumps to the starting blocks, zeroing in on Emmie, my only swimmer, to make the final. The buzzer sounds, and they're off.

It's fireworks.

Not sparklers, not sparks from a fire starting—it's fireworks.

Emmie gets a National Age Group record in the 100-yard freestyle in her first ever meet. Not only does she break the record, she smashes it by almost two full seconds. The sound in the pool is silent as we wait for the results to be official, and then it's just an explosion of noise. Emmie's screaming as she jumps up and down, surrounded by her team who immediately congratulate her. When she launches herself at me for a hug, on her way to get to her brother, she whispers two small words with so much meaning behind them. *"Thank you."*

And I couldn't be prouder.

"So, what's the plan now?" Bryce asks. "Is she wanting to work toward Trials? See if she can make the team?"

I laugh lightly. "If you ask her brother, the first priority is graduating from high school and getting into a good college."

"But..." he presses.

"But if a trip to Los Angeles for the Olympics is part of that, I think he'd be okay with it."

He chuckles. "You're gonna have your hands full, O'Brien. Which is why I'm almost hesitant to ask, do you think you could take on another one?"

My brow furrows. "What are you talking about? Is there another kid you want me to...*Holy shit.*"

When I look at Bryce, he's not looking at me. He's staring out at the pool, a look of longing in his eyes. All those early morning swims, the long sessions in the gym, the few times he's had me time him...it was all starting to click into place.

"Are you fucking kidding me, Clark?"

"I want to go out on my own terms," he comments. "My shoulder is feeling better than it has in years and I miss it."

"Have you talked to Josie about this?"

"Not yet, but I know she'll be excited," he assures me. The last thing I need is his fiancée thinking I talked him into this somehow. "Now all I need is a coach, and there is no one better."

"Don't let Carter hear you say that." It's a joke, but my mind is spinning a hundred miles a minute.

Bryce is giving me yet another reason to stick around. I don't think that's his intent in asking me, but it's there. Plus, I'd seen it in his gaze. There has been a wistfulness there for the last few months; I was just waiting for him to say something.

"Carter's my best friend and I wouldn't have accomplished any of the things I have without him, but this is different. I don't need someone in my corner; I need someone who's not afraid to kick my ass," Bryce says.

I remember watching the Tokyo Games, watching how Bryce could barely pull himself out of the water. There's a difference between being able to see that someone is in pain and knowing firsthand what that pain feels like. I hated watching that, especially when he'd given his all to that race. He got the gold, but I knew it might have been at the cost of the rest of his career.

"You weren't done."

It's not a question, nor is it a statement that needs an answer. It's the truth and we both know it. I've heard about how he coached Carter through his final year, stressing how important it is to make sure you're done. To make sure you're not leaving this sport behind with regrets.

God, I have so many regrets.

"I'm not done. So, man, what do you say? You want to stick around long enough to help a washed-up Olympian make a comeback?"

My brow arches. "Are we calling it a comeback?"

He laughs. "Hell no."

"Then I'm in." I turn enough to shake his hand, which he accepts. "Looks like I'm planning to send two swimmers to the Olympics."

The irony that one of them will be thirty-four while the other won't even be twenty isn't lost on either one of us.

"I guess I should probably go tell my fiancée," he declares, standing. "Seriously, man, Carter and I brought you on for a reason. A reason you just proved. We're happy you're sticking around."

Involuntarily, my gaze drifts past him to where Mia is making her way toward me, stopping to chat with some parents and other swimmers along the way. A warm comfort settles in the pit of my stomach.

I look back toward Bryce, standing as I do so. "I can't thank you enough for giving me this opportunity. I never thought I'd find somewhere I want to stay."

"It's not the somewhere, dude," he replies. "It's the someone."

He means Mia. I know he does, but there's more to it than that. It's this group of people who somehow found one another and came together to create something wonderful. Something full of love, support, and genuine joy in being themselves. Some of our biological families are amazing, some of them suck, but what we've found in one another is bigger than that. We are a family that comes together when biology fails or can't be here.

"You're right," I agree, "but it's still not something I thought I'd ever find."

"It's always been here. Always will be."

Not knowing what else to say, I clap him on his shoulder and let him head toward Josie. With Mia heading my way, I keep standing, waiting for her to reach me.

I will always feel some resentment over what was taken from me, but at least my friends will all get to go out on their own terms. It took me a long time to realize I spent so much time holding on after that accident because I was too afraid it'd be taken from me. I didn't want to repeat history again; I knew where I stood in the public eye, knew where I stood in my family's eye, and I no longer cared about living my own life.

"What are you thinking about?" A hand winds around my bicep, giving it a gentle squeeze. I look down into the eyes that make my stomach swoop, hoping this feeling never goes away. "You didn't hear me talking to you?"

I lean down, pressing a kiss against her cheek, winding my arm around her shoulder. "Sorry about that, beautiful. I've been taking a minute...you know, soaking it all in, and thinking about what's coming next."

For a fraction of a second, her shoulders tense beneath my arm. I hate that I'm part of the reason she has this fear; a knee-jerk reaction to someone else bringing up the future and the possibility that it might not include her. I hate that someone, including me, ever put that thought in her head.

I silently vow to myself that she'll never have to worry about something like this again. At least, not from me. My plans include sticking around until she's so sick of me, she begs me to leave. But even then, I doubt I'd go far.

Her arms wind around my middle, resting her head against my shoulder, which gives me the perfect opportunity to press a kiss against her forehead.

"So, what does the future look like for you now, Ronan O'Brien?"

I grin at the familiar tone. It's the same one she used in every interview she ever conducted for the blog, calm and approachable, but clearly all business. It's been a long time since I've heard that tone. Part of me missed it. "Nothing too extravagant, Miss Sheridan," I tease back. "I want to make my house into a home, take two swimmers to the Los Angeles Olympics, at least, and fall more and more in love...you know, the basics."

Her intense gaze snaps up to mine, a frown creasing her forehead. "What do you mean, take *two* swimmers to the Olympics?"

"That's the part you picked up on?" I ask, brow raised. "Not the falling more and more in love part?"

"Of course not," she scoffs. "If I'm involved, there will be plenty more falling in love. I'm multi-faceted."

My laugh echoes through the emptying pool, bouncing off the walls, and causing a couple of people to turn our way. My entire focus, though, is on Mia. The woman who has so many beautiful sides to her that I can't wait to discover. Even her prickly sides are alluring to me (although, I think I can go a while without having them directed at me again).

"Ronan O'Brien, you better tell me what other swimmer you're going to take to the Olympics!" She pulls away enough to glare at me.

"Well, obviously, I want all the kids on my team to at least make it to Trials. While they can't all make the team, there are two who

I think have a good shot at making it." Her glare darkens. "One of them is a new kid who has a lot to prove. And the other—"

I'm cut off by the sound of a shrill squeal that sends everyone's attention swiveling to find the source. And the source of that sound is a very excited Josie Martin, who's being spun around in Bryce's arms. While most might wonder if a proposal has happened, that ring has been sitting on her finger for weeks now, so those closest to her know it's something else.

"Oh, my god," Mia breathes, turning to focus on me. Her eyes are wide, foggy with tears. "Is Bryce?"

"Yeah," I confirm with a nod. Her hand flies up to cover her mouth, a few tears managing to escape. "He's not done, and if I learned anything from my own experience, it's the importance of not letting someone else take your dream away from you."

"And he asked you to coach him?"

My grin grows. "Yeah, but we're not calling it a comeback. For either one of us."

With Emmie and Bryce, this would be the first time I'm officially putting my name out there as a coach. I've helped hundreds of kids through Operation Fly, coached them myself, but their success was always tied to the organization rather than me as an individual. Bryce's request gives me a different opportunity in this sport. I have an opportunity to help shape champions, to take the hardest lessons I learned and use them to make athletes stronger.

Mia

"Okay, but hear me out," Carter yells over the arguing that's happening in Ronan's library. "What if all the great Olympic swimmers come out of retirement and try to make it to LA? It'd be pretty epic."

"All of them?" I question with a raised brow. "Even those who are dead?"

Carter groans, glaring at me. "No! Obviously not them. I'm talking the Phelps era, maybe a bit younger."

"I don't think anyone can talk Jason Lezak into making a comeback, dude." Ronan steps up behind me, pressing his hand against the small of my back. "Maybe Lezak could take his place."

From the corner of the yard, Lezak lets out a loud bark, clearly pleased with the idea. Whenever I look at him now, I get a little teary-eyed because he's not a small puppy anymore. He's grown so much since I met him, but he's still the same adorable dog. He still wakes up at the ass crack of dawn for workouts with Ronan and then wakes me up with kisses when they get back home. He still trails up and down the length of the pool when we're at work, and watches the swimmers closely like he's their coach instead of Ronan. And he still steals things, including the small box Ronan hid a key in for when he planned to ask me to move in. That time, it was Ronan chasing the dog down the stairs and I was the one he brought his prize to.

Ronan didn't even need to ask the question.

Now the dog sits across the yard with Emmie in the grass beside him. She's trying to play with a small bundle, but the young corgi is much more interested in climbing Lezak like a jungle gym. I still can't believe Bryce caved so easily, the two of them showing up at my door one evening with the tiniest puppy in Josie's hands. They named her Charlotte, Charlie for short, to remember the moment they met for the first time.

In practically the same place Ronan and I met that same spring.

"I think Bryce's comeback is more than enough to focus on," Josie argues from her fiancé's lap. He squeezes her hip. "Oh, right, we aren't calling it a comeback. What is it then? A resurrection? A reverse disappearing act?"

He hides his laugh in her hair.

"No, Josie's right," I cut in. "If all these people come out of retirement to swim at an Olympics on home soil, we might need to restart the blog, and no one has time for that."

Josie groans in commiseration. "There's so much you have to do to run a blog like that. I don't think I remember how."

"Besides," Ronan adds, "Josie is too busy basking in the success of her debut novel!"

Josie released her book *The Gold Between Us* a little over a month ago and has been blown away by the success of it. People are apparently jumping at the chance to read a sports romance based on a real couple. The sales keep pouring in, she's been asked to be a guest on podcasts. Influencers are dying for the chance to work with her. Unable to take credit for her job well done, she insists her success comes from my marketing, which is total bullshit. All the marketing in the world won't make a shitty book sell.

Bryce somehow pulls her closer and whispers something against her ear. Her cheeks turn bright red, and she ducks her head. The look of pure pride on his face tells me everything I need to know.

"Hey, Mia?" I turn to see Liam sticking his head out of the sliding door. "You might want to get in here before Katrina plans to tear the whole kitchen out. Something about stupid bachelor décor?"

"Oh, no, she doesn't!" I'm already moving toward the door. "I want most of it to stay, but yes, the bachelor-ness of it can go."

Ronan wraps an arm around my wrist, tugging me back into him. "What? You don't think I'm going to need the bachelor look anymore?"

My eyes narrow at him, his thumb rubbing over the freshly healed tattoo on the inside of my wrist. "You better not."

He lifts my hand over and brings it up to kiss the skin there. When he stands back up, I take a moment to look at the tattoo. My wrist was one of the few places on my arm I still had space available, and I knew I wanted to see this one every single day. The dark ink stands out on my skin, the drawing nearly perfect as the piece comes together to show three tarot cards: The Four of Cups reversed, The Seven of Wands, and, most importantly, The Lovers.

"Uh, Mia?" Liam sounds panicked now. "Do you want to keep the double oven?"

"Oh, hell no." I gently push Ronan aside. "Carter, I'm about to fire your girlfriend."

"You can't. Ronan hired her!"

"It's her house, too, man," Ronan defends me. "She can fire whoever she wants."

Her house, too.

The sentence is enough to make me melt into a pile of goo. There was a time in my life when I convinced myself Ronan was in my past, and my feelings for him were there, too. Looking back on everything now, I can see the signs of how wrong that thought was. Just because I was mad and hurt, I never stopped caring about him. I cared about him yesterday; I care about him today; and I'll continue to care for the rest of my life, no matter what happens.

But now I can see that care has been morphed into something bigger, something far less tangible, but infinitely sweeter. I love him.

I loved him yesterday; I love him today; and I'm pretty damn sure I'll love him for the rest of our lives.

Maybe even beyond.

Did you love Mia and Ronan's story? Be sure to leave a review! Reviews and ratings help your favorite authors reach more readers.

Can't get enough of the Adair Swimming Crew? Make sure to check out *Maybe One Day* and *Tell Me Tomorrow*!
To read a BONUS scene from *Maybe One Day* and stay up-to-date on all the exciting things happening, sign up for my newsletter!

Acknowledgements

As always, I want to start by thanking YOU, the reader. Whether you're a returning reader or someone new to my writing, welcome. You're among friends here and this is a safe, loving community for all who enter. I don't know where the future of the Adair Swimming series is leading me, but I am taking a step back for a bit, and I wouldn't be confident in that decision without this book. From the minute *Maybe One Day* hit shelves, readers have been begging for this story and I hope I did it justice for you all.

Next, I want to give credit to the people who made this book possible. Due to a scheduling conflict, I had to make a change with my cover designers, as I was too eager to get this book out to you all. Simons & Glade Book Design did an incredible job bringing their own unique artistic style to this cover while still keeping the designs cohesive with the previous two. They nailed everything from Mia and her tattoos, to the enemies to lovers vibe, and, of course, the real star of the show, Lezak. I cannot thank them enough! Next, I want to thank my incredible editor, Ashley, at Earley Editing, LLC. She has worked on every book with me and I'm lucky to have found her!

I also want to thank my incredible group of friends who helped alpha/beta read this and get it to the finalized copy you have in your hands. Amanda, Claire, Katie, and Mary, I'm so grateful for the support you have all shown me in the course of writing this book.

Claire, this book literally would not be possible if you hadn't slid into my Tumblr DMs (can we call them that?) over a decade ago. You have inspired me with your grace, courage, and persistence more times than I can ever say. Mia is you through and through; I wanted to give you the chance to see yourself through the eyes of others, because you're incredible. Thank you for pushing me, thank you for believing in me, thank you for inspiring me, thank you for showing up for me. Most of all, thank you for being exactly who you are and for loving me exactly as I am. Not all soulmates are romantic, and our friendship has proven that to be true time and time again.

To my family: I am so grateful to be surrounded by a family who loves and supports me. My parents have always encouraged my creativity, and my sister is my biggest cheerleader, constantly pushing me to new heights. I am who I am today because of them, and I'd be lost without them. I love you. More than you will ever know.

***

Want to stay in the know of what's happening next? Subscribe to Ashlyn's newsletter and follow her socials. She's cultivated a safe space for all her readers, often recommending other books and keeping readers updated on what's happening in her writing world.

About the Author

Ashlyn Harmon writes books with a little bit of sass, a whole lot of swoon-worthy moments, and characters who are real, and relatable. She loves writing the kinds of female leads she wished she had more access to: unapologetically confident in their bodies and who they are.

She was born and raised in Omaha, Nebraska, and is still daydreaming of getting out one day. When she's not writing, she continues to grow her freelance editing business, where she specializes in all things romance, watching ghost hunting shows, hanging out with her corgi, or with her nose buried in a book.

To stay in the know of what Ashlyn's working on next or what events you can find her at, be sure to follow her on all social media platforms (@ashwritesromance) or check out her website: www.ashlynharmon.com.